THE WORLD'S CLASSICS

THE GOLDEN ASS

APULEIUS was born in the mid-120s AD in Madauros (modern Mdaurusch in Algeria). His father was a *duumvir*, one of the two chief magistrates in the Roman colony, and Apuleius received a superior education at Carthage and then at Athens. He lived in Athens for several years and travelled widely in Greece. Later he lived long enough in Rome to obtain recognition as a literary figure amongst men of social standing. In 155 Apuleius began a journey to Alexandria, but fell ill and had to rest with the family of his friend Pontianus in Oea (modern Tripoli). After his marriage to Pontianus' widowed mother he was indicted on a charge of magic, and in a famous speech, his *Apologia*, he secured his acquittal. He returned to Carthage and there became famous as a writer and lecturer. It is clear that he was still in Carthage during the 160s, but nothing can be established about his life after that date.

P. G. WALSH is Emeritus Professor of Humanity at the University of Glasgow. His publications include *The Roman Novel* (1970, 1995).

THE WORLD'S CLASSICS

APULEIUS

The Golden Ass

*Translated with Introduction
and Explanatory Notes by*

P. G. WALSH

Oxford   New York

OXFORD UNIVERSITY PRESS

Oxford University Press, Great Clarendon Street, Oxford OX2 6DP

Oxford   New York

Athens   Auckland   Bangkok   Bogota   Bombay
Buenos Aires   Calcutta   Cape Town   Dar es Salaam
Delhi   Florence   Hong Kong   Istanbul   Karachi
Kuala Lumpur   Madras   Madrid   Melbourne
Mexico City   Nairobi   Paris   Singapore
Taipei   Tokyo   Toronto   Warsaw

and associated companies in
Berlin   Ibadan

Oxford is a trade mark of Oxford University Press

British Library Cataloguing in Publication Data

Data available

Library of Congress Cataloging in Publication Data

The golden ass/Apuleius; translated with introduction
and explantory notes by P. G. Walsh.
Includes bibliographical references and index.
1. Mythology, Classical—Fiction.   2. Metamorphosis   Fiction.
I. Walsh, P. G. (Patrick Gerard).
PS6209.M3W35   1994   873'.01—dc20   93-37772

ISBN 0-19-282492-9 (Pbk.)

5 7 9 10 8 6

Printed in Great Britain by
Caledonian International Book Manufacturing Ltd
Glasgow

For
John

ACKNOWLEDGEMENTS

This translation was begun and ended in Glasgow, but the greater part of it was completed at Pomona College, at which I spent a pleasant and profitable semester of teaching in 1992. I should like to thank the members of the academic and administrative staff who made our stay a happy one, and who so willingly put the necessary facilities for congenial study at my disposal.

Professor E. J. Kenney offered usefully trenchant criticism of a first draft of a section of Book 4; I hope that his suggestions will be seen to have borne fruit. I have benefited too from the encouraging observations made by the anonymous reader who scrutinized the same specimen translation on behalf of the Press. During our stay in California, Professor Ellen Finkelpearl of Scripps College cast a friendly and expert eye over another section of the translation. Members of my family have also offered useful criticism. None of these helpful adjutants has seen the final version.

It is now more than thirty years since my admiration for *The Golden Ass* induced me to embark on preparatory study for publication of *The Roman Novel* (1970), and later for the chapter on Apuleius in *The Cambridge History of Classical Literature*. In composing this Introduction, I have tried to take account of the more important studies which have subsequently appeared, but the diligent reader will note without surprise some repetition incorporated from those earlier analyses. *The Roman Novel* has now been reissued under the auspices of the Bristol Classical Press (1995), and can serve as a useful companion-volume for this translation.

P. G. W.

CONTENTS

CONTENTS

ABBREVIATIONS

AJP	*American Journal of Philology*
ANRW	*Aufstieg und Niedergang der römischen Welt*
APA	*American Philological Association*
Apol.	*Apology*
CJ	*Classical Journal*
CQ	*Classical Quarterly*
CR	*Classical Review*
CW	*Classical Weekly*
GLK	*Grammatici Latini*, ed. Keil
Flor.	*Florida*
G&R	*Greece and Rome*
JHS	*Journal of Hellenic Studies*
Mnem.	*Mnemosyne*
OCD	*Oxford Classical Dictionary*
Onos	*Lucius or the Ass*
PCPS	*Proceedings of the Cambridge Philological Society*
Philol.	*Philologus*
PP	*Parola del Passato*
RÉA	*Revue des Études Anciennes*
RÉL	*Revue des Études Latines*
RhM	*Rheinisches Museum*
RHR	*Revue de l'histoire des religions*
SHA	*Scriptores Historiae Augustae*
TAPA	*Transactions and Proceedings of the American Philological Association*

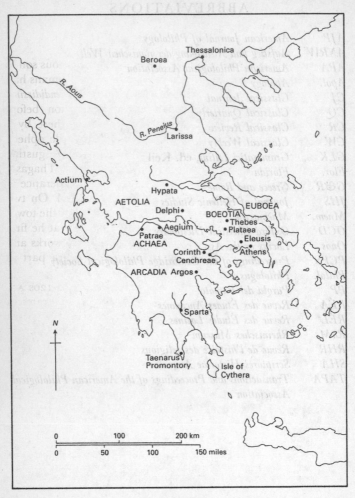

Map of Greece

INTRODUCTION

I

Apuleius (no *praenomen* is attested) was the most famous son of Madauros (modern Mdaurusch in Algeria). The Romans had converted the existing Numidian town into a *splendidissima colonia*, probably in the Flavian era a generation before Apuleius was born. His memory was preserved there by a statue which bore the inscription 'To the Platonist Philosopher', the role in which he was chiefly celebrated. When Augustine two centuries after Apuleius journeyed south from Thagaste to attend this pleasant university town in the furtherance of his education, Apuleius' name there was a byword. On two occasions Augustine associates him specifically with the town; it must have been during his brief studies there that he first gained acquaintance with Apuleius' philosophical works and with *The Golden Ass*, which was to play so large a part in shaping the *Confessions*.[1]

The date of Apuleius' birth there was in the mid-120s AD. His father was a *duumvir*, one of the two chief magistrates in the Roman colony. We may assume from this that Apuleius was bilingual from boyhood; Punic was widely current throughout his native region, but Latin was the official language of the colony. His father had the modest wealth appropriate to his social prominence; at death he bequeathed to his two sons almost two million sesterces. This legacy enabled Apuleius to enjoy a superior education, first at

---

[1] For Madauros as Apuleius' *patria*, Augustine, *CD* 8. 14, *Ep.* 102. 32. Though the town was Numidian, first under Syphax and later under Masinissa (*Apol.* 24), Punic influence was widespread in the region, as inscriptions reveal. For the subsequent Romanization ('splendidissima colonia', *Apol.* 24), see J. Gwyn Griffiths, *Apuleius of Madauros: The Isis Book* (Leiden, 1975), 60 f. For the statue and inscription, J. Tatum, *Apuleius and The Golden Ass* (Cornell, 1979), 106 ff. For *The Golden Ass* and the *Confessions*, Nancy J. Shumate, *Phoenix* (1988), 35 ff.; Walsh, *G&R* (1988), 73 ff. For the prominence of Apuleius' philosophical writings in the *Civ. Dei*, see 4. 2; 8. 14 ff.; 9. 3, 7 ff.

Carthage and later at Athens. He boasts that already at
Carthage he had embarked on the study of philosophy,
though this must have been subsidiary to his rhetorical
studies. At Athens, in his own words, he cultivated 'all nine
Muses with equal enthusiasm', though his chief love was
philosophy 'of which no one can ever drink enough'. He
resided for several years at Athens; his literary studies
imparted a wide familiarity with Greek culture. At Carthage
in later life he lectured in both Latin and Greek.[2]

While resident in Greece he travelled widely, not only on
the mainland but also across the Aegean to Samos and to
Hierapolis in Phrygia. Later he lived long enough in Rome to
obtain recognition as a literary figure amongst men of social
standing.[3]

Shortly afterwards in 155, at the age of about 30, Apuleius
decided to extend his travels with a journey to Egypt;
doubtless his enthusiasm for the Isiac religion, a dominant
theme in *The Golden Ass*, was a leading motive in this decision.
As he was *en route* to Alexandria, he fell ill, and decided to
relieve his indisposition by resting with friends at Oea
(modern Tripoli). There he resumed acquaintance with
Pontianus, with whom he had been on friendly terms as a
fellow-student at Athens. His friend persuaded him to prolong
his stay at Oea, and to take up residence in the family home,
where his brother and his mother, a wealthy widow, shared
his studies. The acquaintance ripened, fostered by Pontianus.
Apuleius stresses that she was no beauty ('non formosa
pupilla, sed mediocri facie mater liberorum'), and indeed she
was about seven years older than he. Discreetly avoiding
mention of money, he claims that he came to love her for her

---

[2] For the date of birth, see Walsh, *The Roman Novel* (Cambridge: CUP, 1970), App.
2. For Punic widespread in the region, n. 1 above, and Gwyn Griffiths, *Apuleius of
Madauros*, 60 ff.; Apuleius' condescending attitude towards the language, *Apol.* 98.
Education at Carthage, *Flor.* 18. 15; at Athens, *Flor.* 20. 4. Lengthy residence at
Athens, *Apol.* 23. 2; still there shortly before 155, *Apol.* 72. 3. Lecturing in Greek and
Latin, *Flor.* 18. 38 f.

[3] Wide travels, *Apol.* 23. 2; Samos, *Flor.* 15. 4; Hierapolis, *De mundo*, 17; Rome,
Flor. 17. 4 (in the circle of Scipio Orfitus, proconsul of Africa, 163–4).

sterling qualities. But relations become soured when Pontianus took a wife. Her father, Herennius Rufus, orchestrated opposition to Apuleius' projected union with Pudentilla, and after the marriage he persuaded Sicinius Aemilianus, brother of Pudentilla's first husband, to indict Apuleius on a charge of magic. The charge was that he had bewitched the rich widow with love-philtres to induce her to marry him; in addition, Pontianus had met with a sudden death, and an additional accusation of murder was initially made though rapidly dropped. The trial was held at Sabrata in 158–9 before the proconsul Claudius Maximus. Conviction for magic under the *lex Cornelia de sicariis et veneficiis*, promulgated in the days of Sulla, was punishable by death. Apuleius defended himself against the charge; his speech, which has survived and is conventionally known as the *Apologia*, secured his acquittal.[4]

Thereafter he returned to his native province and took up residence at Carthage, determining to spend the rest of his life there. His fame as writer and lecturer was so widespread that he was honoured in various cities and at Carthage itself with a public statue. The ex-consul Aemilianus Strabo made the formal proposal in the Carthaginian senate, promising to meet the cost himself. Apuleius' eminence in the city is further attested by his tenure of a select priesthood, and by his being chosen to deliver the parting panegyric to two retiring proconsuls. Public lectures and orations which have survived in part under the title *Florida* document his social prominence; one of them states that his distinction as orator has been celebrated at Carthage for six years. It is therefore clear that he still flourished there in the late 160s, but nothing can be established about his life after that date.[5]

---

[4] Date of arrival at Oea, *Apol.* 55. 10 ('abhinc ferme triennium'); circumstances of encounter with Pontianus, *Apol.* 72. Pontianus' encouragement of the match, and Apuleius' appraisal of Pudentilla's charms, *Apol.* 73. Herennius Rufus as villain, inducing Sicinius Aemilianus to lodge an indictment, *Apol.* 74. For the charges, *Apol.* 2. 2–4.

[5] Decision to reside at Carthage, *Flor.* 16. 3. Statue at Carthage, *Flor.* 16. 39; elsewhere, 16. 37. Priesthood, 16. 38. Panegyrics to departing proconsuls, *Flor.* 9. 17. Six years at Carthage, *Flor.* 18. 16.

II

As a writer, Apuleius has two main claims to fame. As a philosopher without original genius he is important for his transmission of the seminal ideas of Middle Platonism into the increasingly Greekless world of Western Europe from the fourth century to the thirteenth. As a writer of romance, he is the author of the one Latin novel to have survived whole and entire from the Classical period. Its later influence on the vernacular literatures of Europe has been immense. The student of the romance cannot afford to ignore the philosophical works, since its Platonist stance is prominent. Apuleius' other surviving writings, in themselves of subsidiary importance, also contribute to a fuller appreciation of *The Golden Ass*, for there is no doubt that the author in important ways identifies himself with his hero Lucius, and both his speech of self-defence at Sabrata, and his orations at Carthage, provide important elements of autobiography.

Our author's claim that at Athens he cultivated 'all nine Muses' is borne out by the extraordinary range of his subsequent writings, most of them unfortunately lost. It is hardly surprising to find a man of such literary leanings boasting in the *Apology* and the *Florida* that he has composed Catullan love-lyrics, hymns, satirical epigrams, and other forms of poetry; that already at Oea he had published a literary lecture; and that he had written a variety of works of fiction, including an anthology of love-anecdotes, symposium-literature, and a second romance in addition to *The Golden Ass*. What is surprising is that he complemented this literary output with technical treatises which reflect the curiosity of the practical scientist. He wrote treatises on dendrology, agriculture, and medicines. He wrote a work on natural history, and for good measure composed it in Greek. Other monographs deriving from his education in the seven liberal arts were devoted to astronomy, music, and arithmetic.[6]

[6] Love-lyrics and satirical epigrams, *Apol.* 6. 3, 9. 12 ff.; hymns, *Flor.* 17. 18, 18. 37 ff.; other poetry, *Flor.* 9. 27 f., 20. 6; published speeches, *Apol.* 55. 10, Augustine,

These multifarious compositions were, however, incidental to his central passion for philosophy. Just as he proclaimed himself a second Seneca by entitling his work on nature *Quaestiones naturales*, so he followed the footsteps of Cicero in composing a treatise on political philosophy under the heading *De republica*, and in translating Plato's *Phaedo*.[7] These two works are lost, but five others traditionally ascribed to him have survived.

These five treatises are *De deo Socratis*, *De Platone et eius dogmate*, *De mundo*, Περὶ ἑρμηνείας, and *Asclepius*. There is little dispute about the authenticity of the first, and though the second and third are composed in a less exuberant style, the manuscripts and Augustine ascribe them to Apuleius, and the content further encourages the attribution. The fourth, 'On interpretation', appears in a separate manuscript-tradition, and is more jejune in content; the fifth appears to be a Latin translation of a lost Greek hermetic work. These last two works can be safely disregarded in any consideration of Apuleius as novelist dominated by Platonist preconceptions; the content of the first three has an important bearing on *The Golden Ass*.[8]

De deo Socratis ('On the god of Socrates') is more general in its approach than the title suggests; the treatise is devoted to the existence and nature of demons, and is the most systematic exposition of the subject to have emerged from the Graeco-Roman world. After first surveying the separated world of gods (visible stars and invisible members of the Pantheon), Apuleius describes the place of demons in the

---

Ep. 138. 19; love-anecdotes, Lydus, *Mag.* 3. 64; second romance (*Hermagoras*), Priscian in *GLK* 2. 85; dendrology, Servius, *ad Georg.* 2. 126; agriculture, Palladius, 1. 35. 9; medicines, Priscian in *GLK* 2. 203; natural history, *Apol.* 36 ff.; liberal arts, Cassiodorus, *Inst.* 2. 4. 7.

[7] *De rep.*, Fulgentius, p. 122 Helm; *Phaedo*, Sid. Apoll. 2. 9. 5.

[8] On these three treatises, J. Beaujeu's excellent edition (Paris, Budé 1973). On *De mundo*, F. Regen, *Apuleius Philosophus Platonicus* (Berlin, 1971), arguing for Apuleian authorship; on *De interpretatione*, M. W. Sullivan, *Apuleian Logic* (North Holland, 1967), again claiming Apuleius as author. There is a good survey of Apuleius as philosopher by B. L. Hijmans, 'Apuleius, Philosophus Platonicus', *ANRW* II. 36. 1 (Berlin, 1987), 395 ff.

hierarchy of rational beings as intermediaries between gods
and men; they approximate to angels in the Hebraic tradition.
Apuleius divides them into three classes. The first are souls
within human bodies (hence the title *De deo Socratis*). The
second have quitted human bodies to become Lemures, Lares,
Larvae, and Manes. The third group are wholly free of bodily
connections, and are endowed with special powers and special
duties. Somnus and Amor are cited as examples; the story of
Cupid and Psyche at the heart of the romance should be read
with this in mind. The baroque Latinity of the treatise
suggests that it was composed, like *The Golden Ass*, to be
recited in the literary salon, and at a date not too distant from
that of the novel.

By contrast, the second of the three works, *Plato and his
Doctrines*, is a summary of the master's philosophical teaching
composed in a more restrained style for a reading public; it
outlines in two books Plato's physics and ethics. These
summaries are preceded by a hagiographical life on lines
similar to the later biography of Diogenes Laertius. While the
treatment of physics adheres faithfully to Plato's *Timaeus* and
Republic, the section on ethics owes more to Middle Platonism
with its incorporation of Peripatetic and Stoic elements. The
brief appendix on politics reverts more faithfully to the
fundamentals of Plato's *Republic* and *Laws*. This precious
evidence of the teachings of Middle Platonism provides the
reader of *The Golden Ass* with the necessary indications of
Apuleius' philosophical and religious preoccupations.

The third of the philosophical disquisitions, *On the World*, is
a close adaptation of ps.-Aristotle's Περὶ Κόσμου, which
was composed a century or two earlier. The work is divided
into two sections on cosmology and theology. It begins with
an account of the aether and the various aspects of life on
earth. Following a bridging discussion on the harmony
between the earth's constituent parts, the second part
describes how God, known to mankind under different names,
animates and preserves all things; the aretalogy in the final
book of the romance swings sharply into focus here. It is
instructive to observe how the Greek original has been lent a

Roman flavour for a Roman audience. There is abundant
citation of Roman as well as Greek poetry; aspects of city-life
at Rome are adduced to exemplify the harmony existent in the
larger world, just as in his romance Apuleius adds jocose
touches to the Greek story to lend it a Roman flavour. More
important, the distinction in the Greek treatise between God's
transcendent existence beyond the world and his immanent
power within it is adapted to accommodate the demons of *De
deo Socratis*. The style in which this treatise is written is more
akin to *Plato and his Doctrines* than to *The God of Socrates*, though
there are occasional literary evocations and rhythmical riots.
It is tempting to suggest that *Plato and his Doctrines* and *On the
World* are earlier compositions, written before Apuleius' career
as sophist at Carthage, while *The God of Socrates* like *The Golden
Ass* itself was composed for declamation in the literary salons
of the African capital.[9]

Apuleius' speech of self-defence against the charge of magic,
the *Apology*, exhibits remarkable contrasts with the forensic
orations of Cicero delivered two centuries earlier. The speech
is enclosed within the conventional frame of exordium and
peroration, but the heart of the speech, divided into three
sections, begins with a leisurely rebuttal of attacks on the
manner of his private life. So far from pleading urgently for his
very life, Apuleius adopts the manner of the public lecturer,
regaling the court and its president with disquisitions on such
themes as 'The private innocence of the lascivious versifier',
'The enlightened master', 'The true nature of poverty', and
interlarding these themes with a host of quotations from
Greek and Latin poetry. His purpose is clearly to establish
himself as a man of superior culture whom it would be absurd
to accuse of such a degrading activity as magic. In his second
section, he reinforces the impression that he is a lofty
intellectual by demonstrating that the alleged magical mal-
practices were the zoological studies befitting a second

---

[9] On the importance of the Platonic treatises, C. C. Schlam, *The Metamorphoses of
Apuleius* (Chapel Hill: NC, 1992), 11 ff. Middle Platonism is discussed in detail by J.
Dillon, *The Middle Platonists* (Ithaca: NY, 1977).

Aristotle, the medical researches of an aspiring Hippocrates, and the religious devotions befitting a Middle Platonist. The distinction which he draws here between the devotee of magic and the genuine searcher after philosophical truth is an important consideration in the message of *The Golden Ass*. In the final section he adopts a more urgent tone as he delineates the history of his arrival and marriage at Oea. Although the outcome of the trial is not recorded, the issue was clearly in no doubt; Apuleius secured his acquittal.[10]

The speech at many points records incidents similar to those experienced by Lucius in the romance; in particular, the reader must wonder how far the comic account of the trial at the Festival of Laughter, of which there is no sign in the Greek version of the story of Lucius and which has almost certainly been inserted by Apuleius himself, was inspired by the author's own experience.

The *Florida*, the other surviving work, is a collection of twenty-three extracts from the published lectures and speeches of Apuleius after his return to Carthage in the early 160s. These extracts are all taken from the exordia of lectures and speeches; often prefaced by modest disclaimers of his own merits and abilities, they frequently exploit anecdotes which find an echo in some of the inserted stories in *The Golden Ass*. Thus, for example, the story of Asclepiades chancing upon a funeral and discovering that the man to be buried was still alive, recalls the tale of the buried youth and the wise physician at 10.12. The description of the crowds thronging the theatre at the Festival of Laughter at 3.2 is markedly similar to that at *Florida* 16. 11 ff. When the citizens of Hypata propose to erect a public statue in honour of Lucius (3.11), we recall that Apuleius was similarly honoured (*Florida* 16. 41 and 46). These extracts are often not dissimilar in their flowery Latin from the narrative passages of the *Metamorphoses*, suggesting that the romance may have been composed during the same period of Apuleius' residence at Carthage.[11]

[10] For the relevance of the *Apology* to *The Golden Ass*, see Tatum, *Apuleius and the Golden Ass*, ch. 4.   [11] Ibid. 123 ff.

III

Reference is frequently made to our romance by the alternative titles of *Metamorphoses* and *The Golden Ass*. The former is the title found in the manuscripts; the latter is attested by Augustine, who claims that Apuleius himself entitled his work *Asinus aureus* (*CD* 18. 18). In that same passage, however, Augustine states that Apuleius is describing *his own* experience of being transformed into an ass; he is clearly speaking from memory, rather than citing a manuscript before him, which detracts from the reliability of his witness. We have noted our author's fondness for appropriating titles used by Cicero (*De republica*) and Seneca (*Quaestiones naturales*); here we seem to have 'an inescapable reminiscence of Ovid's *Metamorphoses*'.[12] The plural is appropriate: it covers more than Lucius' becoming an ass and reverting to human shape. In his introductory chapter Apuleius describes his theme as the transformation of 'shapes and fortunes', so that Aristomenes' experience in the role of tortoise with his bed over him, and Thelyphron's disfigurement, and Psyche's apotheosis can qualify for inclusion *Metamorphoses*, then is the correct title of the romance, but *The Golden Ass* has become so familiar that it seems pedantic to dispense with it.[13]

The date of the work has been a source of controversy. Many scholars (e.g. Rohde, Purser, Haight) incline to the earlier period of Apuleius' life when he was at Rome, because of the topographical references, the legal jokes, the references to senatorial procedures; it has been further suggested that the racy content and ebullient style befit a younger man.[14] Such arguments are clearly subjective, and can be countered by the claim that the older Apuleius, a man young in heart, was

[12] So E. J. Kenney, *Cupid and Psyche* (Cambridge, 1990), 2.

[13] For a friendlier view of the evidence of Augustine, J. J. Winkler, *Auctor and Actor* (Berkeley, Calif., 1985), 292 ff.

[14] See most recently K. Dowden in J. Tatum and G. Vernazza (eds.), *The Ancient Novel* (Proceedings of the Dartmouth ICAN Conference, Hanover, 1989), 147; on the allegedly youthful style, M. Bernhard, *Der Stil des Apuleius von Madaura*[2] (Amsterdam, 1965), 360.

writing with a Roman audience in mind. Arguments favouring a later date include legal references in the *Cupid and Psyche* story, and the significance of Lucius' claim that the philosopher Sextus as well as Plutarch was an elder relative. Plutarch had probably died about the time Apuleius was born, but Sextus as tutor to the emperor Verus was probably still alive when Apuleius visited Rome. It is unlikely that in a work of fiction such a reference would be made to an eminent author still living. So far as the ebullient style is concerned, we have noted similarly baroque passages to be found in the *Florida*, dating to the 160s. The crucial argument, however, supporting the later date, when Apuleius was in Carthage, is the apparent presence of autobiographical elements in the story such as the offer of a statue to Lucius after the trial at Hypata and to Apuleius likewise at Oea, and the journey to Rome of both hero and author. On balance, the arguments for a date in or after the 160s are overwhelming.[15]

In his prologue, Apuleius informs us that the romance on which he is embarking is the adaptation of a Greek story ('fabulam Graecanicam incipimus'). The original, whose author the ninth-century patriarch Photius calls 'Lucius of Patrae', is now lost, but an abridged version of it appears in the works of Lucian, who is a likely candidate as author of the original.[16] Dispute rages about the length of the original story compared with the abridged version, which bears the title *Lucius or the Ass*, and in which in half-a-dozen places there is evidence of unskilful epitomizing. The most systematic investigation has concluded that *Lucius or the Ass* is at most only five Teubner pages shorter than the original.[17] (If Lucian

[15] For the legal passages, see 6.2, 4, 7, and G. W. Bowersock, *RhM* (1965), 282 n. 31. For Sextus 1, 2 and *SHA, Verus* 2. 5. On the statutes, 3.11, and Augustine *Ep.* 138. 19; see also 6.9, 6 with Kenney's note.

[16] So B. E. Perry, *The Ancient Romances* (Berkeley, Calif., 1967), ch. 4; G. Anderson, *Studies in Lucian's Comic Fiction* (Leiden, 1976), 34 ff.

[17] The text of *Lucius or the Ass* can be consulted in M. D. McLeod's Loeb edn. of Lucian vol. 8. The calculation of length is made by P. Junghanns, *Die Erzählungstechnik von Apuleius Metamorphosen und ihrer Vorlage* (Leipzig, 1932), 118; Perry, *Ancient Romances*, 216, suggests ten pages longer. There is a good discussion of the problem by H. J. Mason in B. L. Hijmans and R. Th. van der Paardt (eds.), *Aspects of Apuleius' Golden Ass* (Groningen, 1978), ch. 1.

were the author, the criterion of the length of his other works would support this judgement.)

This controversy is of some importance for *The Golden Ass*. It is clear from *Lucius or the Ass* that Apuleius followed the main lines of the original as far as the climax of the transformation back into human shape, but that he has inserted additional incidents and anecdotes to point the moral and adorn the tale. Estimates of the extent of these additions have varied. The 'minimalist' position is that the additions are confined to the central *conte* of Cupid and Psyche, the Isis-book at the close of the novel, and the occasional sentimental story, notably the tragic end of Charite. The 'inclusive' thesis, supported by the greater number of scholars, is that virtually all the extended sections not appearing in *Lucius or the Ass* have been added by Apuleius.[18]

A thematic comparison between the abridged Greek version and *The Golden Ass* is helpful as an indication of the insertions (denoted here in italics) made by Apuleius:[19]

	Apuleius	Lucius or the Ass
Bk	Theme	Theme (nos. refer to sections)
1	*Aristomenes and Socrates*	
	Hypata; house of Milo	1–3 Hypata; house of Hipparchus
2	Byrrhena; Photis	3–11 *init*. Abroea; Palaestra
	Thelyphron	
3	*The spoof trial*	
	Metamorphosis and departure	11–17 *init*. Metamorphosis and departure
4	Journey to robbers' cave	17–23 *init*. Journey to robbers' cave
	Three robbers' stories	
	Cupid and Psyche i	
5	*Cupid and Psyche ii*	

[18] See my review of H. van Thiel, *Der Eselsroman*, vol. 1 (Munich, 1971, taking the minimalist view) and of G. Bianco, *La fonte greca delle Metamorfosi di Apuleio* (Brescia, 1971) in *CR* (1974), 215 ff. More recent assessments by Mason in *Aspects*, and Schlam, *Metamorphoses*, 22 ff.

[19] I reproduce this table from Walsh, *Roman Novel*, 147.

Though some scholars demur at such a radical restriction of
the content of the original, even van Thiel would concede that
the lost Greek work can have been no more than twice as long
as *Lucius or the Ass*.[20] It is accordingly clear that Apuleius has
converted a Greek short story into an extended romance with
a tripartite structure. The first three books recount the
undisciplined curiosity of the hero Lucius, which results in his
transformation into an ass; the ensuing seven unfold the saga
of bizarre experiences of his human intellect enclosed in the

[20] Van Thiel, *Der Eselsroman*, ch. 3; Schlam, *Metamorphoses*, 22 f. adopts an
intermediate position.

animal frame; and the final book describes his redemption by the gratuitous grace of Isis and the hero's subsequent submission to the service of the Isiac religion. The curious length of eleven books, unique in works of ancient fiction as in Roman creative literature generally, is worthy of note. It has been reasonably suggested that Book 11 is designed to stand out apart from the rest, to draw attention to the radical difference of its content, and perhaps to underline the significance of the number eleven in Pythagorean and Platonist thought.[21] It is even possible that Augustine acknowledged and imitated this contrast at the close of the novel, for in his *Confessions* he shifts abruptly from autobiography at the close of Book 9 to philosophical and theological reflection in the final books.[22]

IV

The central problem which confronts the interpreter of the romance is to decide whether Apuleius intended it merely as ribald entertainment, or whether he shaped it to be a fable, a story with a moral. The programmatic first chapter seems deliberately designed to beguile; it has rightly been observed that whereas *Lucius or the Ass* plunges directly into I-narrative ('I was once visiting Thessaly . . .'), Apuleius' exordium reads like the prologue of a Latin comedy. He opens the proceedings in the persona of the author, in the spirit of a Terence; he then teasingly combines the promise of risqué narrative of incidents and anecdotes ('the Milesian mode') with hints of a sober connection with Egypt, the implications of which will become clear only in the final book. (This is the initial justification for Winkler's analogy of an Agatha Christie detective story, the suggestion that clues are planted but fully understood only retrospectively at Book 11.) Apuleius as author then slips on the stage-outfit, so to say, and identity of Lucius his hero, and

---

[21] See Kenney, *Cupid and Psyche*, 3; S. Heller, *AJP* (1983), 321 ff. R. Heine, in *Aspects*, 37, speculates on Book 11 as a later addition.

[22] See R. McMahon, *Augustine's Prayerful Ascent* (Athens, Ga., 1989), ch. 4.

proceeds to play the part with relish;[23] thus the potted biography that follows in the first-person narrative belongs to Lucius. It includes a visit to Rome, an experience which has given the Greek youth sufficient Latin to tell the story in that language. When he speaks of himself as a circus-performer leaping from one horse to another, he may obliquely refer to the alternation of fidelity to the Greek source and insertion of additional episodes and anecdotes. The final sentence of the chapter, it should be noted, promises the reader no more than enjoyable entertainment in reading this mélange: 'lector, intende; laetaberis.' There is no hint here of any ulterior motive in the adaptation of the Greek story.

Many perceptive readers from Macrobius onward have thus strong justification for proclaiming that the work is in essence an entertainment. For Winkler it is 'a philosophical comedy about religious knowledge', in which 'all answers to cosmic questions are non-authorised'; 'Book 11 is designed to be not a statement of faith for the reader to accept, but an experience that reproduces the original surprise and wonder of a religious revelation.' G. N. Sandy finds himself in substantial agreement with Farquharson's withering judgement that *The Golden Ass* is 'a mere adventure story, a kind of horrid nightmare, with stories of the Decameron kind but infinitely worse told'; Sandy draws particular attention to the lubricious episodes in the second part of the novel, which appear to be designed 'purely for comic entertainment rather than to put into relief the moral degradation' of Lucius. For B. E. Perry, the *Metamorphoses* is 'a series of mundane stories exploited on their own account as such for the reader's entertainment', and the final book is merely a note of edification employed as 'ballast to offset the prevailing levity

---

[23] In this controversy concerning the spokesman in the first chapter, I agree with Rohde and many successors. For a useful outline of the dispute and various solutions offered, see K. Dowden, *CQ* (1982), 419 ff. Two further suggestions have been made subsequently: S. J. Harrison, *CQ* (1990), 507 ff., argues that the prologue is an address by the book itself; Winkler, *Auctor and Actor*, 203, that the spokesman is 'an itinerant Greek now working as a storyteller in Rome'. I find Rohde's thesis more persuasive than these.

of the preceding ten books', so that Apuleius can 'bow deeply and reverently to his audience'. A critic of similar views, Frances Norwood, describes the final book as 'the climax of *Pilgrim's Progress* tacked on to the end of *Tom Jones*', and suggests that Apuleius exploits the Isiac religion as 'a juggler keeps his best trick for the climax of the performance'.[24]

For those who are content to restrict Apuleius' purposes to those of a literary juggler or entertainer, three lines of enquiry are especially profitable. The first is to study his narrative skills against the presentation of the compendious *Lucius or the Ass*. His careful attention to structure becomes immediately apparent.[25] *Cupid and Psyche* occupies the centre of the novel; as we shall note, it is the projection into myth of the sin, sufferings, and redemption of Lucius. On each side of this central episode, each book is a confluence of contrasting themes, carefully achieved by inserted episodes. In the first book, the comic detail of Lucius' first encounter with his miserly host Milo, adapted from the Greek, is complemented by the insertion of a dramatic story of the death of Socrates by magic; in the second, the social and sexual encounters with his relative and with the maidservant (the Greek continuation of the tale) is offset by the chilling story of the disfigurement of Thelyphron; in the third, the reverse pattern is notable, for here the Greek original has the dramatic content of the metamorphosis of Lucius, and Apuleius prefaces it with an episode of comedy, the Festival of Laughter. Thus throughout the first section of the romance there is a characteristic combination of the comic and the magical. In the second section, following the tale of Cupid and Psyche, this planned variation is continued between the comic on the one hand and the romantic or tragic on the other. Thus in the seventh book

---

[24] Macrobius, *In Somn. Scip.* 1. 2. 8, 'solas aurium delicias profitetur'. Winkler, *Auctor and Actor*, 124 f.; G. Sandy in Hijmans and van der Paardt, *Aspects* 123 ff., citing Farquharson's *Marcus Aurelius* (Oxford, 1951), 99; Perry, *Ancient Romances* 243; F. Norwood, *Phoenix* (1956), 5. Similar views are expressed by E. H. Haight, *Apuleius and his Influence* (NY, 1927), 57.

[25] For more detailed considerations of structure, A. Scobie, in Hijmans and van der Paardt *Aspects*, 43 ff.

the romantic rescue of Charite is juxtaposed with Lucius' privations at the farm; in the eighth, Charite's tragic death, a long episode inserted by Apuleius, is followed by the adventures with the priests, a comic episode derived from the Greek story. Thereafter Apuleius' structure comes under more strain as the Greek version relates Lucius' treatment at the hands of three owners, but the adept balance of themes is still observable: thus in Book 10 two tragic episodes alternate with two jocular accounts.

In addition to such refinements of plot and structure, comparison with *Lucius or the Ass* reveals Apuleius' careful attention to the development of the characters. Thus in the first book Milo the host is a much more miserly skinflint than in the Greek account, and all else is subordinated to this enhanced characterization. In the second book the portrait of the maidservant is more romantically drawn; Photis enchants Lucius with her beauty, whereas in *Lucius or the Ass* her counterpart Palaestra merely lives up to her name as a wrestling-partner. The witch Pamphile in the third book is depicted more horrifically than in the Greek version. Similarly in Lucius' later encounters Charite is a more romantic and ultimately a more tragic figure, the boy to whom he is consigned at the farm is more cruel, the priests of Atargatis are more degenerately effeminate and mendacious, and the baker's wife is more sadistic as well as unfaithful.[26]

The second line of enquiry is to be directed at the inserted episodes and anecdotes, which reveal Apuleius' talents and limitations as a story-teller. These insertions, as we have suggested, successfully integrate comic and dramatic scenes; their underlying purpose is to reflect in different ways the situation of the hero Lucius. In this aim, the stories in the first section of the novel (notably the death of Socrates and the disfigurement of Thelyphron) are closely relevant, and *Cupid and Psyche* has an important bearing on the main theme; the later insertions, however, though illustrative in a general sense

---

[26] For fuller discussion of characterization, see Walsh, *Roman Novel*, 150 ff.

of the degenerate and hazardous world into which the hero
has sunk, are less closely articulated to the fortunes of Lucius,
and indeed Apuleius at some points recounts them with such
lubricious zest that his moralizing purposes all but dis-
appear.

In several of the insertions, Apuleius seeks to demonstrate
his skill at combining different tales (presumably known to his
readers), but not always with conspicuous success; loose ends
are left trailing. Thus in Aristomenes' story in Book 1, where
the point is that Socrates died through his entanglement with
magic, the attempted suicide adds a comic and distracting
element extraneous to the main theme. In the story of
Thelyphron in Book 2, Apuleius is not content to recount the
disfigurement of this character after his rash undertaking to
guard a corpse; he appends a sequel in which the corpse is
reanimated to condemn his widow as a murderess. This
addition allows him to introduce an Isiac priest with magical
powers, but it distracts the reader (some may think intention-
ally) from the relevance of the anecdote, which is the danger of
involvement with magic. The long account in Book 8 of the
deaths of Tlepolemus (at the hands of Thrasyllus) and of
Charite knits together different literary forbears, as we shall
note later. Further examples of such patchwork stories are
seen in Book 10. In the anecdote of the lovesick stepmother
and her reluctant stepson, the story is introduced as a tragedy
on the lines of Euripides' *Hippolytus* and Seneca's *Phaedra*; but
after the stepmother's natural son has drunk the 'poison'
intended for the stepson, it becomes a comedy, for the 'poison'
turns out to be a mere soporific. Most glaring of all these
patchwork creations in its improbabilities is the history of the
female criminal with whom Lucius-turned-ass is to copulate
at the public show in Book 10. She first appears as a jealous
wife who falsely suspects her husband's sister of alienating his
affections, and kills her; but she then transforms herself into
an avaricious shrew who poisons her husband and the
apothecary who furnished the drug, her own daughter and the
apothecary's wife. The ostensible purpose of the story, the
demonstration of the infidelity which stalks through Lucius'

degenerate world, loses all impact because of its inconse-
quentialities.[27]

The third feature worthy of note in this analysis of the
romance as entertainment is the literary texture. In the
Roman system of mandarin education, those who graduated
to the enjoyment of such literature as this were few but well-
read, and the fiction of Petronius and Apuleius could be
enjoyed at two levels; the narrative-content (comic, romantic,
and tragic) provides the running entertainment of an interest-
ing story, and superimposed on this is the more sophisticated
amusement of repeated evocation of earlier masterpieces of
literature. In some episodes, notably *Cupid and Psyche*, the
long inserted narrative of Charite, Tlepolemus, and Thrasyllus
(in which Herodotus, Sophocles, Virgil, Ovid, and Plutarch
are all brought into play), and the Phaedra-story in Book 10
(where Virgil and Seneca are brought continually before our
minds), the literary evocations are prominent in establishing
the structural frame. In other places Apuleius exploits these
familiar texts for glancing parody. For example, when the
sight of Photis in the kitchen excites Lucius to sexual arousal
('obstipui et mirabundus steti, steterunt et membra quae
iacebant ante'), the evocation of the *Aeneid*, 'obstipui,
steteruntque comae', disarms possible puritanical reactions
from the reader. Or again, when in *Cupid and Psyche* Venus
begs Jupiter for the loan of his messenger Mercury and Jupiter
graciously accedes, the phrase which indicates his approval
('nec rennuit Iouis caerulum supercilium') comically echoes a
response of Zeus to Thetis in Homer's *Iliad*.[28]

Like Petronius, Apuleius on occasion burlesques the pre-

---

[27] On the narrative technique in the inserted episodes, see Perry, *Ancient Romances*,
ch. 7, and his earlier articles cited there; E. Paratore, *La novella in Apuleio*[2] (Messina,
1942); J. Tatum, *TAPA* (1969), 487 ff. On the Aristomenes and Thelyphron stories,
see also C. Meyrhofer, *Antichthon* (1975), 8 ff.; on Thelyphron also G. Drake, *Papers in
Language and Literature* (1977), 3 ff. On the story of Charite, W. Anderson, *Philol.*
(1909), 537 ff.; C. Forbes, *CW* (1943), 39 f.; R. van der Paardt, *Symp. Apul.
Gronignanum* (1981), 19 ff. On the stories in Bk. 10, S. Hammer, *Eos* (1923), 6 ff.

[28] See 8.14, 10.3, 2.7, 6.7 with nn.

sentation of Roman historians like Sallust and Livy. When the members of the robber-band drive Lucius-turned-ass to their mountain-lair, Apuleius commences his narrative of events there with the time-honoured formula: 'Res ac tempus ipsum locorum speluncaeque illius . . . descriptionem flagitant.' Later in the romance, the calamities of an estate-owner are prefigured with exotic prodigies; the catalogue of them reminds us of similar prodigy-lists in Livy foretelling, for example, the disasters of Trasimene and Cannae.[29]

Further opportunities for such literary parody are exploited with lawcourt scenes, which figure prominently also in the Greek love-romances. The Festival of Laughter provides the most extended example, with its speeches for the prosecution and defence constructed according to the rules tabulated by Quintilian. The court-scene in the Phaedra episode in Book 10 offers a second example; here the litigants are warned to observe the rules laid down on the Areopagus, and the decision is reached by dropping pebbles in the urn according to the regular Roman procedure. More amusingly, Roman oratory is parodied in a scene outside the courts: when Lucius-turned-ass abandons the cruel boy to be mangled to death by a rampant bear, the boy's rustic mother becomes a veritable Cicero as she assails Lucius in his stall with a splendid parody of a prosecuting counsel's attack.[30]

Beyond purely literary parody, Apuleius introduces Roman legal and procedural motifs for humorous effect, aware that his cultured readers would appreciate the technicalities. It is not only the Greek protagonists who are bound by Roman law; the very gods and goddesses on Olympus respect Roman edicts in matters of inheritance, or marriage, or adultery, or runaway slaves.[31] The deities likewise organize their

---

[29] 4.6 and Sallust, *BJ* 17. 1, 95. 2; 9.33 f. and Livy 21. 62, 22. 1. 8 ff.

[30] 3.3 f. and Quintilian 3. 9; 10. 7 ff.; 7. 27. On Apuleius' literary texture in general I have benefited greatly from discussion with Prof. Ellen Finkelpearl of Scripps College, who hopes eventually to publish a monograph on the subject.

[31] 5.29; 6.9, 22, 4; cf. F. Norden, *Apuleius von Madaura und das römische Privatrecht* (Leipzig, 1912).

assemblies according to Roman convention, with threats of fines for non-attendance and rules of procedure; here Apuleius exploits a comic motif prominent earlier in Ovid and in Seneca's *Apocolocyntosis*.[32]

It is clear beyond doubt, then, that the romance is a literary entertainment, and commentators who wholly reject the notion of an underlying moral purpose are content to explain the final book as Apuleius' exploitation of exotic religious practices solely for the diversion of readers. The rescue of Lucius from his plight through the acknowledgement of the saving power of Isis is visualized as having been inspired by similar *dénouements* in the Greek romances, where hapless lovers are similarly delivered from their privations by the intervention of a kindly deity. In Chariton's novel Aphrodite is the rescuer, in Longus it is Pan; most piquantly of all, in Xenophon of Ephesus the lovers Anthia and Habrocomes address their thanks to Isis, whose role as protector of chastity is emphasized earlier in this novel. Apuleius' entire romance is thus envisaged as literary entertainment in which Apuleius merges the disparate Greek genres of comic short story and extended 'ideal' romance into a novel unity for the pleasurable relaxation of his readers.

V

Yet there is no doubt that designation of the romance merely as entertainment leaves many readers dissatisfied. From the time of Beroaldus and Adlington, the first commentator and the first translator of the novel into English respectively, there was virtual unanimity until the later nineteenth century that it is presented not merely as a moral fable but also as an allegory of the human condition. In his Introductory Address and his Epistle Dedicatory, delivered from University College, Oxford on 18 September 1566, Adlington claims: 'Although the matter therein seeme very light and merry, yet the effect thereof tendeth to a good and vertuous moral . . .'; 'Under the

---

[32] See 6.23. 1 with Kenney, *Cupid and Psyche*, n. ad loc.

wrap of this transformation is taxed the life of mortall men, when as we suffer our mindes so to bee drowned in the sensuall lusts of the flesh, and the beastly pleasure thereof . . . so can we never be restored to the right figure of ourselves except we taste and eat the sweet Rose of reason and vertue, which rather by the mediation of praier we may assuredly attaine.'[33]

It is an absorbing question to ask why many modern critics have earlier poured scorn on this interpretation, and why more recently there has been an increasing tendency to acccept the romance as fable as well as entertainment. One important factor has been the recent rehabilitation of the *philosophus Platonicus* and the greater attention paid to the dominant ideas of Middle Platonism. The contemporaries of Apuleius approached the novel with a greater awareness of the resonances of second-century philosophy in this theme of the deliverance of Lucius-turned-ass by the grace of Isis. A crucial figure in this connection is Plutarch, whose *Moralia* can enlighten us on many aspects of *The Golden Ass*. It is notable that at two important junctures early in the novel, Lucius' descent from Plutarch is stressed; there is no mention of this provenance in *Lucius or the Ass*, and we may assume that Apuleius has added this characterizing detail to suggest that Lucius' family connections should have enabled him to avoid the hazards of curiosity for magic by way of sex. This is the lesson impressed upon him by the priest of Isis in the final book: 'Nec tibi natales . . . uel ipsa qua flores usquam doctrina praefuit.'[34]

The familiar title of the romance, *Asinus aureus*, is conventionally rendered as 'The Prince of Ass-stories', but there may be a purposeful ambiguity here. It has been suggested that the Latin translates the Greek *onos purros*, the 'tawny ass' of

---

[33] *The Eleven Bookes of The Golden Asse* (London, 1566). R. Heine in Hijmans and van der Paardt, *Aspects*, takes the allegorical interpretation back to Fulgentius in the 6th cent., and reminds us that Boccaccio treats the *Cupid and Psyche* episode similarly in his *De genealogiis deorum gentilium libri*. Beroaldus' comm. was pub. in 1500 at Bologna.

[34] Mention of Plutarch at 1. 2. 1, 2. 3. 2. The lesson from the priest, 11. 15. 1.

Typhon which in Plutarch's *De Iside et Osiride* symbolizes the forces of evil. This treatise is of vital importance for a fuller understanding of the romance, since it offers a full explanation of how the Isiac religion is reconciled with the dualist philosophy of Plato. Osiris and Isis represent order and reason; over against them stands Typhon, the principle of irrationality and disorder. We should assign to Isis all that is well-ordered and beautiful in the world, and to Typhon all that lacks measure and order. Isis and Osiris have been transformed from demons into gods, with power above and below the earth.[35]

The ass, 'the most stupid of domestic animals', is assigned to Typhon, the malevolent demon whom it resembles in stupidity and lust. Hence Lucius' transformation into a donkey, and his eventual resumption of human shape, pregnantly signify a relapse into bestial living and re-emergence into authentic humanity. It seems beyond doubt that when Apuleius transformed the climax of the ass-story (which in the Greek version ends on the same note of lubricious comedy which characterizes it throughout) into an apologia for the Isiac religion, he was inspired by Plutarch's *De Iside*. It is true that Plutarch's treatment is the more philosophical, whereas Apuleius emphasizes salient detail of ritual and religious practice; but these variations are attributable to the differing purposes of philosopher and novelist. Even so there are numerous correspondences of detail.[36]

The moral of the *Metamorphoses* is that Lucius' avid curiosity to explore the realm of magic, attained by way of sexual encounter with Photis, was punished because it was a perverted path to universal knowledge. This lesson was already present in the Greek version, but the *curiositas*-motif is

---

[35] For *onos purros*, *Moralia* 362 F; cf. R. Martin, *RÉL* (1970), 332 ff. For the reconciliation of the Isiac religion with Platonism, see *Moralia*, 371 ff., 376–7A. For Isis and Orisis as gods, *Moralia* 361 D.

[36] For the ass and Typhon, *Moralia* 362 F, 371 C. For the parallels, see my 'Apuleius and Plutarch', in H. J. Blumenthal and R. A. Markus (eds.), *Neoplatonism and Early Christian Thought* (London, 1981), 31 n., 25.

much more pervasive and exemplary in Apuleius, who seeks in the *Apology* to establish a distinction between healthy curiosity, which seeks knowledge of the true reality by intellectual effort and religious experience, and the debased curiosity which seeks a false reality by way of magic and sensuality. It is not without significance that this issue is earlier treated in Plutarch's treatise *De curiositate*.[37]

A further important treatise of Plutarch is the *De genio Socratis*. We have already noted that Apuleius' monograph called *De deo Socratis* is of considerable significance for *The Golden Ass* as indicating the preoccupation of Middle Platonism with demons as intermediaries between gods and men. The close similarity between the titles is no coincidence; Apuleius, as we have seen, deliberately selects titles which connect his studies with those of famed forebears. In the first two books of his romance, the stories of the death of Socrates and the disfigurement of Thelyphron underline the malevolent power of witches; they are to be regarded as demons inimical to the human race. The same inference is to be made about the old man in Book 8 who entices one of Lucius' cortege to be devoured by a dragon, and likewise about the witch in Book 10 who is hired by the baker's wife to dispose of her husband.[38]

It will be clear that the reader who approaches *The Golden Ass* with an awareness of Apuleius' philosophical and religious suppositions will suspect from the outset that there is more to the story than mere entertainment. Those without such knowledge, however, are led by the author up the garden path of 'entertainment' until they are suddenly confronted with the moralizing in the final book. But a retrospective survey of

[37] For the two contrasting forms of curiosity, see C. C. Schlam, *CJ* (1968), 120 ff.; G. Sandy, *Latomus* (1972), 179 ff.; J. L. Penwill, *Ramus* (1975), 49 ff. For Plutarch's treatise, *Moralia*, 517 c ff.

[38] The *De genio Socratis* complements *De deo Socratis* on the tenets of Middle Platonism concerning demons. They lodge on the moon; unjust demons commit crimes, while good demons participate in the mysteries, and punish evil deeds. They can rescue individuals from danger if the souls of such persons pay heed to them.

Lucius' experiences must then convince them that Apuleius has created a pattern of events which is summarized in the condemnation by the Isiac priest: 'In the green years of youth, you tumbled on the slippery slope into slavish pleasures, and gained the ill-omened reward of your unhappy curiosity.' The 'slavish pleasures' (*seruiles uoluptates*) are the sexual prelude with Photis, and the 'unhappy curiosity' (*curiositas improspera*) the obsession with magic.[39]

In the first three books which document Lucius' fall from grace, he is given warning after warning of the hazards that attend his fixation on magic, but in spite of his upbringing and learning he remains impervious to them. Aristomenes' story of the death of Socrates posts the initial warning: Socrates forsook his family responsibilities, bound himself by sexual ties to the witch Meroë, and suffered the consequences. But Lucius fails to grasp that *fabula de eo narratur*. A little later at the house of his kinswoman Byrrhena, he examines statuary depicting the myth of Actaeon spying on Diana's naked form, and being turned into a stag to be mangled by his own hunting-dogs; Lucius fails to heed the dangers of such peeping-Tom curiosity (*curioso optutu*) and is to be turned into an ass to be the butt of similar attacks. Byrrhena reinforces the warning by explicit advice about his hostess Pamphile, who enchains handsome youths with the fetters of love, and transforms them to other shapes; Lucius' response is to form a close love-compact with the maid Photis to enable him to gain access to the witch's magical practices. Photis reinforces the warning: 'The honey that tastes so sweet may bring on an attack of bitter bile.' In spite of his superior philosophical knowledge, which he demonstrates in the conversation with his host Milo following the flickering lamp, and in spite of the horrendous warning of the mutilation of Thelyphron (like himself a youthful visitor to Thessaly, land of witches), he tells Photis: 'I am aflame to observe magic with my own eyes.' He adds to this confession of *curiositas* an explicit rejection of family ties in his enslavement to sensual pleasures: 'Now I do

[39] 11.15.

not desire home or hearth; this night with you I count above all that.'[40]

This patterning in the first three books is so crystal-clear, especially on a second reading following awareness of the Isiac priest's condemnation in Book 11, that Apuleius' purpose of converting his entertainment into a fable cannot reasonably be doubted. Difficulty does, however, arise in the second part of the story (Books 4–10), in which the author's task was to portray the punishment incurred by Lucius for his sins. Apuleius' decision to follow the main lines of the Greek story, with its aim no more than comic entertainment, results in his recounting Lucius' good times as well as bad; for example, the favoured treatment which he receives from Charite following her rescue and return home, or again, during the brief interlude with the cooks and their master Thiasus, when with his 'human' tricks he becomes a social attraction. Even so, the main emphases are on his sufferings as an ass in a degenerate world, as in his grisly experiences with the bandits, his privations at the mill, his ordeal at the hands of the sadistic boy, and the degrading nature of his life with the eunuch-priests. The role of Fortune throughout these unhappy experiences should be noted: this victimizing Fortune represents the arbitrary and irrational course of events in a fallen world, and it is significant that the priest of Isis in the final book contrasts her with 'the Fortune with eyes'. Implicit here is the contrasting dominion of Typhon with that of Isis.[41]

Interpenetrating these harsh experiences, earlier recounted by the Greek source, are the insertions and changes introduced by Apuleius himself. In sum they depict a world dominated by deceit, cruelty, and infidelity. The trinity of bandits' exploits, though recounted in a mock-serious tone, none the less reflects

[40] The lesson of Aristomenes, 1.7–8; the statuary, 2.4; Byrrhena's warning, 2.5; Photis' ambivalent rebuke, 2.10; Thelyphron, 2.21 ff. Lucius' abandonment of kin for sensual pleasure, 3.19. The Festival of Laughter, as Photis explains, was the result of Pamphile's magical practices, and posted a further warning.

[41] Favourite of Charite, 7.14; with the cooks and Thiasus, 10.13 ff. For the hostility of Fortune, see 7.2, 3, 16, 17, 25; 8.24; for blind Fortune contrasted with the Fortune with eyes, 11.15.

the world of violence encompassing Lucius. The story of
Charite undergoes a total transformation in Apuleius; in the
Greek version she and her husband Tlepolemus accidentally
perish by drowning, whereas Apuleius composes a story of
cruelty and lust in which Thrasyllus wantonly kills Tlepolemus
in his attempt to obtain Charite's hand in marriage. In the
wanderings of Lucius and his ménage that ensue, Apuleius in
a trinity of episodes depicts a hostile, hateful world of spirits,
nature, and men. The anecdotes that follow repeatedly advert
to sexual lust and magical practices. Four stories centre on
deceiving wives, in one of which the baker's wife engineered
the murder of her husband through the magical arts of a
witch; later Lucius tells the stories of the stepmother's
destructive passion for her stepson, and of the wife whose
jealousy impelled her to mass murder.[42] All these narratives
depict the various facets of the corrupt world into which
Lucius has descended.

VI

It is accordingly clear that Apuleius has artfully converted his
entertainment into a fable. This does not, however, foreclose
his surprises, for in the final book his fable, his story with a
moral, becomes his testament. As *Lucius or the Ass* reveals, the
Greek source reached its climax with a public show mounted
at Thessalonica; there Lucius-turned-ass gulped down some
roses carried by an attendant, was restored to human shape,
and explained his history to the governor, who by a mind-
stretching coincidence happened to know his family, and
facilitated his departure. He then hopefully revisited the lady
who had enjoyed his sexual services when he was an ass, but
he was scornfully rejected by her, whereupon he returned
home. There is dispute about whether the fuller Greek version
ended in precisely this way, but clearly the final book in

---

[42] Bandits' stories, 4.9 ff.; Charite and Thrasyllus, 8.1 ff.; trinity of episodes, 8.
17–22; adulterous wives, 9.5, 16 ff. The baker murdered by magic, 9.30; the
stepmother and the mass-murderess, 10.2 ff., 23 ff.

Apuleius' romance presents a wholly original climax to the tale.[43]

If Apuleius had wished merely to edify his readers by appending a moralizing close, it would have been sufficient to describe how Lucius recovered his human shape by eating the roses proffered to him by the priest of Isis, and how the remonstration of the priest pointed the moral. Instead of this, Apuleius transfers the *mise-en-scène* from Thessalonica in the Greek original to Corinth and its suburb Cenchreae, presumably because he had personal acquaintance with its importance as a centre of Isiac worship. On the shore at Cenchreae Lucius addresses despairing prayers to Isis, and when by her aid he has resumed his human shape, he becomes her votary. The lyrical prayers, the rapt meditation before her statue, the account of the cult-initiation, and the description of other ceremonials make this book the most detailed account of the Isis-liturgy that we possess from antiquity. Apuleius is not content even with this; he records how Lucius upon the advice of Isis travelled to Rome, and there underwent two further initiations. Prior to the first of these, the priest who was to initiate him received a divine message that *a man from Madauros*, the native city of Apuleius, was to be admitted as a votary. The author therefore identifies himself at this point with his hero, so that there is a clear case for calling Book 11 a personal testament. The propaganda elements in his account are conspicuous. There is emphasis on the number of initiates of all ranks and ages; the antiquity of the cult is stressed; the bystanders who have witnessed Lucius' recovery of his human form are urged to amend their lives. 'Let unbelievers observe you, and . . . recognize the errors of their ways.'[44]

Elsewhere I have speculated that this fervid recommendation of the religion of Isis may represent a counterblast to the

---

[43] The various theories about the ending of the Greek *Metamorphoses* are helpfully summarized by Schlam, *Metamorphoses*, 24 ff.

[44] For Cenchreae as a centre of Isiac worship, Gwyn Griffiths, *Apuleius of Madauros*, 14 ff. A man from Madauros, 11.27; initiates, 11.10; antiquity, 11.5; unbelievers, 11.15.

meteoric spread of Christianity in Africa in the later second century. This suggestion has been sceptically received, but it is worth summarizing the arguments here, which depend on the thesis that the romance was written in Carthage in the later second century, after earlier residence in Athens and Rome. It seems probable that in Rome he encountered Christian apologies proliferating there; that composed by Marcianus Aristides contains a scathing attack on Isis, who by this date had been accepted as an honoured inmate in the *curia deorum*. His return to Carthage coincided with the extraordinary flowering of Christianity in North Africa. Madauros, Apuleius' own birthplace, is mentioned as the first focal point of Christian witness; more important, however, is the evidence of Tertullian's *Apology*, which claims that the whole province of Africa was in ferment in the 190s because of the inroads made by Christianity.[45]

If this were the sum of evidence, and the speculation rested merely on the vague claim that 'Genuine conversion to paganism will appear . . . only when Christianity had become so powerful that its rival was, so to speak, made an entity by opposition and contrast', the thesis would lack substance. Two further factors, however, must be taken into account. The first is a remarkable statement by Tertullian that at least some fellow-Africans believed that Christians worshipped *an ass's head* (*somniastis caput asininum esse deum nostrum*), and that a condemned man in the amphitheatre aped the Christian god by equipping himself with ass's ears and a hoof, and by carrying the inscription 'The God of the Christians, Offspring of an Ass'. Tertullian explains this strange notion by suggesting that it was a distortion of Tacitus' excursus on Jewish practices in his *Histories* (5. 3 ff.). This popular belief that Christians worshipped the ass is also retailed by

---

[45] On this theory that Apuleius was reacting to Christian inroads, see *Phoenix* (1968), 151 ff.; Walsh, *Roman Novel*, 186 ff. Marcianus Aristides, *Apol.* 12. 3: 'If Isis is a goddess, and could not help her own brother and husband, how can she help anyone else?' Madauros as a Christian centre, Augustine, *Ep.* 16. 2. Tertullian's evidence, *Apol.* 37 (date AD 197).

Minucius Felix, and it is accordingly possible to interpret Lucius' metamorphosis into an ass, and his restoration to human shape, as the adoption and later renunciation of Christian beliefs.[46]

The second factor worthy of consideration relates to the condemnation of the baker's wife in Book 9: 'Instead of adhering to a sure faith, she sacrilegiously feigned bold awareness of a deity whom she proclaimed to be the only God.' This condemnation must obviously be directed at either Jewish or Christian beliefs and practices, and given the increased Christian presence in Africa, Christianity is the likelier target. The claims made for the Isiac religion certainly swing into sharper focus if considered against the competing claims of Christianity. The emphasis on the *numen unicum multiformi specie* of Isis, the consecration of Lucius' entire lifespan to her, the prominence lent to contemplation, the preoccupation with sexual chastity all gain greater significance when considered in this defensive light against the external challenge.[47]

VII

At the centre of this unprecedented synthesis of entertainment, fable, and testament is the inserted story of Cupid and Psyche.[48] The purpose of this story within a story (a technique familiar to educated readers from both Alexandrian and

---

[46] For the quotation on conversion to paganism, see A. D. Nock, *Conversion* (Oxford, 1933), 14. The Tertullian passage is at *Apol.* 16; cf. Minucius Felix, *Oct.* 9. 4, 28. 8.

[47] The baker's wife, 9.14; cf. L. Herrmann, *Latomus* (1953), 188 ff. For Isis' *numen unicum* and compassionate care, 11.1–2; consecration of Lucius' life-span, 11.6; cf. A. J. Festugière, *Personal Religion among the Greeks* (Berkeley, Calif., 1960), 80; contemplation, 11–17 ff.; sexual chastity, 11.6, 19, 23 (for Christian emphasis on this virtue, Hermas, 29. 1 ff.; Justin, *1 Apol.* 15; Tertullian, *Apol.* 9).

[48] The *conte* of Cupid and Psyche has been recently ed. by E. J. Kenney with a comprehensive introduction and bibliography. L. C. Purser's edn. (London, 1910) is still serviceable; P. Grimal has published a French edn. (Paris, 1963). G. Binder and R. Merkelbach have assembled a collection of essays in *Amor und Psyche* (Wege der Forschung, 126, Darmstadt, 1968).

Roman literature) is to illuminate the larger whole; Apuleius has projected into the wider world of myth the central thread of *The Golden Ass*. Like the romance proper, the *conte* is introduced with the beguiling promise of an elegant narration, a programmatic parallel. Like Lucius, Psyche indulges her curiosity, in spite of repeated warnings; as punishment she wanders like Lucius-turned-ass forlornly through the world; her deliverance is preceded by a series of trials which correspond with the initiation of Lucius into the Isiac mysteries in the final book. The correspondence is especially marked in the final trial, in which Psyche is required to visit the realm of the dead; Lucius likewise in his initiation treads 'the threshold of Persephone'. After successfully performing these tasks, Psyche is rescued by Cupid from the suspended death brought on by her curiosity; she is transported to heaven, and bears a child who is called Pleasure, just as Lucius' intimate relationship with Isis brings him pleasure beyond telling (*inexplicabilis uoluptas*).[49]

This striking series of connections led Merkelbach to argue that the entire romance was a *roman-à-clef* rooted in the Isiac mystery-religion, and meaningful only to the initiates. This view has, however, failed to win wide acceptance.[50]

The source or sources on which Apuleius drew for his story cannot be definitely established. The basic themes of the beautiful girl with two jealous sisters, her courtship by an enchanted suitor reputed to be a monster, the enforced separation from him because of the breaking of a taboo, the oppression by a witch who imposes impossible trials upon her, and the ultimate reconciliation with her lover, can all be paralleled in widespread versions of folklore tales; the existence of a North African version is of particular interest. It was Apuleius' brilliant achievement to convert this *Märchen*

[49] For the technique of a story within a story, see esp. Catullus, 64 (and Kenney, *Cupid and Psyche*, 12 f.). The culminating trial of Psyche and the initiation of Lucius, 6. 20 and 11.21, 23. Birth of Voluptas and *inexplicabilis uoluptas*, 6.24 and 11.24.

[50] The notion of *The Golden Ass* as sacral myth was earlier propounded by R. Reitzenstein and K. Kerényi. Merkelbach has argued that all the extant Greek romances except Chariton's, as well as that of Apuleius, are coded documents in this sense.

into a *Kunstmärchen* for his special purpose of illuminating the career of Lucius.[51]

In this adaptation of a traditional story, our author's Platonist preoccupations are especially prominent; he has grafted on to his source the names of the protagonists to indicate that Psyche's separation from, and ultimate reunion with, Cupid is an allegory for the soul's restless aspiration to attain the divine, as Plato depicts it in his *Phaedrus*. Beyond this, it has been suggested that the Platonist doctrine of the two Venuses, as first recounted by Pausanias in the *Symposium* and reproduced by Apuleius in his *Apology*, is central to the story. Just as the higher Venus ('recommending virtues by beauty of character to those who love her') and the lower Venus ('binding in her embrace enslaved bodies') contend for mastery over Lucius, so in *Cupid and Psyche*, it is suggested, the two Venuses (and the two Cupids or forms of love) compete for the soul of Psyche. The thesis is clearly valid in the case of Lucius, for the higher Venus prevails when Isis replaces Photis as the object of his affections. It seems, however, less relevant in the career of Psyche, for though the character of Cupid is schizoid, his less reputable persona is never revealed to her, and her sexual role as *matrona* is clearly different from Lucius' random sensuality. Nor does Apuleius characterize Venus in deliberately contrasted philosophical roles; she is a many-sided literary creation.[52]

Apuleius did not invent the story of the love between Cupid and Psyche; that relationship, stemming from the influence of Plato, was already celebrated in the art and literature of the

[51] For the folk-tale and its diffusion see J. O. Swähn, *The Tale of Cupid and Psyche* (Lund, 1955); J. R. G. Wright, *CQ* (1971), 273 ff. For the N. African version, see O. Weinreich in Binder and Merkelbach, *Amor und Psyche*, 293 ff., with earlier bibliography. It seems perverse to argue that Apuleius created rather than adapted the basic tale, as suggested by D. Fehling, *Amor und Psyche* (Wiesbaden, 1977).

[52] For Psyche (the soul) and her aspiration to the divine in Plato, see esp. *Phaedrus* 248c and compare 5.24 here. For the two Venuses, *Symp.* 180d–181b and Apuleius, *Apol.* 12; see E. J. Kenney, 'Psyche and her mysterious Husband', in D. A. Russell (ed.), *Antonine Literature* (Oxford, 1990), 175 ff., and his *Cupid and Psyche* at 5.6. 9, where he suggests that 'Psyche tempts Cupid physically as Photis had tempted Lucius'. But the two situations (marital bliss and random sensuality) are wholly different.

Hellenistic age. Erōs, the wanton boy who inflames with passion both deities and human beings, frequently appears in the poems of the Palatine Anthology, on occasion suffering the love-torments which he inflicts on others; Psyche by name is more fugitive, but in Hellenistic statuary the love-relationship of Cupid with a winged maiden is a frequent theme, and must relate to the Platonist myth as depicted in the *Phaedrus* and *Symposium*.[53]

The schizoid character of Cupid—now the sober husband, now the wanton boy of Hellenistic literature—is best explained as the combination of the traditional portrayal of the enchanted suitor with the literary stereotype. It is notable that throughout his relationship with Psyche—except when she breaks the taboo by gazing on him in his sleep—the wanton boy with his torch and arrows is wholly absent; on the other hand, in his dealings with his mother Venus and with other deities, including Jupiter, he is invariably depicted as the mischievous ne'er-do-well. Venus is a composite of a purely literary kind, depicted with affectionate ribaldry now as the irascible Juno of the *Aeneid*, now as the self-inflating creator of all new life as in Lucretius, now as the prickly Aphrodite in Apollonius Rhodius.[54]

Psyche's portrayal is even more diverse. Initially she is cast in the role of Chariton's Callirhoe, the sweet heroine of the Greek love-romance. When her father exposes her as bidden on a deserted rock, she becomes the tragic heroine like an Iphigenia or a Polyxena. After her sisters have persuaded her that she must behead her monstrous husband, she acts the irresolute heroine as depicted in the dramas of Euripides and Seneca, and (more directly) in the *Metamorphoses* of Ovid. When, now pregnant, she embarks on her journey of pilgrimage through the world, she becomes a second Io, the

---

[53] For the texts in the *Palatine Anthology* see Walsh, *Roman Novel*, 195 f. For the representations in art, C. C. Schlam, *Cupid and Psyche: Apuleius and the Monuments* (*APA*, University Park, 1976), esp. 4 ff.

[54] For Venus playing the role of Juno and of Lucretius' Venus, see 4.29–30; for the reincarnation of Aphrodite in Apollonius Rhodius, 5.29; see also the endnotes on those sections.

mortal maiden pursued by a goddess's spite in Aeschylus and Ovid. In the final trial imposed by Venus, when she must visit Hades, she becomes a second Aeneas. These are the more sustained evocations, but throughout the story Apuleius the literary opportunist (to exploit the phrase without denigration) entertains his learned readers with a host of poetic reminiscences from Greek and Latin predecessors.[55]

VIII

It is salutary to recall that the influential *Nachleben* of *The Golden Ass* from the time of the Italian Renaissance onwards depended on the precarious survival of a single manuscript **F** (Florence Laur. 68.2), copied at Monte Cassino in the late eleventh century. This manuscript derives ultimately from a double recension made by a certain Sallustius, first at Rome in 395 and then at Constantinople in 397. At that date the pagan Macrobius and the Christian Augustine attest their knowledge of the romance; a century later Fulgentius, bishop of Ruspe in North Africa, indicates that it was still being read in that province. But it is hardly surprising that Apuleius' philosophical works were more in evidence in the ensuing Christian centuries.[56]

The eleventh-century Manuscript **F**, illegible at some points, was happily copied a century or two later, probably also at Monte Cassino. This copy, identified by the siglum φ, usefully supplements the readings of **F**, though the scribe was negligent. During the Italian Renaissance of the fourteenth and fifteenth centuries further copies were made, not from **F** or φ, but from another copy of **F** subsequently lost; the text as

---

[55] Most recently gathered in Kenney's excellent commentary. For Psyche as a second Callirhoe, 4.28 and Chariton 1. 1. 2; for the irresolute heroine in Ovid, Kenney on 5.21. For Psyche as a second Io (cf. Ovid, *Met.* 1. 588 ff.), see Walsh, *Roman Novel*, 52 f. On Psyche and Aeneas, Ellen Finkelpearl, *TAPA* (1990), 333 ff. On Apuleius' exploitation of Virgil in general; C. Lazzarini, *Studi Classici e Orientali* (Pisa, 1985), 131 ff.

[56] For Macrobius and Augustine, nn. 24 and 1 above. For Fulgentius' allegorical interpretation of *Cupid and Psyche*, see *Mitologiae* 3. 6 (ed. Helm; the text is reproduced in Binder and Merkelbach, *Amor und Psyche*, 435 ff.)

now established is based primarily on **F** and φ, and to a minor degree on readings from these Renaissance copies. The autograph copy of Boccaccio (Florence Laur. 54. 32) survives as a literary curiosity, but is of no importance for the establishment of the text.[57]

A textual curiosity worthy of note is the *spurcum additamentum* inserted in φ after the first sentence of 10.21 but omitted from all modern editions and accordingly not included in this translation. The hand has been identified as that of Zanobi da Strada (d. 1361), who may have been responsible for conveying this and other manuscripts from Monte Cassino to Florence.[58]

Following the pioneering commentary of Beroaldus published at Bologna in 1500, other notable annotated editions were produced by Oudendorp (Leiden, 1786) and Hildebrand (Leipzig, 1842). These established the scholarly base for a trinity of notable modern editions, those of Helm (Leipzig, 1909, rev. 1955), Giarratano-Frassinetti (Turin, 1960), and Robertson (Paris, 1940; repr. 1956), on the last of which this translation is based.[59]

IX

In the half-century following publication of the *editio princeps* by Bussi in 1469, further imprints of all Apuleius' works appeared at Vicenza, Venice, Milan, and Florence, and separate editions of *The Golden Ass* at Bologna and Venice. (Even a century before 1469, Petrarch and Boccaccio had possessed their own copies; Boccaccio not only offered an allegorized interpretation of *Cupid and Psyche*, but also

[57] For the history of the text, see D. S. Robertson's introduction to the Budé edn. of the *Met.* (Paris, 1940); and earlier in *CQ* (1924), 27 ff., 85 ff. There are briefer accounts by P. K. Marshall in L. D. Reynolds (ed.), *Texts and Transmission* (Oxford, 1983), and in Kenney, *Cupid and Psyche*, 38.

[58] On the *spurcum additamentum*, E.˙ Fraenkel, *Eranos* (1953), 151 ff. On Zanobi's role in conveying the MSS to Florence, G. Billanovich, *I primi umanisti* (Fribourg, 1953), 31 ff.

[59] For a useful tabulation of editions and commentaries, see Hijmans and van der Paardt, *Aspects*, 247.

incorporated three of the adultery-stories from Book 9 into his *Decameron*.) The romance gained an even wider circulation in 1518, when following the influential commentary of Beroaldus (1500), Boiardo's celebrated translation was published in 1518, to be followed thirty years later by Firenzuola's free version, which through numerous reprints became one of the most widely read books in Western Europe. The book promoted an explosion of social satire on the central theme of *asinità*, in which Giordano Bruno was especially prominent.[60]

Meanwhile in Spain López de Cortegana, archdeacon of Seville, had exploited Beroaldus' commentary to produce his Spanish translation, probably in 1525. This was to exercise considerable influence on the birth of the picaresque in Spain. *Lazarillo de Tormes* (1554) contains no direct verbal reminiscences, but the general similarities of the I-narrative, the emphasis on the role of Fortune, the satire directed against men of religion, and the characterization of the hero all suggest Apuleian influence. Aleman's *Guzmán de Alfarache* (1599) more obviously reflects the influence of *The Golden Ass*; not only is Guzmán repeatedly described as an ass, but the novel contains a description of a festival of Isis. In other Spanish novels of the period, such as Úbeda's *La picara Justina* (1605) and Vincente Espinel's *Vida del escudero Marcos de Obregon* (1618), the debt to Apuleius is either acknowledged or clearly implicit. Whether Cervantes was directly evoking Apuleius in his *Don Quixote* is controverted, but certain scenes, especially Lucius' engagement with the wineskins, reappear in the Spanish novel.[61]

[60] For the early edns. of Apuleius, see J. E. Sandys, *A History of Classical Scholarship* (Cambridge, 1903–8), ii. 96. For Boccaccio's allegorization of *Cupid and Psyche, De genealogiis* (op. cit. n. 33 above), 5.22; the adultery-tales, see endnotes on 9.4 and 9. 22. For the translations by Boiardo and Firenzuola, see A. Scobie in Hijmans and van der Paardt, *Aspects*, 214 ff. For the subsequent explosion of *asinità*, see E. H. Haight, *Apuleius and his Influence* (London, 1927), 117 ff., underlining the importance of Bruno.

[61] See Walsh, *Roman Novel*, 235 ff., for discussion of such Apuleian influence; more cautious estimates in A. Scobie, *Aspects of the Ancient Romance* (Meisenheim, 1969), 91 ff., and Hijmans and van der Paardt, *Aspects*, 218 ff.

In Germany the Latin romance was translated by Johann
Sieder (1538), in France by Michel (1522) and again by
Louveau (1586), and in England by William Adlington,
Fellow of University College Oxford (1566). Adlington's
version, heavily indebted to his Continental predecessors, was
immediately 'ransacked to furnish the playhouses of London';
it went through five editions by 1600. Aside from dramatic
performances, 'almost every one of the major English writers
of the period . . . made use of *The Golden Asse*, sometimes along
with the Latin original'. Sidney's *Arcadia*, Spenser's *The Faerie
Queene*, Marlowe's *Hero and Leander*, Milton's *Comus* and
Paradise Regained exemplify this adaptation of Apuleian themes
in non-dramatic works. Shakespeare among dramatists is the
exemplar *par excellence* of those who repeatedly evoke episodes,
and indeed the language, of Adlington's rendering of the
romance.[62]

Of the Shakespearian plays *A Midsummer Night's Dream*
reflects the clearest influence; it is true that works such as
Reginald Scot's *Discovery of Witchcraft* (1584) may also have
been influential, but the two features of Bottom's transformation into an ass, and Titania's obsessive attachment to his
animal form, make the thesis of direct borrowing from
Apuleius persuasive. In *Much Ado About Nothing*, in which
Dogberry on six occasions describes himself as an ass, there
are several scenes and incidents which recall the privations of
Lucius. Even more obvious is the parallel between Othello
and Psyche, as both plan the execution of their spouses. Both
victims awake as the assassins address the light ('Put out the
light, and then put out the light.'). Just as a drop of burning
oil from Psyche's lamp falls on the recumbent Cupid, so a tear
from Othello's eye awakens Desdemona. Similarities of

[62] For the later influence of *The Golden Ass* in Germany, see A. Rode and E. Burck,
Metamorphosen oder Der goldene Esel (Hamburg, 1961), 256 ff., for the French
translations, R. R. Bolgar, *The Classical Heritage and its Beneficiaries* (Cambridge,
1954), 526. The quotations (the first reproduced from Stephen Gosson (1582)) are to
be found in J. J.M. Tobin, *Shakespeare's Favorite Novel* (University Press of America,
Lanham, Md., 1984), p. xiii. I have derived the substance of this and the next
paragraph from Tobin's book.

language in this scene make the inspiration from *The Golden Asse* clear-cut. *Hamlet*, too, with similarities of episodes (poisoned husband, widow warned by husband's ghost, sexual tension between stepmother and stepson as in Apuleius' inserted stories), contains striking verbal expressions unique in the Shakespearian canon and occurring in Adlington. This is a mere selection of the more obvious parallels; less conspicuous echoes from Apuleius can be cited from other plays of Shakespeare.[63]

The influence of *Cupid and Psyche* on the art and literature of post-Renaissance Europe is even more pervasive. The reflection in art begins with Raphael's famous frescos in the Villa Farnesina, which portray twelve facets of the love-relationship. Raphael's pupil, Pierino del Vaga, similarly painted nine panels on the theme in the Castel Sant' Angelo. Giulio Romano in the Palazzo del Tè at Mantua depicted a running sequence of episodes from the story. From this period onward many of the greatest painters of Europe, including Titian, Caravaggio, Rubens, Velasquez, and Van Dyck, pay their tribute to the love-theme. The subject is prominent in the history of tapestry, as Boucher's eighteenth-century sets demonstrate. In sculpture perhaps the most famous representations are those of Canova and Rodin.[64]

We have already noted some of the creative writers on whom *Cupid and Psyche* exercised a potent spell, including Boccaccio and Spenser, whose *Faerie Queene* contains a poetic summary of the story. Heywood's *Love's Mistris*, a dramatic exposition of the *conte*, was staged by Inigo Jones before King James I in 1636. In his Preface, Heywood says: 'The Argument is taken from Apuleius, an excellent Morall if truely understood . . .'. A year later his friend Marmion published,

---

[63] On *A Midsummer Night's Dream*, J. Dover Wilson, *Shakespeare's Happy Comedies* (Evanston, Ill., 1963), points to seven close similarities with *The Golden Ass*. For the ass-references in *Much Ado About Nothing*, see esp. IV. ii and v. i. Othello reflects Apuleian influence esp. in v. ii. *Hamlet* reveals 'the pervasive use of *The Golden Ass*' (so Tobin, *Shakespeare's Favorite Novel*, 86). Tobin analyses the plays of Shakespeare in chronological order to demonstrate the extraordinary influence which Adlington's translation exercised on him throughout his composition of them.

[64] See Haight, *Apuleius and his Influence*, 171 ff.

in heroic couplets, 'a Morall Poem intituled the Legend of Cupid and Psyche', an allegorical epic in two books. Another celebrated seventeenth-century production was Joseph Beaumont's *Psyche, or Love's Mystery* in which the author exploits the story to 'represent a soul led by divine Grace'.

The romantics of the nineteenth century revived the interest of English readers in the tale. John Keats before composing his *Ode to Psyche* had identified with the creative impulse of Apuleius ('So felt he, who first told how Psyche went | On the smooth winds to realms of wonderment'), and he prefaced the Ode with a letter which underlines the reverence with which he regarded the story. Later, William Morris in his *Earthly Paradise*, and Robert Bridges in *Eros and Psyche*, wrote poetic versions of the story, Bridges patronizingly claiming that Psyche 'deserves more care in handling the motives of her conduct than was perhaps felt in Apuleius' time and country'. Perhaps the outstanding tribute to the *conte* in the nineteenth century was the creative translation which Walter Pater enclosed in his novel *Marius the Epicurean* (1885).[65]

X

Several modern translations of Apuleius' romance have been issued. The Bohn translator (1853) claims that '*The Golden Ass* has been several times presented to the English public, but, it is believed, never so completely or faithfully';[66] like other volumes in the Bohn series, its aim is primarily to assist readers struggling with the Latin rather than to present a version to be read independently. The translation of F. D. Byrne (London, 1905) is praiseworthy; B. E. Perry considered it the best of the modern renderings. H. E. Butler's two volumes (Oxford, 1910) suffer from the squeamishness of his day; he omits passages which he regards as sexually

---

[65] Ibid. 138 ff.; see also L. C. Purser's edn. of *Cupid and Psyche* (London, 1910), pp. lxvi ff. For Apuleius and Pater, see E. J. Brenk in Hijmans and van der Paardt, *Aspects*, 231 ff.

[66] Doubtless with reference to the versions of Thomas Taylor (London, 1822), and of Sir George Head (London, 1851), as well as to that of Adlington.

indelicate without offering any indication of where his axe falls. Moreover, he is out of sympathy with Apuleius' flamboyant presentation, simplistically condemning 'a style which, by whatever canons it be judged, was intrinsically bad'. In North America, Jack Lindsay's racy version (New York, 1932) is widely popular, but it contains many errors and some infelicities.

Finally comes Robert Graves's Penguin version (1950), recently reissued with a foreword and some tactful revision by Michael Grant. The poet-craftsman's enviably supple use of the English language makes this translation attractive to read independently of the Latin, but it is by no means always faithful to the original, and in places seems merely to offer a paraphrase of Adlington. Of Graves a similar judgement can be passed as of Adlington; literary skill and versatility, not exact scholarship, is the primary requirement for the popular success of a translation. There is a disastrous exordium with 'Apuleius' address to the reader', in which the miniature biography which belongs to the hero Lucius is attached to the author; the translation misleads at some points and condenses at others. But the jocose spirit of the original is well captured, and one may confidently predict an extended life for this version.

Any justification of a new translation rests largely on the claim that greater understanding of the Latinity of Apuleius has been achieved over the past half-century. Robertson's text has provided a more satisfactory base. The new critical editions of individual books, notably those produced at Groningen and the two British contributions of Kenney (*Cupid and Psyche*) and Gwyn Griffiths (Book 11) are particularly useful in this respect. The new Loeb version of J. A. Hanson (1989), which has replaced that of Gaselee, is admirable in every respect. I have constantly consulted it. Kenney's facing translation in his edition of *Cupid and Psyche* has also furnished valuable aid.

SELECT BIBLIOGRAPHY

This is a selection of the more important publications of recent years. For fuller bibliographies, consult from the list below Scobie, *Comm. on Met. I*, 6 ff.; Gwyn Griffiths, 360 ff.; Hijmans-van der Paardt, *Aspects*, 247 ff.; Schlam, *The Metamorphoses*, 157 ff.; Kenney, *Cupid and Psyche*, 226 ff. See also G. N. Sandy, *CW* (1974), 321 ff. (*ANRW* announces that in its forthcoming volume, II. 34. 2 (?1994), the following contributions will appear: G. Sandy, 'Apuleius' *Metamorphoses* and the Ancient Novel'; W. S. Smith, 'Style and Character in *The Golden Ass*: "Suddenly an Opposite Appearance" '; L. Callebat, 'Traditions formelles et création de langage dans l'œuvre d'Apulée'; H. J. Mason, 'Greek and Latin Versions of the Ass Story'; B. L. Hijmans, 'Apuleius Orator: *Pro se de magia* (*Apologia*) and *Florida*'; M. G. Bajoni, 'Il linguaggio filosofico di Apuleio: aspetti linguistici e letterari del *De mundo*'.)

1. *Editions and Commentaries*

R. HELM, *Apulei opera quae supersunt* (Leipzig, 1907; repr. with additions, 1955).

C. GIARRATANO and P. FRASSINETTI, *Apulei Metamorphoses Libri XI* (Turin, 1960).

D. S. ROBERTSON and P. VALLETTE, *Apulée: Les Métamorphoses* (Paris, Budé, 1940–5).

A. Scobie, *Apuleius: Metamorphoses I* (Meisenheim am Glan, 1975).

R. T. VAN DER PAARDT, *A Commentary on Book III* (Amsterdam, 1971).

B. L. HIJMANS Jun., A. TH. VAN DER PAARDT, *et al.*, *Book IV. 1–27* (Groningen, 1977).

P. GRIMAL, *Apulei Metamorphoseis IV. 28–VI. 24* (Paris, 1963).

E. J. KENNEY, *Cupid and Psyche* (Cambridge, 1990).

B. L. HIJMANS *et al.*, *Books VI. 25–VII* (Groningen, 1981).

—— *Book VIII* (Groningen, 1985).

J. GWYN GRIFFITHS, *Apuleius of Madauros: The Isis-Book* (Leiden, 1975).

J. C. FREDOUILLE, *Apulée: Métamorphoses Liber XI* (Paris, 1975).

Philosophical Works

J. BEAUJEU, *Apulée: Opuscules philosophiques* (Paris, Budé, 1973).

Apology and Florida

P. VALLETTE, *Apulée: Apologie, Florides*[2] (Paris, Budé, 1960).
B. MOSCA, *Apuleio: La Magia* (Florence, 1974).

Lucius or the Ass

M. D. MACLEOD, *Lucian VIII* (London, Loeb, 1967).

2. *Translations*

(Eng.) F. D. BYRNE, *The Golden Ass of Apuleius* (London, 1905).
H. E. BUTLER, *The Metamorphoses or Golden Ass of Apuleius of Madaura* (Oxford, 1910).
J. LINDSAY, *The Golden Ass of Apuleius* (New York, 1932).
R. GRAVES, *The Transformations of Lucius* (Harmondsworth, 1950).
J. A. HANSON, *Apuleius, Metamorphoses* (new Loeb edn. London, 1989).
(Fr.) P. GRIMAL, *Romans grecs et latins* (Paris, 1958).
(Ger.) A. RODE and E. BURCK, *Metamorfosen oder Der goldene Esel* (Hamburg, 1961).
(Ital.) Q. CATAUDELLA (ed.), *Il romanzo antico greco e latino* (Florence, 1973).

3. *General*

ANDERSON, G. *Eros Sophistes: Ancient Novelists at Play* (APA, Chico, Calif., 1982).
—— *The Novel in the Graeco-Roman World* (Beckenham, 1984).
BERNHARD, M., *Der Stil des Apuleius von Madaura* (repr. Amsterdam, 1965).
BIANCO, G., *La fonte greca delle Metamorfosi di Apuleio* (Brescia, 1971).
BINDER, G., and MERKELBACH, R. (eds.), *Amor und Psyche* (Wege der Forschung 126, Darmstadt, 1968. Incl. essays by P. Grimal, L. Friedländer, F. Liebrecht, G. Heinrici, R. Reitzenstein, R. Helm, D. Weinreich, H. Jeanmaire, L. Bieler, H. Erbse, H. Wagenfoort, R. Merkelbach, S. Lancel).
CALLEBAT, L., *Sermo Cotidianus dans les Métamorphoses d'Apulée* (Caen, 1968).
CIAFFI, V., *Petronio in Apuleio* (Turin, 1960).
DERCHAIN, P., and HUBEAUX, J., 'L'affaire du marché à Hypata dans la Mét. d'Apulée', *AC* (1958), 100 ff.
DILLON, J., *The Middle Platonists* (Ithaca, NY, 1977).

DOWDEN, K., 'Apuleius and the Art of Narration', *CQ* (1982), 419 ff.

—— 'Psyche on the Rock', *Latomus* (1982), 336 ff.

DRAKE, G., 'Candidus. A Unifying Theme in Apuleius' *Met.*', *CJ* (1968/9), 102 ff.

—— 'Lucius' "Business" in the *Met.* of Apuleius', *PLL* (1969), 339 ff.

—— 'The Ghost Story in The Golden Ass by Apuleius', *PLL* (1977), 3 ff.

ENGLERT, J., and LONG, T., 'Functions of Hair in Apuleius' *Met.*', *CJ* (1972/3), 236 ff.

FEHLING, D., *Amor und Psyche* (Wiesbaden, 1977).

FERGUSON, J., 'Apuleius', *G&R* (1961), 61 ff.

FESTUGIÈRE, A. J., *Personal Religion among the Greeks* (Berkeley, Calif., 1960).

FINKELPEARL, E., 'Psyche, Aeneas and an Ass: *Met.* 6. 10–21', *TAPA* (1990), 333 ff.

—— 'The Judgment of Lucius: *Met.* 10. 29–34', *CA* (1990), 221 ff.

FLIEDNER, H., *Amor und Cupido* (Meisenheim, 1974)

FORBES, C., 'Charite and Dido', *CW* (1943), 39 f.

GRIMAL, P., 'Le calame égyptien d'Apulée', *REA* (1971), 343 ff.

Groningen Colloquia 1981 (ed. B. L. Hijmans and V. Schmidt), 1988 (ed. H. Hofmann).

HÄGG, T., *The Novel in Antiquity* (Oxford, 1983).

HAIGHT, E. H., *Apuleius and his Influence* (London, 1927).

—— 'Apuleius and Boccaccio', in *More Essays on Greek Romances* (New York, 1945), 113 ff.

HANI, J., 'L'âne d'or et l'Égypte', *RP* (1973), 274 ff.

HEISERMAN, A., *The Novel before the Novel* (Chicago, 1977).

HELLER, S., 'Apuleius, Platonic Dualism, and Eleven', *AJP* (1983), 321 ff.

HERRMANN, L., L'Ane d'Or et le Christianisme', *Latomus* (1953), 188 ff.

HICTER, M., *Apulée, Conteur Fantastique* (Brussels, 1942).

—— 'L'autobiographie dans l'âne d'or d'Apulée'. *AC* (1944), 95 ff., (1945), 61 ff.

HIJMANS, B. L., and VAN DER PAARDT, R. TH. (eds.), *Aspects of Apuleius' Golden Ass* (Groningen, 1978). Incl: H. J. Mason, 'Fabula Graecanica: Apuleius and his Greek Sources'; P. G. Walsh, 'Petronius and Apuleius'; R. Heine, 'Picaresque Novel versus Allegory'; A. Scobie, 'The Structure of Apuleius' Met.';

A. G. Westerbrink, 'Some parodies in Apuleius' Met.'; R. Th. van der Paardt, 'Various Aspects of Narrative Technique in Apuleius' *Met.*'; C. C. Schlam, 'Sex and Sanctity: the Relationship of Male and Female in Apuleius' *Met.*'; B. L. Hijmans, 'Significant Names and their Function in Apuleius' *Met.*'; G. N. Sandy, 'Book 11; Ballast or Anchor?'; J. Gwyn Griffiths, 'Isis in the *Met.* of Apuleius'; A. Scobie, 'The Influence of Apuleius' *Met.* in Renaissance Italy and Spain'; E. J. Brenk, 'Apuleius, Pater, and the Bildungsroman'; (also papers by L. Callebat and B. L. Hijmans on prose-style, and by E. Visser on Couperus and Apuleius)).

JAMES, P. *Unity in Diversity* (Hildesheim, 1987).

JONES, C. P., 'Apuleius' *Met.* and Lollianus' Phoinikika', *Phoenix* (1980), 243 ff.

JUNGHANNS, P., *Die Erzählungstechnik von Apuleius' Met. und ihrer Vorlage* (Leipzig, 1932).

KENNEY, E. J., 'Psyche and her Mysterious Husband', in D. A. Russell (ed.), *Antonine Literature* (Oxford, 1990), 175 ff.

KENNY, B., 'The Reader's Role in The Golden Ass', *Arethusa* (1974), 187 ff.

LABHARDT, A., '*Curiositas*: notes sur l'histoire d'un mot et d'une notion', *Mus. Helv.* (1960), 206 ff.

LANCEL, S., '*Curiositas* et préoccupations spirituelles chez Apulée', *RHR* (1961), 25 ff.

LAZZARINI, C., 'Il modello Virgiliano nel lessico delle *Met.* di Apuleio', *Studi Classici e Orientali* (Pisa, 1985), 131 ff.

LESKY, A., 'Apuleius von Madaura und Lukios von Patrai', *Hermes* (1941), 43 ff.

MACKAY, L. A., 'The Sin of the Golden Ass', *Arion* (1965), 474 ff.

MARTIN, R., 'Le sens de l'expression Asinus Aureus et la signification du roman apuléen', *RÉL* (1970), 332 ff.

MASON, H. J., 'Lucius at Corinth', *Phoenix* (1971), 160 ff.

—— 'The distinction of Lucius in Apuleius' *Met.*', Phoenix (1983), 135 ff.

MAZZARINO, A., *La Milesia e Apuleio* (Turin, 1950).

MERKELBACH, R., *Roman und Mysterium in der Antike* (Munich, 1962).

METTE, H. J., 'Curiositas', in H. Erbse, (ed.), *Festschr. Bruno Snell* (Munich, 1956), 227 ff.

MEYRHOFER, C., 'On Two Stories in Apuleius', *Antichthon* (1975), 8 ff.

MILLAR, F., 'The World of the Golden Ass', *JRS* (1981), 63 ff.

MORESCHINI, C., 'La demonologia medioplatonica et le *Met.* di Apuleio', *Maia* (1965), 30 ff.

—— *Apuleio e il Platonismo* (Florence, 1978).

NETHERCUT, W., 'Apuleius' Literary Art; Resonance and Depth in the Met.', *CJ* (1968), 110 ff.

NEUMANN, E., *Amor and Psyche* (New York, 1962).

NOCK, A. D., *Conversion* (Oxford, 1933).

NORDEN, F., *Apulejus von Madaura und das römische Privatrecht* (Leipzig, 1912).

NORWOOD, F., 'The Magic Pilgrimage of Apuleius', *Phoenix* (1956), 1 ff.

PARATORE, E., *La novella in Apuleio*² (Messina, 1942).

PENWILL, J. L., 'Slavish Pleasures and Profitless Curiosity', *Ramus* (1975), 49 ff.

PERRY, B. E., *The Ancient Romances* (Berkeley, Calif., 1967) (cf. *CP* (1923), 229 ff., (1929), 231 ff.; *TAPA* (1923), 196 ff., (1926), 238 ff.); *CJ* (1968/9), 97 ff.)

REGEN, F., *Apuleius Philosophus Platonicus* (Berlin, 1971).

REITZENSTEIN, R., *Hellenistische Wunderezählungen* (Stuttgart, 1963).

RIEFSTAHL, H., *Der Roman des Apuleius* (Frankfurt, 1938).

SANDY, G. N., 'Knowledge and Curiosity in Apuleius' Met.', *Latomus* (1972), 179 ff.

—— 'Foreshadowing and Suspense in Apuleius' Met.', *CJ* (1973), 232 ff.

—— '*Serviles voluptates* in Apuleius' Met.', *Phoenix* (1974), 234 ff.

SCAZZOSO, P., *Le Metamorfosi di Apuleio* (Milan, 1951).

SCHLAM, C. C., 'The Curiosity of the Golden Ass', *CJ* (1968), 120 ff.

—— 'Platonica in the *Metamorphoses* of Apuleius', *TAPA* (1970), 477 ff.

—— *Cupid and Psyche: Apuleius and the Monuments* (*APA*, Penn., 1976).

—— 'Apuleius and the Middle Ages', in Bernardo and Levin (eds.), *The Classics in the Middle Ages* (Binghampton, NY, 1990), 363 ff.

—— *The Metamorphoses of Apuleius* (Chapel Hill, NC, 1992).

SCOBIE, A., *Aspects of the Ancient Romance and its Heritage* (Meisenheim, 1969).

—— *More Essays on the Ancient Romance and its Heritage* (Meisenheim, 1973).

—— *Apuleius and Folklore* (London, 1983).

SHUMATE, N., 'The Augustinian Pursuit of False Values as a Conversion Motif in Apuleius' Met.', *Phoenix* (1988), 35 ff.

SMET, R. DE, 'The Erotic Adventures of Lucius and Photis in Apuleius' *Met.*', *Latomus* (1987), 613 ff.

SMITH, W. S., 'The Narrative Voice in Apuleius' *Met.*', *TAPA* (1972), 513 ff.

STABRYLA, S., 'The Functions of the Tale of Cupid and Psyche in the Structure of the *Met.* of Apuleius', *Eos* (1973), 261 ff.

STEPHENSON, W. E., 'The Comedy of Evil in Apuleius', *Arion* (1964), 87 ff.

SUMMERS, R. G., 'Apuleius Juridicus', *Historia* (1972), 120 ff.

—— 'A Note on the date of the Golden Ass', *AJP* (1973), 375 ff.

SWAHN, J. Ö., *The Tale of Cupid and Psyche* (Lund, 1955).

TATUM, J., 'The Tales in Apuleius' Metamorphoses', *TAPA* (1969), 487 ff.

—— 'Apuleius and Metamorphosis', *AJP* (1972), 306 ff.

—— *Apuleius and The Golden Ass* (Ithaca, NY, 1979).

THIBAU, R., 'Les Mét. d'Apulée et la théorie Platonicienne de l'Eros', *Stud. Phil. Gand.* (1965), 89 ff.

TOBIN, J. J. M., *Shakespeare's Favorite Novel* (New York, 1984) (cf. also *Shakespeare Survey* (1978), 33 ff.; *English Studies* (1978), 199 ff.; *Studia Neophilologica* (1979), 225 ff.; *Notes and Queries* (1978), 120 f.

VAN DER PAARDT, R. 'The Unmasked "I"; Apuleius, *Met.* XI 27', *Mnem.* (1981), 96 ff.

VAN THIEL, H., *Der Eselsroman (*2 vols. Munich, 1971).

VEYNE, P., 'Apulée a Cenchrées', *RP* (1965), 241 ff.

WALSH, P. G., 'Was Lucius a Roman?' *CJ* (1968), 264 ff.

—— *The Roman Novel* (Cambridge, 1970).

—— 'Apuleius and Plutarch', in H. J. Blumenthal and R. A. Markus (eds.), *Neoplatonism and Early Christian Thought* (London, 1981), 20 ff.

—— 'Apuleius', in E. J. Kenney and W. K. Clausen (eds.), *The Cambridge History of Classical Literature* (Cambridge, 1982), 774 ff.

—— 'The Rights and Wrongs of Curiosity', *G&R* (1988), 73 ff.

WINKLER, J. J., *Auctor & Actor* (Berkeley, Calif., 1985).

WITTMAN, W., *Das Isisbuch des Apuleius* (Stuttgart, 1938).

WLOSOK, A., 'Zur Einheit der *Met.* des Apuleius'. *Philol.* (1969), 68 ff.

WRIGHT, C. S., 'No Art at all. A Note on the Proemium of Apuleius' *Met.*', *CP* (1973), 217 ff.

WRIGHT, J. R. G., 'Folk-Tale and Literary Technique in *Cupid and Psyche, CQ* (1971), 273 ff.

SMITH, R. DE, *The Erotic Adventures of Lucius and Photis in Apuleius*, MW, Trondheim (1987), 613 ff.

BOOK 1

Journey to Hypata: The Exemplar of Socrates

1 What I should like to do is to weave together different tales
in this Milesian mode of story-telling and to stroke your
approving ears with some elegant whispers, as long as you
don't disdain to run your eye over Egyptian paper inscribed
with the sharpened point of a reed from the Nile. I want you
to feel wonder at the transformations of men's shapes and
destinies into alien forms, and their reversion by a chain of
interconnection to their own. So let me begin! Who is the
narrator? Let me briefly explain: my antique stock is from
Attic Hymettus, the Ephyrean Isthmus, and Spartan Taenarus,
fertile territories established for ever in yet more fertile works
of literature. In those regions, in the initial campaigns of
boyhood, I became a veteran in Attic speech. Later in Rome,
as a stranger to the literary pursuits of the citizens there, I
tackled and cultivated the native language without the
guidance of a teacher, and with excruciating difficulty. So at
the outset I beg your indulgence for any mistakes which I
make as a novice in the foreign language in use at the Roman
bar. This switch of languages in fact accords with the
technique of composition which I have adopted, much as a
circus-rider leaps from one horse to another, for the romance
on which I am embarking is adapted from the Greek. Give it
your attention, dear reader, and it will delight you.

2 I was on my way to Thessaly to transact some business. My
family on my mother's side hails from that region, and the
prominence lent to it by the famous philosopher Plutarch, and
later by his nephew Sextus, lends us esteem. I was riding on
my home-bred horse, which is pure white in colour. After we
had crossed high mountain tracks, slippery paths in the
valleys, dew-laden pastures, and churned-up ploughlands, I
dismounted, for the horse was now tired, and I too needed to
invigorate myself by walking, for I was saddle-sore. I

attentively wiped the sweat from the horse's brow, fondled his
ears, loosened the reins, and took him along at a slow and
gentle pace until nature in its usual protective way could
relieve the strain of his tiredness. With his head bent low and
his mouth turned sideways, he took a walking breakfast from
the fields through which he passed. In the course of the walk,
I made myself a third to two companions who happened to be
journeying a little way ahead. I overheard what they were
saying. One of them guffawed, and said: 'Spare me this tissue
of crazy and monstrous lies.' Now I am always interested in
unusual stories, so on hearing this I demurred, and said: 'Do
tell me all about it. I am not inquisitive, but am the type
which likes to know about everything, or at least about most
things. And your elegant and amusing tales will lighten the
rigours of the hill which we are beginning to climb.'

3   But the man who had spoken earlier said: 'Surely this lying
tale of yours is only as true as the claim that when magic
formulae are whispered, running rivers go backward, the sea
is stopped and becomes idle, the winds die down and cease to
blow, the course of the sun is halted, the moon runs dry of
dew, the stars are plucked from the sky, daylight is blotted
out, and darkness prevails.' At this I broke in with some
assurance. 'Come on,' I urged the story-teller, 'don't be
ashamed or reluctant to spin out the rest of the story, now that
you have recounted the earlier part.' Then I addressed the
other man. 'Because your ears are deadened and your mind is
closed, you are contemptuous of reports that may well be true.
Heavens, man, you aren't too bright in your quite perverse
belief that all that seems unfamiliar to the ear, or unprecedented to the eye, or even too hard for our thoughts to
grasp, is to be accounted lies. Investigate such features a little
more carefully, and you will find that they are not merely
open to discovery, but are also easily performed.

4   'For example, yesterday evening I was trying to compete
with fellow-guests in greedily bolting down a largish portion
of cheesecake. Because the stuff was so soft and sticky, it stuck
in my throat and impeded my breathing so that I very nearly
choked. Yet recently at Athens I saw with my own two eyes a

contortionist performing in front of the Painted Porch; he swallowed a razor-sharp cavalry-sword with a lethal point. Then he was offered a small coin, and this encouraged him to thrust a hunting-spear deep into his gizzard, with the mortally dangerous end going in first. Then to my astonishment a handsome nancy-boy climbed up above the metal section, where the upturned shaft protruded from the man's throat up towards his head. With sinuous movements he performed a ballet-routine as though there was not a single sinew or bone in his body. Everyone watching was amazed; you would have said that it was the noble serpent which coils itself in slippery embraces round the staff of the god of healing, that knotted club with half-sheared branches which the god carries round with him. So do, please, now run through the story again which you had begun. I'll believe it, if this man won't, and I'll stand you lunch at the first inn we reach on our journey. That is the reward that I have in store for you.'

5 The man replied: 'There is no need for your fair and kind offer. I'll certainly embark on the story I began earlier, but first I'll swear to you by the sun-god who gazes down on us that what I'm telling you is true. You will harbour no further doubts once you reach the next town in Thessaly, because what happened for the world to see is common gossip there. But first let me tell you where I'm from: I'm a native of Aegium. You should hear as well how I make a living: I trade in honey, cheese, and the like with the women who run hostelries, and I journey to and fro throughout Thessaly, Aetolia, and Boeotia. So when I heard that some fresh and succulent cheese was on the market for a modest price at Hypata, the leading city in all Thessaly, I made my way quickly there to buy the lot. But I got off on the wrong foot, as often happens, and was disappointed in my hope of profit, because a wholesale merchant called Lupus had bought it all up the previous day. I was exhausted by this fruitless dash, so I made my way to the baths just as the evening star came up.

6 'Whom should I spy there but my old friend Socrates? He was sitting on the ground, only half-covered by a torn and dingy cloak, so pale as to be almost unrecognizable, and

shrunk to a mere shadow, like one of Fortune's outcasts who often beg for pennies at street-corners. I approached him because he was a close and intimate friend, but with some reluctance because of his appearance. "Good Lord, Socrates, whatever is the matter? How ghastly you look! What a scandal this is! They are weeping and mourning your death at home. Guardians have been appointed for your children by decree of the provincial judge. Your wife has performed the routine of mourning; she is ravaged after months of grief and sorrow, her eyes almost blind with weeping. Her parents are urging her to lighten the unhappiness of the household with the joys of a new marriage. And here you are, looking like a ghost, and bringing down the utmost shame on us!"

' "Aristomenes," said Socrates, "it is clear that you are innocent of the treacherous twists and turns, the unsteady assaults and see-sawing changes our fortunes bring." As he spoke, he drew his patched cloak over his face, which had been blushing with embarrassment all this time, with the result that he uncovered the rest of his body from the navel to his private parts. At that moment I could bear the wretched sight of his hardships no longer. I took his hand, and tried to bring him to his feet.

7   'But he would not budge, and kept his head covered. "Leave me, let me be!" he cried, "Let Fortune feast her eyes longer on me as the token of her victory!" But I induced him to accompany me, and at the same time I slipped off one of my two shirts, and hastily clothed him, or rather covered him up. There and then I hauled him off to the baths, coughed up for the oil and towels, and vigorously scrubbed off a huge deposit of filth. Once he was well cleaned up, I took him to an inn, supporting his exhausted body with great difficulty, for I too was tired out. I made him lie down to recover, gave him a good meal and a relieving drink, and chatted with him to enable him to relax. In no time he showed an eager desire to talk; he joked, even indulging in some clever repartee and unassuming wit. But then he heaved a tortured sigh from the depths of his heart, and beat his forehead repeatedly and savagely with his hand.

' "What a mess I'm in!" he began. "I have fallen into this misfortune through seeking a diversion at a celebrated gladiatorial show. You will remember that I made for Macedonia on a business-trip. I was busy there for nine months and more, and was making my way home with a good bit of money in my pocket. Shortly before reaching Larissa, where I intended to take in the show as I was passing through, I was making my way along a trackless, pitted valley when I was held up by some brigands of massive physique who robbed me of all my money. When I finally got away I stopped at an inn, because I was badly shaken up. It was run by a woman called Meroë, who was getting on in years, but was still quite attractive. I explained to her the circumstances of my long period away from home, my eagerness to get back, and the robbery that I had suffered. Her reaction was to treat me with extraordinary sympathy. She set me down without payment in front of a welcome supper, and then as she was feeling sexy she took me to her bed. From the moment I slept with her my misery began. The scourge of a long and baneful association sprang from that one act of sexual intercourse. Even the shabby clothes which those generous brigands had left me to cover my body I surrendered to her, and every penny I earned as a porter, as long as I still had my strength. So the combination of such a kind wife as this and malevolent Fortune has brought me to the condition which you have just witnessed."

8 ' "Good Lord!" I exclaimed. "You certainly deserve to suffer the worst possible fate, if there is anything worse than your recent experiences, because you put the pleasures of sex and a leather-skinned whore before your home and children." Socrates put his index-finger to his lips, registering shocked alarm. "Hush!" he said, looking round to see if it was safe to speak. "Don't mention the prophetess in case your loose tongue brings you harm."

' "Really?" I replied. "What sort of woman is this mighty queen of inn-keepers?"

' "She's a witch", he said, "with supernatural powers. She can bring down the sky, raise the earth, freeze running waters, melt mountains, raise ghosts, dispatch gods to the world below, black out the stars, and light up hell itself!" •

' "Come, come," I said, "ring down the tragic curtain, fold up the backcloth, and do please use the language of every day."

' "Would you care to hear one or two of her magic feats, or still better, a whole string of them? She makes not only the locals fall madly in love with her, but also Indians, both lots of Ethiopians, and even Antipodeans, but such things as these are trivial aspects of her art, mere play. Just hear what she brought about with dozens of people watching.

9   ' "A lover of hers went after another woman. With one word the witch transformed him into a beaver. Why a beaver? Because that animal in fear of captivity escapes its pursuers by biting off its own genitals, and she wanted the same fate to befall him likewise for having made love to this other woman. Then there was a neighbouring innkeeper competing for custom with her; she changed him into a frog, and now the old man swims in a barrel of his own wine, and as he squats in the lees he greets his former customers with dutiful croaks. Another man she changed into a ram because he was a barrister who prosecuted her, and now it's as a ram that he pleads his cases. Then there was the wife of a lover of hers who was heavy with child. Because she made witty and disparaging remarks about the witch, Meroë has condemned her to an indefinite pregnancy by sealing up her womb and postponing the birth. The general estimate is that the poor woman has now been carrying her burden for eight years, and is so misshapen it's as though she were giving birth to an elephant.

10   ' "Because of these periodic outrages that brought harm to many there was a general swell of indignation, and the community decreed that on the following day she should suffer the extreme punishment of stoning. But she anticipated this plan by the potency of her spells. You remember the case of Medea, who won a respite of a single short day from Creon, and ignited his whole house and daughter and the old man himself with flames which burst out from the bridal crown? Well, Meroë confided to me recently, when she was drunk,

that she dug a trench and performed rites of black magic in it by invoking the spirits of the dead. By this means she locked the entire community in their houses by the silent powers of supernatural spirits, so that for two whole days they could not break the bars, force open the doors, or even tunnel through the walls. Eventually the citizens bolstered each other and made a united appeal to her, swearing by all that was holy that they would not lay a finger on her, and that if anyone had ideas to the contrary, they would rescue her. Once they had appeased her in this way, she set the whole town free. As for the man who had summoned the public gathering, she shifted him and his entire barred dwelling—walls, floor and foundations—to another community at dead of night. This town was a hundred miles away, perched on the tip of a rugged mountain, and waterless owing to its position. But the houses of the residents there were so closely packed that they allowed no room for a new arrival, so the witch just dumped the house in front of the town gate, and made off."

11 ' "This account of your experience", I rejoined, "is remarkable, and as harrowing as it is strange. Indeed, it has pricked me with no small anxiety or rather fear; I feel not so much niggling doubt as sharp apprehension that the old hag may exploit the aid of her supernatural power in the same way to learn of this conversation of ours. So we must retire to bed quite early, and once our tiredness is relieved by sleep, we must hasten away before dawn, and put the greatest possible distance between ourselves and this place."

'While I was still urging this course, my good friend Socrates was overcome by the unaccustomed drinking and by protracted exhaustion. He fell asleep, and began to snore quite heavily. So I closed and bolted the door, pushed my bed up against the hinges to fasten them securely, and then lay down. At first my fear kept me awake for a while, but then about half way through the night I began to nod off. I had just fallen asleep when the doors were suddenly flung open, with a violence greater than you would associate with robbers; indeed, the hinges were smashed and torn from their sockets, and the doors sent crashing to the ground. My bed was small and decrepit, and had a broken leg; it was overturned by the savage force of the assault. I myself was thrown out, and as the bed landed upside down, it covered and concealed me.

12   'At that moment I recognized that certain feelings naturally give birth to their opposites, for just as tears often flow as the result of joy, so even at that moment of extreme fear I could not restrain my laughter at being transformed from Aristomenes into a tortoise. As I lay sprawled on the ground hidden by my wise old bed, I squinted out to see what was happening, and caught sight of two elderly women. One was carrying a blazing lamp, and the other a sponge and an unsheathed sword. With these objects in their hands they stood on each side of Socrates, who was sleeping soundly. The woman with the sword spoke first: "This, sister Panthia, is my dear Endymion, my Ganymede who has abused my tender years day and night, but now considers my love beneath him. Not only does he malign me with his insults, but he is also planning his escape. I suppose I am to play the role of Calypso abandoned by the guileful Ulysses and doomed to lament my loneliness for ever!" Then she extended her finger, and pointed me out to her dear Panthia: "This good fellow", she said, "is Aristomenes the counsellor. He proposed the escape, and now he lies close to death. He is lying on the ground, stretched out beneath the bed, watching all that is going on, and thinking that he will get away scot-free with insulting me. I'll make him sorry one day—in fact I'll do it now, at this very moment—for his earlier facetiousness and his insistent curiosity."

13   'In my desperate plight as I heard this, I broke out in a cold sweat, and my stomach turned over with fright, so that my shaking even disturbed the bed, which bounded up and down in spasms on my back. Then the kindly Panthia said: "Wouldn't it be a good idea, then, sister, to deal with him first, to tear him to pieces as the frenzied Bacchants did, or to tie his legs together and cut off his manhood?" Meroë answered her; I recognized who she was, as the name accorded so well with the stories Socrates had told about her. What she said was: "No; he shall live at least long enough to

bury this wretch's body in a shallow grave." She then drew Socrates' head to one side, and plunged the sword right down to the handle through the left side of his neck. As the blood spurted out, she caught it in a leather bottle which she applied to the wound, so that not a single drop was visible anywhere. I witnessed this with my own eyes. Then the good lady stuck her right hand deep into the wound, probed around for my poor friend's heart, and drew it out. No doubt she wished to observe the proprieties of a sacrifice. When the impact of the weapon had cut his throat, Socrates uttered a sound or rather an inarticulate gurgle through the wound, as he breathed out his life's breath. Panthia then applied the sponge to seal the wide expanse of the wound, and addressed it: "Listen, sea-born sponge; be sure not to float away in the following stream." After these words, they departed. On their way they both pushed aside the bed, sat astride me, and voided their bladders over my face until they had doused me in their noisome urine.

14   'As soon as they left the premises, the doors reverted undamaged to their previous position. The hinges settled back in their sockets, the bars were restored to the doorposts, the bolts jumped back into the locks. I remained still stretched out on the ground, lifeless and naked, shivering and soaked in urine. I was like a new-born baby just out of its mother's womb, or like someone on the point of death; or more precisely, like someone who has survived death and been born posthumously—at any rate, like someone doomed to the inevitable gibbet. "What will become of me", I asked myself, "when Socrates here is seen in daylight with his throat cut? Who will believe that my story is at all plausible, though I recount the truth? What people will say is: 'You could at least have clamoured for help, even if a man of your size couldn't withstand a mere woman. What, you watched a man have his throat cut, and you kept quiet? And how did you escape from that murderous incursion? How was it that the perpetrators of such bestial cruelty spared you, when you were clearly a witness and could denounce the crime? Because you managed to avoid death, death is now your point of return.' "

'These were the thoughts which repeatedly preoccupied my mind as night began to advance towards day. My best course of action therefore seemed to be to steal away before daybreak and take to the road, however fearful my progress would be. I collected my haversack, inserted the door-key, and drew back the bars. But those honest and faithful doors, which had sprung ajar of their own accord during the night, opened only with the greatest reluctance and after repeated turning of the key.

15 ' "Hullo, there!" I cried. "Where are you? Open the inn-gate. I want to leave before daybreak." The doorman, who was lying behind the inn-gate and who was still half-asleep, replied: "What, setting out at this time of night? Don't you know that the roads are infested with robbers? You may be keen to die because you have some crime on your conscience, but I'm not such a blockhead as to perish on your behalf." "But daylight isn't far off", I rejoined. "Besides, what can robbers take from a wholly indigent traveller? You dolt, you must surely know the saying that as many as ten wrestlers can't strip a man when he's already naked." The janitor's reaction in his fragile and somnolent state was to turn over on his other side. "How do I know", he asked, "that you haven't cut the throat of that fellow-traveller with whom you booked in late yesterday, and that you aren't now covering yourself by running away?" At that moment, as I recall, the earth yawned open. I caught a glimpse of Tartarus deep below, and of Cerberus waiting to make a meal of me to relieve his hunger. I realized that the good Meroë's clear intention had been not to spare my throat out of pity, but to preserve me for the gibbet out of savage spite.

16 'So I went back into the dormitory, and began to ponder my quickest mode of death. Fortune, however, afforded me no death-dealing weapon other than my little bed. "My dear little bed," I said to it, "so dear to my heart! You have endured with me so many trials, and you observed the events of last night. You are the sole witness I can adduce at my trial to declare my innocence. As I hasten on the path to join the shades below, furnish me with some weapon which will

extricate me." Saying this, I began to unwind the rope with which the bed was corded. I threw and attached one end of it over a beam which jutted out beneath the window on the inside. The other end I knotted firmly into a noose. I then got off the floor and mounted the bed to kill myself, inserting my head into the noose. But just as I was kicking away with one foot the support of the bed, so as to allow the rope to tighten on my throat, and by taking the weight of my body to deprive it of its function of breathing, the rope which was old and rotten suddenly broke. I fell headlong, right on top of Socrates whose bed was next to mine, and we rolled down together on the ground.

17   'At that very moment the janitor burst in, yelling at the top of his voice. "Where have you got to? You were straining at the leash while it was still dark, and now you are snoring in your blankets!" Socrates was first on his feet before me, wakened either by my fall or by the janitor's tuneless bellow. "It's not surprising", he remarked, "that guests hate the sight of all these janitors. This nosy character has burst cheekily in, doubtless trying to lay his hands on some possession of ours, and with his loud bawling he has wakened me when I was fast asleep from utter exhaustion."

'At this I shot up, alight with enthusiasm and in a transport of unexpected joy. "Take a look, honest doorman. This is my companion, my father and brother, whom you wrongly accused me of killing during the night when you were in your cups." Even as I spoke, I embraced and kissed Socrates, but he was put off by the odour of that foulest of liquids which those witches had deposited on me, and he pushed me violently away. "Keep your distance," he said. "You stink like a filthy urinal!" and he began to enquire genially about the reasons for the foul smell. In my depression I made some ridiculous joke on the spur of the moment, and then diverted his thoughts to another topic. I laid my hand in his, and said: "Let's go and enjoy the pleasures of an early-morning journey." I seized my haversack, and paid the innkeeper the bill for our stay. Then we set out.

18   'After we had travelled a fair distance, the sun came up and

brought light to the world. I kept a careful and watchful eye on the patch of my friend's throat where I had seen the sword make its entry, and I said to myself: "You fool! You had too much wine to drink, and you had a terrible nightmare. You can see that Socrates is untouched and healthy and unharmed. There is no sign of the wound or the sponge, or indeed of that deep and fresh incision." Then I said to Socrates: "Reliable doctors are quite right in their belief that when people have stuffed themselves with food and too much wine, they have harsh and disturbing dreams. I myself drank too much last evening, and had a bad night which brought such dreadful and troublesome dreams that I still feel as if I'm spattered and polluted with human blood."

'Socrates grinned, and countered: "It's not blood that spattered you; you merely wet yourself. Mind you, I too had a dream in which I seemed to get my throat cut. I felt a sharp pain in my neck here, and I thought that my heart was being torn out. Even now I feel out of breath; my knees are knocking, and my progress is unsteady. I need a bite of food to restore myself." "Here you are," I said, "breakfast is served." With that I took my haversack off my shoulder, and hastily handed him some bread and cheese. "Let's sit by that plane tree," I added.

19   'We did this, and I got myself something to eat from my pack. As he greedily wolfed the food, I paid closer attention to him, and I noted that he was fainting; his face was gaunt and as pale as boxwood. In a word, his deathly pallor had so altered his appearance that I was terrified, picturing again those Furies of the night, so much so that the first crust of bread that I had taken, small though it was, got stuck in my throat, and I could neither swallow nor regurgitate it. An additional cause of my panic was the absence of other travellers, for who was likely to believe that when one of a pair of companions had been killed, the other was innocent?

'Once Socrates had had enough to eat, he began to feel an intolerable thirst, for he had greedily wolfed a large slice of excellent cheese. Not far from the roots of the plane-tree was a quiet stream, glistening like silver or glass, its motion as gentle

as a tranquil pond. "There you are," I said. "You can quench
your thirst from the milky waters of the stream." He stood up,
and for a moment sought out a more level section of the bank.
Then he got down on his knees, and bent greedily over the
water to take a drink. He had not quite touched the surface of
the water with parted lips than the wound in his neck yawned
deep and wide. The sponge suddenly tumbled out, and with it
only a drop or two of blood. Then his lifeless body almost
keeled over into the stream, but I managed to grab one foot,
and after a hard struggle I dragged the corpse to the top of the
bank. There I mourned my unhappy companion as much as
time allowed, and then buried him in sandy soil to dwell for
ever close to the stream. I fled for my life in fear and trembling
through remote and trackless wastes, and now, like a man
obsessed with human blood on his hands, I have quitted my
native region and home, and have embraced voluntary exile. I
now live in Aetolia, and have married again there.'

20   This was what Aristomenes told us. His companion from
the very beginning had shown stubborn disbelief and contempt
for his account. 'I've never heard a taller story than this, nor a
more stupid one than this tissue of lies', he said. Then he
turned to me, and said: 'Your clothes and deportment show
that you are a man of culture; can you believe that the story is
true?' 'I consider nothing impossible,' I replied, 'for I believe
that people undergo all that their fates decree. My view is that
you and I and the whole world experience many strange,
almost impossible happenings which lose their credibility
when recounted to one who is unaware of them. Not only do I
believe our friend— indeed I do—but I am most grateful to
him for distracting us with such an amusing and elegant tale,
so that I have completed this rough and extensive lap of my
journey without strain or boredom. I suspect that my mount
too is grateful for the favour, since I have not tired him out,
and have ridden all the way to the city gate not on his back,
but on my ears.'

21   This made an end to our conversation and joint journey, for
my companions both went off to a small farmhouse on the left
of the road, while I made for the first inn that I saw, and at

once made enquiries of the old woman who kept the tavern. 'Is this town Hypata?' I asked. She nodded. 'Do you know of a man named Milo, one of the outstanding citizens?' She smiled, and said: 'He is rightly labelled an outstanding citizen of this district, for he stands outside the city boundary; in fact, he lives outside the town.' 'Now joking apart, dear mother, would you please tell me something of his background, and which house he lives in?' 'Do you see the last set of windows looking out on the town, with the entrance on the other side facing the nearest alley-way? Mister Moneybags Milo lives there. Though he is extremely wealthy, he is notorious for being an absolute miser, living in utter squalor. He is a money-lender on a large scale, charging high interest and taking gold and silver as security. Yet he lives in that tiny house, spending all his time counting his mildewed coins. He has a wife who shares his run-down life. The only servant he feeds is one young girl. He walks about dressed like a beggar.'

On hearing this I let out a laugh. 'My friend Demeas has certainly been kind and far-seeing in attending to my interests! So this is the kind of man to whom he introduces me at the outset of my travels, so I need have no fear of kitchen-smoke or foul-smelling fumes in his lodging.'

22   After making this observation, I walked on a little further, and reached the entrance to the house. The door was close-barred, and I began to shout and hammer on it. Eventually a young girl emerged. 'Hello there!' she said. 'You've certainly given the door a good wallop! What security do you intend to offer for a loan? You surely can't be the only one who is unaware that the only pledge we accept is gold or silver.' 'This is hardly a promising start,' I remarked. 'I'd much rather you tell me whether I find your master at home.' 'Yes, he is' she said. 'Why do you ask?' 'I have a letter addressed to him from Demeas of Corinth.' 'Just wait for me here', she replied, 'until I tell him.' With that she barred the door again, and vanished inside. After a while she returned, and held open the door. 'He asks you to come in,' she said.

When I made my way in, I found Milo reclining on quite a small couch, and on the point of starting his dinner. His wife sat by his feet, and there was a table before them with nothing on it. He pointed to it, and said, 'Share our board.' 'That's kind!', I said, at once passing across the letter from Demeas. He hastily scanned it, and said: 'I'm grateful to my friend Demeas for introducing me to such an important guest.'

23   With that he ordered his wife to quit the couch, and bade me take her place. When I still demurred out of good manners, he grabbed me by the shirt and pulled me down. 'Sit here,' he said, 'we're so afraid of robbers that we can't buy chairs or even enough table-ware.'

I sat down. 'I could rightly have guessed from your civilized appearance and your quite innocent modesty that you come from a good family, and Demeas confirms this in his letter. I beg you not to look with contempt on our small and unpretentious dwelling. You will have the adjoining bedroom here, to afford you decent privacy. Do have a pleasant stay with us. You will add dignity to our house by consenting to stay here, and if you rest content with our small abode, you will bring great credit on yourself, for you will be imitating the virtues of your father's namesake Theseus, who did not spurn the tiny lodging of the aged Hecale.' Milo then summoned the young maid. 'Photis,' he said, 'take our guest's baggage, and store it carefully in the bedroom over there. Then go quickly to the store-cupboard, and bring oil, towels, and whatever else he requires for oiling and rubbing-down. After that, escort my guest to the baths close by, for he is tired after his long and quite taxing journey.'

24   On hearing these words I reflected on Milo's parsimony, and sought to instal myself more closely in his affections. 'I have no need of any of those things,' I said, 'for they accompany me everywhere on my travels, and I can easily ask the way to the baths. My chief concern is for my horse, which has had a hard time getting me here. Take these coins, Photis, and buy him some hay and barley.'

After these exchanges my luggage was deposited in the bedroom, and I set out for the baths. But first I made for the market, to obtain some food for supper, and I saw there some fish of good quality on sale. I enquired about the cost, turned down the asking price of a hundred sesterces, and got them for twenty denarii. I was just leaving the market when I encountered one Pythias, formerly a fellow-student of mine at Athens in Attica. He greeted me with affectionate signs of recognition after such a long time, and embraced and kissed me jovially. 'My dear Lucius,' he said, 'it's quite a long time since I saw you last. Heavens, the last time was when we said farewell to our master Clytius. What business brings you this way?' 'You'll find out tomorrow,' I said. 'But what's all this? Congratulations are in order, for I see you now have the attendants and rods and dress befitting a magistrate.' 'That's right,' he said, 'I'm charged with the corn-supply, and I have the rank of aedile. If you wish to buy provisions, I'm most ready to help you.' I refused the offer, because I had already provided myself with plenty of fish for supper. But then Pythias noticed my basket, and he shook the fish about to get a better view of them. 'How much have you paid for this load of rubbish?' he asked. 'I had difficulty getting the fishmonger to reduce the price to twenty denarii for them,' I replied.

25   On hearing this he at once seized my arm and took me back into the market. 'From which of these traders did you buy that trash?' he enquired. I pointed out an elderly man sitting in a corner. Pythias at once invoked his aedile's authority to rebuke him in the harshest terms. 'So', he said, 'you have no compunction in exploiting friends of mine, or indeed any strangers whatsoever. By putting such high prices on your wretched fish you are turning this desirable region of Thessaly into nothing but a rocky desert. But you won't get away with it. I'll make you realize how unscrupulous traders are to be kept in check while I'm in charge.' With that he threw the parcel of fish on the ground in front of us, and ordered his attendant to jump on the fish, and crush them all underfoot. Dear Pythias was pleased with this stern demonstration of righteousness, and he urged me to leave, saying: 'I'm well pleased, Lucius, with the dressing-down which we've handed out to the old man.' I was bowled over and struck utterly dumb by this performance. I retired to the baths, robbed of both my money and my supper by this stern sermon from my

wise fellow-student. After taking my bath, I turned back to Milo's lodging and made for my bedroom.

26 The maid Photis then appeared. 'Your host is asking for you,' she said. I was already au fait with Milo's niggardliness, so I made the courteous excuse that I had decided to dispel the trials of travelling with sleep rather than with food. On hearing this, he came in person, placed his arm in mine, and began gently to constrain me to accompany him. As I hesitantly and meekly demurred, he said: 'I refuse to leave until you come with me'. He swore an oath on this, and when I reluctantly acceded to his insistence, he led me to that little couch of his. When I was seated on it, he asked: 'How is our friend Demeas? And his wife? And his children? And the family-slaves?' I answered the queries one by one. He questioned me also in some detail about the reasons for my journey. I conscientiously explained. He then conducted an exhaustive enquiry about my native region, its prominent citizens, and finally the governor himself. At last he realized that in addition to the upset of such a taxing journey, I was further exhausted by this continuing patter, for I kept nodding off midway through a conversation, and I was now so weary that I was slurring out meaningless comments in my replies. So finally he allowed me to go to bed, enabling me to escape from the noisome old man's feast, which was long on words but short on victuals. So, heavy with sleep but not with food (for I had dined on nothing but gossip), I retired to my bedroom, and sought the rest for which I longed.

BOOK 2

Further Warnings at Byrrhena's: The Exemplar of Thelyphron

1 As soon as the darkness was dispelled and a new sun ushered in the day, I rose from my couch the moment I awoke from sleep, for I was generally buoyed up, and most eager to discover the weird and wonderful features of the place. I recalled that I was in the heart of Thessaly, the source of those spells of the magic art which are famed by common consent through the entire world. I remembered too that the tale recounted by Aristomenes, that best of companions, had its origin in this city. So in expectation and enthusiasm alike I was quite alert, and I studied each feature with some care. I did not believe that anything which I gazed on in the city was merely what it was, but that every single object had been transformed into a different shape by some muttered and deadly incantation. I thought that the stones which caused me to trip were petrified persons, that the birds which I could hear were feathered humans, that the trees enclosing the city-limits were people who had likewise sprouted foliage, that the waters of the fountains were issuing from human bodies. I imagined that at any moment the statues and portraits would parade about, that the walls would speak, that oxen and other cattle would prophesy, that the very sky and the sun's orb would suddenly proclaim an oracular message.

2 In this trance, or rather hypnosis, induced by such tortured longing, I went round examining everything, but without finding a suggestion or even a trace of what I passionately sought. I wandered from door to door like a man seeking some extravagant and dissolute diversion, and all unknowing I suddenly found myself at the food-market. I caught sight of a woman walking through it, surrounded by a sizeable retinue, and I quickened my step and overtook her. Her jewellery was gold-inlaid and her clothes gold-

embroidered, undoubtedly signalling that she was an upper-class matron. Walking close to her side was a man of advanced years. As soon as he set eyes on me he exclaimed: 'Heavens, it's Lucius!' and he gave me a kiss of greeting. At once he whispered something in the lady's ear which I could not overhear. 'This is your aunt,' he said. 'You must approach her yourself, and greet her.' 'I'm shy of doing that', I said, 'for I do not know her.' Whereupon I blushed all over, and kept my distance with my head bowed.

The lady then turned to stare at me. 'My goodness,' she said, 'he has the manners of a gentleman. He gets them from his mother Salvia who is a model of goodness. And damn me if his appearance generally isn't just right! He is tall, but not lofty; he's slim, but there is spunk there; his colour is moderately ruddy, his hair is blonde but not foppish; his green eyes have a watchful look, quick to focus, sharp as an eagle's. His face looks healthy from every angle, and his walk is pleasing and natural.'

3   Then she added: 'Lucius, these hands of mine reared you. That was as it should be, for not only am I your mother's blood relation, but we were brought up together. We are both descended from Plutarch's household, we had the same wet-nurse, and we grew up together as inseparable sisters. The one thing that distinguishes us is our social standing. She contracted marriage with a prominent public figure, whereas I married a private citizen. I'm called Byrrhena; you may recall the name through mention of it among those who brought you up. So don't be shy of accepting our hospitality; in fact our house is yours.'

These remarks of hers had given me time to disguise my blushes, and I spoke up in reply. 'Dear aunt,' I said, 'I could hardly bid my host Milo goodbye without his feeling aggrieved. I shall make every effort to do what I can, short of breaching my obligation to him. Whenever any occasion for a journey this way arises in future, I shall always lodge with you.' In the course of these and similar exchanges, the short journey we had made on foot brought us to Byrrhena's house.

4   The reception-area was very fine. Pillars stood at each

corner, supporting statues representing the goddess Victory.
In these representations, her wings were outspread but
motionless, and her dewy feet stood on tiptoe on the slippery
surface of a revolving sphere, momentarily joined to it but
giving the impression of imminent flight. But the notable
feature was Parian marble chiselled into the likeness of Diana,
which occupied the centre of the whole atrium, and was raised
off the ground. The statue gleamed spectacularly; with her
garment breeze-blown, her lively figure was hastening forward as if to confront the incomer with the august majesty of
her godhead. Hounds, likewise executed in marble, escorted
the goddess on both flanks. Their eyes were threatening, their
ears pricked up, their nostrils flaring, their maws savage. If
barking sounded loudly from anywhere near at hand, you
would think that it issued from those mouths of marble. But
the highest feat of craftsmanship achieved by that genius of a
sculptor was that the hounds were rearing breast-high, and
their hind legs were braking while their forelegs were in rapid
motion.

To the rear of the goddess rose a rock forming a cave. Out
of the stone sprouted moss, green plants, foliage and
brushwood; vines on one side were set off against miniature
trees on the other. Within the cave the reflection of the statue
shone out because of the smooth brightness of the marble.
Apples and grapes hung from the lower edge of the rock; their
highly artistic finish, depicted with a skill rivalling nature's,
made them lifelike, so that you could imagine that some of
them could be plucked for eating once the maturing autumn
endowed them with the colour of ripeness. If you bent low and
gazed into the water which skirted the goddess's feet as it
lapped in gentle waves, you would think that the bunches of
grapes hanging from the rock possessed the faculty of
movement as well as other lifelike qualities. In the middle of
the marble foliage a statue of Actaeon was visible, fashioned
in marble and reflected in the water; his neck craned forward
as he gazed with curiosity towards the goddess. He was
already animal-like, on the point of becoming a stag as he
waited for Diana to take her bath.

5   As I repeatedly ran my eye over this scene with intense
delight, Byrrhena remarked: 'All that you see is yours.' After
saying this, she had a private word with all the others, and
asked them to leave us. When they had all been sent away, she
said to me: 'Dearest Lucius, I swear by the goddess here; I am
troubled and fearful for you. Since you are my cherished son, I
should like to give you warning well in advance. Watch out for
yourself. Take stringent precautions against the wicked arts
and evil enticements of the notorious Pamphile, the wife of
Milo, who you say is your host. She is reputed to be a witch of
the first rank, a specialist in all forms of necromancy. She has
only to breathe on twigs, pebbles, and common objects of that
kind, and she can plunge all this light of day which descends
from the starry heavens into the lowest depths of Tartarus,
reducing it to the chaos of old. Then as soon as she catches
sight of any handsome young man, she is captivated by his
charms, and at once focuses her eyes and her attention on
him. She sows the seeds of allurements, dominates his will,
and proceeds to imprison him in eternal bonds of deep love. If
those who are less amenable prove worthless to her because
they scorn her, she transforms them in a trice into stones or
cattle or any animal you can think of, while others she utterly
destroys. These are the fears I have for you, and I think that
you should be on your guard against them, for she is
constantly ablaze with desire, and your youth and handsome
bearing make you a suitable target for her.' These were the
troubled thoughts which Byrrhena shared with me.

6   But I was already disposed to curiosity, and as soon as I
heard mention of the art of magic which I had always prayed
for, so far from taking precautions against Pamphile, I was
eager even without compulsion to undergo such schooling
willingly, and to pay a heavy price for it. In short, I was all for
taking a running jump and landing myself headlong in those
murky depths. So with lunatic haste I freed myself from
Byrrhena's detaining hand as if from a confining chain, and
bade her a hasty farewell. I then flew off at top speed to Milo's
lodging. As I redoubled my steps like one demented, I said to
myself: 'Lucius, look alive, and keep your wits about you.

This is the chance you were praying for. You will be able to achieve that long-standing ambition of yours, and obtain your heart's content of wonderful stories. Dismiss your childish fears, come to grips with the issue at close quarters and without cowardice. You must steer clear of any love-relationship with your hostess, and scrupulously respect the good Milo's marriage-bed. Make a bee-line instead for the maidservant Photis. She is attractive, she has amusing ways, and she is quite sharp. Last night when you retired to sleep, she genially escorted you to your room, fussed over you in getting you to your bed, tucked you in quite affectionately, kissed your forehead, and showed by her face her unwilling-ness to leave. In fact she kept halting and looking back. So even though it has its hazards, Photis must be your target. The best of luck in your endeavours.'

7   These were the arguments occupying my mind as I made for Milo's door. I voted with my feet, as the expression goes. I found neither Milo nor his wife at home, but only my dear Photis. She was cooking minced pork for stuffing, and slices of meat, and some very spicy sausage of which I had already caught a whiff. She was wearing an elegant linen dress, with a bright red belt fastened up supporting her breasts. As she turned the casserole-dish round and round with her petal-like fingers, and shook it repeatedly in its circular motion, she simultaneously rotated her body. Her hips moved lightly in rhythm, and as she wiggled her supple spine, her person rippled most attractively. I was spellbound at the sight, and stood there lost in admiration. The parts of me that were asleep before now stood to attention. Finally I managed to speak to her; 'My dear Photis,' I said, 'how lusciously and attractively you wiggle that wee pot, and your bottom with it! That's a succulent dish you have in readiness there! How lucky a fellow would be if you let him stick his finger in—he'd be on top of the world!'

That pert and witty girl at once replied: 'Keep clear, poor boy, keep clear as far as possible from this stove of mine. If once my little flame shoots out and as much as sears you, you will be all ablaze inside, and I'll be the only one who can put your fire out. The spices which I incorporate are sweet. I'm an expert at pleasurably shaking a bed as well as a pot.'

8   With these words she looked me in the eye, and grinned. I did not leave her presence until I had carefully studied all the features of her appearance. Of her other charms I need say nothing, for it has always been my one obsession first to examine a person's head of hair thoroughly and openly outside, and then to take pleasure in it privately indoors. I have a secure and well-established justification for preferring this criterion of beauty. First comes the fact that the head is the outstanding part of the body; it is exposed and prominent, and is the first feature to meet the eye. Secondly, whereas the other physical parts are made attractive by the gay colour of bright clothing, it is the head's own natural sheen which achieves this. Lastly, most women when they wish to demonstrate their personal attractions disrobe and remove all their clothes in their eagerness to show off their naked beauty, seeking to please the eye more with the rosy blush of their skin than with the golden colour of their dress. But if you were to scalp some lady of outstanding beauty, and thus rob her face of its natural adornment—this is a sacrilegious suggestion, and I pray that so grisly an illustration of my point may never materialize—it would not matter if she came down from heaven, or rose from the sea, or was sprung from the waves. In other words, it would not matter if she were Venus herself, flanked by a whole choir of Graces, accompanied by the entire body of Cupids, wearing that belt of hers around her waist, diffusing the scent of cinnamon and bedewing the air with balsam; if she appeared without her hair, she would not give pleasure even to her Vulcan.

9   How enchanting is a woman's hair when its pleasing colour and glossy sheen shines out! When it faces the sun's rays, it is enlivened and flashes fire, or gently reflects the sunlight. Sometimes it offers contrasting pleasures by varying its appearance. Hair with a golden glow subsides into the soft shaded colour of honey. Hair which is raven-black seeks to rival the ultramarine necks of doves. Hair oiled with drops of Arabian perfume, parted with the fine teeth of a sharp comb,

and gathered at the back, serves as a mirror when it confronts the lover's eyes, and affords him a more flattering reflection. Sometimes numerous strands are combined to form a thick wedge on top of the head, or they flow down the back, extending in a long plait. Such in fact is the lofty status of a woman's hair that she can appear before us adorned with gold, fine clothes, jewellery and the rest of her finery, but unless she has ordered her hair she cannot be regarded as well-groomed.

My Photis, however, had not fussed over hers, and yet its tousled arrangement lent her added charm. Her abundant hair had been let hang soft and free down from her head over her neck, and having rested briefly on the golden border of her dress, it had finally been gathered and fastened in a knot on top of her head.

10   I could no longer endure the fierce torture of my extreme pleasure. I leaned over her, and implanted the sweetest of honeyed kisses where her hair reached the crown of her head. She then twisted her neck to face me, and gave me a sidelong look with devouring eyes. 'Hey there, schoolboy,' she said, 'the savoury dish you're sampling is bitter as well as sweet. Just watch out; that honey which tastes so sweet may bring on a lengthy attack of bitter bile.'

'How can you say that, light of my life?' I asked. 'I am ready to be laid and grilled on this fire of yours, once you have roused me with one little kiss.' As I spoke I grasped her tightly in my arms, and started to kiss her. In a moment she was as abandoned as I was, as she rose to the same heat of passion. With unrestrained desire she showed her longing for me; the breath from her open lips was like cinnamon, and the thrust of her tongue was like nectar as it met mine. I said to her: 'This is killing me! Indeed, I'm already dead unless you take pity on me.' She gave me another long kiss, and answered: 'Don't worry. That longing which we share makes me your slave, and our pleasure will be postponed no longer. As soon as the first lamp is lit, I'll be in your bedroom. So be off with you, and make your preparations. I shall engage you in an all-night battle with the strength of passion.'

11   After this genial exchange and others of a similar kind, we parted. Just after midday Byrrhena sent over to me some guest-presents: a fat pig, five chickens, and a cask of vintage wine. I summoned Photis then, and said to her: 'Look at this! Bacchus, the spokesman and squire of Venus, has turned up without prompting. All this wine we must drink today so as to dispel the cowardice induced by embarrassment, and instil into ourselves the onset of sexual pleasure. These are the only provisions needed on Venus' barque to ensure that throughout the night-watch we have plenty of oil in the lamp and plenty of wine in the cup.'

      We devoted the rest of the day to the baths and then to supper, for I had been invited to that elegant little board of Milo. I took my place on the couch as safely remote from his wife's eye as I could, for I had Byrrhena's warning in mind, and I watched her face with as much apprehension as if I were gazing into Lake Avernus. But repeated glances at Photis as she served at table restored my spirits. As darkness closed in, Pamphile peered at the lamp, and remarked: 'We are to have quite a storm tomorrow.' When her husband asked her how she knew, she replied that the lamp foretold it to her. Milo greeted this reply with a laugh. 'What a splendid Sibyl we are nurturing in the lamp here! From her observatory on the lampstand she observes all the activities in the sky, and the sun as well.'

12   At this point I interposed. 'I have had experience of this kind of prophecy, but there is nothing surprising about it. It is true that this tiny flame is insignificant and fashioned by human hands, but it is mindful of the greater fire in the heavens, which is, so to say, its progenitor. So by a divine foreknowledge it is itself aware, and communicates to us, what the sun intends to bring forth in the height of the heavens. At this very time in the city of Corinth where I live there is a Chaldaean visitor who with his remarkable responses is causing absolute mayhem. For a small fee he makes public the secret decrees of the fates. He advises on a day for a wedding which will make the marriage stable, or the day on which to lay wall-foundations to ensure that they last, or a day which

will profit the business-man, or which will be auspicious for a traveller, or suitable for vessels to commence their voyage. When I questioned him on how this journey of mine would turn out, his lengthy reply was quite surprising and varied. He said that at one time my fame would blossom considerably, and at another I would be the subject of a lengthy story, an unbelievable tale spread over several books.'

13   Milo grinned at this. 'This Chaldaean of yours—what sort of appearance has he, and what is his name?' 'He's tall', I said, 'and on the dark side. His name is Diophanes.' 'The very one,' said Milo. 'He's been here as well, making many similar forecasts to many people. His takings were not just in pennies; in fact he had already made a fortune. But then the poor chap found Lady Luck capricious, or it would be truer to say, vicious.

'One day he was hemmed in by a large crowd gathered round him, and he was predicting futures for the circle of bystanders when a business-man called Cerdo approached him. He wanted to know the right day for starting a journey. Diophanes selected and apportioned a day, and Cerdo laid down his purse, poured out the coins, and counted out a hundred denarii as Diophanes' fee for the prophecy. At this moment a young nobleman crept up in Diophanes' rear, seized him by the cloak, and pulled him round. He then embraced and kissed him with great warmth. Diophanes returned the kiss, and made the young man sit down beside him. In his surprise at his sudden appearance, he forgot the transaction which he was conducting. "How long is it since you got here?" he asked. "I have been so looking forward to your arrival." The other man replied: "It was just before dark yesterday. But tell me about yourself, brother. When you sailed in some haste from the island of Euboea, how did the rest of your voyage and the journey overland go?"

14   'That distinguished astrologer Diophanes was still distracted, and had not yet recovered his wits. "I only pray", he said, "that all our enemies public and private may experience so grim a journey; it was as bad as that of Ulysses. The ship in which we were sailing was battered by competing storm-

winds. We lost both rudders, and just managed to run
aground on the fringe of the opposite shore. There the ship
went straight down, and we barely managed to swim ashore,
with the loss of all our possessions. Such things as we
managed to gather through the compassion of strangers or the
kindness of friends were all purloined by a band of brigands,
and to crown it all my only brother Arignotus tried to resist
their violent attack, and the poor man had his throat cut
before my very eyes."

'Diophanes was still sadly recounting these experiences
when Cerdo the business-man grabbed the coins which he
had laid out as payment for his forecast, and at once took to
his heels. It was only then that Diophanes awoke to the
situation, and realized his foolish mistake, once he saw that
every single one of us had collapsed in gales of laughter. But
doubtless the Chaldaean foretold the truth for you, Master
Lucius, if for no one else in the world. Good luck to you, and
have a prosperous journey!'

15   While Milo was giving us this long rigmarole, I was silently
seething, hugely annoyed with myself for having precipitated
needlessly one unseasonable anecdote after another, with the
result that I was losing a large part of the evening, and the
most welcome pleasure which it would yield. Eventually I
swallowed all feelings of decency, and I said to Milo: 'Well,
then, let Diophanes bear with his fortune, and once again
consign to sea and land alike the spoils which he has gained
from my countrymen. You will have to pardon me, but I am
still feeling the effects of yesterday's exhausting journey, and I
should like to retire to bed early.'

I made off even as I was speaking, and hastened to my
bedroom. There I found that the arrangements for the
celebration were quite as they should have been. The slaves
had their floor-space arranged as far as possible away from
the door; I imagine that this was so that they would not be
near enough to overhear our chat during the night. Close to
my bed stood a small table on which were laid acceptable left-
overs from all the courses of the dinner. There were generous
cups already half-filled with wine, awaiting only the necessary

dilution, and by them was a flagon, its neck already smoothly cut so that it lay open for easy pouring. These, then, were the apposite preliminaries for our gladiatorial combat of love.

16 I had just climbed into bed when my Photis, having tucked her mistress in, made her smiling entrance. She wore a garland of roses, and had a rose-blossom tucked between her breasts. She kissed me hard, put garlands round my neck, and sprinkled petals over me. Then she seized a cup, poured hot water into the wine, and gave it to me to drink. Just before I downed the lot, she took gentle possession of the cup, and with her eyes fixed on me, she charmingly sipped the rest, allowing it slowly to vanish between her lips. A second and third cup was shared between us as we passed it quickly from hand to hand. By now the wine had gone to my head, and I felt restless and randy physically as well as in mind. For some little time now I had felt my wound swelling. I pushed my clothes clear of the groin, and showed Photis that I could not delay the love-encounter any longer. 'Take pity,' I said, 'come to my aid with all speed. As you can see, the war which you declared on me without employing the services of the fetials, is now imminent, and I am extended in readiness. Once I felt the impact of cruel Cupid's first arrow in the depth of my heart, I stretched my bow strongly likewise, and I am mortally afraid that the string may break through being drawn too tightly. Now indulge me a little further; let your hair run free and flow over me in waves as you offer me your love-embrace.'

17 At once she hastily removed all the food-dishes. She stripped off her clothes, and let her hair flow loose. Then with a show of genial wantonness she adopted the charming pose of Venus treading the ocean waves. She even for a moment covered her hairless parts with her rosy little hand, a deliberate gesture rather than modest concealment. 'Engage,' she said, 'and do so bravely. I shall not yield before you, nor turn my back on you. Direct your aim frontally, if you are a man, and at close quarters. Let your onslaught be fierce; kill before you die. Our battle this day allows no respite.' As she spoke she mounted the bed, and eased herself slowly down on

top of me. She bounced up and down repeatedly, manœuvring her back in supple movements, and gorged me with the delight of this rhythmical intercourse. Eventually our spirits palled as our bodies lost their zest; we collapsed simultaneously in a state of exhaustion as we breathlessly embraced each other. Engaged in these and similar grapplings we remained awake almost until dawn. From time to time we refreshed our weary bodies with wine, which fired our sexual urges and renewed our pleasure. Several other nights we spent similarly, taking that first night as our model.

18   One day it chanced that Byrrhena pressed me strongly to have dinner at her house, and though I made valiant excuses, she would have none of them. So I had to approach Photis and seek her advice—taking the auspices, so to say, to discover her will. Though she was reluctant to let me go more than a nail's breadth from her, she genially allowed me a short furlough from our love-campaign. But she added this proviso: 'Be sure to come back from your dinner reasonably early, because there is a lunatic band of upper-class youths disturbing the peace of the streets. You will see the corpses of murdered people lying in various places on the public highways. The provincial governor's forces cannot rid the city of all this killing, because they are so far away; and your conspicuous status, together with their lack of respect for a stranger travelling abroad, may cause them to lie in wait for you.'

'Photis, my dear,' I said, 'let me reassure you. In the first place I should much prefer my own pleasures here to dining with strangers. Secondly, I shall dispel this fear of yours by returning early, and I shall not be unattended, because with my short sword buckled by my side I shall be bearing the guarantee of my safety.' I duly took this precaution, and made my way to the dinner.

19   There was quite a crowd of guests. The hostess was a leading figure locally, so the élite of the town was there. The expensive tables gleamed with citrus-wood and ivory, the couches were draped with golden coverlets, the large cups though not a matching set were equally costly as each other.

One was of glass skilfully inlaid, a second of unblemished crystal; others were of bright silver, gleaming gold, amber marvellously hollowed out, precious stones shaped into drinking-vessels. There were cups there which you would have said were impossible to fashion. Several waiters strikingly dressed were expertly serving heaped-up dishes, while curly-haired boys in splendid uniforms regularly circulated with jewelled cups of vintage wine. Once the lamps were brought in, conversation at table became animated. Laughter was rife, wit ran free, and repartee was exchanged.

Byrrhena then began to speak to me. 'How pleasant is your stay in our region turning out?' she asked. 'My information is that our temples, baths, and other public buildings are much superior to those of all other towns, and that we are also plentifully equipped with the practical requirements for living. Here at any rate the man of leisure is free to roam, the business-man from abroad finds a population similar to that at Rome, and the guest of modest means can relax in a country house. In short, we serve as the holiday centre in this entire province for the pleasure-seeker.'

20   I acknowledged this claim. 'What you say is true. My belief is that nowhere in the world have I been so free as here. But I am quite apprehensive of the dark dens where magic is practised, and which cannot be sidestepped. People say that not even the tombs of the dead are safe, and that human remains, parts of human bodies, are extracted from graves and funeral-pyres to encompass deadly disaster for the living. At the very moment when a body is being borne out to burial, there are aged sorceresses who move at high speed and reach the burial plots of strangers before anyone else.'

Another guest took up the topic and carried it further. 'Why,' he said, 'in this place they don't even spare the living. There was some fellow or other who had just such an experience, for he had his face completely disfigured and mutilated.' At these words the entire table exploded into ribald laughter, and all turned their heads and eyes towards a man reclining by himself in a corner. He was embarrassed by this general attention paid to him, and made as if to rise, muttering at this unkind treatment. But Byrrhena interjected. 'No, don't go, dear Thelyphron. Stay for a little while, and in your civilized fashion tell us again that tale of yours, so that my son Lucius here may enjoy your genial and elegant account.' Thelyphron responded: 'You, my lady, continue to show your unimpeachable good manners, but there are some people here whose arrogance is intolerable.' His words reflected his annoyance, but Byrrhena swore on her own life that he must stay, and so overcame his reluctance that she finally induced him to consent to speak.

21   So then Thelyphron piled up the couch-coverlets, and raised himself partly upwards on the couch by leaning on them with his elbow. He then stretched out his right hand, deploying an arm as orators do, with the two smaller fingers bent and the others extended, and with the thumb gently but accusingly pointed upward. This was how he began.

'As a young lad I set out from Miletus to attend the Olympic games, and as I was eager to visit this region of the celebrated province as well, I travelled the length and breadth of Thessaly, and arrived at Larissa in an evil hour. My travel-funds were now running low, so as I wandered about viewing all the sights, I was looking out for some means of relieving my poverty. I saw in the middle of the market-place a tall old man standing on a stone. He was making a public announcement that if any person was willing to guard a corpse, the fee could be negotiated. I remarked to one of the passers-by: "Whatever is this all about? Do corpses often take to their heels in these parts?" "Hush!" he replied. "You are just a boy and a mere stranger, so naturally you are unaware that the Thessaly in which you are lodging contains witches who in different localities bite morsels off dead men's faces, and use them as additional materials for their practice of magic."

22   ' "Do please tell me," I replied, "What does this protection of a corpse involve?" "To begin with", he said, "you must keep intensive watch all night through, keeping your eyes trained unblinkingly and continuously on the body. Your gaze must not be distracted in the slightest, not even so much as by a swivelling of the eyes. Those most repellent hags change

their outward appearance by transforming themselves into any creature, and they creep in so surreptitiously that they easily escape the eyes even of the sun-god himself and of the goddess Justice, for they take on the shape of birds, or again of dogs, or mice, or even flies. Then by their dread spells they shroud the watchers in sleep. No individual could properly assess the number of hidden tricks which those most wicked women devise to attain their lustful desires. Yet the payment offered for this mortally dangerous task is no more than about four or six gold pieces. Oh yes, and there is a further point which I had almost forgotten. If the watcher does not hand over the body intact in the morning, he is forced to make good any feature which has been prised off, wholly or partly, with the equivalent feature cut off from his own face."

23 'On hearing this, I exhibited a manly spirit, and at once approached the man making the announcement. "You can stop shouting now," I said, "I'm ready to stand guard. Tell me the fee." "A thousand sesterces will be credited to you", he said. "But look here, young man; you must be scrupulously careful to guard with care the son of leading citizens of this town from those wicked Harpies." "What you tell me is stuff and nonsense," I rejoined. "The person you see before you is a man of steel, whose eyes never close and whose sight is certainly keener than that of Lynceus himself, or of Argus. In fact he is eyes personified."

'He barely heard me out, but at once led me to a house whose entrance was barred. He ushered me inside through a tiny rear door, and opened up a room deep in shadow, since the windows were shuttered. He pointed out a tearful matron clothed in black, and he approached her side. "This man has commissioned himself to guard your husband, and has arrived full of confidence." The lady pushed her overhanging hair to each side, revealing a face which was attractive even in grief. She turned her eyes on me, and said: "Do please ensure that you perform the task with the greatest vigilance." "Have no worries on that score," I replied, "as long as you have ready the appropriate payment."

24 'When this was agreed, she rose and led me to another

retiring-room. There in the presence of seven witnesses who were brought in, she uncovered with her own hand the body, which was shrouded by gleaming linen sheets. For some time she wept over it, and then she tremblingly pointed out each feature of the corpse, asking those present to witness them. One of them committed to tablets the formal inventory: "Observe", she said, "the nose intact, the eyes undamaged, the ears unharmed, the lips untouched, the chin entire. Good citizens, solemnly witness to this." After these words the tablets were sealed up, and she rose to withdraw. I said to her: "Give instructions that everything I need is made available to me." "What is it you need?" she asked. "An outsize lamp," I said, "enough oil to keep it alight till daylight, hot water with jars of wine and a cup, and a plate bearing the left-overs from your dinner." "Away with you, you silly man," she said, tossing her head. "The house is in mourning, and yet you ask for dinners and courses? In this house not a whiff of smoke has been visible for days on end. Do you think that you have come here to a drinking-party? The proper fare for you here is grief and tears." As she said this, she looked round at a little maid-servant, and said: "Myrrhine, bring a lamp and some oil quickly. Lock the guard in this room, and then leave at once."

25   'So I was left alone to console the corpse. I massaged my eyes, and prepared them for the night-watch. As I sought to soothe my spirits by singing songs, dusk fell, and night came on. Soon it got darker, and then as bedtime came, darker still, until finally it was dead of night. I began to get more and more jittery, when suddenly a weasel crept in and halted facing me, fixing me with the sharpest gaze imaginable. It showed such extraordinary self-assurance for such a tiny animal that it quite upset me. Finally I said to it: "Clear off, you filthy creature. Go and hide with your mates in the garden, before you feel the force of my arm here and now. Be off!"

'It retreated, and scuttled out of the room at once. A minute later I was overpowered by a deep sleep which plunged me suddenly into a bottomless gulf. Even the god of Delphi could not easily have decided which of the two of us there was more dead than the other. I lay there lifeless, needing a second guard to watch over me. It was almost as if I were not present.

26   'The crowing of crested cocks was just proclaiming a truce to the invasion of night when I finally awoke. I was absolutely aghast, and I rushed over to the corpse. I held the lamp up to it, and uncovered the dead man's face, peering at each feature, but all were unharmed. The wretched wife now came bursting in, tearful and troubled, accompanied by the witnesses of the previous day. She at once descended on the corpse. After kissing it long and hard, she examined all its features under the revealing witness of the lamp. She then turned away, and called for her steward Philodespotus, instructing him to pay the faithful guard his reward at once. There and then the money was handed over. "Young man", she said "we are most grateful to you. I swear that from now on we will regard you as one of our intimate friends, because of this conscientious service which you have performed."

'I was ecstatic with joy at this turn of events, and at the profit which I had obtained against all expectation. Those gleaming gold coins I jangled repeatedly in my hand, gazing in wonder at them. "My lady," I said, "think of me not as a friend, but as one of your servants. Whenever you need my assistance you can call on me with assurance." No sooner were the words out of my mouth than the whole ménage at once attacked me, grabbing any weapon to hand and cursing this outrageous suggestion of future misfortune. One battered my face with his fists, another elbowed me betwen the shoulder-blades, a third pummelled my ribs violently with his hands. They kicked me, pulled my hair, ripped my clothes. I was ejected from the house, lacerated and torn apart like the arrogant Aonian, or the Pipleian poet who sang his poems.

27   'Out in the street close by I recovered my breath. I realized all too late that my words had been ill-omened and thoughtless, and I ruefully acknowledged that I had deserved a worse beating than I had sustained. But by now the corpse had emerged and was being greeted with tears and the final lamentations. Since the dead man was from the upper class, he was being conducted through the forum in a public funeral-procession according to ancestral ritual. Then an old

man clad in black confronted the cortège; he showed his distress by weeping and tearing at his noble white hair. He laid hold of the coffin with both hands, and spoke in strained tones, punctuated by frequent sobbing. "Citizens," he said, "I beg you by your sense of honour and devotion to the state to avenge this murdered citizen, and to punish harshly this wicked and criminal woman for her most pernicious crime. She and no other has poisoned this wretched young man, the son of my sister, to win the favour of her adulterous lover, and to lay hands on the spoil of his inheritance."

'These were the tearful complaints loudly voiced by the old man to one and all. The crowd meanwhile was becoming aggressive, for the plausibility of the accusation inclined them to lend credence to the charge. They called for torches, demanded stones, encouraged urchins to finish off the woman. She confronted the attack with crocodile tears, and swore by all the gods as reverently as she could that she was guiltless of such a dread crime.

28   'In consequence the old man said: "Then let us refer judgement of the truth to the foresight of the gods. Zatchlas, a leading Egyptian prophet, is here. Some time ago he promised on payment of a large fee to bring back for a short time this spirit from the dead, and to instil into this body the life which it enjoyed before death." As he spoke, he introduced a young man clad in linen garments, with palm-leaf sandals on his feet. His head was wholly shaven. For some time the old man kissed the prophet's hands and clasped his knees, saying: "Have pity, O priest, have pity! By the stars of heaven, by the powers of hell, by the elements of the universe, by the silences of the night, by the sacred shrines of Coptus, by the floods of the Nile, by the mysteries of Memphis and the rattles of Pharos, grant a momentary loan from the sun and inject some modest light into these eyes which are forever closed. We do not seek to defy fate, or to deny to the earth its possession, but we implore a brief moment of life to obtain the consolation of vengeance."

'The prophet was won over by these words, and placed one small herb on the corpse's mouth, and another on the heart.

Then he turned to the east, and silently prayed to the nascent rising of the venerable sun. The sight of this awesome drama roused those present to vie in eagerness to witness so great a miracle.

29   'I slipped into the midst of the crowd of the dead man's associates, and perched on a rock behind the bier. The rock was a little higher, and I surveyed the whole scene with inquisitive eyes. The dead man's chest first began to swell, his life-giving veins began to throb, and his body filled with breath. Then the corpse sat up, and the young man spoke. "Why, I implore you, now that I have drunk of the cups of Lethe and am swimming in the marshy waters of the Styx, why do you haul me back to life's duties for a brief moment? Cease to summon me, cease, I beg you; allow me to return to my rest." These were the words heard from the corpse, but the prophet addressed him rather sharply: "Why do you not recount the details and reveal to the citizens the secrets of your death? Are you not aware that the Furies can be summoned by my curses on you, and that your weary limbs can be subjected to torture?" The dead man raised himself from the bier, and uttering the hollowest of groans he addressed the people in these words: "I was destroyed by the evil arts of my new bride. I was sentenced to drink a cup of poison, and I surrendered my bed while it was still warm to an adulterer."

'Then that most worthy wife adopted a bold stratagem suited to the moment, and with sacrilegious spirit confronted her husband, and argued with him as he condemned her. The citizens were fired up, but took opposite stances. Some claimed that this was the worst woman alive, and that she should be buried with her husband's body, while others argued that no credence should be lent to the lying words of the corpse.

30   'But the next words of the young man removed this hesitation. Once again he uttered a hollow groan, and said: "Very well, I shall offer you, yes, offer you, clear proofs of the untainted truth. I will reveal what no person whosoever other than myself will know or prophesy." He then pointed me out

with his finger. "When this most prudent guardian of my corpse was keeping a careful watch over me, some aged sorceresses were hovering close to my remains. They transformed themselves several times to get at me, but in vain, because they failed to beguile his conscientious diligence. Finally they invested him in a cloud of sleep, and immured him in deep slumber. Then they never ceased summoning me by name until my immobile joints and cold limbs made sluggish attempts to render obedience to their magic art. This fellow here was actually alive, and merely dead to the world in sleep. He bears the same name as I, and at the calling of his name he rose up all unknowing, and stepped out of his own accord like the ghost of a dead man. Though the doors of the chamber had been barred carefully, there was a hole in them, and through it the witches cut off first his nose and then his ears. In this way he took my place in undergoing such surgery. Then, to ensure that their deceit would pass unnoticed in what followed, they shaped wax to represent the ears which they had cut off, and gave him a perfect fit. Likewise they fashioned a nose like his own. The poor man now standing here gained a reward not for being diligent, but for being mutilated."

'At these words I was panic-stricken, and proceeded to investigate my face. I clapped my hand to my nose; it came away. I pulled at my ears, and they too fell off. The bystanders identified me by pointing me out with their fingers, and turning their heads towards me, and they broke out into shrieks of laughter. I was in a cold sweat, and I slipped away, threading my path between their feet. Because of my mutilated appearance I am a risible figure, and I have been subsequently unable to return to my ancestral home. I have concealed the loss of my ears by letting my hair grow on both sides of my face, and the unsightly appearance of my lost nose I have made respectable by covering it with this linen bandage which is tightly wrapped over it.'

31   As soon as Thelyphron had finished this story, the drinkers, who were now well into their cups, renewed their guffaws. As they demanded their customary toast to the god Laughter,

Byrrhena explained to me: 'Tomorrow is a feast-day which was established in the early days of this city. We are the only people who on this day seek the benevolence of the god Laughter in an amusing and joyful ritual. Your presence will make the day more pleasant for us. My wish is that you may devise some happy entertainment from your store of wit to honour the god, so that in this way our offering to the great deity may be enlarged and enhanced.'

'That is a good suggestion', I replied, 'and I will follow your instruction. I only hope that I can think of some material to enable the great god to deck himself out in a flowing mantle.' Then, at the prompting of my slave, who warned me that darkness had fallen, I hastily rose from the table. By now I was as bloated with drink as the rest, and with an abrupt farewell to Byrrhena I started to weave my way homeward.

32   But as soon as we reached the nearest street, the torch on which we depended was blown out by a sudden gust of wind. We could scarcely escape the grip of the blinding darkness, and as we wearily made our way back to the lodging, we bruised our toes on the cobble-stones. As we held on to each other, we were now nearing our goal when suddenly three lusty figures with massive frames pushed against our doors with all their weight. They showed not the slightest concern at our arrival, but battered the doors with greater violence, vying with each other in their assaults. We both, and I myself in particular, reasonably assumed that they were ruffians of the most violent kind, so I at once extricated and gripped my sword which I had concealed beneath my clothing, and had carried abroad for just such an occasion as this. Without hesitation I flew into the band of robbers, and drove my sword up to the hilt into each one that I encountered in the struggle. Eventually they lay before my feet, punctured by numerous gaping wounds, and they gasped out their last breath.

The din of this engagement had roused Photis, and she opened the door. I crept in, panting and bathed in sweat. I at once retired to bed and sleep, for I was wearied with this battle against three brigands, which had been a re-enactment of the slaughter of Geryon.

BOOK 3

The Festival of Laughter: Lucius Becomes an Ass

1 Just as Aurora with her crimson trappings brandished her rosy arm and began to drive her chariot across the sky, I was wrenched out of untroubled sleep as the night restored to me the light of day. Anxiety assailed my mind as I recalled the incident of the previous evening. With my feet tucked beneath me and my hands clasped over my knees with fingers interlocked, I sat squatting on my bed and wept floods of tears, picturing before my mind now the forum as the scene of the trial, now the sentence, and finally the very executioner. 'Will any juror', I asked myself, 'show himself so merciful and well-disposed to me as to be able to declare me innocent, gore-stained as I am after that triple slaughter, and steeped in the blood of so many citizens? Was this the journeying which the Chaldaean Diophanes proclaimed with such assurance would bring me fame?' As I turned these thoughts over repeatedly in my mind, I lamented my misfortune.

2 Meanwhile there was a banging on the door, and our portals echoed with the shouting of a crowd outside. At once the house was thrown open, and a great number burst in. The whole place was jammed with magistrates, their officials, and an assorted mob. Two attendants proceeded to lay hands on me on the instruction of the magistrates, and began to drag me off as I offered no resistance. As soon as we reached the nearest street, the whole township poured out and followed us in astounding numbers. As I walked along dejectedly with head bowed towards the ground (or rather, towards the denizens of hell), I observed from the corner of my eye a most surprising sight. Of the thousands of people milling about, there was not a single one who was not splitting his sides with laughter. After being paraded through all the streets—for they led me round from one corner to another, as if they were expiating the threat of portents by driving round sacrificial

victims in ceremonies of purification—I was dragged before
the tribunal in the forum.

The magistrates now took their seats on the raised
platform, and the city-herald loudly demanded silence.
Suddenly from all present there was a concerted demand that
since the huge crowd was in danger of being crushed because
of the excessive numbers, this important case should be tried
in the theatre. At once from every side the people darted off
and with astonishing speed packed the auditorium. They even
jammed the aisles and the concourse at the top. Several
wound their legs round columns, others hung from statues, a
few were partly visible through the windows and ornamental
trellis-work. All were indifferent to the hazards threatening
their physical safety in this curious eagerness to observe the
proceedings. Then the city officials escorted me like a
sacrificial victim across the stage, and made me stand in the
orchestra.

3   The prosecutor, an elderly man, was then summoned by a
further loud cry from the herald. As he rose, water was poured
into a small vessel, which was finely perforated like a colander
to allow it to run out drop by drop; this was to regulate the
time allowed for speaking. The man addressed the assembly
as follows:

'The case before us, august citizens, is no trivial one. It has
a bearing on the peace of the whole community, and will be
valuable for the stern example it sets. Hence it is all the more
fitting that one and all here present, in the interests of the
dignity of this our city, should carefully ensure that this
impious killer may not escape punishment for the multiple
butchery which he has bloodily perpetrated. Pray do not
believe that I am fired by private enmity, or that I am
indulging savage hatred of a personal kind. My job is as
commander of the night-patrol, and I believe that my
sleepless supervision can be censured by no one up to this very
day.

'I shall now turn to the matter in hand, and scrupulously
recount the events of last night. Just after midnight I patrolled
the city, scrutinizing in careful detail every area door by door.

I caught sight of this most savage youth with his dagger drawn, wreaking slaughter all around, and before his feet I observed three victims slain by his savagery. They were still breathing, their bodies suffering convulsions in pools of blood. This man was justly apprehensive because he knew that he had committed this great outrage, and so he at once fled, slipping away under cover of darkness into some house where he lay hidden throughout the night. But the gods' foresight allows no respite to evildoers, and early this morning I waited for him before he could escape by unobserved paths, and I ensured that he was haled before this most austere court which exacts sacred oaths. Here, then, you have a defendant sullied by numerous murders, a defendant caught in the act, a defendant who is a stranger to our city. So cast your votes responsibly against this foreigner, who is charged with an offence for which you would heavily punish even a fellow-citizen.'

4   With these words that most incisive prosecutor ended his monstrous indictment. The herald bade me at once to embark upon whatever response I wished to make. But at that moment I could come out with nothing but tears, caused by contemplating not so much that remorseless indictment as my own afflicted conscience. But then I felt the accession of heaven-sent courage, so I made this response to the charges.

'I am well aware how difficult it is for a man accused of murder to persuade this large crowd of his innocence when the bodies of three citizens lie here before your eyes. This would be the case even if he speaks the truth and acknowledges the deed without prompting. But if with collective good-will you consent to grant me a cursory hearing, I shall readily persuade you that it is through no fault of mine that I am burdened with this capital charge. Rather, the considerable odium of the accusation is baselessly imposed on me through the chance outcome of my reasonable indignation.

5   'I was making my way back from dinner at a rather late hour. Admittedly I had taken too much to drink, and I shall not deny the truth of that. But as I turned in at the house of your fellow-citizen, the honest Milo, I saw before the very

entrance to the lodging some most ruthless robbers seeking to force their way in. They were trying to wrench the house-doors off their hinges; all the bars which had been most securely installed had been violently torn away. The robbers were plotting with each other the murder of those within. Then one of them, more eager for action and of more imposing physique than the others, began to rouse them to the same pitch with exhortations like these: "Come on, lads, let's attack them, while they sleep, with all our manly spirit and ready vigour. Away with all feelings of hesitation and cowardice! Let slaughter stalk with drawn sword throughout the house. Let's cut down those who lie sleeping, and run through those who try to resist. We shall make good our retreat unscathed only if we leave no one in the house unscathed."

'I freely confess, citizens, that I sought to frighten off and rout these desperadoes. I was armed with a short sword which accompanied me in case of dangers of this kind, and I thought such action the duty of a good citizen. I was also extremely apprehensive for the safety of my hosts and myself. But those utterly savage and monstrous men did not take to their heels, and though they saw that I was armed, they none the less boldly confronted me.

6   'Their battle-line was now assembled. The leader and standard-bearer of the gang promptly assailed me with brute force. He seized me by the hair with both hands, bent my head backward, and intended to batter me with a stone. But while he was urging that one be handed to him, my sword-thrust was true, and I successfully laid him low. A second robber was hanging on to my legs with his teeth; I killed him with a well-directed blow between the shoulder-blades. A third who rushed blindly at me I finished off with a thrust to the heart.

'This was how I maintained the peace, and defended the house of my hosts and the safety of the townsfolk. I believed that I would not merely escape punishment, but would also win public praise. I had never been indicted before on even the most trivial charge. As one highly respected in my community, I had always placed unblemished behaviour before any advantage. I can see no justification for now having to stand trial here on account of the just vengeance which impelled me to take action against these despicable criminals. No one can point to any previous enmity between them and myself, or indeed to any previous acquaintance whatsoever with these robbers. If it is believed that a desire for ill-gotten gains was the incentive for so great a crime, at least let such gains be produced.'

7   Tears again rose to my eyes at the close of this utterance. I stretched out my hands in doleful entreaty to one section of the audience after another, appealing to their common humanity and to the love which they bore for their dear ones. Once I was satisfied that the compassion of all was roused, and that my tears had stirred their pity, I called to witness the eyes of the Sun and of Justice, and recommended my immediate plight to the gods' future care. But when I raised my gaze a little higher, I saw that the whole gathering without exception was splitting its sides with loud laughter, and that even my kind host and patron Milo was unable to contain himself, and was laughing loudest of all. At that moment I reflected: 'So this is the nature of good faith and awareness of right conduct! Here am I, a killer indicted on a capital charge through ensuring the safety of my host, and he is not satisfied with refusing me his consoling support; he laughs aloud at my undoing as well!'

8   At this moment a woman, sobbing and tear-stained, wearing mourning black and carrying a baby in her lap, came running down through the theatre. Behind her came a second figure, an old hag clad in repulsive rags, and equally tearful. Both brandished olive-branches. They stationed themselves on each side of the bier on which the corpses of the slain were shrouded, and they raised a din of lamentation dismally bewailing their fate: 'We entreat you by the sense of compassion which you share, and in the name of the universal rights of mankind. Show pity for these young men un-deservedly slain. By taking vengeance afford some consolation to the one of us now widowed, and to the other left forlorn, or at any rate lend support to the fortunes of this little child

orphaned in his infancy, and do justice to your laws and to
public order with the blood of this ruffian.'

Next the senior magistrate rose and addressed the people:
'Not even the perpetrator himself can deny this crime which
deserves stern punishment. Only one problem remains for us
to deal with: we must seek out the associates in this dreadful
deed, for it is unlikely that one man on his own took the lives
of three such vigorous young men. So the truth must be
extracted from this man by torture. The slave who supported
him has escaped unnoticed. We have now reached the stage at
which the defendant under interrogation must reveal his
accomplices in this crime, so that we may once and for all
dispel all our fear of this grim band.'

9   In accordance with Greek custom, fire and a wheel were
brought in, together with every variety of whip. My
consternation certainly grew; in fact it was redoubled at the
prospect of my not being allowed to die unmutilated. But the
old woman whose weeping had roused general indignation
said: 'Good citizens, before you nail to the cross this ruffian
who has murdered the wretched victims who are my dear
ones, allow the corpses of the slaughtered men to be
uncovered. By gazing on their youthful and handsome bodies
you may be further roused to just indignation, and inflict
harsh punishment which fits the crime.'

Applause greeted these words, and at once the magistrate
ordered me to uncover with my own hands the bodies laid out
on the bier. In spite of my struggles and lengthy refusal to
revive the memory of my earlier crime by displaying the
bodies afresh, at the command of the magistrates the
attendants exerted the greatest physical pressure on me to
compel me to do so. In short, they forced my hand from where
it was dangling at my side to wreak its own doom by guiding it
on to the corpses. I was finally compelled to yield; I drew back
the pall with the greatest reluctance, and uncovered the
bodies.

Heavens, what a sight met my eyes! What an extraordinary
thing! What a sudden reversal of my fortunes! A moment
before I had been consigned as a slave to the household of

Proserpina and Orcus, but now I was stopped in my tracks and dumbfounded at this transformation. I have no adequate words to explain the nature of that strange sight: those corpses of the slain turned out to be three inflated wineskins which had been slit open in various places. The gaping holes appeared where, as I cast my mind back to the battle of the previous night, I recalled having wounded those brigands.

10   At that moment the laughter which some had guilefully repressed for a short time now burst out without restraint to engulf the entire crowd. Some cackled in paroxysms of mirth, others pressed their hands to their stomachs to relieve the pain. In one way or another the entire audience was overcome with hilarity, and as they quitted the theatre, they kept looking back at me. From the moment when I seized the coverlet I myself stood rooted there, frozen into stone like one of the statues or pillars in the theatre. I did not return to life until my host Milo came up. As I held back, and sobbed repeatedly with the tears again welling in my eyes, he laid his hand on me, and with gentle force drew me along with him. He took me home by a circuitous route wherever he spotted deserted streets, and he sought to console me in my despondency and my continuing apprehension by discoursing on various matters. But he could not succeed in mitigating in any way my anger at the insult which had struck me to my heart's depths.

11   Now, however, the magistrates in person clad in their robes of office entered our residence and sought to mollify me with an explanation on these lines. 'Master Lucius, we are well aware of your high rank, and also of your family's pedigree, for the nobility of your famous house is known to the whole province. We assure you that the humiliation which you so bitterly resent was not intended as an insult, and so you must banish all the melancholy which at present fills your heart, and dispel your mental anguish. This festival, which we regularly celebrate in public as each year comes round, in honour of Laughter, the most welcome of the gods, always owes its success to some novel subterfuge. This deity will

favourably and affectionately accompany everywhere the person who arouses and enacts his laughter, and he will never allow you to grieve in mind, but will implant continual joy on your countenance with his sunny elegance. The whole community has now bestowed outstanding honours on you for the pleasure you have given them; for they have enrolled you as patron, and have decreed that your statue be set up in bronze.' To this address I replied: 'The gratitude that I accord to this most glorious and unique city of Thessaly matches the distinctions which you offer me, but I urge you to reserve your statues and portraits for worthier and greater persons than myself.'

12 With this modest response I raised a fleeting smile, pretending as best I could to be cheerful, and as the magistrates departed I bade them a friendly farewell. Suddenly a servant came hastening in. 'Your aunt Byrrhena summons you,' he said. 'She wishes to remind you of the dinner-party which late last night you promised to attend and which will shortly begin.' But I was apprehensive, and even at a distance I shuddered at the thought of her house. So I made the following reply: 'How I wish, dear aunt, that I could obey your bidding, if only I could do so in good faith. But my host Milo has made me promise to have dinner with him today, invoking the deity who is in close attendance on us. He does not leave my side, and does not permit me to leave his, so we must postpone that promise of dinner.'

While I was still dictating this, Milo put his arm firmly in mine, and conducted me to the baths close by, giving instructions that the toiletries should accompany us. I sought to avoid everyone's eyes and made myself inconspicuous as I walked along at his side, avoiding the laughter of passers-by which I had myself promoted. My embarrassment was such that I do not recall how I bathed and towelled and returned to the house again, for I was distraught and paralysed as the eyes and nods and fingers of all present marked me down.

13 The outcome was that having enjoyed a hasty and extremely modest supper at Milo's table, I pleaded as excuse a sharp headache brought on by my continual weeping

earlier, and I readily obtained leave to retire to bed. I threw myself down on my little couch, and in my depression I recalled every detail of what had happened. Eventually my Photis came in, after having seen her mistress to bed. Her demeanour was quite different from before, for she did not look cheerful, nor was her conversation spiced with wit. She wore a sombre look, wrinkling her face into a frown.

At last she spoke hesitantly and timidly. 'I have to confess', she said, 'that I caused this discomfiture of yours.' As she spoke, she produced a strap from under her dress, and handed it to me. 'Take your revenge, I beg you,' she said, 'on a woman who has betrayed you, or exact some punishment even greater than this. But I implore you not to imagine that I deliberately planned this painful treatment for you. God forbid that you should suffer even the slightest vexation on my account. If anything untoward threatens you, I pray that my life-blood may avert it. It was because of a mischance that befell me, when ordered to perform a different task, that the damage was inflicted on you.'

14   Impelled by my habitual curiosity and eager to have the hidden cause of the incident of the previous night revealed, I then replied: 'This is a wicked and most presumptuous strap, since you have allotted it the task of beating you. I shall destroy it by cutting it up or by slashing it to pieces rather than have it touch your skin, which is soft as down and white as milk. But tell me truthfully: what action of yours was attended by the perversity of savage Fortune, and resulted in my downfall? I swear by that head of yours which is so dear to me that I can believe no one, and you least of all, in the suggestion that you laid any plan for my undoing. In any case, a chance happening, or even a detrimental occurrence, cannot convert innocent intentions into guilty deeds.' As I finished speaking, I thirstily applied my mouth to the moist and trembling eyes of my Photis, which were languid with uncontrolled desire, and were now half-closed as I pressed hungry kisses upon them.

15   Her high spirits now restored, 'Please wait a moment', she said, 'until I carefully close the bedroom door. I don't wish to

commit a grievous error by carelessly and sacrilegiously letting my tongue run free.' As she spoke, she thrust home the bolts and fastened the hook securely. Then she came back to me, and took my neck in both her hands. In a low and quite restrained voice, she said: 'I am fearful and mortally terrified of revealing the secrets of this house, and of exposing the hidden mysteries wrought by my mistress. But I have considerable trust in you and your learning. In addition to the noble distinction of your birth and your outstanding intellect, you have been initiated into several sacred cults, and you are certainly aware of the need for the sacred confidentiality of silence. So all that I entrust to the sanctuary of your pious heart you must for ever enclose and guard within its confines, and thus repay the ingenuous trust of my revelations with the steadfast security of your silence. The love which holds me fast to you compels me to reveal to you things which I alone know. You are now to gain acquaintance with the entire nature of our household, with the wondrous and secret spells of my mistress. To these the spirits hearken and the elements are enslaved, and by them the stars are dislocated and the divine powers harnessed. But for no purpose does my mistress have recourse to the power of this art so much as when she eyes with pleasure some young man of elegant appearance, and indeed this is a frequent practice of hers.

16   'At the moment she is passionately obsessed with a young and extremely handsome Boeotian, and she eagerly deploys every device and every technique of her art. Only this evening I heard her with my own ears threatening the sun itself with cloud cover and unbroken darkness because it had not retired from the sky quickly enough, and had yielded to nightfall too late for her to practise the enticements of magic. Yesterday, when she was on her way back from the baths, she happened to catch sight of the young man sitting in the barber's, and she ordered me to remove secretly his hair which had been snipped off by the scissors and was lying on the floor. As I was carefully and unobtrusively gathering it, the barber caught me at it. Now we in this city have a bad name for practising the art of sorcery, so he grabbed me brusquely and rebuked

me. "You brazen hussy, is there no end to your repeatedly stealing the hair of eligible young men? If you don't finally stop this criminal practice, I'll have you up at once before the magistrates." He followed up his words with action; he thrust his hands between my breasts, felt around, and angrily extracted some hair which I had already hidden there. I was extremely concerned at this turn of events, remembering my mistress's usual temper. She often gets quite annoyed if she is frustrated in this way, and she takes it out on me most savagely. I actually thought of running away from her, but the thought of you at once caused me to reject the idea.

17   'I was just returning dispirited and afraid to go back empty-handed from the barber's, when I saw a man paring some goatskins with scissors. Once I watched the skins inflated, tightly tied, and hanging up, and the hair from them lying on the ground and of the same blonde colour as that of the young Boeotian, I abstracted a quantity of it and passed it to my mistress, concealing its true provenance. So it was that in the first hours of darkness, before you returned from your dinner, my mistress Pamphile in a fit of ecstatic madness climbed up towards the overlapping roof. On the far side of the house there is an area which is uncovered and exposed to the elements. It commands every view on the eastern side, as well as those in other directions. So it is especially convenient for those magical arts of hers, and she practises them there in secret. First of all she fitted out her infernal laboratory with the usual supplies, including every kind of aromatic plant, metal strips inscribed with unintelligible letters, the surviving remains of ill-omened birds, and a fairly large collection of corpses' limbs, earlier mourned over by relatives and in some cases even buried. Noses and fingers were in a heap in one place, and in another, nails from the gibbet to which there still clung flesh from the men hanged there. In yet another place the blood of slaughtered men was kept, and also gnawed skulls, torn from the fangs of wild beasts.

18   'Then, after chanting spells over quivering entrails, she poured propitiating offerings of various liquids—now spring-water, now cow's milk, now mountain-honey; she also poured

out mead. She twisted and entwined the locks of hair with each other, and placed them on live coals to be burnt with a variety of fragrant plants. Immediately, through this combination of the irresistible power of her magic lore and the hidden energy of the harnessed deities, the bodies from which the hair was crackling and smoking acquired human breath, and were able to feel and walk. They headed for the place to which the stench from the hair they had shed led them, and thus they took the place of the Boeotian youth in barging at the doors, in their attempt to gain entrance. At that moment you appeared on the scene, drunk with wine and deceived by the darkness of the sightless night. You drew your short sword, and armed yourself for the role of the mad Ajax. But whereas he inflicted violence on living cattle and lacerated whole herds, you much more courageously dealt the death-blow to three inflated goatskins. Thus you laid low the enemy without shedding a drop of blood, so that I can embrace not a homicide but an utricide.'

19   This elegant remark of Photis made me smile, and I responded in the same joking spirit. 'Well then,' I said, 'I can regard this as the first trophy won by my valour, in the tradition of Hercules' twelve labours, for I can equate the body of Geryon which was in triplicate, or the three-formed shape of Cerberus, with the like number of skins that I slew. But to obtain as you desire my forgiveness willingly for the entire error by which you involved me in such great distress, you must grant me the favour which is my dearest wish. Let me watch your mistress when she sets in train some application of her supernatural art. Let me see her when she summons the gods, or at any rate when she changes her shape. I am all agog to witness magic from close up. Mind you, you yourself do not seem to be a novice wholly innocent of such things. I have come to be quite convinced of this, for your flashing eyes and rosy cheeks, your shining hair, your kisses with parted lips, and your fragrant breasts hold me fast as your willing slave and bondsman, whereas previously I always spurned the embraces of matrons. So now I have no thought of returning home or planning my departure there;

there is nothing which I count better than spending a night with you.'

20   'Lucius,' she replied, 'I should dearly love to grant your wish, but her surly disposition aside, Pamphile invariably seeks solitude and likes to perform such secret rites when no one else is present. However, I shall put your wish before my personal danger. I shall watch out for a favourable occasion, and carefully arrange what you seek. My only stipulation, as I said at the beginning, is that you must promise to maintain silence in this momentous matter.'

As we chatted away, our desire for each other roused the minds and bodies of both of us. We threw off the clothes we wore until we were wholly naked, and enjoyed a wild love-orgy. When I was wearied with her feminine generosity, Photis offered me a boy's pleasure. Finally this period of wakefulness caused our eyes to droop; sleep invaded them, and held us fast until it was broad daylight.

21   After we had spent a few nights in such pleasurable pursuits, one day Photis came hurrying to me trembling with excitement. Her mistress, she said, was having no success in her love-affair by other means, and so she intended on the following night to invest herself with a bird's plumage, and to join her beloved by taking wing. I should accordingly be ready to observe with due circumspection this astonishing feat. So just as darkness fell, Photis led me silently on tiptoe to that upper chamber, and instructed me to witness what was happening there through a chink in the door.

Pamphile first divested herself of all her clothing. She then opened a small casket and took from it several small boxes. She removed the lid from one of these, and extracted ointment from it. This she rubbed for some time between her hands, and then smeared it all over herself from the tips of her toes to the crown of her head. She next held a long and private conversation with the lamp, and proceeded to flap her arms and legs with a trembling motion. As she gently moved them up and down, soft feathers began to sprout on them, and sturdy wings began to grow. Her nose became curved and hard, and her nails became talons. In this way Pamphile became an owl; she uttered a plaintive squawk as she tried out her new identity by gradually forsaking the ground. Soon she rose aloft, and with the full power of her wings quitted the house.

22   This was how Pamphile deliberately changed her shape by employing techniques of magic. I too was spellbound, but not through any incantation. I was rooted to the ground with astonishment at this event, and I seemed to have become something other than Lucius. In this state of ecstasy and riveted mindlessness, I was acting out a waking dream, and accordingly I rubbed my eyes repeatedly in an effort to discover whether I was awake. Finally I returned to awareness of my surroundings, and seizing Photis' hand I placed it on my eyes. 'While the chance allows', I begged her, 'do please allow me one great and unprecedented boon bestowed by your affection. Get me, my honey-sweet, a little ointment from that same box—by those dear breasts of yours I beg you. Bind me as your slave for ever by a favour which I can never repay, and in this way ensure that I shall become a winged Cupid, drawing close to my Venus.'

'Is that what you're after, my foxy lover?' she asked. 'Are you trying to force me to apply an axe to my own limbs? When you are in that vulnerable state, I can scarcely keep you safe from those two-legged Thessalian wolves! And where shall I seek you, when shall I see you, once you become a bird?'

23   'The gods preserve me from perpetrating such an outrage,' I replied. 'Even if I were to fly through the entire heavens on the soaring wings of an eagle, as the appointed messenger or happy squire of highest Jove, would I not sweep down from time to time from the enjoyment of such distinction on the wing to this fond nest of mine? I swear by this sweet knot that binds your hair and has enmeshed my heart, there is no other girl I prefer to my dear Photis. A second thought comes to my mind: once I have smeared myself and have become a bird like that, I shall have to keep a safe distance from all habitations. What a handsome and amusing lover I should make for matrons to enjoy when I'm an owl! If those night-

birds do get inside a house, the residents, as we see, take care
to catch them and nail them to their doors, to expiate by their
sufferings the threatened destruction to the household
occasioned by their ill-omened flight. But I almost forgot to
ask: what word or action do I need to discard those feathers
and to return to my being Lucius?' 'You have no worries in
ensuring that,' she answered, 'for my mistress has shown me
each and every substance that can restore to human form
those who have adopted such shapes. Do not imagine that she
did this out of mere goodwill; it was so that I could aid her
with an efficacious remedy on her return. Observe with what
cheap and everyday herbs such a great transformation is
achieved. You wash yourself with water in which a sprig of
dill and some bay-leaves have been steeped, and drink some of
it.'

24   She made this claim repeatedly, and then with great
apprehension she crept into the chamber, and took a box from
the casket. First I hugged and kissed it, and prayed that it
would bring me happy flying hours. Then I hastily tore off all
my clothes, dipped my hands eagerly into the box, drew out a
good quantity of the ointment, and rubbed all my limbs with
it. I then flapped my arms up and down, imitating the
movements of a bird. But no down and no sign of feathers
appeared. Instead, the hair on my body was becoming coarse
bristles, and my tender skin was hardening into hide. There
were no longer five fingers at the extremities of my hands, for
each was compressed into one hoof. From the base of my spine
protruded an enormous tail. My face became misshapen, my
mouth widened, my nostrils flared open, my lips became
pendulous, and my ears huge and bristly. The sole consolation I could see in this wretched transformation was the
swelling of my penis—though now I could not embrace
Photis.

25   As I helplessly surveyed the entire length of my body, and
came to the realization that I was not a bird but an ass, I tried to
complain at what Photis had done to me. But I was now
deprived of the human faculties of gesture and speech; all I
could do by way of silent reproach was to droop my lower lip,

and with tearful eyes give her a sidelong look. As soon as she saw what I had become, she beat her brow with remorseful hands and cried: 'That's the end of poor me! In my panic and haste I made a mistake; those look-alike boxes deceived me. But the saving grace is that the remedy for this transformation is quite easy and available. Just chew some roses, and you will stop being an ass and at once become my Lucius again. I only wish that I had plaited some garlands this evening as I usually do, and then you would not have had the inconvenience of even one night's delay. But as soon as dawn breaks, the remedy will be set before you with all speed.'

26   She kept wailing on like this. Though I was now a perfect ass, a Lucius-turned-beast, I still preserved my human faculties, and I gave long and serious thought to whether I should end the life of that most nefarious and abominable woman by kicking her repeatedly with my hooves and by tearing her apart with my teeth. But second thoughts deterred me from that rash course, for I feared that if Photis suffered the punishment of death, I should lose all my prospects of saving help. So angrily shaking my drooping head from side to side, I swallowed the indignity for the time being, and submitted to this most bitter of misfortunes. I retired to the stable to join the horse which had served as my trusty mount. I found another ass stabled there, which belonged to Milo my former host. I imagined that if dumb animals shared a silent comradeship bestowed by nature, that horse of mine would register some acknowledgement and pity for me, and would offer me hospitality and a decent lodging. But Jupiter, god of hospitality, and Faith, who has withdrawn her divinity from men, can testify how differently things turned out. That reputable mount of mine and the ass put their heads together and at once plotted my destruction. I can only assume that their concern was for their provender. Scarcely had they spotted me approaching the stall when they laid back their ears, and with flying hooves launched a frenzied attack on me. I was forced back as far as possible from the barley which earlier in the evening I had set down with my own hands in front of that most grateful serving-animal of mine.

27   Such treatment forced me to seek my own company, and I
retired to a corner of the stable. There I reflected on the
arrogance of my fellow-beasts, and I planned revenge on my
disloyal horse next day, when with the aid of roses I would
return to being Lucius. These thoughts were interrupted by
my catching sight of a statue of the goddess Epona seated in a
small shrine centrally placed, where a pillar supported the
roof-beams in the middle of the stable. The statue had been
devotedly garlanded with freshly picked roses. So in an
ecstasy of hope on identifying this assurance of salvation, I
stretched out my forelegs and with all the strength I could
muster, I rose energetically on my hind legs. I craned my neck
forward, and pushed out my lips to their full extent, making
every possible effort to reach the garlands. My attempt was
frustrated by what seemed to be the worst of luck; my own
dear servant, who always had the task of looking after my
horse, suddenly saw what was going on, and jumped up in a
rage. 'For how long', he cried, 'are we to endure this clapped-
out beast? A minute ago his target was the animals' rations,
and now he is attacking even the statues of deities! See if
I don't maim and lame this sacrilegious brute!' At once he
looked around for a weapon, and chanced upon a bundle of
wood which happened to be lying there. In it he spotted a
cudgel with its leaves still attached which was bigger than the
rest. He did not lay off beating my wretched body until there
was a loud explosion. The doors were staved in with an
almighty din, and there were fearful shouts from close
at hand of 'Robbers!' At this my slave took to his heels in
panic.

28   At that very moment the doors were violently forced open,
and a band of robbers burst into the whole house. Each area
of it was ringed by an armed contingent, and as people rushed
from every side to lend help, the marauders swiftly positioned
themselves to block their progress. All the robbers were
equipped with swords and torches which brightened the
darkness, for the flames and weapons gleamed like the rising
sun. They then attacked and split open with heavy axes the
treasure-store, which was situated in the middle of the house,

and was secured and bolted with bars of considerable strength; it was packed with Milo's precious stones. When they had forced their way in from every side, they bore off the entire store of treasures, each taking his share in hastily accumulated bundles. But these when assembled proved too many for those who were to carry them, for the extraordinary abundance of their rich haul caused them quite a headache. So they then led the two asses and my horse out of the stable, and loaded us as far as they could with the heavier bundles. They then drove us off from the plundered house with threats from their cudgels, leaving behind one of their comrades to report on the enquiry into the outrage. With repeated beatings they drove us pell-mell over the trackless expanse of mountain.

29   By this time I was as good as dead from the weight of all the baggage, the steep climb over the mountain-top, and the quite lengthy trek. Then—better late than never—the idea occurred to me to appeal to the civil authority, and to free myself from all these hardships by appealing to the august name of the emperor. So when we were now passing in full daylight through a crowded village with a busy market, as I made my way through knots of people I tried to call out Caesar's venerable name in my native Greek tongue. I repeatedly declaimed the 'O' eloquently and loudly enough, but nothing further; the rest of the appeal, the name of Caesar, I could not articulate. The robbers took badly to my unmusical recital, and cut my wretched hide on both sides so severely that they left it useless even as a straining-cloth.

Finally, however, the Jupiter whom we all know handed me an unexpected prospect of salvation. After we had passed many farmhouses and large estates, I sighted a quite pleasing little garden, in which among other attractive plants some virgin roses were in full flower in the morning dew. I drew nearer, with my eyes glued on them. Hope of deliverance made me eager and cheerful. My lips were already working up and down as I made for them. But then a much more salutary plan occurred to me. Undoubtedly, if I shrugged off my ass-identity and returned to being Lucius, I should meet a sticky end at the hands of the robbers, whether because they might suspect me of magical arts, or allege that I would lay evidence against them. So necessity compelled me to steer clear of the roses. I continued to bear with my present plight, and I champed at the bit as though I were an ass.

BOOK 4

At the Bandits' Hideout. Cupid and Psyche (i)

1 At about midday, when the heat was already intense from the blazing sun, we took lodgings in some village with elderly acquaintances whom the bandits knew well. This intimacy became clear to me, even though I was an ass, from their initial encounter, their torrent of talk, and their exchange of kisses. Moreover, the robbers presented their hosts with some gifts unloaded from my back, and they were evidently explaining in whispered chatter that they were stolen goods. Next they relieved us of all the baggage, and let us out into the nearest meadow to graze at will. But having an ass and my own horse as grazing-companions could hold no pleasures for me, unused as I yet was to a normal diet of grass. However, I caught sight of an allotment behind the stable, and as I was now desperate with hunger I broke boldly into it, and stuffed myself liberally with the vegetables, raw though they were. Then with a prayer to the entire company of gods I ran my eye over the whole expanse in the hope of finding a rose-bed standing out with its colour from the neighbouring allotments. The fact that I was now alone made me optimistic; being out of the way, under cover and well hidden, I thought that I could gulp down the antidote, and while unobserved could renounce the bent gait of a four-footed beast, and resume the upright stance of a man.

2 So as my mind tossed on this sea of thought, I saw at some distance a valley shaded by a leafy wood. Glinting among diverse smaller plants and the most luxuriant shrubbery were some bright roses of ruddy hue. Since my finer feelings were not wholly bestial, that grove seemed to me to be the abode of Venus and the Graces; in its shady recesses that delightful blossom shone out with its brightness of royal crimson. At once I bounded forward at a gallop, with a prayer to the smiling deity Success on my lips; and heaven help me, that

swift burst of speed made me feel like a racehorse rather than an ass. But alas, that superlatively nimble performance failed to outpace my Fortune's perverse hostility. On drawing near to the spot, I saw no soft and enticing roses, all moist with the dew and nectar of heaven, sprouting from their luxuriant bushes and blessed thorns; there was not even a valley anywhere. Instead there was merely the lip of a river-bank enclosed by thickly intertwining trees. These trees with their abundant foliage look like laurels, and bear pale red, cup-shaped blossoms opening out like the scented flower. Indeed, though they have virtually no smell, uneducated folk call them by their country-name of laurel-roses. If eaten they are deadly to all grazing animals.

3   Caught fast in this net of fate, I disregarded my personal safety, and was ready and eager to swallow those poisoned roses. But as I hesitantly drew near to crop them, a young man (I presumed him to be the allotment-holder whose entire crop of vegetables I had plundered) on observing the extent of his losses came rushing at me in a rage with a huge stick. He grabbed me, and rained blows all over my body; he would have put my very life in danger if I had not finally used my brains, and become my own helper. I raised my rear end high, kicked out at him repeatedly with my hind legs, and made good my escape, leaving him badly bruised on the nearby hill-slope. But at that moment a woman (doubtless the man's wife) looked down from the summit, and on seeing him stretched out lifeless she at once came bounding down to him, shrieking and bawling. The pity she meant to arouse was sure to spell my imminent end, for all the villagers, roused by her crying, at once together called out their dogs, and set them on me from every side to charge me in a mad frenzy and rend me to pieces. At that moment I was undoubtedly on the threshold of death, for I could see that the dogs, massive in size and many in number, a match for bears and lions, were marshalled and being roused against me. So I adapted my plan to the situation, abandoned my flight, and at full gallop retired to the stable where our lodgings were. The villagers held off the dogs with some difficulty, laid hold of me, and

fastened me to a ring with a most secure strap. Once again I would certainly have been finished off by their beatings, but my belly became constricted by the pain from their blows. It was crammed with the raw vegetables, and caused me to be afflicted with diarrhoea. The shit shot out in a stream; some of them were forced back from my now battered haunches when sprayed with this most putrid of fluids, and others with the stench of the stinking fumes.

4   As the sun's bright orb bent low towards the south, the bandits immediately loaded us, and especially myself, with much heavier burdens, and led us out of the stable. We had now travelled most of the way. I was exhausted by the long journey, sagging under the weight of the baggage, wearied by the blows from the cudgels, and now lame and tottering as well, since my hooves were worn out. So I halted by a small stream of gently winding water, and seized with alacrity this splendid opportunity, planning to flex my legs adroitly and to throw my body headlong in. I had made up my mind that no beatings would cause me to rise and continue the journey; I was even ready to die, not merely under the cudgel but also at the point of a sword. I reasoned that in my utter exhaustion and weakness I deserved a compassionate discharge, or at any rate that the bandits, both impatient at delay and eager to hasten their flight, would allot the burden on my back between the two other beasts, and abandon me as prey to the wolves and vultures rather than exact a heavier vengeance.

5   But this splendid plan was nipped in the bud by the most grievous misfortune, for the other ass guessed and forestalled my intention. He at once collapsed, baggage and all, with feigned exhaustion. He lay there like one dead, and made no attempt to rise, in spite of cudgels, goads, and hauling on his tail, ears and legs from every side. Finally the bandits grew weary and abandoned hope of him. They held a parley, and to avoid postponing their flight by tending for so long a dead or rather petrified ass, they divided his load between the horse and myself. They then drew a sword, cut his hamstrings right through, dragged him a little way off the road, and hurled him still breathing over the top of the cliff headlong into the

nearest valley below. As I reflected on the fate of my wretched comrade-in-arms, I decided to renounce guile and deceit, and to show myself a good ass to my masters, especially as I had heard them telling each other that we were about to lodge close by, and that this would form a peaceful end to our entire journey, for it was the base where they lived. We then climbed over a gentle hill, and reached the appointed spot. There all the baggage was unloaded from us, and stowed inside. Freed from my burdens, in place of a bath I sought to relieve my weariness by rolling in the dust.

6   Both subject and occasion demand that I offer an account of the region and of the cave which was the bandits' abode, for at one and the same time I shall stretch my mind and also enable you to measure carefully whether I was an ass in thought and feeling as well as in body. A bristling mountain rose up, shadowy with its woodland foliage, to a towering height. Its slanting and precipitous slopes, girt with rocks which were razor-sharp and therefore insurmountable, were flanked by valleys full of hollows and cavities, from which thorn-bushes rose like gigantic ramparts; they formed a natural defence since they faced every side. From the summit a spring gushed out, forming huge bubbles. As it tumbled headlong down, it disgorged its silvery waters, opening out into several rivulets, watering the valleys with a succession of pools, and enclosing the whole area like an encompassing sea or a slow-moving river. A high tower rose over the cavern where the mountain's edges ended. There was a sturdy pen with a strong fence suitable for housing sheep; its sides extended all ways, and served in place of a regular wall before the tiny path which formed the entrance. You could call it— pardon the joke—the bandits' reception room. There was nothing else nearby except a small hut carelessly roofed with reeds, in which as I later discovered look-outs chosen by lot from the complement of bandits kept watch at night.

7   The robbers crouched and crept down into the cave one by one, having tied us with strong straps just outside the entrance. Inside was an old hag doubled up with age, the single individual to whom the safety and care of this

numerous and youthful band seemed to be entrusted. They accosted her with these unfriendly words: 'Hey, you body overdue for burning, you prime insult to the human species, hell's unique reject, are you going to go on sitting at home like this, enjoying yourself? Aren't you going to give us a long-delayed meal to comfort and restore us after our great and dangerous trials? Here you are as usual, doing nothing whatever day and night except greedily pouring strong wine into that demanding belly!' The old woman trembled at this, and fearfully replied in a hoarse whisper: 'My most gallant and faithful protectors, everything is ready, and plenty of it. The stew is cooked and tastes delicious; there's lots of bread, and generous helpings of wine in spotless cups; and the usual hot water is ready for a quick wash-down.' As she finished speaking, they at once stripped off. The heat of the roaring fire gave new life to their naked bodies; they sluiced themselves with hot water, and rubbed oil on themselves. Then they sat at the tables which were generously laden with food.

8   They had just reclined at table when another, much larger group of young men arrived, at once equally recognizable as bandits, for they too brought in their loot of gold and silver coin and vessels, as well as silk garments interwoven with gold thread. Like the others, they too had a wash to revive themselves, and then they took their places on the couches among their comrades. Next they drew lots to act as waiters. Their eating and drinking was uncouth; they devoured pounds of stew, mounds of bread, and buckets of wine. They sported noisily, sang lustily, joked contentiously; their behaviour generally resembled nothing so much as that of the semi-bestial Lapiths and Centaurs at table. Then the strongest of them all said: 'We for our part stoutly and successfully stormed the house of Milo at Hypata, and not only have we acquired this mass of riches by our courage, but we have returned to base without casualties, and if it's worth mention-ing, we have come back eight feet richer. Whereas you who made Boeotian cities your target have lost your most valiant leader Lamachus, and have returned with a reduced force. I should rightly put Lamachus' safety higher than all these

bundles which you have brought back. However it was that his outstanding courage caused his death, the memory of that great man will be famed as much as that of glorious kings and battle-leaders, whereas you, model robbers that you are, in your mean and despicable thieving carry on your rag-and-bone trade by creeping fearfully through baths and old women's lodgings.'

9   One of the later arrivals took up the cudgels. 'Surely everyone knows that larger houses are much easier to storm? Why? Because even if there is a considerable household living in a grand manor, they all take more thought for their own skins than for their master's property. But people who live alone on a modest scale, whether they have a small fortune or, come to that, a large one, hide it away as if it didn't exist, keep a sharper eye on it, and defend it to the point of endangering their life's blood. What happened to us will bear me out. As soon as we reached Thebes with its seven gates, we carefully investigated the inhabitants' finances. We became aware that a certain money-changer called Chryseros had a large fortune, but concealed his wealth by elaborate ruses for fear of having to shoulder public services and shows. In short, he lived alone without a companion, quite happy in his small but well-guarded shack, generally shabby and unkempt, but sitting on his bags of gold. So we decided to make him our first target, thinking nothing of a struggle with one man, and imagining that we could make off with all his riches without trouble and at leisure.

10   'So as soon as night fell we waited at the entrance to his house. We decided not to lift the outer door off its hinges, or to force it, or even to break it down in case the din from the doors roused the entire neighbourhood, and made an end of us. So then Lamachus, our splendid standard-bearer, showing all the confidence of his proven courage, gingerly pushed his hand through the opening made for the key, and tried to dislodge the bar. But Chryseros, that most worthless specimen of all who walk on two feet, had been spying on us all the time, and was watching our every move. On tiptoe and in dead silence he gradually edged his way to the door. Then

suddenly with the utmost force he impaled our leader's hand on the door-panel with a massive nail. He left him there to his fate, with his hand pinned as to a gibbet, and climbed on to the roof of his shack, from where he kept shouting at the top of his voice, imploring the help of his neighbours. He called on each of them by name, warning them of the danger they all faced, giving it out that his house was suddenly engulfed by fire. So one and all panicked at the imminent danger so close at hand, and anxiously rushed to lend help.

11 'This put us on the horns of a dilemma; either we would be overpowered or our comrade abandoned. So with his consent we contrived a drastic solution dictated by the circumstances. With a nicely judged blow right through the joint where the arm is attached to the shoulder, we hacked our leader's arm right off and abandoned it there. We staunched the wound with a bundle of rags so that the drops of blood should not betray our tracks, and we hastily made off, taking with us the rest of Lamachus. We were agitated by our sense of obligation to him, and this afflicted and greatly confused us; but fear of pressing danger frightened us into flight. Our magnanimous, lion-hearted leader could neither make haste to follow us, nor find safety in staying behind. He plaintively urged us with repeated appeals and repeated prayers by Mars' right hand and by the sacred trust of our oath to deliver our goodly comrade from both pain and capture. Why, he demanded, should a brave bandit live on without the hand which alone could rob and strangle? He would be quite happy at the prospect of self-sought death at a comrade's hand. But when none of us could be induced to accede to his eager plea that we slay our father, with his remaining hand he drew his sword, planted a lingering kiss upon it, and with the fiercest of thrusts plunged it into his heart. We then paid our respects to the brave spirit of our stout-hearted leader. We carefully wrapped his body's remains in a linen cloth, and entrusted him to the safe anonymity of the sea. Our Lamachus now lies buried with an entire element for his grave.

12 'Lamachus, then, appended to his life an end worthy of his virtues. But Alcimus could not distract Fortune's savage will

from his ingenious plan. He broke into the tiny hut of an old woman as she slept, and climbed to her room above. But instead of throttling the life out of her as he ought to have done, he decided first to sling out her possessions one by one through the window, which was quite broad, so that we could bear them off. He heaved them all out enthusiastically, and he was disinclined to forgo even the couch on which the poor old thing was sleeping, so he rolled her off her little bed. He was about to throw down with it the rest of the bedclothes which he pulled from under her, when that shameless creature grovelled at his knees and pleaded with him: "Tell me, son, why are you presenting these measly, bedraggled possessions of a wretched old lady to my rich neighbours whose house is overlooked by this window?" Alcimus was taken in by the crafty guile of these words. Thinking that she was telling the truth, he feared that all that he had earlier dropped down, as well as what he was about to throw out, would be directed not to his comrades but into the house of strangers. He was now convinced of his mistake, so he hung out of the window to take a careful look all around, and in particular to assess the wealth of the neighbouring house which the old woman had mentioned. While concentrating on trying to do this, he was off his guard, and that wicked old woman gave him a push. It wasn't violent, but it was sudden and unexpected. He was balanced precariously, and focusing too on the scene outside. So she sent him flying down. Not only did he tumble from a great height, but he also landed on a huge boulder lying near the house. His rib-cage was shattered and burst open, and he spewed out streams of blood from deep down inside. After he had told us what had happened, he died without suffering much longer. We buried him as we did his predecessor, so Lamachus gained from our hands a good second-in-command.

13   'Under the blow of this double bereavement, we then abandoned our operations in Thebes, and moved up to Plataea, the nearest town. There we heard some common gossip about a certain Demochares who was soon to mount a gladiatorial show. This leading noble was fabulously wealthy and outstandingly generous, and he was laying on a public

entertainment matching the splendour of his fortune. I doubt if anyone has the talent or eloquence to describe properly the individual features of his diverse preparations. On one side were gladiators of celebrated prowess, on another hunters of renowned fleetness of foot, on another criminals whose prospects of reprieve were bleak; these last were the means by which the wild beasts would feast and fatten themselves. As part of a complex contraption there were gaily painted wooden towers assembled in stories to form a mobile house, and handsome animal-cages intended for the hunting-entertainment soon to be enacted. And then the number of beasts, and the different species! Why, in his boundless enthusiasm, Demochares had also imported from abroad the noble beasts which were to entomb the condemned criminals. In addition to the other furnishings of this splendid show, he had used every penny he inherited on purchasing a large number of huge she-bears; besides those he had trapped in local hunts and those he had bought at great expense, there were those which his friends had vied in bestowing on him on various occasions, and he had the costly business of upkeep and of careful feeding on them.

14 'But this bright and arresting provision of public entertainment did not escape Envy's baleful eyes. The bears, wearied by their long captivity, emaciated by the summer heat, and enervated by idle inactivity, succumbed to a sudden epidemic, so that scarcely one remained. You could see the hulks of half-dead beasts cast up like wrecks in street after street. Thereupon the common herd, compelled by sordid poverty and monotony of diet to seek any disgusting addition of free food for their shrunken bellies, fell on this feast which lay everywhere. This inspired Eubulus here and myself to devise a crafty plan. We carried off one of the bears, the biggest of the lot, to our hide-out as if to prepare it for eating. We carefully separated the flesh from the skin, adroitly keeping the claws whole and undamaged, and leaving the beast's head in place down to the neck-joint. We then carefully thinned out the skin by scraping it, sprinkled it with fine ash, and left it in the sun to dry. While the blazing heat of

heaven was absorbing the moisture, we stuffed ourselves manfully with the bear-meat, and allotted duties for the forthcoming operation. One of our number (it would be the person who excelled the rest in mental resolve rather than in physical strength, and who above all must be a volunteer) was to cover himself in the skin, and assume the appearance of a bear. He would be led into Demochares' house, and would exploit the quiet of the night to give us ready access through the gate.

15   'This crafty idea had induced quite a number of our most valiant brotherhood to volunteer for the role. Thrasyleon was chosen in preference to the rest by the vote of the band, and he submitted to the hazard of this uncertain contrivance. With untroubled face he enclosed himself in the skin, now supple and easily adjusted. We then sewed the edges of it together with tiny stitches, and we covered the slight slit, where we had joined the skin together, with the thick surrounding bristles. Then we forced Thrasyleon's head into the narrow confines of the throat where the animal's neck had been cut out. We made small holes around the nose and eyes to allow him to breathe and to see, and then we guided our most intrepid of comrades, now a hundred per cent beast, to a cage which we had bought quite cheaply for the job. Of his own accord he crept hastily in, bravely and eagerly. After thus making the initial preparations, we proceeded to complete the deception.

16   'We elicited the name of a certain Nicanor, a Thracian by origin who cultivated the closest ties of friendship with Demochares, and then we composed a letter purporting to convey that this good friend had devoted the first fruits of his hunting to adorn the show. By now evening had come on, so we exploited the cover of darkness to consign to Demochares the cage containing Thrasyleon, together with the forged letter. He marvelled at the size of the beast, and showed delight at his friend's timely munificence. Generous fellow that he was, he ordered ten gold pieces to be counted out of his money-box and presented to us as the agents of his joy. The novelty of such a sight usually draws people's attention, and hordes of folk gathered to admire the beast. Our comrade

Thrasyleon was clever enough to keep their nosy inspection at bay by repeatedly and threateningly advancing on them. The citizens with one voice kept hymning Demochares as a quite god-favoured, blessed man, for after the great disaster which had befallen the bears, he was somehow managing to challenge Fortune by obtaining a new supply. He ordered the beast to be taken at once to his country estate, and later brought back again with the utmost care.

17   'But I broke in: "This bear, sir, is exhausted by the sun's heat and the long journey. You should be chary about putting her amongst a great herd of animals which I hear are unwell. Better instead to look for an open, airy space in your residence here, if possible somewhere cool close to a pond. You surely know that this kind of animal usually makes its home in wooded groves, moist caves, and by pleasant streams?" Demochares was chastened by these warnings, recalling the number of beasts which he had lost. He agreed without reluctance, and readily allowed us to position the cage where we thought best. "We are also quite ready", I said to him, "to stay here and keep watch on the cage overnight. The animal is exhausted by the trials of the heat and the upheaval, and we can be more careful in giving him his meals on time, and his usual drink." "There is no need for us to put you to this trouble", answered Demochares, "as virtually the whole household is used to feeding bears through long practice."

18   'We then said our goodbyes and departed. After emerging from the city gate, we caught sight of a tomb in a remote and hidden spot well away from the road. In it were scattered about some coffins, occupied by the dust and ashes of the departed, their lids only half-fastened through time's decay. These we opened so that they could serve as storage for our prospective loot. Then, following the routine of our school, we waited for the time of night when the moon has set, when sleep launches its initial attack on men's minds, and then invades them in greater force and subdues them. We positioned our detachment, armed with swords, at the very entrance to Demochares' house to demonstrate our intention to plunder it. Thrasyleon, no less active, crept out of his cage

at the precise hour of night which robbers favour. With his
sword he at once disposed of every single guard heavily asleep
nearby, and then killed the doorman himself. He abstracted
the key, opened the doors, and as we rushed in eagerly and
made for the inside of the house, he pointed out to us the
strongroom where he had smartly observed a quantity of
silver being stored the evening before. By a combined assault
we at once forced our way in. I ordered each of the comrades
to pick up all the gold and silver they could carry, hide it with
haste in that abode of our faithful friends the dead, and run
back at top speed for another load. In the interests of all of us
I would wait alone at the door and keep a careful eye on the
proceedings until they returned. And the sight of the bear
charging at large through the middle of the house seemed
enough to deter any of the household who might happen to be
awake. However valiant and fearless any of them was, on
sighting the monstrous shape of the huge beast, and especially
at night, he would surely take to his heels at once, and shut
himself in with fear and trembling, barring the door of his
room behind him.

19   'But after we had duly organized all this with meticulous
planning, a sinister incident befell us. While I was waiting on
tenterhooks for my comrades to return, a slave-boy was
roused by the noise; doubtless it was the will of heaven. He
crept softly out, and sighted the beast charging around at
large all over the house. Maintaining complete silence, he
turned in his tracks and managed to inform everyone in the
house of what he had seen. The whole place was at once
overflowing with the teeming hordes of the household. The
darkness was brightened with torches, lamps, tapers, candles,
and other means of nocturnal illumination. Not one of that
great crowd emerged unarmed; each and all stood guard over
the doorways armed with cudgels, lances, and even drawn
swords. There were hunting-dogs too, long-eared, shaggy
creatures, being egged on to pin down the beast.

20   'While the confusion was still mounting, I imperceptibly
stole away, retreating backwards, but as I lurked behind the
door I could clearly see Thrasyleon putting up a marvellous

struggle against the dogs. Though heading close to life's finishing-post, he did not forget his honour or ours, nor his long-standing courage, but he continued to fight in the very jaws of the gaping Cerberus. In short, as long as life lasted he continued in the role which he had willingly undertaken. Now retreating, now holding fast, with various postures and body-movements he finally slipped out of the house. Yet though he had escaped into the open, he could not flee to safety, for all the fierce dogs from the next alley-way formed a column in great numbers and attached themselves to the hunting-dogs, which had likewise at that moment come pouring out of the house in pursuit. It was a grim and deadly sight to see; our Thrasyleon encircled and besieged by packs of savage dogs, and ripped apart by repeated bites. Finally, I could not bear the great strain. I joined myself to the milling crowd, and sought to lend a hidden hand to my good comrade by the only means I could, and to deter the leaders of the chase. "What a monstrous, unforgivable scandal!" I said, "we are destroying a great and truly precious beast!"

21   'But my artful words did not avail that most ill-starred young man, for a tall, strong fellow burst out of the house, and without hesitation plunged his lance into the beast's heart. A second man did the same, and a crowd of them, their fear now dispelled, vied with each other in plunging their swords also into him from close at hand. But Thrasyleon, that matchless glory of our band, did not betray the sanctity of his oath by any cry, let alone an exclamation of pain. It was not his endurance, but rather the breath of life in him which was finally overcome, though it deserved immortality. Now ripped apart by the hounds' teeth and slashed by swords, with resolute roaring and bestial howling he bore his imminent fate with noble animation, surrendering his life to its due end, but gaining glory for himself. He had thrown the mob into such panic-stricken and terrified confusion that until dawn broke, and in fact until it was fully daylight, not one man dared to lay so much as a finger on the beast, though it lay prostrate. But at last a butcher who was somewhat bolder than the rest gingerly and fearfully slit open the beast's belly, and stripped

our noble bandit of his bear. This was how Thrasyleon joined the ranks of our dead, but his fame will never die. We rapidly fastened up the baggage which the faithful corpses had preserved for us, and left the confines of Plataea at top speed. We repeatedly reflected how true it was that in this life of ours Lady Loyalty is not to be found, for in loathing at our treachery she has taken herself off to the world of the spirits and the dead below. So utterly exhausted by the weight of our baggage and the rigours of the journey, we have carted back this booty which lies before your eyes, mourning the loss of three of our comrades.'

22 Following the close of this speech, they poured libations of unmixed wine from golden cups in memory of their dead comrades. Then they appeased the god Mars with some hymns, and took a short nap. As for us, the old woman provided fresh barley in such unstinted abundance that my horse on receiving such a large allowance all to himself thought that he must be tucking into a dinner for the Salian priests. But I had never dined on raw barley previously, having always eaten it chopped up and softened from prolonged boiling. So when my eyes lit on the corner where the loaves surviving from the whole mob's depredations had been stacked, I vigorously exercised my jaws, which were weak from long hunger, and covered with cobwebs from long disuse. Then suddenly later in the night the bandits roused themselves, and packed up. They prepared themselves in various ways, some arming themselves with swords, some disguising themselves as ghosts, and rushed out at full speed. But even beckoning sleep could not restrain my urgent and overpowering appetite. Earlier, when I was Lucius, I would be satisfied with one or two bread-rolls and would then quit the table, but on this occasion I chewed through almost three basketfuls, for the belly I had to minister to was bottomless. Daylight broke as I devoted myself single-mindedly to this task.

23 Finally, my donkey's sense of decency induced me to abandon the bread with the greatest reluctance, and I quenched my thirst at the stream close by. At that moment

the bandits returned, wearing deeply worried and serious frowns. They had no bags of loot to show, not so much as an old rag. For all their swords, all their hands, all the combined force of their gang, all that they brought with them was one young girl. Her appearance proclaimed her to be free-born; her ladylike outfit showed that she was one of the local aristocracy. Heavens, she could have put ideas into the head of even an ass like me! She was crying, and tearing at her hair and clothes. They escorted her into the cave, and spoke to her to temper her distress. 'Your life and virtue are in no danger. Be patient with us for a short time until we get our cut. The pressures of poverty have driven us to this occupation. Your parents are rather grasping, but they will be prompt in paying the proper ransom out of their large money-bags on behalf of their own flesh and blood.'

24   But blarney such as this totally failed to soothe the girl's distress, and no wonder. She put her head between her knees, and wept uncontrollably. Whereupon the bandits called the old woman in, and told her to sit by the girl and talk to her as best she could in soft and consoling words. They then reverted to the routine of their profession. But no words of the old hag could distract the girl from her tears now in spate. Her laments rose higher, and she sobbed her heart out unceasingly, so that she forced the tears out of my eyes as well. She said; 'Here am I, as wretched as can be, deprived of my nice home and large household and affectionate slaves and respected parents, a mere chattel, the unhappy loot of a smash-and-grab raid, shut up like a slave in this rock-walled prison, stripped of all the comforts of my birth and upbringing, unsure of my safety, exposed to an executioner's torture, among all these dreadful bandits, this mob of horrid gangsters. How can I stop weeping, or even go on living?' After this outburst of crying, she was worn out with mental grief, constriction of the throat and mental weariness, and she let her languid eyes droop in sleep.

25   She had merely dropped off for a moment, when suddenly she jerked out of sleep like a madwoman, and began to maltreat herself much more severely. She started to beat her

breast with heavy blows and to belabour that bright face of hers, and though the old woman most pressingly sought the reasons for this fresh renewal of grief, her sighs grew deeper. Then she began: 'Now it's all up with me for sure, now I'm utterly finished, now I've lost all hope of being saved. The noose or the sword must be my only recourse, or at any rate I must throw myself off a cliff, no doubt about that.' The old woman's response was rather sharp. With a sterner face she told the girl to explain why the deuce she was crying, or what had suddenly caused her to renew her wild wailing after being sound asleep. 'I suppose you're trying to deprive my young men of their sizeable reward from ransoming you. If you go on like this, I'll have you burnt alive! I'll just ignore these tears of yours; bandits don't take much account of them.'

26   The girl was brought up short by these words. She kissed the old woman's hand, and said: 'Dear mother, forgive me. Call to mind the milk of human kindness, and give me some little support in this grimmest of misfortunes. Surely at your advanced age with its venerable grey hairs your sense of pity has not withered. Just contemplate the tragedy that has befallen me. I have a handsome young man, outstanding among his peers. The entire city voted him "favourite son of the community". He is in fact my cousin, just three years older than myself. From babyhood he was reared with me, and now that he's grown up we have been inseparable, sharing the same dear house, in fact the same room and bed. We are pledged to each other with fond feelings of sacred love, and for some time he has been bound by nuptial vows to marry me. With my parents' consent he has actually been registered as my husband. Just prior to the wedding he was sacrificing victims in the temples and public shrines, dutifully attended by a crowd of kith and kin. Our whole house was adorned with laurels and bright with torches as it re-echoed the marriage-hymn. At that moment my unhappy mother was holding me in her arms, and clothing me in the wedding-dress for the occasion. She was showering me with honeyed kisses, and murmuring anxious prayers to foster the hope of children to come. But then there was a sudden incursion as footpads

burst in; it was a scene of savage battle as they flashed their
naked weapons menacingly. But they did not turn their hands
to slaughter or plunder, but at once in close-packed formation
they rushed into the bedroom. None of our household fought
them off or so much as raised a finger to oppose them as they
grabbed me, distressed and fainting with cruel fear, from my
mother's fearful grasp. This was how they broke up and
ruined my wedding; it was like the experience of Attis or of
Protesilaus over again.

27 'Just now I had a terrible dream; the whole of my
misfortune has been renewed or rather redoubled. I seemed to
be forcibly dragged from my house, apartment, chamber,
from my very couch, and to be calling on my most wretched
husband's name through a trackless waste. Just torn from my
embraces, still drenched in perfume and adorned with
garlands of flowers, he chased after me as I fled on feet which
did not belong to me. Then with piercing cry he complained
that his lovely wife had been kidnapped, and called for the
people's help. But one of the bandits was enraged by being
hounded in this troublesome way. He grabbed a big stone
lying by his feet, struck my unhappy young bridegroom with
it, and killed him. I was fearstruck at this dreadful vision, and
in panic was jerked out of that lethal sleep.'

The old woman sighed in sympathy with the girl's tears,
and began to speak. 'Cheer up, my lady; don't be frightened
by the baseless fancies of dreams. For one thing, dreams in
daylight hours are held to be false, and for another, even
night-dreams sometimes tell of untruthful happenings. So
tears, beatings, even murders sometimes portend a profitable
and favourable outcome, while on the other hand, smiles,
bellyfuls of honey-cakes and pleasurable love-encounters
foretell future affliction with melancholy, physical illness, and
all such hardships. Come then, here and now I'll divert you
with the pretty story of an old wife's tale.' This is how she
began.

The Tale of Cupid and Psyche

28 In a certain city there lived a king and queen with three notably beautiful daughters. The two elder ones were very attractive, yet praise appropriate to humans was thought sufficient for their fame. But the beauty of the youngest girl was so special and distinguished that our poverty of human language could not describe or even adequately praise it. In consequence, many of her fellow-citizens and hordes of foreigners, on hearing the report of this matchless prodigy, gathered in ecstatic crowds. They were dumbstruck with admiration at her peerless beauty. They would press their hands to their lips with the forefinger resting on the upright thumb, and revere her with devoted worship as if she were none other than Venus herself. Rumour had already spread through the nearest cities and bordering territories that the goddess who was sprung from the dark-blue depths of the sea and was nurtured by the foam from the frothing waves was now bestowing the favour of her divinity among random gatherings of common folk; or at any rate, that the earth rather than the sea was newly impregnated by heavenly seed, and had sprouted forth a second Venus invested with the bloom of virginity.

29 This belief grew every day beyond measure. The story now became widespread; it swept through the neighbouring islands, through tracts of the mainland and numerous provinces. Many made long overland journeys and travelled over the deepest courses of the sea as they flocked to set eyes on this famed cynosure of their age. No one took ship for Paphos, Cnidos, or even Cythera to catch sight of the goddess Venus. Sacrifices in those places were postponed, shrines grew unsightly, couches become threadbare, rites went unperformed; the statues were not garlanded, and the altars were bare and grimy with cold ashes. It was the girl who was entreated in prayer. People gazed on that girl's human countenance when appeasing the divine will of the mighty goddess. When the maiden emerged in the mornings, they

sought from her the favour of the absent Venus with sacrificial victims and sacred feasts. The people crowded round her with wreaths and flowers to address their prayers, as she made her way through the streets. Since divine honours were being diverted in this excessive way to the worship of a mortal girl, the anger of the true Venus was fiercely kindled. She could not control her irritation. She tossed her head, let out a deep growl, and spoke in soliloquy:

30   'Here am I, the ancient mother of the universe, the founding creator of the elements, the Venus that tends the entire world, compelled to share the glory of my majesty with a mortal maiden, so that my name which has its niche in heaven is degraded by the foulness of the earth below! Am I then to share with another the supplications to my divine power, am I to endure vague adoration by proxy, allowing a mortal girl to strut around posing as my double? What a waste of effort it was for the shepherd whose justice and honesty won the approval of the great Jupiter to reckon my matchless beauty superior to that of those great goddesses! But this girl, whoever she is, is not going to enjoy appropriating the honours that are mine; I shall soon ensure that she rues the beauty which is not hers by rights!'

She at once summoned her son, that winged, most indiscreet youth whose own bad habits show his disregard for public morality. He goes rampaging through people's houses at night armed with his torch and arrows, undermining the marriages of all. He gets away scot-free with this disgraceful behaviour, and nothing that he does is worthwhile. His own nature made him excessively wanton, but he was further roused by his mother's words. She took him along to that city, and showed him Psyche in the flesh (that was the girl's name). She told him the whole story of their rivalry in beauty, and grumbling and growling with displeasure she added:

31   'I beg you by the bond of a mother's affection, by the sweet wounds which your darts inflict and the honeyed blisters left by this torch of yours: ensure that your mother gets her full revenge, and punish harshly this girl's arrogant beauty. Be willing to perform this single service which will compensate

for all that has gone before. See that the girl is seized with consuming passion for the lowest possible specimen of humanity, for one who as the victim of Fortune has lost status, inheritance and security, a man so disreputable that nowhere in the world can he find an equal in wretchedness.'

With these words she kissed her son long and hungrily with parted lips. Then she made for the nearest shore lapped by the waves. With rosy feet she mounted the surface of the rippling waters, and lo and behold, the bright surface of the sea-depths was becalmed. At her first intimation, her retinue in the deep performed her wishes, so promptly indeed that she seemed to have issued instructions long before. Nereus' daughters appeared in singing chorus, and shaggy Portunus sporting his blue-green beard, and Salacia, the folds of her garment sagging with fish, and Palaemon, the elf-charioteer on his dolphin. Bands of Tritons sported here and there on the waters, one softly blowing on his echoing shell, another fending off with silk parasol the heat of the hostile sun, a third holding a mirror before his mistress's face, while others, yoked in pairs to her chariot, swam below. This was the host of Venus' companions as she made for the Ocean.

32   Meanwhile, Psyche for all her striking beauty gained no reward for her ravishing looks. She was the object of all eyes, and her praise was on everyone's lips, but no king or prince or even commoner courted her to seek her hand. All admired her godlike appearance, but the admiration was such as is accorded to an exquisitely carved statue. For some time now her two elder sisters had been betrothed to royal suitors and had contracted splendid marriages, though their more modest beauty had won no widespread acclaim. But Psyche remained at home unattached, lamenting her isolated loneliness. Sick in body and wounded at heart, she loathed her beauty which the whole world admired. For this reason the father of that ill-starred girl was a picture of misery, for he suspected that the gods were hostile, and he feared their anger. He sought the advice of the most ancient oracle of the Milesian god, and with prayers and sacrificial victims begged from that mighty deity a marriage and a husband for that slighted maiden.

Apollo, an Ionian Greek, framed his response in Latin to accommodate the author of this Milesian tale:

33   Adorn this girl, O king, for wedlock dread,
        And set her on a lofty mountain-rock.
        Renounce all hope that one of mortal stock
        Can be your son-in-law, for she shall wed
        A fierce, barbaric, snake-like monster. He,
        Flitting on wings aloft, makes all things smart,
        Plaguing each moving thing with torch and dart.
        Why, Jupiter himself must fearful be.
        The other gods for him their terror show,
        And rivers shudder, and the dark realms below.

The king had formerly enjoyed a happy life, but on hearing this venerable prophecy he returned home reluctant and mournful. He unfolded to his wife the injunctions of that ominous oracle, and grief, tears and lamentation prevailed for several days. But now the grim fulfilment of the dread oracle loomed over them. Now they laid out the trappings for the marriage of that ill-starred girl with death; now the flames of the nuptial torch flickered dimly beneath the sooty ashes, the high note of the wedding-flute sank into the plaintive Lydian mode, and the joyous marriage-hymn tailed away into mournful wailing. That bride-to-be dried her tears on her very bridal-veil. Lamentation for the harsh fate of that anguished household spread throughout the city, and a cessation of business was announced which reflected the public grief.

34   But the warnings of heaven were to be obeyed, and unhappy Psyche's presence was demanded for her appointed punishment. So amidst intense grief the ritual of that marriage with death was solemnized, and the entire populace escorted her living corpse as Psyche tearfully attended not her marriage but her funeral. But when her sad parents, prostrated by their monstrous misfortune, drew back from the performance of their monstrous task, their daughter herself admonished them with these words:

'Why do you rack your sad old age with protracted weeping? Or why do you weary your life's breath, which is dearer to me than to yourselves, with repeated lamentations?

Why do you disfigure those features, which I adore, with
ineffectual tears? Why do you grieve my eyes by torturing
your own? Why do you tear at your grey locks? Why do you
beat those breasts so sacred to me? What fine rewards my
peerless beauty will bring you! All too late you experience the
mortal wounds inflicted by impious envy. That grief, those
tears, that lamentation for me as one already lost should have
been awakened when nations and communities brought me
fame with divine honours, when with one voice they greeted
me as the new Venus. Only now do I realize and see that my
one undoing has been the title of Venus bestowed on me.
Escort me and set me on the rock to which fate has consigned
me. I hasten to embark on this blessed marriage, I hasten to
behold this noble husband of mine. Why should I postpone or
shrink from the arrival of the person born for the destruction
of the whole world?'

35   After this utterance the maiden fell silent, and with resolute
step she now attached herself to the escorting procession of
citizens. They made their way to the appointed rock set on a
lofty mountain, and when they had installed the girl on its
peak, they all abandoned her there. They left behind the
marriage-torches which had lighted their way but were now
doused with their tears, and with bent heads made their way
homeward. The girl's unhappy parents, worn out by this
signal calamity, enclosed themselves in the gloom of their
shuttered house, and surrendered themselves to a life of
perpetual darkness.

But as Psyche wept in fear and trembling on that rocky
eminence, the Zephyr's kindly breeze with its soft stirring
wafted the hem of her dress this way and that, and made its
folds billow out. He gradually drew her aloft, and with
tranquil breath bore her slowly downward. She glided down
over the sloping side of that high cliff, and he laid her down in
the bosom of the flower-decked turf in the valley below.

BOOK 5

Cupid and Psyche (continued)

1 In that soft and grassy arbour Psyche reclined gratefully on the couch of the dew-laden turf. The great upheaval oppressing her mind had subsided, and she enjoyed pleasant repose. After sleeping long enough to feel refreshed, she got up with carefree heart. Before her eyes was a grove planted with towering, spreading trees, and a rill glistening with glassy waters.

At the centre of the grove close to the gliding stream was a royal palace, the work not of human hands but of divine craftsmanship. You would know as soon as you entered that you were viewing the bright and attractive retreat of some god. The high ceiling, artistically panelled with citron-wood and ivory, was supported on golden columns. The entire walls were worked in silver in relief; beasts and wild cattle met the gaze of those who entered there. The one who shaped all this silver into animal-forms was certainly a genius, or rather he must have been a demigod or even a god. The floors too extended with different pictures formed by mosaics of precious stones; twice blessed indeed, and more than twice blessed are those whose feet walk on gems and jewels! The other areas of the dwelling, too, in all its length and breadth, were incalculably costly. All the walls shimmered with their native gleam of solid gold, so that if the sun refused to shine, the house created its own daylight. The rooms, the colonnade, the very doors also shone brilliantly. The other riches likewise reflected the splendour of the mansion. You would be justified in thinking that this was a heavenly palace fashioned for mighty Jupiter when he was engaged in dealings with men.

2 Psyche, enticed by the charming appearance of these surroundings, drew nearer, and as her assurance grew she crossed the threshold. Delight at the surpassing beauty of the

scene encouraged her to examine every detail. Her eyes lit upon store-rooms built high on the other side of the house; they were crammed with abundance of treasures. Nothing imaginable was missing, and what was especially startling, apart from the breath-taking abundance of such riches, was the fact that this treasure-house had no protection whatever by way of chain or bar or guard.

As she gazed on all this with the greatest rapture, a disembodied voice addressed her: 'Why, my lady, do you gaze open-mouthed at this parade of wealth? All these things are yours. So retire to your room, relieve your weariness on your bed, and take a bath at your leisure. The voices you hear are those of your handmaidens, and we will diligently attend to your needs. Once you have completed your toilet a royal feast will at once be laid before you.'

3   Psyche felt a blessed assurance being bestowed upon her by heaven's provision. She heeded the suggestions of the disembodied voice, and after first taking a nap and then a bath to dispel her fatigue, she at once noted a semicircular couch and table close at hand. The dishes laid for dinner gave her to understand that all was set for her refreshment, so she gladly reclined there. Immediately wine as delicious as nectar and various plates of food were placed before her, brought not by human hands but unsupported on a gust of wind. She could see no living soul, and merely heard words emerging from thin air: her serving-maids were merely voices. When she had enjoyed the rich feast, a singer entered and performed unseen, while another musician strummed a lyre which was likewise invisible. Then the harmonious voices of a tuneful choir struck her ears, so that it was clear that a choral group was in attendance, though no person could be seen.

4   The pleasant entertainment came to an end, and the advent of darkness induced Psyche to retire to bed. When the night was well advanced, a genial sound met her ears. Since she was utterly alone, she trembled and shuddered in fear for her virginity, and she dreaded the unknown presence more than any other menace. But now her unknown bridegroom arrived and climbed into the bed. He made Psyche his wife, and

swiftly departed before dawn broke. At once the voices in attendance at her bed-chamber tended the new bride's violated virginity. These visits continued over a long period, and this new life in the course of nature became delightful to Psyche as she grew accustomed to it. Hearing that unidentified voice consoled her loneliness.

Meanwhile her parents were aging in unceasing grief and melancholy. As the news spread wider, her elder sisters learnt the whole story. In their sadness and grief they vied with each other in hastily leaving home and making straight for their parents, to see them and discuss the matter with them.

5   That night Psyche's husband (he was invisible to her, but she could touch and hear him) said to her: 'Sweetest Psyche, fond wife that you are, Fortune grows more savage, and threatens you with mortal danger. I charge you: show greater circumspection. Your sisters are worried at the rumour that you are dead, and presently they will come to this rock to search for traces of you. Should you chance to hear their cries of grief, you are not to respond, or even to set eyes on them. Otherwise you will cause me the most painful affliction, and bring utter destruction on yourself.'

Psyche consented and promised to follow her husband's guidance. But when he had vanished in company with the darkness, the poor girl spent the whole day crying and beating her breast. She kept repeating that now all was up with her, for here she was, confined and enclosed in that blessed prison, bereft of conversation with human beings for company, unable even to offer consoling relief to her sisters as they grieved for her, and not allowed even to catch a glimpse of them. No ablutions, food, or other relaxation made her feel better, and she retired to sleep in floods of tears.

6   At that moment her husband came to bed somewhat earlier than usual. She was still weeping, and as he embraced her, he remonstrated with her: 'Is this how the promise you made to me has turned out, Psyche my dear? What is your husband to expect or to hope from you? You never stop torturing yourself night and day, even when we embrace each other as husband and wife. Very well, have it your own way, follow your own

hell-bound inclination. But when you begin to repent at leisure, remember the sober warning which I gave you.'

Then Psyche with prayers and threats of her impending death forced her husband to yield to her longing to see her sisters, to relieve their grief, and he also allowed her to present them with whatever pieces of gold or jewellery she chose. But he kept deterring her with repeated warnings from being ever induced by the baleful prompting of her sisters to discover her husband's appearance. She must not through sacrilegious curiosity tumble headlong from the lofty height of her happy fortune, and forfeit thereafter his embrace.

She thanked her husband, and with spirits soaring she said: 'But I would rather die a hundred times than forgo the supreme joy of my marriage with you. For I love and cherish you passionately, whoever you are, as much as my own life, and I value you higher than Cupid himself. But one further concession I beg for my prayers: bid your servant the Zephyr spirit my sisters down to me, as he earlier wafted me down.' She pressed seductive kisses on him, whispered honeyed words, and snuggled close to soften him. She added endearments to her charms: 'O my honey-sweet, darling husband, light of your Psyche's life!' Her husband unwillingly gave way before the forceful pressure of these impassioned whispers, and promised to do all she asked. Then, as dawn drew near, he vanished from his wife's embrace.

7   Psyche's sisters enquired about the location of the rock on which she had been abandoned, and they quickly made their way to it. There they cried their eyes out and beat their breasts until the rocks and crags echoed equally loudly with their repeated lamentations. Then they sought to conjure up their sister by summoning her by name, until the piercing notes of their wailing voices permeated down the mountain-side, and Psyche rushed frantically and fearfully from the house. 'Why', she asked, 'do you torture yourselves to no purpose with your unhappy cries of grief? Here I am, the object of your mourning. So cease your doleful cries, and now at last dry those cheeks which are wet with prolonged tears, for you can now hug close the sister for whom you grieved.'

She then summoned the Zephyr, and reminded him of her husband's instruction. He speedily obeyed the command, and at once whisked them down safely on the gentlest of breezes. The sisters embraced each other, and delightedly exchanged eager kisses. The tears which had been dried welled forth again, prompted by their joy. 'Now that you are in good spirits', said Psyche, 'you must enter my hearth and home, and let the company of your Psyche gladden your hearts that were troubled.'

8　　Following these words, she showed them the magnificent riches of the golden house, and let them hear the voices of her large retinue. She then allowed them the rich pleasure of a luxurious bath and an elegant meal served by her ghostly maids. But when they had had their fill of the copious abundance of riches clearly bestowed by heaven, they began to harbour deep-seated envy in their hearts. So one of them kept asking with nagging curiosity about the owner of those divine possessions, about the identity and status of her husband. Psyche in her heart's depths did not in any way disobey or disregard her husband's instructions. She invented an impromptu story that he was a handsome young man whose cheeks were just darkening with a soft beard, and who spent most of his day hunting in the hills of the countryside. But she was anxious not to betray through a slip of the tongue her silent resolve by continuing the conversation, so she weighed her sisters down with gold artefacts and precious jewels, hastily summoned the Zephyr, and entrusted them to him for the return journey.

9　　This was carried out at once, and those splendid sisters then made their way home. They were now gnawed with the bile of growing envy, and repeatedly exchanged loud-voiced complaints. One of them began: 'Fortune, how blind and harsh and unjust you are! Was it your pleasure that we, daughters of the same parents, should endure so different a fate? Here we are, her elder sisters, nothing better than maidservants to foreign husbands, banished from home and even from our native land, living like exiles far from our parents, while Psyche, the youngest and last offspring of our mother's weary womb, has obtained all this wealth, and a god for a husband! She has not even a notion of how to enjoy such abundant blessings. Did you notice, sister, the quantity and quality of the precious stones lying in the house, the gleaming garments, the sparkling jewels, the gold lying beneath our feet all over the house? If she also has as handsome a husband as she claims, no woman living in the whole world is more blessed. Perhaps as their intimacy continues and their love grows stronger, her god-husband will make her divine as well. That's how things are, mark my words; she was putting on such airs and graces! She's now so high and mighty, behaving like a goddess, with those voices serving her needs, and winds obeying her commands! Whereas my life's a hell; to begin with, I have a husband older than my father. He's balder than an onion as well, and he hasn't the virility of an infant. And he keeps our house barricaded with bars and chains.'

10   The other took up the grumbling. 'I have to put up with a husband crippled and bent with rheumatism, so that he can succumb to my charms only once in a blue moon. I spend almost all my day rubbing his fingers, which are twisted and hard as flint, and burning these soft hands of mine on reeking poultices, filthy bandages, and smelly plasters. I'm a slaving nursing attendant, not a dutiful wife. You must decide for yourself, sister, how patiently or—let me express myself frankly—how menially you intend to bear the situation; I can't brook any longer the thought of this undeserving girl falling on her feet like this. Just recall how disdainfully and haughtily she treated us, how swollen-headed she'd become with her boasting and her immodest and vulgar display, how she reluctantly threw at us a few trinkets from that mass of riches, and then at once ordered us to be thrown out, whisked away, sent off with the wind because she found our presence tedious! As sure as I'm a woman, as sure as I'm standing here, I'm going to propel her headlong off that heap of riches!

'If the insulting way she's treated us has needled you as well, as it certainly should have, we must work out an effective plan together. We must not show the gifts in our possession to our parents or anyone else. We must not even betray the slightest awareness that she's alive. It's bad enough that we've witnessed the sorry situation ourselves, without our having to spread the glad news to our parents and the world at large. People aren't really fortunate if no one knows of their riches. She'll realize that she's got elder sisters, not maid-servants. So let us now go back to our husbands and homes, which may be poor but are honest. Then, when we have given the matter deeper thought, we must go back more determined to punish her arrogance.'

11   The two wicked sisters approved this wicked plan. So they hid away all those most valuable gifts. They tore their hair, gave their cheeks the scratching they deserved, and feigned renewed grief. Their hastily summoned tears depressed their parents, reawakening their sorrow to match that of their daughters, and then swollen with lunatic rage they rushed off to their homes, planning their wicked wiles—or rather the assassination of their innocent sister.

Meanwhile Psyche's unknown husband in their nightly conversation again counselled her with these words: 'Are you aware what immense danger overhangs you? Fortune is aiming her darts at you from long range and, unless you take the most stringent precautions, she will soon engage with you hand to hand. Those traitorous bitches are straining every nerve to lay wicked traps for you. Above all, they are seeking to persuade you to pry into my appearance, and as I have often warned you, a single glimpse of it will be your last. So if those depraved witches turn up later, ready with their destructive designs, and I am sure they will, you must not exchange a single word with them, or at any rate if your native innocence and soft-heartedness cannot bear that, you are not to listen to or utter a single word about your husband. Soon we shall be starting a family, for this as yet tiny womb of yours is carrying for us another child like yourself. If you conceal our secret in silence, that child will be a god; but if you disclose it, he will be mortal.'

12   Psyche was aglow with delight at the news. She gloried in the comforting prospect of a divine child, she exulted in the fame that such a dear one would bring her, and she rejoiced at

the thought of the respected status of mother. She eagerly counted the mounting days and departing months, and as a novice bearing an unknown burden, she marvelled that the pinprick of a moment could cause such a lovely swelling in her fecund womb.

But now those baneful, most abhorrent Furies were hastening on their impious way aboard ship, exhaling their snakelike poison. It was then that Psyche's husband on his brief visit again warned her: 'This is the day of crisis, the moment of worst hazard. Those troublesome members of your sex, those hostile blood-relations of yours have now seized their arms, struck camp, drawn their battle-line, and sounded the trumpet-note. Your impious sisters have drawn their swords, and are aiming for your jugular. The calamities that oppress us are indeed direful, dearest Psyche. Take pity on yourself and on me; show dutiful self-control to deliver your house and your husband, your person and this tiny child of ours from the unhappy disaster that looms over us. Do not set eyes on, or open your ears to, these female criminals, whom you cannot call your sisters because of their deadly hatred, and because of the way in which they have trodden underfoot their own flesh and blood, when like Sirens they lean out over the crag, and make the rocks resound with their death-dealing cries!'

13 Psyche's response was muffled with tearful sobs. 'Some time ago, I think, you had proof of my trustworthiness and discretion, and on this occasion too my resolution will likewise win your approval. Only tell our Zephyr to provide his services again, and allow me at least a glimpse of my sisters as consolation for your unwillingness to let me gaze on your sacred face. I beg you by these locks of yours which with their scent of cinnamon dangle all round your head, by your cheeks as soft and smooth as my own, by your breast which diffuses its hidden heat, as I hope to observe your features as reflected at least in this our tiny child: accede to the devoted prayers of this careworn suppliant, and grant me the blessing of my sisters' embraces. Then you will give fresh life and joy to your Psyche, your own devoted and dedicated dear one. I no longer

seek to see your face; the very darkness of the night is not oppressive to me, for you are my light to which I cling.' Her husband was bewitched by these words and soft embraces. He wiped away her tears with his curls, promised to do her bidding, and at once departed before dawn broke.

14   The conspiratorial pair of sisters did not even call on their parents. At breakneck speed they made straight from the ships to the familiar rock, and without waiting for the presence of the wafting wind, launched themselves down with impudent rashness into the depths below. The Zephyr, somewhat unwillingly recalling his king's command, enfolded them in the bosom of his favouring breeze and set them down on solid earth. Without hesitation they at once marched with measured step into the house, and counterfeiting the name of sisters they embraced their prey. With joyful expressions they cloaked the deeply hidden deceit which they treasured within them, and flattered their sister with these words: 'Psyche, you are no longer the little girl of old; you are now a mother. Just imagine what a blessing you bear in that purse of yours! What pleasures you will bring to our whole family! How lucky we are at the prospect of rearing this prince of infants! If he is as handsome as his parents—and why not?—he is sure to be a thorough Cupid!'

15   With this pretence of affection they gradually wormed their way into their sister's heart. As soon as they had rested their feet to recover from the weariness of the journey, and had steeped their bodies in a steaming bath, Psyche served them in the dining-room with a most handsome and delightful meal of meats and savouries. She ordered a lyre to play, and string-music came forth; she ordered pipes to start up, and their notes were heard; she bade choirs to sing, and they duly did. All this music soothed their spirits with the sweetest tunes as they listened, though no human person stood before them. But those baleful sisters were not softened or lulled even by that music so honey-sweet. They guided the conversation towards the deceitful snare which they had laid, and they began to enquire innocently about the status, family background, and walk of life of her husband. Then Psyche's

excessive naïvety made her forget her earlier version, and she concocted a fresh story. She said that her husband was a business-man from an adjoining region, and that he was middled-aged, with streaks of grey in his hair. But she did not linger a moment longer in such talk, but again loaded her sisters with rich gifts, and ushered them back to their carriage of the wind.

16   But as they returned home, after the Zephyr with his serene breath had borne them aloft, they exchanged abusive comments about Psyche. 'There are no words, sister, to describe the outrageous lie of that idiotic girl. Previously her husband was a young fellow whose beard was beginning to sprout with woolly growth, but now he's in middle age with spruce and shining grey hair: What a prodigy he must be! This short interval has brought on old age abruptly, and has changed his appearance! You can be sure, sister, that this noxious female is either telling a pack of lies or does not know what her husband is like. Whatever the truth of the matter, she must be parted from those riches of hers without delay. If she does not know what her husband looks like, she must certainly be married to a god, and it is a god she's got for us in that womb of hers. Be sure of this, that if she becomes a celebrity as the mother of a divine child—which God forbid— I'll put a rope round my neck and hang myself. For the moment, then, let us go back to our parents and spin a fairy story to match the one we concocted at first.'

17   In this impassioned state they greeted their parents disdainfully, and after a restless night those despicable sisters sped to the rock at break of day. They threw themselves down through the air, and the wind afforded them his usual protection. They squeezed their eyelids to force out some tears, and greeted the girl with these guileful words: 'While you sit here, content and in happy ignorance of your grim situation, giving no thought to your danger, we in our watchful zeal for your welfare lie awake at night, racked with sadness for your misfortunes. We know for a fact—and as we share your painful plight we cannot hide it from you—that a monstrous dragon lies unseen with you at night. It creeps

along with its numerous knotted coils; its neck is blood-stained, and oozes deadly poison; its monstrous jaws lie gaping open. You must surely remember the Pythian oracle, and its chant that you were doomed to wed a wild beast. Then, too, many farmers, local huntsmen, and a number of inhabitants have seen the dragon returning to its lair at night after seeking its food, or swimming in the shallows of a river close by.

18   'All of them maintain that the beast will not continue to fatten you for long by providing you with enticing food, and that as soon as your womb has filled out and your pregnancy comes to term, it will devour the richer fare which you will then offer. In view of this, you must now decide whether you are willing to side with your sisters, who are anxious for your welfare which is so dear to their hearts, and to live in their company once you escape from death, or whether you prefer to be interred in the stomach of that fiercest of beasts. However, if you opt for the isolation of this rustic haunt inhabited only by voices, preferring the foul and hazardous intimacy of furtive love in the embrace of this venomous dragon, at any rate we as your devoted sisters will have done our duty.'

Poor Psyche, simple and innocent as she was, at once felt apprehension at these grim tidings. She lost her head, and completely banished her recollection of all her husband's warnings and her own promises. She launched herself into the abyss of disaster. Trembling and pale as the blood drained from her face, she barely opened her mouth as she gasped and stammered out this reply to them.

19   'Dearest sisters, you have acted rightly in continuing to observe your devoted duty, and as for those who make these assertions to you, I do not think that they are telling lies. It is true that I have never seen my husband's face, and I have no knowledge whatsoever of where he hails from. I merely attend at night to the words of a husband to whom I submit with no knowledge of what he is like, for he certainly shuns the light of day. Your judgement is just that he is some beast, and I rightly agree with you. He constantly and emphatically warns

me against seeing what he looks like, and threatens me with great disaster if I show curiosity about his features. So if at this moment you can offer saving help to your sister in her hour of danger, you must come to my rescue now. Otherwise your indifference to the future will tarnish the benefits of your previous concern.'

Those female criminals had now made their way through the open gates, and had occupied the mind of their sister thus exposed. They emerged from beneath the mantlet of their battering-ram, drew their swords, and advanced on the terrified thoughts of that simple girl.

20   So it was that one of them said to her: 'Our family ties compel us, in the interests of your safety, to disregard any danger whatsoever which lies before us, so we shall inform you of the one way by which you will attain the safety which has exercised us for so long. You must whet a razor by running it over your softening palm, and when it is quite sharp hide it secretly by the bed where you usually lie. Then fill a well-trimmed lamp with oil, and when it is shining brightly, conceal it beneath the cover of an enclosing jar. Once you have purposefully secreted this equipment, you must wait until your husband ploughs his furrow, and enters and climbs as usual into bed. Then, when he has stretched out and sleep has begun to oppress and enfold him, as soon as he starts the steady breathing which denotes deep sleep, you must slip off the couch. In your bare feet and on tiptoe take mincing steps forward, and remove the lamp from its protective cover of darkness. Then take your cue from the lamp, and seize the moment to perform your own shining deed. Grasp the two-edged weapon boldly, first raise high your right hand, and then with all the force you can muster sever the knot which joins the neck and head of that venomous serpent. You will not act without our help, for we shall be hovering anxiously in attendance, and as soon as you have ensured your safety by his death, we shall fly to your side. All these riches here we shall bear off with you with all speed, and then we shall arrange an enviable marriage for you, human being with human being.'

21   Their sister was already quite feverish with agitation, but these fiery words set her heart ablaze. At once they left her, for their proximity to this most wicked crime made them fear greatly for themselves. So the customary thrust of the winged breeze bore them up to the rock, and they at once fled in precipitate haste. Without delay they embarked on their ships and cast off.

But Psyche, now left alone, except that being harried by the hostile Furies was no solitude, tossed in her grief like the waves of the sea. Though her plan was formed and her determination fixed, she still faltered in uncertainty of purpose as she set her hands to action, and was torn between the many impulses of her unhappy plight. She made haste, she temporized; her daring turned to fear, her diffidence to anger, and to cap everything she loathed the beast but loved the husband, though they were one and the same. But now evening brought on darkness, so with headlong haste she prepared the instruments for the heinous crime. Night fell, and her husband arrived, and having first skirmished in the warfare of love, he fell into a heavy sleep.

22   Then Psyche, though enfeebled in both body and mind, gained the strength lent her by fate's harsh decree. She uncovered the lamp, seized the razor, and showed a boldness that belied her sex. But as soon as the lamp was brought near, and the secrets of the couch were revealed, she beheld of all beasts the gentlest and sweetest, Cupid himself, a handsome god lying in a handsome posture. Even the lamplight was cheered and brightened on sighting him, and the razor felt suitably abashed at its sacrilegious sharpness. As for Psyche, she was awe-struck at this wonderful vision, and she lost all her self-control. She swooned and paled with enervation; her knees buckled, and she sought to hide the steel by plunging it into her own breast. Indeed, she would have perpetrated this, but the steel showed its fear of committing so serious a crime by plunging out of her rash grasp. But as in her weariness and giddiness she gazed repeatedly on the beauty of that divine countenance, her mental balance was restored. She beheld on his golden head his luxuriant hair steeped in ambrosia; his

neatly pinned ringlets strayed over his milk-white neck and rosy cheeks, some dangling in front and some behind, and their surpassing sheen made even the lamplight flicker. On the winged god's shoulders his dewy wings gleamed white with flashing brilliance; though they lay motionless, the soft and fragile feathers at their tips fluttered in quivering motion and sported restlessly. The rest of his body, hairless and rosy, was such that Venus would not have been ashamed to acknowledge him as her son. At the foot of the bed lay his bow, quiver, and arrows, the kindly weapons of that great god.

23   As Psyche trained her gaze insatiably and with no little curiosity on these her husband's weapons, in the course of handling and admiring them she drew out an arrow from the quiver, and tested its point on the tip of her thumb. But because her arm was still trembling she pressed too hard, with the result that it pricked too deeply, and tiny drops of rose-red blood bedewed the surface of the skin. So all unknowing and without prompting Psyche fell in love with Love, being fired more and more with desire for the god of desire. She gazed down on him in distraction, and as she passionately smothered him with wanton kisses from parted lips, she feared that he might stir in his sleep. But while her wounded heart pounded on being roused by such striking beauty, the lamp disgorged a drop of burning oil from the tip of its flame upon the god's right shoulder; it could have been nefarious treachery, or malicious jealousy, or the desire, so to say, to touch and kiss that glorious body. O you rash, reckless lamp, Love's worthless servant, do you burn the very god who possesses all fire, though doubtless you were invented by some lover to ensure that he might possess for longer and even at night the object of his desire? The god started up on being burnt; he saw that he was exposed, and that his trust was defiled. Without a word he at once flew away from the kisses and embrace of his most unhappy wife.

24   But Psyche seized his right leg with both hands just as he rose above her. She made a pitiable appendage as he soared aloft, following in his wake and dangling in company with him as they flew through the clouds. But finally she slipped down

to earth exhausted. As she lay there on the ground, her divine lover did not leave her, but flew to the nearest cypress-tree, and from its summit spoke in considerable indignation to her.

'Poor, ingenuous Psyche, I disregarded my mother Venus' instructions when she commanded that you be yoked in passionate desire to the meanest of men, and that you be then subjected to the most degrading of marriages. Instead, I preferred to swoop down to become your lover. I admit that my behaviour was not judicious; I, the famed archer, wounded myself with my own weapon, and made you my wife—and all so that you should regard me as a wild beast, and cut off my head with the steel, and with it the eyes that dote on you! I urged you repeatedly, I warned you devotedly always to be on your guard against what has now happened. But before long those fine counsellors of yours will make satisfaction to me for their heinous instructions, whereas for you the punishment will be merely my departure.' As he finished speaking, he soared aloft on his wings.

25   From her prostrate position on the ground Psyche watched her husband's flight as far as her eyes allowed, and she tortured her heart with the bitterest lamentations. But once the sculling of his wings had removed him from her sight and he had disappeared into the distance, she hurled herself headlong down from the bank of a river close by. But that kindly stream was doubtless keen to pay homage to the god who often scorches even the waters, and in fear for his person he at once cast her ashore on his current without injuring her, and set her on its grassy bank. The rustic god Pan chanced to be sitting at that moment on the brow of the stream, holding the mountain deity Echo in his arms, and teaching her to repeat after him all kinds of songs. Close by the bank nanny-goats were sporting as they grazed and cropped the river-foliage here and there. The goat-shaped god was well aware of the calamity that had befallen Psyche. He called her gently to him, lovesick and weary as she was, and soothed her with these consoling words.

'You are an elegant girl, and I am a rustic herdsman, but my advanced years give me the benefit of considerable experience. If my hazard is correct—sages actually call such guesswork divine insight—I infer from your stumbling and frequently wandering steps, from your excessively pale complexion and continual sighs, and not least from your mournful gaze, that you are suffering grievous love-pains. On that account you must hearken to me: do not seek again to destroy yourself by throwing yourself headlong or by seeking any other means of death. Cease your sorrowing, lay aside your sadness, and instead direct prayers of adoration to Cupid, greatest of gods, and by your caressing attentions win the favour of that wanton and extravagant youth.'

26   Psyche made no reply to this advice from the shepherd-god. She merely paid reverential homage to his divine person, and proceeded on her way. After wandering with weary steps for a considerable distance, as night fell a certain path led her all unknowing to a city where the husband of one of her sisters had his realm. Psyche recognized it, and asked that her arrival be announced to her sister. She was then ushered in, and after they had greeted and embraced each other, her sister enquired why she had come.

Psyche began to explain. 'You recall that plan of yours, by which you both persuaded me to take a two-edged razor and slay the beast who used to lie with me falsely claiming to be my husband, with the intention of later devouring my poor self with his greedy maw? I fell in with your proposal, but when the lamp which conspired with me allowed me to gaze on his face, the vision I beheld was astonishing and utterly divine: it was the son of the goddess Venus, I mean Cupid himself, who lay peacefully sleeping there. I exulted at the sight of such beauty, and was confused by the sense of overwhelming delight, and as I experienced frustration at being unable to enjoy relations with him, the lamp by a dreadful mischance shed a drop of burning oil on his shoulder. At once the pain caused him to start from his sleep, and when he saw me wielding the steel and the flame, he said: "This is a dreadful deed you have done. Leave my bed this instant, and take your goods and chattels with you. I shall now take your sister"—at this point he cited your name specifically—"in solemn marriage." At once he then ordered the Zephyr to waft me outside the bounds of his estate.'

27   Psyche had not yet finished speaking when her sister, goaded by mad lust and destructive envy, swung into action. She devised a lying excuse to deceive her husband, pretending that she had learnt of her parents' death; she at once boarded ship, and then made hot-foot for the rock. Although the wrong wind was blowing, her eagerness was fired by blind hope, and she said: 'Take me, Cupid, as your worthy wife; Zephyr, take your mistress aboard!' She then took a prodigious leap downward. But not even in death could she reach that abode, for her limbs bounced on the rocky crags, and were fragmented. Her insides were torn out, and in her fitting death she offered a ready meal to birds and beasts.

The second punitive vengeance was not long delayed. Psyche resumed her wanderings, and reached a second city where her other sister similarly dwelt. She too was taken in by her sister's deception, and in her eagerness to supplant Psyche in the marriage which they had befouled, she hastened to the rock, and fell to her deadly doom in the same way.

28   While Psyche was at this time visiting one community after another in her concentrated search for Cupid, he was lying groaning in his mother's chamber, racked by the pain of the wound from the lamp. But then the tern, the white bird which wings her way over the sea-waves, plunged swiftly into the deep bosom of ocean. She came upon Venus conveniently there as the goddess bathed and swam; she perched beside her, and told her that her son had suffered burning, and was lying in considerable pain from the wound, with his life in danger. As a result the entire household of Venus was in bad odour, the object of gossip and rebuke on the lips of people everywhere. They were claiming that Cupid was relaxing with a lady of easy virtue in the mountains, and that Venus herself was idly swimming in the ocean, with the result that pleasure and favour and elegance had departed from the world; all was unkempt, rustic, uncouth. There were no weddings, no cameraderie between friends, none of the love which children inspire; all was a scene of boundless squalor, of unsavoury

tedium in sordid alliances. Such was the gossip which that garrulous and prying bird whispered in Venus' ear, tearing her son's reputation to shreds.

Venus was absolutely livid. She burst out: 'So now that fine son of mine has a girl-friend, has he? Come on, then, tell me her name, since you are the only one who serves me with affection. Who is it who has tempted my innocent, beardless boy? Is it one of that crowd of nymphs, or one of the Hours, or one of the band of Muses, or one of my servant-Graces?' The garrulous bird did not withhold a reply. She said: 'I do not know, mistress; I think the story goes that he is head over heels in love with a girl by the name of Psyche, if my memory serves me rightly.' Then Venus in a rage bawled out at the top of her voice: 'Can it really be true that he is in love with that Psyche who lays claim to my beauty and pretends to my name? That son of mine must surely have regarded me as a procuress, when I pointed the girl out to him so that he could win her acquaintance.'

29   As she grumbled she made haste to quit the sea, and at once made for her golden chamber. There she found her son lying ill as she had heard, and from the doorway she bellowed out as loudly as she could: 'This is a fine state of affairs, just what one would expect from a child of mine, from a decent man like you! First of all you trampled underfoot the instructions of your mother—or I should say your employer—and you refused to humble my personal enemy with a vile love-liaison; and then, mark you, a mere boy of tender years, you hugged her close in your wanton, stunted embraces! You wanted me to have to cope with my enemy as a daughter-in-law! You take too much for granted, you good-for-nothing, loathsome seducer! You think of yourself as my only noble heir, and you imagine that I'm now too old to bear another. Just realize that I'll get another son, one far better than you. In fact I'll rub your nose in it further. I'll adopt one of my young slaves, and make him a present of these wings and torches of yours, the bow and arrows, and all the rest of my paraphernalia which I did not entrust to you to be misused like this. None of the cost of kitting you out came from your father's estate.

30   'Ever since you were a baby you have been badly brought
up, too ready with your hands. You show no respect to your
elders, pounding them time after time. Even me your own
mother you strip naked every day, and many's the time you've
cuffed me. You show me total contempt as though I were a
widow, and you haven't an ounce of fear for your stepfather,
the bravest and greatest of warriors. And why should you?
You are in the habit of supplying him with girls, to cause me
the pain of having to compete with rivals. But now I'll make
you sorry for this sport of yours. I'll ensure that you find your
marriage sour and bitter.

   'But what am I to do, now that I'm becoming a laughing-
stock? Where shall I go, how shall I curb in this scoundrel?
Should I beg the assistance of my enemy Sobriety, so often
alienated from me through this fellow's loose living? The
prospect of having to talk with that unsophisticated, hideous
female gives me the creeps. Still I must not despise the
consolation of gaining revenge from any quarter. She is
absolutely the only one to be given the job of imposing the
harshest discipline on this rascal. She must empty his quiver,
immobilize his arrows, unstring his bow, extinguish his torch,
and restrain his person with sharper correction. Only when
she has sheared off his locks—how often I have brushed them
shining like gold with my own hands!—and clipped those
wings, which I have steeped in my own breast's liquid nectar,
shall I regard the insult dealt to me as expiated.'

31   These were her words. Then she bustled out, glowering and
incensed with passionate rage. At that moment Ceres and
Juno came up with her. When they observed her resentful
face, they asked her why she was cloaking the rich charm of
her radiant eyes with a sullen frown. 'You have come, she
answered, 'at a timely moment to fulfil my wishes, for I am
seething inside. I ask you to search with might and main for
that fickle runaway of mine called Psyche. I'm sure that the
scandalous gossip concerning my household, and the
behaviour of that unspeakable son of mine, have not passed
you by.' They knew quite well what had happened, and they
sought to assuage Venus' raging temper. 'My lady, how is it

that your son's peccadillo has caused you to war on his pleasures in this unrelenting way, and also to desire to destroy the girl that he loves? What harm is there, we should like to know, in his giving the glad eye to a nicely turned-out girl? Don't you realize that he is in the prime of manhood, or are you forgetting his age? Just because he carries his years well, does he strike you as a perpetual Peter Pan? You are a mother, and a sensible one at that. Are you always going to pry nosily into your son's diversions, and condemn his wanton ways, censure his love-life, and vilify your own skills and pleasures as practised by your handsome son? What god or what person on earth will bear with your scattering sensual pleasures throughout the world, when you sourly refuse to allow love-liaisons in your own house, and you close down the manufacture of women's weaknesses which is made available to all?'

This was how the two goddesses sucked up to Cupid, seeking to win his favour, though he was absent, by taking his part, for they feared his arrows. But Venus was affronted that the insults which she sustained were treated so lightly. She cut the two of them short, turned on her heel, and stalked quickly off to the sea.

BOOK 6

*Cupid and Psyche (continued):
The Frustrated Escape*

1 Meanwhile Psyche in her random wanderings was suffering torment, as she sought day and night to trace her husband. She was restless in mind, but all the more eager, in spite of his anger, to soften him with a wife's endearments, or at any rate to appease him with a servant's entreaties. She spied a temple perched on the peak of a high mountain, and she said: 'Perhaps this is where my lord dwells?' She made her way quickly there, and though her feet were utterly weary from her unremitting labours, her hope and aspiration quickened them. She mounted the higher ridges with stout heart, and drew close to the sacred shrine. There she saw ears of wheat in a heap, and others woven into a garland, and ears of barley as well. There were sickles lying there, and a whole array of harvesting implements, but they were in a jumbled and neglected heap, thrown carelessly down by workmen's hands, as happens in summer-time. Psyche carefully sorted them out and ordered them in separate piles; no doubt she reflected that she should not neglect the shrines and rites of any deity, but rather implore the kindly pity of each and all.

2 Kindly Ceres sighted her as she carefully and diligently ordered these offerings, and at once she cried out from afar: 'Why, you poor Psyche! Venus is in a rage, mounting a feverish search for your traces all over the globe. She has marked you down for the sternest punishment, and is using all the resources of her divinity to demand vengeance. And here you are, looking to my interests, with your mind intent on anything but your own safety!'

Then Psyche grovelled at the goddess's feet, and watered them with a stream of tears. She swept the ground with her hair, and begged Ceres' favour with a litany of prayers. 'By your fruitful right hand, by the harvest ceremonies which assure plenty, by the silent mysteries of your baskets and the winged courses of your attendant dragons, by the furrows in your Sicilian soil, by the car which snatched and the earth which has latched, by Proserpina's descent to a lightless marriage, and by your daughter's return to rediscovered light, and by all else which the shrine of Attic Eleusis shrouds in silence—I beg you, lend aid to this soul of Psyche which is deserving of pity, and now entreats you. Allow me to lurk hidden here among these heaps of grain if only for a few days, until the great goddess's raging fury softens with the passage of time, or at any rate till my strength, which is now exhausted by protracted toil, is assuaged by a period of rest.'

3   Ceres answered her: 'Your tearful entreaties certainly affect me and I am keen to help you, but I cannot incur Venus's displeasure, for I maintain long-standing ties of friendship with her—and besides being my relative, she is also a fine woman. So you must quit this dwelling at once, and count it a blessing that I have not apprehended and imprisoned you.' So Psyche, in suffering this reverse to her hopes, was now beset by a double grief. As she retraced her steps, she noticed in a glimmering grove in the valley below an elegantly built shrine. Not wishing to disregard any means, however uncertain, which gave promise of brighter hope, and in her eagerness to seek the favour of any divinity whatsoever, she drew close to its sacred portals. There she observed valuable offerings, and ribbons inscribed with gold letters pinned to the branches of trees and to the doorposts. These attested the name of the goddess to whom they were dedicated, together with thanks for favours received. She sank to her knees, and with her hands she grasped the altar still warm from a sacrifice. She wiped away her tears, and then uttered this prayer.

4   'Sister and spouse of mighty Jupiter, whether you reside in your ancient shrine at Samos, which alone can pride itself on your birth, your infant cries, and your nurture; or whether you occupy your blessed abode in lofty Carthage, which worships you as the maiden who tours the sky on a lion's back; or whether you guard the famed walls of the Argives, by

the banks of the river-god Inachus, who now hymns you as bride of the Thunderer and as queen of all goddesses; you, whom all the East reveres as the yoking goddess, and whom all the West addresses as Lucina, be for me in my most acute misfortunes Juno the Saviour, and free me from looming dangers in my weariness from exhausting toils. I am told that it is your practice to lend unsolicited aid to pregnant women in danger.'

As she prayed like this, Juno at once appeared before her in all the venerable majesty of her divinity. There and then the goddess said: 'Believe me, I only wish that I could crown your prayers with my consent. But shame prevents me from opposing the will of Venus, my daughter-in-law whom I have always loved as my own daughter. There is a second obstacle—the legislation which forbids sanctuary for runaway slaves belonging to others, if their owners forbid it.'

5 Psyche was aghast at this second shipwreck devised by Fortune. Unable to meet up with her elusive husband, she abandoned all hope of salvation, and had recourse to her own counsel. 'What other assistance can I seek or harness to meet my desperate plight? Even the goodwill of goddesses however well-disposed has been of no avail to me. Now that I am trapped in a noose as tight as this, where can I make for, under what roof or in what dark corner can I hide, to escape the unwinking eyes of mighty Venus? Why don't you show a manly spirit, and the strength to renounce idle hope? Why don't you surrender yourself voluntarily to your mistress, and soften her savage onslaught by showing a humble demeanour, however late in the day? You never know, you may find the object of your long search in her house.' This was how she steeled herself for the uncertain outcome of showing obedience, or rather for her certain destruction, as she mentally rehearsed the opening lines of the plea she was to utter.

6 Venus now despaired of a successful search for her by earthly means, and she made for heaven. She ordered her carriage to be prepared; Vulcan had lovingly applied the finishing touches to it with elaborate workmanship, and had given it to her as a wedding-present before her initiation into

marriage. The thinning motion of his file had made the metal gleam; the coach's value was measured by the gold it had lost. Four white doves emerged from the large herd stabled close to their mistress's chamber. As they strutted gaily forward, turning their dappled necks from side to side, they submitted to the jewelled yoke. They took their mistress aboard and delightedly mounted upwards. Sparrows sported with the combined din of their chatter as they escorted the carriage of the goddess, and the other birds, habitually sweet songsters, announced the goddess's approach with the pleasurable sound of their honeyed tunes. The clouds parted, and heaven admitted his daughter; the topmost region delightedly welcomed the goddess, and the tuneful retinue of mighty Venus had no fear of encounter with eagles or of plundering hawks.

7   She at once made for the royal citadel of Jupiter, and in arrogant tones sought the urgent use of the services of the spokesman-god Mercury. Jupiter's lowering brow did not refuse her. Venus happily quitted heaven at once with Mercury accompanying her, and she spoke seriously to him: 'My brother from Arcadia, you surely know that your sister Venus has never had any success without Mercury's attendance, and you are well aware for how long I have been unable to trace my maid who lies in hiding. So I have no recourse other than that you as herald make public proclamation of a reward for tracking her down. So you must hasten to do my bidding, and clearly indicate the marks by which she can be recognized, so that if someone is charged with unlawfully concealing her, he cannot defend himself on the plea of ignorance.' With these words she handed him a sheet containing Psyche's name and other details. Then she at once retired home.

8   Mercury did not fail to obey her. He sped here and there, appearing before gatherings of every community, and as instructed performed the duty of making proclamation: 'If anyone can retrieve from her flight the runaway daughter of the king, the maidservant of Venus called Psyche, or indicate her hidden whereabouts, he should meet the herald Mercury

behind the *metae Murciae*. Whoever does so will obtain as reward from Venus herself seven sweet kisses, and a particularly honeyed one imparted with the thrust of her caressing tongue.'

Longing for this great reward aroused eager competition between men everywhere when Mercury made the proclamation on these lines, and this above all ended Psyche's hesitation. As she drew near to her mistress's door, a member of Venus's household called Habit confronted her, and at once cried out at the top of her voice: 'Most wicked of all servants, have you at last begun to realize that you have a mistress? Or are you, in keeping with the general run of your insolent behaviour, still pretending to be unaware of the exhausting efforts we have endured in searching for you? How appropriate it is that you have fallen into my hands rather than anyone else's. You are now caught fast in the claws of Orcus, and believe me, you will suffer the penalty for your gross impudence without delay.'

9   She then laid a presumptuous hand on Psyche's hair, and dragged the girl in unresisting. As soon as she was ushered in and presented before Venus' gaze, the goddess uttered the sort of explosive cackle typical of people in a furious rage. She wagged her head, scratched her right ear, and said: 'Oh, so you have finally condescended to greet your mother-in-law, have you? Or is the purpose of this visit rather to see your husband, whose life is in danger from the wound which you inflicted? You can rest assured that I shall welcome you as a good mother-in-law should.' Then she added: 'Where are my maids Melancholy and Sorrow?'

They were called in, and the goddess consigned Psyche to them for torture. They obeyed their mistress's instruction, laid into poor Psyche with whips and tortured her with other implements, and then restored her to their mistress's presence. Venus renewed her laughter. 'Just look at her,' she said. 'With that appealing swelling in her belly, she makes me feel quite sorry for her. I suppose she intends to make me a happy grandmother of that famed offspring; how lucky I am, in the bloom of my young days, at the prospect of being hailed as a grandma, and having the son of a cheap maidservant called Venus's grandson! But what a fool I am, mistakenly calling him a son, for the wedding was not between a couple of equal status. Besides, it took place in a country house, without witnesses and without a father's consent, so it cannot be pronounced legal. The child will therefore be born a bastard— if we allow you to reach full term with him at all!'

10   Saying this, she flew at Psyche, ripped her dress to shreds, tore her hair, made her brains rattle, and pummelled her severely. She then brought some wheat, barley, millet, poppy-seed, chickpeas, lentils and beans. She mingled them together in an indiscriminate heap, and said to her: 'You are such an ugly maidservant that I think the only way you win your lovers is by devoted attendance, so I'll see myself how good you are. Separate out this mixed heap of seeds, and arrange the different kinds in their proper piles. Finish the work before tonight, and show it to me to my satisfaction.' Having set before her this enormous pile of seeds, she went off to a wedding-dinner. Psyche did not lay a finger on this confused heap, which was impossible to separate. She was dismayed by this massive task imposed on her, and stood in stupefied silence. Then the little country-ant familiar to us all got wind of her great problem. It took pity on the great god's consort, and cursed the vindictive behaviour of her mother-in-law. Then it scurried about, energetically summoning and assembling a whole army of resident ants: 'Have pity, noble protegées of Earth, our universal mother; have pity, and with eager haste lend your aid to this refined girl, who is Cupid's wife.' Wave after wave of the sespedalian tribe swept in; with the utmost enthusiasm each and all divided out the heap grain by grain, and when they had sorted them into their different kinds, they swiftly vanished from sight.

11   As night fell, Venus returned from the wedding-feast flushed with wine and perfumed with balsam, her whole body wreathed with glowing roses. When she observed the astonishing care with which the task had been executed, she said: 'This is not your work, you foul creature; the hands that accomplished it are not yours, but his whose favour you

gained, though little good it's done you, or him either!' The goddess then threw her a crust of bread, and cleared off to bed.

Meanwhile Cupid was alone, closely guarded and confined in a single room at the back of the house. This was partly to ensure that he did not aggravate his wound by wanton misbehaviour, and partly so that he would not meet his dear one. So the lovers though under the one roof were kept apart from each other, and were made to endure a wretched night. But as soon as Dawn's chariot appeared, Venus summoned Psyche, and spoke to her like this: 'Do you see the grove there, flanked by the river which flows by it, its banks extending into the distance and its low-lying bushes abutting on the stream? There are sheep in it wandering and grazing unguarded, and their fleeces sprout with the glory of pure gold, I order you to go there at once, and somehow or other obtain and bring back to me a tuft of wool from a precious fleece.'

12   Psyche made her way there without reluctance, but with no intention of carrying out this task. She wanted to seek the cessation of her ills by throwing herself headlong from a cliff above the river. But from that stretch of stream one of the green reeds which foster sweet music was divinely inspired by the gentle sound of a caressing breeze, and uttered this prophecy: 'Psyche, even though you are harrowed by great trials, do not pollute my waters by a most wretched death. You must not approach the fearsome sheep at this hour of the day, when they tend to be fired by the burning heat of the sun and charge about in ferocious rage; with their sharp horns, their rock-hard heads, and sometimes their poisonous bites, they wreak savage destruction on human folk. But once the hours past noon have quelled the sun's heat, and the flocks have quietened down under the calming influence of the river-breeze, you will be able to conceal yourself under that very tall plane-tree, which sucks in the river-water as I do myself. Then, as soon as the sheep relax their fury and their disposition grows gentle, you must shake the foliage in the neighbouring grove, and you will find golden wool clinging here and there to the curved stems.'

13   This was how the reed, endowed with human qualities of openness and kindness, told Psyche in her extremity how to gain safety. She did not disregard this careful instruction and suffer accordingly; she followed out every detail, and the theft was easily accomplished. She gathered the soft substance of yellow gold in her dress, and brought it back to Venus. But the hazard endured in this second trial won her no favourable acknowledgement from her mistress at least, for Venus frowned heavily, smiled harshly, and said: 'I know quite well that this too is the work of that adulterer. But now I shall try you out in earnest, to see if you are indeed endowed with brave spirit and unique circumspection. Do you see that lofty mountain-peak, perched above a dizzily high cliff, from where the livid waters of a dark spring come tumbling down, and when enclosed in the basin of the neighbouring valley, water the marshes of the Styx and feed the hoarse streams of the Cocytus? I want you to hurry and bring me back in this small jug some icy water drawn from the stream's highest point, where it gushes out from within.' Handing Psyche a vessel shaped from crystal, she backed this instruction with still harsher threats.

14   Psyche made for the topmost peak with swift and eager step, for she was determined there at least to put an end to her intolerable existence. But the moment she neared the vicinity of the specified mountain-range, she became aware of the lethal difficulty posed by her daunting task. A rock of huge size towered above her, hard to negotiate and treacherous because of its rugged surface. From its stony jaws it belched forth repulsive waters which issued directly from a vertical cleft. The stream then glided downward, and being concealed in the course of the narrow channel which it had carved out, it made its hidden way into a neighbouring valley. From the hollow rocks on the right and left fierce snakes crept out, extending their long necks, their eyes unblinkingly watchful and maintaining unceasing vigil. The waters themselves formed an additional defence, for they had the power of speech, and from time to time would cry out 'Clear off!' or 'Watch what you're doing!', or 'What's your game? Look

out!', or 'Cut and run!', or 'You won't make it!' The hopelessness of the situation turned Psyche to stone. She was physically present, but her senses deserted her. She was utterly downcast by the weight of inescapable danger; she could not even summon the ultimate consolation of tears.

15   But the privations of this innocent soul did not escape the steady gaze of benevolent Providence. Suddenly highest Jupiter's royal bird appeared with both wings outstretched: this is the eagle, the bird of prey who recalled his service of long ago, when following Cupid's guidance he had borne the Phrygian cupbearer up to Jupiter. The bird now lent timely aid, and directed his veneration for Cupid's power to aid his wife in her ordeal. He quitted the shining paths of high heaven, flew down before the girl's gaze, and broke into speech: 'You are in all respects an ingenuous soul without experience in things such as this, so how can you hope to be able to steal the merest drop from this most sacred and unfriendly stream, or even apply your hand to it? Rumour at any rate, as you know, has it that these Stygian waters are an object of fear to the gods and to Jupiter himself, that just as you mortals swear by the gods' divine power, so those gods frequently swear by the majesty of the Styx. So here, hand me that jug of yours.' At once he grabbed it, and hastened to fill it with water. Balancing the weight of his drooping wings, he used them as oars on right and left to steer a course between the serpents' jaws with their menacing teeth and the triple-forked darting of their tongues. He gathered some water in the face of its reluctance and its warning to him to depart before he suffered harm; he falsely claimed that Venus had ordered him to collect it, and that he was acting in her service, which made it a little easier for him to approach.

16   So Psyche joyously took the filled jug and hastened to return it to Venus. Even so, she was unable to conciliate the harsh goddess's resolve. Venus flashed a menacing smile as she addressed her with threats of yet more monstrous ill-treatment: 'Now indeed I regard you as a witch with great and lofty powers, for you have carried out so efficiently commands of mine such as these. But you will have to

undertake one further task for me, my girl. Take this box' (she handed it over) 'and make straight for Hades, for the funereal dwelling of Orcus himself. Give the box to Proserpina, and say: "Venus asks you to send her a small supply of your beauty-preparation, enough for just one day, because she has been tending her sick son, and has used hers all up by rubbing it on him." Make your way back with it as early as you can, because I need it to doll myself up so as to attend the Deities' Theatre.'

17   Then Psyche came to the full realization that this was the end of the road for her. All pretence was at an end; she saw clearly that she was being driven to her immediate doom. It could not be otherwise, for she was being forced to journey on foot of her own accord to Tartarus and the shades below. She lingered no longer, but made for a very high tower, intending to throw herself headlong from it, for she thought that this was the direct and most glorious possible route down to the world below. But the tower suddenly burst into speech, and said: 'Poor girl, why do you seek to put an end to yourself by throwing yourself down? What is the point of rash surrender before this, your final hazardous labour? Once your spirit is sundered from your body, you will certainly descend to the depths of Tartarus without the possibility of a return journey.

18   'Listen to me. Sparta, the famed Achaean city, lies not far from here. On its borders you must look for Taenarus, which lies hidden in a trackless region. Dis has his breathing-vent there, and a sign-post points through open gates to a track which none should tread. Once you have crossed the threshold and committed yourself to that path, the track will lead you directly to Orcus' very palace. But you are not to advance through that dark region altogether empty-handed, but carry in both hands barley-cakes baked in sweet wine, and have between your lips twin coins. When you are well advanced on your infernal journey, you will meet a lame ass carrying a load of logs, with a driver likewise lame; he will ask you to hand him some sticks which have slipped from his load, but you must pass by in silence without uttering a word. Immediately after that you will reach the lifeless river over

which Charon presides. He peremptorily demands the fare, and when he receives it he transports travellers on his stitched-up craft over to the further shore. (So even among the dead, greed enjoys its life; even that great god Charon, who gathers taxes for Dis, does not do anything for nothing. A poor man on the point of death must find his fare, and no one will let him breathe his last until he has his copper ready.) You must allow this squalid elder to take for your fare one of the coins you are to carry, but he must remove it from your mouth with his own hand. Then again, as you cross the sluggish stream, an old man now dead will float up to you, and raising his decaying hands will beg you to drag him into the boat; but you must not be moved by a sense of pity, for that is not permitted.

19   'When you have crossed the river and have advanced a little further, some aged women weaving at the loom will beg you to lend a hand for a short time. But you are not permitted to touch that either, for all these and many other distractions are part of the ambush which Venus will set to induce you to release one of the cakes from your hands. Do not imagine that the loss of a mere barley-cake is a trivial matter, for if you relinquish either of them, the daylight of this world above will be totally denied you. Posted there is a massive hound with a huge, triple-formed head. This monstrous, fearsome brute confronts the dead with thunderous barking, though his menaces are futile since he can do them no harm. He keeps constant guard before the very threshold and the dark hall of Proserpina, protecting that deserted abode of Dis. You must disarm him by offering him a cake as his spoils. Then you can easily pass him, and gain immediate access to Proserpina herself. She will welcome you in genial and kindly fashion, and she will try to induce you to sit on a cushioned seat beside her and enjoy a rich repast. But you must settle on the ground, ask for coarse bread, and eat it. Then you must tell her why you have come. When you have obtained what she gives you, you must make your way back, using the remaining cake to neutralize the dog's savagery. Then you must give the greedy mariner the one coin which you have held back, and

once across the river you must retrace your earlier steps and
return to the harmony of heaven's stars. Of all these
injunctions I urge you particularly to observe this: do not seek
to open or to pry into the box that you will carry, nor be in any
way inquisitive about the treasure of divine beauty hidden
within it.'

20   This was how that far-sighted tower performed its prophetic
role. Psyche immediately sped to Taenarus, and having duly
obtained the coins and cakes she hastened down the path to
Hades. She passed the lame ass-driver without a word,
handed the fare to the ferryman for the river crossing, ignored
the entreaty of the dead man floating on the surface,
disregarded the crafty pleas of the weavers, fed the cake to the
dog to quell his fearsome rage, and gained access to the house
of Proserpina. Psyche declined the soft cushion and the rich
food offered by her hostess; she perched on the ground at her
feet, and was content with plain bread. She then reported her
mission from Venus. The box was at once filled and closed out
of her sight, and Psyche took it. She quietened the dog's
barking by disarming it with the second cake, offered her
remaining coin to the ferryman, and quite animatedly
hastened out of Hades. But once she was back in the light of
this world and had reverently hailed it, her mind was
dominated by rash curiosity, in spite of her eagerness to see
the end of her service. She said: 'How stupid I am to be
carrying this beauty-lotion fit for deities, and not to take a
single drop of it for myself, for with this at any rate I can be
pleasing to my beautiful lover.'

21   The words were scarcely out of her mouth when she opened
the box. But inside there was no beauty-lotion or anything
other than the sleep of Hades, a truly Stygian sleep. As soon
as the lid was removed and it was laid bare, it attacked her
and pervaded all her limbs in a thick cloud. It laid hold of her,
so that she fell prostrate on the path where she had stood. She
lay there motionless, no more animate than a corpse at rest.

But Cupid was now recovering, for his wound had healed.
He could no longer bear Psyche's long separation from him,
so he glided out of the high-set window of the chamber which

was his prison. His wings were refreshed after their period of rest, so he progressed much more swiftly to reach his Psyche. Carefully wiping the sleep from her, he restored it to its former lodging in the box. Then he roused Psyche with an innocuous prick of his arrow. 'Poor, dear Psyche,' he exclaimed, 'see how as before your curiosity might have been your undoing! But now hurry to complete the task imposed on you by my mother's command; I shall see to the rest.' After saying this, her lover rose lightly on his wings, while Psyche hurried to bear Proserpina's gift back to Venus.

22   Meanwhile Cupid, devoured by overpowering desire and with lovelorn face, feared the sudden arrival of his mother's sobering presence, so he reverted to his former role and rose to heaven's peak on swift wings. With suppliant posture he laid his case before the great Jupiter, who took Cupid's little cheek between his finger and thumb, raised the boy's hand to his lips and kissed it, and then said to him: 'Honoured son, you have never shown me the deference granted me by the gods' decree. You keep piercing this heart of mine, which regulates the elements and orders the changing motion of the stars, with countless wounds. You have blackened it with repeated impulses of earthly lust, damaging my prestige and reputation by involving me in despicable adulteries which contravene the laws—the *lex Iulia* itself—and public order. You have transformed my smiling countenance into grisly shapes of snakes, fires, beasts, birds, and cattle. Yet in spite of all this, I shall observe my usual moderation, recalling that you were reared in these arms of mine. So I will comply with all that you ask, as long as you know how to cope with your rivals in love; and if at this moment there is on earth any girl of outstanding beauty, as long as you can recompense me with her.'

23   After saying this, he ordered Mercury to summon all the gods at once to an assembly, and to declare that any absentee from the convocation of heavenly citizens would be liable to a fine of ten thousand sesterces. The theatre of heaven at once filled up through fear of this sanction. Towering Jupiter, seated on his lofty throne, made this proclamation: 'You gods whose names are inscribed on the register of the Muses, you

all surely know this young fellow who was reared by my own hands. I have decided that the hot-headed impulses of his early youth need to be reined in; he has been the subject of enough notoriety in day-to-day gossip on account of his adulteries and all manner of improprieties. We must deprive him of all opportunities; his juvenile behaviour must be shackled with the chains of marriage. He has chosen the girl, and robbed her of her virginity, so he must have and hold her. Let him take Psyche in his embrace and enjoy his dear one ever after.'

Then he turned to address Venus. 'My daughter,' he said, 'do not harbour any resentment. Have no fear for your high lineage and distinction in this marriage to a mortal, for I shall declare the union lawful and in keeping with the civil law, and not one between persons of differing social status.' There and then he ordered that Psyche be detained and brought to heaven through Mercury's agency. He gave her a cup of ambrosia, and said: 'Take this, Psyche, and become immortal. Cupid will never part from your embrace; this marriage of yours will be eternal.'

24   At once a lavish wedding-feast was laid. The bridegroom reclined on the couch of honour, with Psyche in his lap. Jupiter likewise was paired with Juno, and all the other deities sat in order of precedence. Then a cup of nectar, the gods' wine, was served to Jupiter by his personal cup-bearer, that well-known country lad, and to the others by Bacchus. Vulcan cooked the dinner, the Hours brightened the scene with roses and the other flowers, the Graces diffused balsam, and the Muses, also present, sang in harmony. Apollo sang to the lyre, and Venus took to the floor to the strains of sweet music, and danced prettily. She had organized the performance so that the Muses sang in chorus, a Satyr played the flute, and one of Pan's people sang to the shepherd's pipes. This was how with due ceremony Psyche was wed to Cupid, and at full term a daughter was born to them. We call her Pleasure.

25 This was the tale told to the captive maiden by that crazy, drunken old hag. I was standing close by, and God only

knows how sorry I was not to have writing-tablets and a stilus to set down such a pretty story! Then suddenly the robbers turned up, heavily laden; they had been involved in some hard fighting, but several of the livelier spirits were keen to leave the wounded at home tending their wounds, and to take off again. They said they wanted to collect the remaining bundles hidden in a cave. So they quickly gobbled down their dinner, and then led my horse and myself out on to the road, beating us with sticks all the while; we were to carry back their spoils. After an exhausting journey over many hills and winding paths, as night came on they brought us to a cave. There they loaded us with heaps of baggage, and without giving us a minute to recover our breath they swiftly got us back on the road. They were in such agitated haste that in driving me forward and belabouring me with repeated blows, they caused me to tumble over a rock at the roadside. They kept raining blows on me, and forced me to get up again, but only with difficulty because my right leg and left hoof were injured.

26   One of them said: 'How long are we to waste our time feeding this broken-down ass now that he is lame as well?' A second added: 'And what's more, he has brought bad luck on our house. We haven't made a penny profit since his arrival— just wounds and the slaughter of our bravest men.' A third chipped in: 'What I intend to do, as soon as the unwilling beast has finished carrying these sacks, is to push him over the cliff at once to make a welcome meal for the vultures.' Whilst these gentlest of souls were arguing with each other about how to finish me off, we had now returned home, for fear had lent wings to my hooves. They hurried to remove our loads, and without thought for our welfare or indeed for my execution, they took with them their comrades, who all this time had stayed behind nursing their wounds, and they rushed back to pick up the rest of the loot themselves, saying that they were tired of our delaying tactics.

Even so I was consumed with considerable anxiety at the thought of the death in store for me. I said to myself: 'Why are you standing here, Lucius, waiting for the worst? The robbers have passed sentence of death, death most painful, on you. It won't require much of an effort from them. You see these clefts close at hand with sharp rocks protruding from them; before you have tumbled all the way down they will impale you, and your limbs will be scattered in pieces, for that fine magic of yours has given you merely the appearance and the labours of an ass, and not an ass's thick hide but a leech's thin skin. Why not pluck up a man's courage, and give thought to your safety while you can? You have a perfect chance to escape while the robbers are away. You're surely not afraid of that hag with one foot in the grave who is guarding you? You could finish her off with one kick even of your wounded foot. But where in the world shall I take refuge, and who will give me shelter? Yet that is a foolish thought, quite worthy of an ass, for what traveller would not be delighted to make off with a mount to carry him?

27   So there and then I yanked hard at the tether by which I had been secured. I split it and plunged forward on my four feet. But I failed to evade the vigilance of that old hag, for she had eyes like a kite's. When she saw that I had broken free, she seized the tether with a daring that belied her sex and age, and she tried to pull me round and force me back. But that murderous intention of the robbers was in my mind, so I felt no tenderness towards her. I kicked out at her with my rear hooves and sent her flying to the ground. But though she was sprawled out there, she still clung grimly to the halter, and as I galloped forward she was dragged along with me for a fair distance. At once she let out noisy shrieks, begging the aid of stronger hands. But the din that she raised with her crying was futile, for the only person near who could come to help was the imprisoned girl. The shouting roused her, and she came racing out. Heavens, what a dramatic and memorable scene she witnessed! There was the old woman playing Dirce, but clinging to an ass and not a bull. With a man's resolution the girl performed the noblest deed of daring: she tugged the halter from the old hag's hands, whispered soothing words to draw me back from bolting, nimbly leapt on my back, and spurred me into a renewed gallop.

28   The desire to flee on my own account and my eagerness to free the girl were reinforced by the encouraging slaps which she gave me as a frequent reminder of our plight. So I sped along like a horse, hammering the ground at a four-footed gallop. I whinnied in response to the girl's honeyed words, and while pretending to scratch my back I kept bending my neck round and kissing the girl's dainty feet. Then she gave a deep sigh, turning her troubled face skywards. 'You gods in heaven,' she said, 'now at last lend me your aid in my desperate peril; and Fortune, now that you have shown your grimmer face, relent from your savage rage. These wretched torments of mine have appeased you enough. As for you, guardian of my freedom and my safety, if you deliver me home safe and sound, and restore me to my parents and my handsome suitor, what thanks I shall render you, what distinctions I shall confer on you, what dishes I shall serve up to you! First I shall lovingly comb this mane of yours, and adorn it with my childhood trinkets. After curling the hair on your brow, I shall part it neatly. Your tail, which is all matted and spiky because no one has washed it, I shall spruce up and make it glossy. You will be decked with lots of gold medals, so that you will shine like the stars of heaven as you celebrate your triumph in a joyous procession of the people. I shall stuff you every day with nuts and softer delicacies carried in the folds of my silk apron, hailing you as my saviour!

29   'As you enjoy your choice food, abundant leisure, and lifelong happiness, you will be accorded also the prestige of fame, for I intend to commemorate with an enduring memorial the fortune which divine providence has bestowed on me today. I shall have a picture painted of this flight of mine, and consecrate it in the atrium of my house. This unprecedented theme, "A noble maiden escaping captivity on an ass's back", will be on view, will be heard in common gossip, and will be immortalized by the pens of learned men. You too will have your place among the wonder-tales of old, cited as an example from real life to inspire our belief that Phrixus swam across the sea on a ram, that Arion piloted a dolphin, that Europe straddled a bull. If it is true that it was

Jupiter who bellowed in the form of a bull, there may lurk within my donkey some human identity or divine personality.'

Such were the words which the girl repeatedly uttered as she mingled repeated sighs with her prayers. We now reached the intersection of three roads. The girl grabbed the halter, and struggled hard to direct me to the right, doubtless because that was the road which led to her parents. But I knew that the robbers had taken that route to gather the rest of the loot, so I resisted stubbornly, and remonstrated with her in the silence of my heart. 'Wretched girl, what have you in mind? What are you doing? Why are you hell-bound so fast, and why use my feet to try to get there? You will be the death not only of yourself, but of me as well.' As we pulled in opposite directions, engaged in a boundary-dispute about land-rights or rather about rights of way, the robbers laden with their spoils caught us red-handed. In the bright moonlight they recognized us from a distance, and hailed us with waspish laughter.

30   One of the party greeted us like this: 'Where are you off to, moonlighting in such a hurry along this road? Aren't you afraid of ghosts and spirits abroad at dead of night? I suppose that as the most dutiful of girls you were hastening to visit your parents? Well, now, we shall escort you, since you are alone, and we shall show you a short-cut to your family.' Suiting the action to the word, he laid hold of the halter and turned me back the other way. He was carrying a knotted club, and did not spare me my customary beating. Since I was now on my way back to face an unwelcome and immediate death, I recalled the pain in my hoof, and I began to limp and let my head sag. 'So,' said the one who had pulled me round, 'are you stumbling and staggering again? Those worthless feet of yours can take off well enough, but now they cannot walk! Only a minute ago you were flying faster than the winged Pegasus!'

While my friendly companion was making these jokes at my expense and brandishing his cudgel, we had reached the outer enclosure of their base. The sight that greeted us was of the old hag with a rope round her neck, hanging from a branch of a tall cypress. They dragged her down, and unceremoniously trussed her up with her own rope, and threw her headlong over the cliff. At once they bound the girl tightly with ropes, and then they ravenously attacked the dinner which the poor old woman had prepared with devotion which survived her death.

31   As they tucked into the entire spread with gluttonous greed, they now began to discuss with each other the punishment to be meted out to us as their revenge. Opinions varied, as you would expect in such a discordant mob. The first man proposed that the girl be burnt alive, the second recommended that she be thrown to the beasts, the third urged that she be nailed to a gibbet, and the fourth suggested that her body be mangled by torture. They agreed unanimously on the one thing, that she be put to death. When the hubbub had died down, one of them said dispassionately:

'It is not in keeping with the philosophy of our brotherhood, with the civilized attitude of each of us, or indeed with my own moderation to allow you to indulge in barbaric excesses beyond what her crime demands. Wild beasts, the gibbet, firebrands, torture, even the precipitate darkness of a speedy death are inappropriate suggestions. So if you listen to my advice, you will grant the girl her life, but the life that she deserves. Doubtless you have not forgotten your earlier resolution about the ass here, which is always bone-idle, eats us out of house and home, and now falsely pretends to be lame, though he was the agent and minister of the girl's flight. You should accordingly vote to slit his throat tomorrow, and to sew the girl naked inside his belly, since he would rather have her than us. Leave only her face protruding, and let him enclose the rest of her body in his bestial embrace. Then you must expose him stuffed and fattened on some jagged rock, leaving him to the sun's blazing heat.

32   'In this way both of them will endure your righteous decree. The ass will meet his death, long and justly deserved; the girl will experience the teeth of wild animals as the worms draw his limbs apart, and fiery burning when the sun roasts his belly with excessive heat, and the tortures of the gibbet when

dogs and vultures drag out her inmost entrails. Consider too
the aggregate of her other agonies and tortures. While she is
still alive, her dwelling-place will be a dead beast's belly; the
oppressive stench will scorch her nostrils; the deadly hunger
of continued fasting will cause her to waste away; and she will
not be able to contrive her death, for her hands will not be
free.'

On hearing these words, the robbers voted for the proposal
with acclamation, but as I took it in with my long ears, I could
only shed tears for the corpse that I would be tomorrow.

BOOK 7

Charite (and Lucius) Rescued: Further Ordeals of Lucius

1 As soon as day dawned to dispel the darkness, and the sun's gleaming chariot brought brightness to the world, there was a fresh arrival. He belonged to the gang of robbers, as their ritual greeting to each other revealed. He was panting as he took his seat by the entrance to the cave. Once he had recovered his breath, this was the message that he brought to the company. 'We can stop worrying and breathe easily so far as Milo's house at Hypata is concerned, the house which we plundered the other day. After you had valiantly carried everything off and returned to base here, I mingled with the crowd of citizens, pretending to be indignant and outraged. I took note of the plans being laid to investigate the crime, whether they would decide to track down the robbers and to what extent this would be carried out, so that I could report everything to you according to your instructions. The whole crowd had reasonable grounds rather than doubtful arguments for accusing a certain Lucius as the clear culprit of the crime. A few days earlier he had brought a forged letter of introduction. He passed himself off to Milo as an honest man, winning his confidence so intimately that he was even welcomed as a guest and treated as a close friend. He had stayed a few days in the house, and had inveigled himself into the affections of Milo's maidservant by pretending to be in love with her. By this means he had carefully reconnoitred the bars on the gate, and the very rooms in which all the family wealth was usually kept.

2 'The evidence pointing to his being the miscreant was not slight, for he had made off at the very time when the crime was committed, and had not been seen anywhere since. His means of escape had been ready at hand, enabling him to outstrip his pursuers and to go to ground further and further

away, for he had kept with him the conspicuous white horse on which to make a getaway. The assumption was that his slave, who was discovered in his lodging there, would reveal his master's crimes and future intentions, but though the magistrates had taken him into state custody, and next day had inflicted sundry tortures on him, almost squeezing the life out of him, he had not made any such declaration. However, several investigators had been dispatched to the native region of this Lucius in order to search out the culprit, and make him pay the penalty for the crime.'

As the man recounted his tale, I was mentally contrasting the earlier condition of the happy Lucius I had been with the immediate hardships of the wretched ass I had become. I groaned in the depths of my heart, acknowledging that learned men of old had good grounds for envisaging and describing Fortune as blind and utterly sightless. That goddess, I mused, ever bestows her riches on the wicked and the unworthy, never favouring anyone by discerning choice, but on the contrary preferring to lodge with precisely the people to whom she should have given a wide berth, if she had had eyes to see. Worst of all, she foists on us reputations at odds with and contrary to the truth, so that the evil man boasts in the glory of being honest, while by contrast the transparently innocent man is afflicted with a damaging reputation.

3   In my case, Fortune by launching her most savage attack had transformed me into a four-footed beast of the most menial condition. Though my predicament seemed deserving of the distress and compassion of even the bitterest enemy, here I was being indicted for robbing a host who was most dear to me, a charge more truly deserving the label of parricide and not merely robbery. Yet I was unable to plead my case, or even to say one word to refute the charge. So I tried to avoid giving the impression that through a guilty conscience I was admitting to so wicked a crime by remaining silent. Unable to restrain myself, I sought merely to say 'Non feci', 'Not guilty'. I got the first word out repeatedly, but the second I wholly failed to articulate. I got stuck on the first

word, and kept braying 'Non, non', however much I waggled my drooping lips to form as round a circle with them as I could. But why do I go on lamenting Fortune's hostility? She had not even baulked at my becoming the fellow-slave and mate of my own serving mount, my horse.

4   This was the sea of troubles on which I tossed, but then a more pressing anxiety took hold of me: I recalled the robbers' decision that I be sacrificed to the shades of the maiden. I kept eyeing my belly, feeling the sensation of having already given birth to that poor girl. Then the robber who had just made the lying allegation about me produced a thousand gold coins which he had sewn in the lining of his coat. He explained that he had relieved various travellers of them, and was now demonstrating his probity by donating them to the common chest. He further began to enquire with concern about the safety of his comrades. On being told that some of them, in fact the bravest, had met their deaths on active service through various misfortunes, he recommended that for the moment they should concentrate on enrolling fresh comrades, making peaceful trips and pronouncing a truce on all conflicts. By recruiting fresh blood they could bring up the complement of their fighting-force to its earlier strength. Reluctant individuals could be press-ganged by intimidation, and volunteers enticed by rewards; and quite a number would prefer to renounce the degradation of slavery, and to enhance their way of life to that enjoyed by princes. He personally had already met a candidate who was tall, young, well-built and powerful. He had worked on him, and finally persuaded him to turn his hands, which were flaccid from long idleness, to better account, so that he might enjoy the blessings of rude health as long as he could, and instead of holding out his powerful hand to beg for pennies, he could use it for raking in gold.

5   All the robbers applauded these words, and voted to enrol the candidate who seemed already to have passed muster, and to search out others to complement their number. The speaker then went out, and only minutes later brought in a young man as huge as had been promised. None of the present

company could apparently match him, for in addition to his powerful physique he was a whole head higher than all of them. A soft beard was spreading over his cheeks. His body was only half-covered with a patchwork cloak which was ill-fitting and roughly stitched together, and between the gaps in it his chest and belly rippled with close-packed muscles.

On making this entrance the newcomer spoke. 'Greetings, followers of Mars most valiant of gods, henceforth to be my trusty comrades. Give a warm welcome to a willing warrior of valorous vigour, one readier to sustain wounds in body than to gain gold in hand, and one who despises the death which others fear. Do not count me destitute or mean, nor judge my merits by the rags I wear. I was the leader of a most mighty band with which I despoiled the entire land of Macedonia. I am that celebrated brigand Haemus the Thracian, a man at whose name whole provinces tremble, son of Theron who was likewise a famous bandit. Human blood served as my milk, and I was reared among the platoons of my father's gang, to be his heir and rival in valour.

6   'But within a short time I lost that entire complement of brave comrades of old, and the great resources which we possessed. The cause was my having misguidedly attacked the emperor's financial agent as he was passing through. After earning a salary of 200,000 sesterces, he had lost his job through a stroke of bad luck. But to acquaint you with what happened I'll describe it from the beginning.

'This man had become a prominent celebrity at Caesar's court, and the emperor himself thought a lot of him. But he was falsely accused by certain deceitful persons, and harsh envy consigned him to exile. Now his wife Plotina was a woman of unique loyalty and matchless chastity, and she had established a firm family-foundation for her husband by ten terms of child-bearing. She rejected and disdained the pleasures of high life at Rome to accompany her exiled husband and to share his privations. Her hair was cropped, and her appearance mannish. All her valuable jewellery and gold coins she carried in bulging belts fastened round her, and she passed fearlessly among the bands of military guards as they brandished their unsheathed swords. She shared all her husband's dangers and kept ceaseless watch over his safety, facing unbroken hardships with the spirit of a man. At this time he had endured the many difficulties of the land-journey and the terrors of the sea, and he was making for Zacynthus, which the decree of fate had assigned to him as his temporary abode.

7   'He had just disembarked on the coast at Actium, at a time when we had slipped down from Macedonia and were prowling in the neighbourhood. Late at night we invaded a little inn lying close in to the shore and the ship; they were sleeping there to avoid being tossed on the ocean-waves. We plundered everything in it, but before we got away we faced considerable danger, for as soon as Plotina heard the door being forced open, she rushed into the dormitory and with agitated cries created wholesale disturbance as she summoned the soldiers, and her servants by name, and the entire neighbourhood as well, to lend help. However, we succeeded in escaping unharmed because they all took fright and hid out of fear for their own skins. But I must give the lady her due. That greatest integrity and matchless loyalty which she showed gained favour through such virtuous conduct, for there and then she sent a petition to the divine person of the emperor. This won a swift recall for her husband, and utter revenge on us for the attack we made on them. In short, Caesar refused to allow Haemus' brotherhood to exist any longer, and it was at once dissolved, for even a nod from the mighty emperor achieves this result. So military units hunted down our whole gang, which was suppressed and hacked to pieces. I managed with some difficulty to steal away un-accompanied, and to escape from the enveloping jaws of Orcus. I'll tell you how it happened.

8   'I put on a lady's dress with a floral pattern which spread out in billowing folds, and a woven turban to cover my head, and the kind of neat white shoes which women wear. In this way I disguised myself, passing myself off as a member of the other sex. I seated myself on an ass laden with ears of barley, and rode through the ranks of enemy troops which allowed me

free passage, for they thought that I was a woman mounted on
an ass, since my cheeks at the time were hairless and glowing
with the smooth sheen of boyhood. Though I trembled a bit at
being within range of these weapons of war, I was not untrue
to my father's fame or to my own valour, but under cover of
my strange disguise I launched attacks single-handed on
farm-houses and villages, thus scraping together the expenses
of my journey.'

He then ripped open his ragged outfit, and poured out
before them two thousand gold pieces. 'Here is my contribution,' he said, 'or rather my dowry, which I gladly present to
your brotherhood. I further offer myself to you as a most
trusty leader, and if you do not reject me, it will not be long
before I turn this stone dwelling of yours into a house of gold.'

9   The robbers without hesitation or delay voted unanimously
to appoint him as leader. They dug out a respectable outfit for
him to wear, in place of the patchwork cloak which had
proved so rich. In this new guise he kissed each of them, took
his place at the head of the table, and made his debut as
leader over dinner and some heavy drinking. In the ensuing
conversation he learned of the maiden's flight on my back and
of the hideous death appointed for both of us. He asked where
she was, and they led him to her. When he saw her weighed
down with chains, he turned up his nose in disgust, and
withdrew.

'I am not so ignorant, or at least not so rash, as to veto your
decision,' he said, 'but I shall have a guilty conscience if I
conceal my own attitude. But you must first trust in my
concern for your welfare, especially as you can revert to the
ass-plan if my suggestion does not find favour. My view is that
robbers with good sense should put no consideration before
their own profit, not even revenge, which often brings harm to
others as well as to its victims. So if you plant the girl in the
ass and finish her off, you will merely vent your annoyance on
her, and gain no profit. My alternative proposal is that she be
taken to some town and sold there; a young girl like this one
will fetch quite a high price. I myself have a long acquaintance with some brothel-keepers, and I imagine that one or

other of them will be willing to pay quite a few talents for this girl to be employed in a brothel, a suitable price for one of such high birth. She won't make her getaway from there as she did before, and her service in the bordello will give you adequate revenge. In my view this is an advantageous proposal, but you yourselves have discretion over the planning of your affairs.'

10   With these words the secretary of the robbers' chest had been pleading our case, becoming the noble saviour of both the girl and the ass. The other robbers held a lengthy discussion; their delay in reaching a decision tore at my innards and made me hold my breath anxiously. But finally they consented to the new bandit's proposal, and at once loosed the girl from her bonds. As soon as she had set eyes on that young man, and had heard mention of the brothel and its keeper, she began to perk up and to smile all over her face. My natural reaction was to criticize the whole sex when I observed that this girl, who had pretended to be in love with her young suitor and to long for a chaste marriage, welcomed the prospect of a foul and filthy brothel. At that moment the whole female sex and its morals lay perilously poised on the judgement of an ass.

The young man then spoke up again. 'So should we not address a prayer to Comrade Mars, and depart to sell the girl and search out fresh comrades? But I see that we have not a single beast to sacrifice, nor even abundance or sufficiency of wine to drink. So appoint ten representatives to accompany me; that will suffice to attack the nearest village, and enable me to bring back a meal fit for Salian priests.' So he set out; the rest laid a huge fire, and set up an altar to Mars on the green turf.

11   A little later they arrived back carrying wine-skins and driving a whole flock of farm-animals before them. From it they selected a huge billy-goat, old and shaggy, and sacrificed it to Mars, Follower and Comrade. At once they prepared a lavish spread, and then the presiding host said: 'You should regard me as your energetic leader not merely in your looting campaigns, but also in your entertainments.' He set to with

remarkable efficiency, organizing everything in lively fashion. He swept the floor, laid the table, cooked the meat, stuffed the sausages. He deftly served out the food, and above all he drowned them in huge goblets of wine, which he repeatedly replenished. From time to time he would pretend to take from the store-cupboard what the company needed; this allowed him to keep approaching the girl, and with a smile to offer her tit-bits which he had surreptitiously removed, and cups of wine which he had sampled. She would eagerly swallow them, and several times she readily assented to give him the kisses which he sought.

I was quite put out by this. 'Dear me, young lady, have you forgotten your marriage and your groom who shares your passion? Are you now preferring this blood-stained, murderous outsider to your newly-wed husband, whoever he is, to whom your parents have joined you in marriage? Isn't your conscience pricking you? Have you trodden your affection underfoot, that you like to play the wanton here among these spears and swords? Suppose the other bandits spot what is going on? I hope that you won't make a beeline for the ass again, and cause my downfall once more! It's another's hide that you are certainly putting at risk, and not your own!'

12   As I continued berating her and making these accusations with the liveliest displeasure, I became aware from some ambivalent remarks of theirs, which were not hard for a wise ass to fathom, that this fellow was not Haemus the notorious bandit but Tlepolemus the girl's bridegroom; for as the exchanges between them proceeded, he spoke in a louder voice, ignoring my presence as if I were actually dead. 'Take heart, dearest Charite,' he said, 'for all these enemies will soon be your prisoners.' All the time and with greater insistence he kept plying the wine, now undiluted and slightly warmed, upon the bandits, while he himself was not touching a drop. And bless me if it didn't strike me that he was mixing some soporific drug in with their cups. In the end every man jack of them lay out for the count with the wine; they were all as good as dead. It was no trouble then to shackle them very tightly

with chains, and when he had trussed them up to his liking, he put the girl on my back and made for their home town.

13   As soon as we got there, the whole town turned out to see the one they had been praying for. Parents, relatives, dependants, young wards, and slaves came dashing out, delight on their faces, ecstatic with joy. What a parade was on view—men and women, young and old, and a truly unforgettable sight, the girl riding in triumph on an ass! Then I too felt all the elation proper for a man to feel. Not wishing to be excluded as one detached from the celebrations, I pricked up my ears, flared my nostrils, and brayed enthusiastically; indeed, I sounded forth like a thunderclap. The girl's parents took her to her room, and fussed over her affectionately. Tlepolemus at once took me back to the cave with a great crowd of mules and citizens. I was not unwilling to go; apart from my habitual nosiness, I was keen at that moment to see the bandits under lock and key. We found them still in the grip of the wine more than of their bonds. So the citizens uncovered and brought out all the loot, and loaded us up with the gold, silver, and the rest of the booty. Some of the bandits still in their chains they then rolled headlong over into the nearest gorges; others they slew with their own swords, and left them exposed there. We then returned to the town, elated and in good spirits, having taken our revenge. The treasures they committed to public keeping, and they gave Tlepolemus legal rights over the girl whom he had rescued.

14   From then on Charite, now a married lady, addressed me as her saviour and tended me devotedly. On her wedding-day she ordered my manger to be stocked with heaps of barley, and enough hay left there to feed a Bactrian camel. But what grim curses pronounced on Photis would have been adequate for me? She had transformed me into an ass, not a dog; and there was I, watching the dogs, all of them stuffed and swollen with the left-overs and pickings from that magnificent banquet!

After that special night when she was initiated into love-making, the new bride never stopped recalling her gratitude to me in the presence of her parents and her husband, until she induced them to grant me the highest honours. So they met in council with their more reflective friends to decide how I could be most suitably rewarded. One proposal had been that I be granted a life of leisure indoors, stuffed with choice barley, beans, and vetch. But the second suggestion won the day; this envisaged giving me unrestricted freedom in country pastures, where I could sport at will among the herds of horses, and present the owners with a crowd of mule-foals by my superior services in mounting the mares.

15   So the groom in charge of the horses was at once summoned. After some lengthy words of explanation, I was put in his charge to be led away. I was naturally in good spirits and elated as I trotted ahead. I now had the prospect of release from lugging baggage and other burdens, and having gained my freedom I was sure to find some roses, since with the advent of spring the fields were sprouting. Then a second thought struck me as well; since so much gratitude and so many distinctions had been showered on me as an ass, I would be the recipient of many more generous awards once I regained my human shape.

But as soon as the groom drove me well away from the city, no luxuries and not even freedom awaited me. His wife, a greedy, utterly unscrupulous woman, at once harnessed me to the grinding-mill, punishing me from time to time with a leafy stick, as at the expense of my hide she prepared to make bread for her household and herself. She was not satisfied with wearing me out merely to provide herself with food; she hired me out to grind her neighbours' corn as I pounded round and round, and she did not give my wretched body even the standard rations for such heavy labours. For she would sell my barley, which I had crushed and ground under the same millstone by my own circling movements, to neighbouring farmers, while she would put before me, after a day harnessed to the exhausting contraption, some husks of bran, unsifted and grimy, with lots of rough gravel permeating it.

16   My head was already down because of these hardships, but cruel Fortune consigned me to fresh tortures, doubtless to enable me to take pride in my high renown through the

proverbial 'deeds of valour done at home and abroad'. At long
last that exemplary herdsman followed his master's instructions, finally allowing me admission to the herds of horses. In
my joy at being free at last, I pranced and capered gently
around, and began to mark down the mares which would
make the most suitable bed-mates for me. But even this
happier prospect led to disastrous ruin. The stallions, well fed
and long fattened from their lengthy period at stud, scared me
stiff anyway, being certainly too powerful for any ass, but in
addition they felt challenged by me, and were bent on
preventing any adultery with an inferior breed. So they failed
to observe the compact of hospitality laid down by Jupiter;
they regarded me as a rival, and attacked me with rage and
utter hatred. One raised his massive chest aloft, and with
brow held high and rearing head, pummelled me with his
front hooves. A second turned his ample, muscle-bound rump
upon me, and launched a long-range attack with his hind legs.
A third whinnied in threatening and hostile fashion; laying
back his ears and baring white teeth like axes, he bit me all
over. I had read of a similar happening in the story of a king of
Thrace, who would throw his wretched guests to wild horses
to be torn to pieces and devoured; that most powerful of all
tyrants was so economical with his barley that he sated the
hunger of his gluttonous beasts by generous provision of
human bodies.

17   I too was similarly lacerated by these varied attacks of the
horses, so that I longed to be back doing the rounds with the
millstone. But Fortune, never satisfied with the tortures she
inflicted on me, devised yet a further plague against me. I was
given the job of carting timber down from a mountain, and
the boy in charge of me was the most abominable youth in
creation. Climbing the high ridge of the mountain exhausted
me, and my hooves were chafed through collision with sharp
rocks; this was bad enough, but I was also so savagely beaten
by repeated blows from cudgels that the pain from the
beatings penetrated deep down into my marrow. The boy
kept raining blows on the one spot on my right hip, so that the
skin was broken, and the huge sore beneath formed into a

cavity; I say a cavity, but it was more like a well or a window. He never stopped thumping the blood-smeared wound over and over again. Moreover, he weighed me down with such a load of timber that you would have thought that the pile of logs had been assembled for an elephant rather than an ass to carry. Then, whenever the load became top-heavy and slid over to one side, instead of removing some of the faggots from the side where it had shifted over, and thus giving me momentary relief by lessening the pressure, or at any rate equalizing the weight by transferring them to the other flank, instead he would pile up some stones on top, and seek to balance the uneven weight by that means.

18   Even then, following those very painful experiences of mine, he was not satisfied with burdening me with this monstrous load; for when we were crossing the stream which happened to flow alongside the road, he wanted to prevent the water soaking his boots, so he would jump on my hind-quarters and perch there, though I suppose this made only a slightly additional weight to that massive load. If I chanced to slip on the ridge of the river-bank, which was treacherous with slimy mud, and I collapsed through inability to maintain the weight, that peerless groom lent me no help in my exhaustion. He might have given me a hand, pulled me upright by the halter, raised me by the tail, or at any rate removed a part of the heavy load until I could stand up again. But instead he would seize his huge stick, and starting with my head or rather with my very ears, he would beat me all over until the blows themselves served as a sort of poultice and brought me to my feet. The boy then thought up a further torture for me. He fastened together some very sharp thorns, which had a lethally effective sting, into a bundle joined with a twisted knot, and he then attached them to my tail as a dangling weapon of torture. They came into play and became effective when I started walking, and with their deadly points they pierced me savagely.

19   So my suffering was twofold. If I galloped forward to avoid the boy's most painful beatings, I was smitten more sharply by the impact of the thorns, and if on the other hand I halted

for a moment to relieve the agony, his blows forced me to break into a trot. That criminal youth seemed to have nothing in mind except to finish me off one way or another, and in fact several times he threatened with an oath to do so. Then an incident occurred which clearly fired his unspeakable malice to more despicable action. One day my endurance snapped because of his extreme impudence, and I lashed out at him strongly with my hooves. The result was that he contrived this wicked design against me: he loaded a fair-sized bundle of tow on to my back, secured it carefully with ropes, and led me out on to the road. Then he stole a glowing coal from the nearest farm-house, and inserted it into the middle of the bundle. Once the fire grew hot as it was nourished by the thin tow, it burst into flame, and I was engulfed with the heat that spelt death. No escape was in sight from this most ghastly of afflictions, no consoling prospect of salvation. Such a conflagration admits of no delay; it moves too fast for well-considered remedies.

20   But in this grim plight Fortune smiled on me with kindlier eye. Perhaps she was preserving me to face future hazards, but at any rate she freed me from the immediate sentence of death. I chanced to observe close by a pool of muddy water caused by the previous day's rain. Without a thought and at one bound I hurtled headlong into it. The flames were completely doused, and eventually I emerged, both lightened of my load and delivered from destruction. But that most depraved, inconsiderate youth pinned the blame on myself for that dastardly trick of his. He assured all the herdsmen that when roaming of my own accord among braziers belonging to our neighbours, I had staggered and slipped, and wilfully brought the fire down over me. Then he added with a grin, 'How much longer, then, shall we go on feeding this fire-raiser to no effect?'

Not many days elapsed before he sought me out with a far more reprehensible ruse. He had sold the wood on my back to the next-door cottage, and as he led me along without a load, he bawled out that he could no longer cope with my evil ways. He said that he was giving up the impossible, wholly wretched job of looking after me, and he fabricated complaints on these lines:

21 'Do you see this lazy brute, this utterly slow, wholly asinine creature? To crown all his other villainies, he now causes further trouble by exposing me to fresh dangers. Whenever he spies a traveller—it could be an elegant lady, a grown-up girl, or an innocent young boy—he hastily shrugs off his load, sometimes throwing off his saddle as well, and makes a wild dash towards them; ass though he is, he aspires to be a lover of humans. He knocks them to the ground, eyes them fondly, and seeks to indulge his bestial urges with love-making at which Venus frowns. He even makes pretence of kissing, as with his filthy features he nuzzles and bites. This is a practice which will land us in fierce exchanges and disputes, perhaps even in criminal charges. Just now, for example, he caught sight of a splendid young woman. The wood he was carrying went flying off in all directions, and he made a mad dive at her. Jolly gallant that he is, he had her down on the filthy ground, for all the world as if he were going to mount her there and then before everyone's eyes. If her weeping and wailing hadn't roused some travellers to rush to her defence, to snatch her from between his hooves and free her, the poor woman would have been trampled on and torn apart. Her fate would have been agonizing, and for us the upshot would have been the penalty of death.'

22 He combined other allegations with lies like this to afflict my modest silence even more sorely, and to effect my destruction he pitilessly inflamed the anger of the herdsmen against me. Then one of them said: 'So why don't we solemnly sacrifice this marriage-partner who performs in public—or to put it better, this adulterer who offers his services to all? These unnatural love-liaisons would make him a suitable victim.' He added: 'So come on, boy, butcher him on the spot, throw his guts to our dogs, and then keep the rest of the meat for the workmen's dinner. We can stiffen his hide with a sprinkling of ashes, take it back to our masters, and easily invent a story that the ass was killed by a wolf.' My accuser was himself the guilty party, but now that he was appointed to carry out the

shepherds' sentence, he gleefully jeered at my predicament, and recalled the kicking which I bitterly regretted had not achieved its aim. Without delay he began there and then to sharpen his sword on a whetstone.

23   But then one of the gang of countrymen spoke up. 'It would be wrong', he said, 'to slaughter this fine ass like that, and to forgo such vital help and service just because we have charged him with immorality and sexual misbehaviour. An alternative is to hack off his genitals so that love-making is out for him; that way he can relieve you of all fear of danger. That's one advantage, and in addition he can become much stouter and heavier. I know of a number of animals, not just idle asses but also the most fiery horses, which suffered from excessive lust for coupling, and for that reason became recalcitrant and wild. But once they were castrated they at once became tame and manageable, quite ready to carry loads and submitting to their other duties. So as long as my advice doesn't meet with your disapproval, I can pick up the proper instruments from home and be back here shortly; I've been planning to visit the nearest market, so it will take me a little time. But then I can force this obstinate and unpleasant gallant's thighs apart, rob him of his manhood, and make him gentler than any wether in the flock.'

24   This proposal delivered me from the grasping clutches of Orcus, but I was most unhappy at this highly barbaric punishment in prospect. The thought that my body's rear end was to lose all its life made me weep. At that moment my idea was to dispose of myself by hunger-strike or by jumping off a height; I would die surely enough, but I would die with all my parts secure. While I was preoccupied with choosing my mode of death, that youthful executioner of mine led me out again early in the morning up the usual mountain track. He then tethered me to a branch dangling from a massive oak, climbed a little higher off the path, and began to wield his axe to chop wood to take down into the plain. All at once a deadly she-bear poked her monstrous head out of a nearby cave and sidled forth. As soon as I saw her, I was panic-stricken and aghast at her sudden appearance. I shifted the whole weight

of my body on to my back legs, raised my neck high in the air, broke the halter which tethered me, and took off promptly at high speed. It wasn't a matter of first feet forward; I threw my whole body hurtling pell-mell downward to the fields below, fleeing with the utmost urgency from that monstrous bear, and from the boy who was worse than the bear.

25   At that moment a traveller spotted me wandering without an owner. He took possession of me, quickly mounted, and beating me with the stick which he carried, he guided me along a byway which was new to me. I willingly co-operated with this course, as I was escaping from that most repulsive scheme of butchering my manhood. The beating I did not greatly mind, for I was used to such ritual assaults with the cudgel.

But Lady Fortune whom I knew well was bent on my undoing. With a speed which spelt misery for me, she pre-empted the timely prospect of concealment, and laid a fresh ambush. The herdsmen who had charge of me were hunting a lost heifer. After combing different areas, they chanced on us and recognized me at once. They seized me by the halter, and started to drag me off. But the traveller offered strong and bold resistance, appealing to the faith of men and gods: 'Why are you using force to drag me away? Why attack me?' 'What?' they responded. 'Are you saying that we are being rough with you when you have stolen our ass and are making off with him? You'd better tell us instead where you have hidden the beast's groom; presumably you've killed the boy.' They then pulled him to the ground, clobbered him with their fists, and put the boot in. He reacted with an oath, swearing that he had seen no rider; he had taken the ass when it was roaming free and unattended so as to obtain the reward for retrieving it, and he intended to restore it to its owner. 'I just wish', he added, 'that the ass himself—I wish to God that I'd never set eyes on him—could break into human speech and attest my innocence. If he did, you would certainly be ashamed of manhandling me like this.' But his protests were ineffectual; the herdsmen grabbed him by the neck and angrily dragged him back to the woodland glades of the mountain, where the boy usually gathered his wood.

26   There was no sign of the boy anywhere on the horizon, but a body was visible, torn limb from limb and scattered about, and it was obviously his. I knew beyond doubt that the bear's teeth were the perpetrators, and I would certainly have divulged this knowledge if the faculty of speech had been granted me. I did all that I could do; I silently welcomed this vengeance, delayed though it was. Eventually the herdsmen recovered the whole corpse, fitted the scattered parts together with some difficulty, and buried it in the earth there and then. As for my Bellerophon, they charged him with being caught red-handed as a thief and blood-stained assassin, and led him in chains to temporary confinement in their huts, so that as they said he could be turned over to the magistrates for punishment next day.

Meanwhile, as the boy's parents were beating their breasts in tearful lamentation, who should appear but the countryman, true to his promise and demanding to carry out the surgery as arranged. One of the mourning party said: 'The pernicious ass is not to blame for our present bereavement, but tomorrow you can certainly lop off not only his manhood but his head as well, and you can count on the help of these herdsmen.'

27   So my ordeal was postponed until next day, and I offered my thanks to that kind boy because at least in death he had granted me a stay of execution for one short day. But even this small respite afforded no chance of thanksgiving or rest, because the boy's mother burst into my stable, lamenting her son's bitter death. She was sobbing tearfully, dressed in sombre black, tugging her grey hair coated in ashes with both hands, moaning and bawling incessantly, beating and tearing violently at her breasts.

Then she broke into speech: 'Here he is, happily reclining in his manger, a slave to gluttony, perpetually stuffing and expanding that greedy, bloated belly, showing no pity for my distress, without a thought for the gruesome ill-fortune of his dead master! Doubtless he spurns and despises the infirmity of my old age, and imagines that he will survive this abominable crime without paying for it. But then, I suppose, he considers himself innocent; it is the usual way when people behave atrociously to expect no repercussions, in spite of a guilty conscience. You utterly worthless four-footed creature, God knows that even if you could acquire a human voice to plead your case, you could not persuade the dimmest fool that you are innocent of this horrible deed! You could have defended my poor little boy with your feet, and shielded him with your teeth. O yes, you could lash out at him time and time again with your hooves, so why couldn't you show the same readiness to prevent his death? The least you could have done was to hoist him on your back and clear off at once, saving him from that violent brigand's blood-stained hands! Above all, you should not have forsaken and abandoned your fellow-slave and master, your comrade and herdsman, to escape yourself. Do you not know that those who have failed to lend help to save people in danger of death are often punished for acting in such a despicable manner? But you will not laugh at my misfortunes any longer, you murderer. You will find that my wretched grief has a strength all its own—I'll see to that!'

28   As she spoke, she thrust her hands beneath her dress, loosened her breast-band, wound it round each of my feet separately, and lashed them together as tightly as she could, so that I would have no resource with which to seek revenge. She seized the bar used to reinforce the stable-doors, and proceeded to beat me with it until her strength was sapped with exhaustion, and the stick slipped from her grasp, borne down with its own weight. Then, grumbling at how quickly her arms grew tired, she ran to the hearth, seized a burning brand, and thrust it between my buttocks. This continued till I had recourse to my sole remaining means of defence. I unleashed at close quarters a stream of excrement, and covered her face and eyes with the foul liquid. That menace was at last forced back from me by that blinding and malodorous substance; otherwise this ass would have been a second Meleager, consigned to death by the firebrand of a maddened Althea.

BOOK 8

Charite's Revenge and Death: Lucius with the Catamite Priests

1 As cockcrow signalled the end of night, a young man arrived from the neighbouring city. I assumed that he was one of the servants of Charite, the girl who had endured hardships as trying as mine at the hands of the brigands. As he sat by the fire in the company of his fellow-slaves, he reported the strange and sacrilegious saga of the girl's death and the disaster which had struck her whole house. This was what he told them.

'Grooms, shepherds and herdsmen, our Charite is dead. Poor thing, she has departed to the shades below through the harshest of fates, but she has not gone alone. So that you may know the whole story, I shall tell you what happened from the beginning. It is a sequence of events which persons more learned than I, writers whom Fortune has invested with fluency of the pen, can appropriately commit to paper as an example of historical narrative.

'In a nearby town lived a young man of high birth, his nobility matched by his wealth. But he spent his time in the degenerate pursuits of the tavern, the brothel, and day-long drinking. This had led him to evil association with gangs of robbers, so that his hands were even stained with human blood. His name was Thrasyllus. Rumour circulating about him was matched by the reality.

2 'As soon as Charite had reached marrying-age, he had become one of her chief suitors. He devoted the greatest energy to the task of courting her; but though he was the leading contender among all those of his social rank, and sought to obtain her parents' consent with lavish gifts, his character as a reprobate led to the ignominy of rejection. Our young mistress was then joined in marriage to the worthy Tlepolemus, but Thrasyllus continued to nurture intensely

the love for which he had been utterly rejected, and with it he mingled his resentment at having been refused marriage. He then sought an opportunity to commit a bloodstained crime. Eventually he gained a suitable pretext for attendance on the couple, and he made preparations for the outrage which he had long planned.

'On the day when the girl was delivered from the threatening daggers of the robbers by the crafty and courageous deeds of her bridegroom, Thrasyllus mingled with the crowd of those who felicitated her, and he made a show of his delight. He expressed joy at the recent deliverance of the newly-weds, and at the prospect of children to be born to them. Their acknowledgment of the distinction of his glittering parentage led them to admit him to our household as one of our most honoured guests. He concealed his wicked design, and falsely played the role of the truest of friends. Soon by regular conversation, continual association, and occasional dinners and drinks together, he grew closer and closer to them, until gradually and without realizing it he had fallen headlong into the destructive depths of lust for Charite. This was inevitable, for the flame of fierce love when it burns low gives pleasure with its initial warmth, but once fed by familiarity it becomes a fierce fire, scorching our whole bodies with uncontrollable heat.

3   'It had long preoccupied Thrasyllus that he could find no suitable opportunity for secret conversation with Charite. He now saw that the possibilities of adulterous love were increasingly barred by the number of retainers guarding her, and he realized that the bond of the couple's new and growing affection was so strong that it could not be severed. Moreover, even if the girl showed willing, an impossible supposition, her inexperience of conjugal deceit was an obstacle. Yet he was driven on towards the impossible goal by the destructive striving which made it seem attainable. When love strengthens day by day, what at first is regarded as difficult to achieve seems easy to accomplish. So now observe—I ask you to pay attention closely here—the violent outcome of the onset of his mad lust.

4   'One day Tlepolemus went hunting in company with
Thrasyllus. His quarry was wild animals, but only in the
sense that mountain-goats are wild, for Charite did not allow
her husband to hunt beasts armed with tusks or horns. Soon
the hunt reached a leafy eminence, where the thick cover of
branches cast its shadow. There were goats enclosed there,
hidden from the view of the trackers. The pedigree hounds,
trained for their tracking faculties in the hunt, were released
with the command to attack the animals crouching in their
lairs. Without hesitation they recalled the smart training they
had received, and they spread out to cover all the means of
entry. At first they confined themselves to low growls, but
then on receipt of a sudden signal they caused all hell to be let
loose with their fierce and discordant barking. But what
emerged was no she-goat, no fearful young deer, no hind (that
gentlest of all creatures in the wild), but a monstrous boar of
unprecedented size. His coarse flesh bulged with muscle; his
hide was disfigured with spiky hair; his back was shaggy with
bristles standing erect. He foamed at the mouth as he loudly
ground his tusks; fire flashed from his menacing eyes; the
savage onset of his ranting jaws moved like a bolt of lightning.
At first he lunged with his tusks this way and that, to slash
and slaughter the more adventurous hounds which had
ventured to close quarters. Then he trampled underfoot the
flimsy net which had held up his first attacks, and then made
his escape over it.

5   'While all the rest of us in panic took cover behind foliage or
tree-trunks (for usually our hunting expeditions were not
dangerous, and on this occasion we had no weapons or means
of defence), Thrasyllus exploited an opportune trick to
achieve his treachery. He craftily said to Tlepolemus: "Why
are we so thunderstruck, showing the same sort of idle fear as
our grovelling slaves here, or the lack of spirit of terrified
women, in letting such a splendid prize slip from our grasp?
Why don't we mount and chase after him at full speed? Here,
you take a hunting-spear and I shall grab a lance."

'They did not delay for a moment, but at once leapt on their
horses and pursued the beast with the greatest vigour. The

boar, still conscious of its native strength, wheeled round to attack. Aglow with the savage fire of rage, it whetted its tusks as it peered at them, in doubt whom to attack first. Tlepolemus was first to hurl the spear which he carried, and he pierced the animal's back from above. Thrasyllus, however, did not attack the beast, but with a blow of his lance cut the rear hamstrings of Tlepolemus' mount. The horse collapsed in a pool of its own blood, fell full length on its back, and unintentionally threw its master to the ground. The boar lost no time in savagely attacking his prostrate form. With repeated lunges of its tusks, it tore first at his clothing and then at Tlepolemus himself as he sought to rise. His good friend showed no compunction for his criminal deed, and could not even find full satisfaction in observing the sacrificial victim of his cruelty in such mortal danger. In fact he plunged his lance through his comrade's right thigh, as Tlepolemus in panic vainly sought to protect his crippled limbs and pitiably implored the other's help. Thrasyllus assailed him all the more confidently in his belief that wounds inflicted by the steel would resemble those ripped open by the tusks. He also ran through the beast itself with practised hand.

6   'After the youthful Tlepolemus had been dispatched in this way, the members of his retinue were all roused from our various hiding-places, and hastily gathered with downcast faces. Thrasyllus was delighted at having achieved his wish by bringing his enemy low, but he wiped the joy from his face, wore a troubled look, feigned sorrow, and affectionately embraced the corpse which he himself had slain. Indeed, he made practised pretence of performing all observances of mourners except for his tears alone, which refused to flow. In this way he modelled his actions on the rest of us who were genuinely mourning, and he kept blaming the beast for the foul deed inflicted by his own hand.

'The crime had scarcely been fully perpetrated when Rumour slipped from the scene and guided her twisted course first to the house of Tlepolemus, where she smote the ears of the hapless bride. As soon as Charite took in the message, the like of which she will never hear again, she became deranged and fired by madness. She rushed wildly about in a frenzy, coursing through crowded streets and the fields of the countryside, bewailing with demented cries her husband's misfortune. Sad bands of citizens gathered; they followed and drew up with her to share her grief. The entire city was deserted in the citizens' desire to look on her. What a scene it was as she rushed towards her husband's remains, and with gasping breath threw her whole body on the corpse! There and then she virtually surrendered to her dead husband the life that she had pledged to him. With some difficulty she was torn away from him by the hands of her kinsfolk, and she unwillingly survived. The dead body was conducted to burial with the whole citizen-body attending the funeral-train.

7   'Thrasyllus made a show of crying out and beating his breast all too vehemently. Doubtless under the stimulus of mounting joy, he now shed the tears which he could not summon when he first expressed grief. He beguiled Truth herself with his many expressions of affection, as he called on his friend, his contemporary, his comrade, and to crown all his brother, citing him by name as well. From time to time he would also draw Charite's hands back from beating her breasts, quieten her grief, restrain her lamentation, dull the sharp pain of her sorrow with soothing words, and weave a web of consolations by adducing various instances of wide-ranging misfortunes. Yet while performing all these observances of feigned devotion, he was indulging his eagerness to fondle the lady, and nurturing his own hateful love by seeking to arouse a perverse pleasure in her.

'But as soon as the funeral observances were over, the girl at once made haste to join her husband below. She tried every possible avenue, or at any rate the route that is non-violent and leisurely and needs no weapon to accomplish it, but is akin to peaceful rest. In short, she wretchedly starved herself, and foully neglected her person. She hid herself in the deepest darkness, and no longer had dealings with the light of day. But Thrasyllus applied constant pressure partly by his own efforts, partly through her other friends and relatives, and finally through the girl's very parents. He finally constrained

her to tend her body, now almost lifeless in its pallid and filthy
state, by washing and later by eating. She was a girl who in
general respected her parents, and though reluctant, she
yielded to the dictates of her sense of duty. So she performed
as bidden the routine tasks of the living, not smilingly but with
a calmer countenance than before. But in her heart, indeed in
the depths of her being, grief and sadness were gnawing at her
mind. All her days, all her nights she now spent in the grief of
longing. She had statues of her dead husband made in the
likeness of the god Liber; she made herself his votary, and
paid him divine honours in worship, thus torturing herself in
the very act which consoled her.

8   'Thrasyllus, however, was temperamentally impulsive and
rash, living up to his name. Tears had not yet sated Charite's
grief; the uncontrolled emotions of her disturbed mind had
not yet subsided; her sorrow had not worn itself out through
its protracted vehemence. She was still weeping after her
husband, still rending her garments, still tearing her hair. Yet
he did not hesitate to broach the possibility of marriage. The
lapse of an unguarded moment led him to disclose his
unspeakable treachery, which in silence and secrecy he had
hugged to his heart. Charite was appalled at this sacrilegious
disclosure, and she abominated it. It hit her like a thunderclap, or an explosive downpour in the rainy season, or a bolt
of lightning from heaven. It shattered her physically, and
made her mind a blur. Gradually, however, her spirit revived.
Over and over again she moaned like an animal. She now saw
through the unspeakable Thrasyllus' pretence, but in order to
refine a plan of action she sought a delay to the aspiration of
her suitor.

     'During this moratorium the shade of Tlepolemus, so
wretchedly slain, disturbed his wife's chaste sleep. He raised
his face, gore-stained and unsightly in its pallor, before her. "I
greet you as my wife", he said, "though no other will be able
to call you mine. Even if remembrance of me is now firm in
your heart, and the calamity of my bitter death does not sever
the bond of our love, you must find greater happiness in
marriage to another, provided that you do not accept the

sacrilegious hand of Thrasyllus. Do not speak with him, or recline at table with him, or share his bed; shun the bloodstained hand of my assassin. Do not embark upon a marriage initiated by the murder of your kin. Those wounds whose blood your tears washed away are not all the work of tusks; it was the lance of the wicked Thrasyllus which has set me apart from you." Further words which he spoke revealed the nefarious plot in its entirety.

9   'Charite slumbered on, her face sunk into the couch as it had been when sleep first overtook her in her melancholy. Her tears streamed forth and bedewed her cheeks. Then she was roused from sleep as if some weapon of torture had jolted her, and her grief was renewed. She uttered prolonged wailing, tore her nightgown, and with merciless hands beat her pretty arms. But she did not divulge the vision of that night to anyone; the revelation of the crime she kept wholly secret. She silently decided both to punish the iniquitous assassin and to detach herself from a life which had become intolerable.

'The abominable Thrasyllus now made a further appearance. In pursuit of his thoughtless pleasure, he assailed with talk of marriage the ears which she kept firmly barred. But her rejection of his address was gentle, and her role-playing was performed with admirable guile. In response to his insistent chatter and obsequious pleading, she said: "The handsome face of your fraternal friend, my dearest husband, is still vivid before my eyes; the cinnamon-like fragrance of his body with its scent of ambrosia still pervades my nostrils; handsome Tlepolemus is still alive in my heart's depths. So you will show proper and exemplary prudence if you grant the required period of lawful mourning to this woman in her great misery, until the remainder of the year is completed by the months still to elapse. This delay is in the interests of both my modesty and the good of your health; otherwise, by marrying too early we may fire my husband's ghost to bitterness and justified anger, and he may bring about your death."

10   'These words of hers did not induce sobriety in Thrasyllus, or even hearten him with their distant promise. He continued to press her repeatedly with suggestive whispers from his

wearying tongue. Finally Charite pretended to yield, and
answered him. "Very well, Thrasyllus, but at least grant me
this pressing request: our intimate relations must in the
meantime be conducted silently and in secrecy. No member of
the household must become privy until the remaining days of
mourning are past."

'Thrasyllus bowed in defeat to this deceitful promise of the
lady, and he enthusiastically endorsed the suggestion of secret
love-encounters, for his own unprompted longing aspired to
the night and the cover of darkness. He relegated all else to
the single desire to possess her. "But be sure", added Charite,
"to come well concealed by a cloak, and with no companion.
Make your way silently, just after dark, to my gate. A single
whistle will suffice; wait for this nurse of mine here, who will
have her hand on the bolt, watching out for your arrival. She
will likewise open the house, let you in, and guide you to my
bedroom without the conspiratorial help of a lamp."

11 'This staging of a marriage with death appealed to
Thrasyllus. With no suspicion of anything amiss, he was in a
turmoil of expectation, and his only complaint was that the
day was long and the night slow in coming. But when the sun
finally yielded to darkness, he clothed himself as Charite
demanded. The sight of the nurse astutely posted on watch
deceived him; he crept into the bedroom hell-bent on gaining
his desire. The old nurse had received her instructions from
her mistress. She fawned on him, and then unobtrusively
brought out goblets and a wine-jar containing a sleeping-
draught mixed with the wine. Greedily and without suspicion
he drained his cup several times; the nurse had lyingly
excused her mistress's late arrival by claiming that she was at
the bedside of her sick father. Without difficulty she soon had
him sleeping like the dead; once he was laid out and
vulnerable to any assault, Charite was summoned in. She was
animated by a man's courage as she strode to the assassin
with steely aggression and fierce rage. She stood over him,
and said:

12   ' "Here he is, my husband's faithful comrade, a huntsman
beyond compare, my own dear spouse! Here is the hand that

shed my blood, here is the breast that devised a deceitful fraud
to encompass my destruction! These are the eyes which found
perverted pleasure in gazing on me. But already here they
anticipate the darkness which is to descend on them, and they
have foresight of the punishment to visit them. Take your
untroubled rest, enjoy your blessed dreams! I shall not assault
you with sword or steel, for I would not have you ranked with
my husband by your sharing the nature of his death. You will
live, but your eyes will perish; only when you sleep will you
exercise your sight. I shall ensure that you regard your
enemy's death as more blessed than your life. What is certain
is that you will not see the light of day, and that you will need
a companion's guiding hand. You will not embrace Charite or
enjoy marriage with her. You will neither gain renewed vigour
by the tranquillity of death, nor take joys in the pleasures of
life. Instead you will wander between the regions of hell and of
the sun, a dubious image of a living man. You will spend long
days seeking the hand that stormed your eyesight, and your
suffering will be compounded by your wretched ignorance of
whom to blame. The blood from your eyes will be the libation
which I shall pour on the tomb of my Tlepolemus; those eyes
will constitute the sacrifice which I shall make to his sacred
shade.

' "But why do I grant you the boon of a respite from the
torture you deserve, and perhaps allow you to dream of
baneful embraces with me? Emerge from the shadows of sleep,
awake to that other darkness which will be your punishment.
Lift up your eyeless face, acknowledge this my vengeance,
apprehend your misery, take stock of your sufferings. This is
how your eyes have gained the favour of a chaste woman; this
is how the marriage-torches have lit your bridal chamber.
Your bridesmaids will be the avenging Furies; blindness will
be your groomsman, and the prick of undying guilt."

13   'This was how she prophesied his future. She then took a
pin from her hair, and pierced his eyeballs through, leaving
him totally sightless. As he shook off his drunken sleep
through the pain which he could not identify, she seized the
unsheathed sword which Tlepolemus had been accustomed to

buckle on, and she burst out at a frenzied pace through the middle of the city. It was clear that she had some criminal deed in mind as she made straight for her husband's tomb. We and the entire citizen-body quitted all our houses and anxiously overtook her, urging each other to wrest the sword from her crazed hands. But Charite took her stand by Tlepolemus's coffin, and drove each of us back with the gleaming sword. As she surveyed the copious tears which we were all shedding, and our discordant wailing, she said: "Dry your untimely tears, renounce the grief which is out of keeping with my valorous deeds. I have exacted vengeance from the bloodstained murderer of my husband; I have punished the plunderer who brought death to my marriage. It is now time for me to seek through this sword the downward path to Tlepolemus."

14   'She then recounted in sequence all that her husband had told her in her dream, and the trickery she had employed to deceive and to lay hands on Thrasyllus. She then drove the sword below her right breast, and slid to the ground. As she writhed in her own blood, she stuttered some last incoherent words, and died like a man. Her kinsfolk then hastened to wash poor Charite's body with devoted care, and restored her to her husband in their common burial-place to be his spouse for ever.

'When Thrasyllus heard all that had happened, he found himself unable to bring this present tragedy to its appropriate close, for he was convinced that not even death by the sword was meet for such a foul crime. At his request he was led to the tomb, where he repeatedly cried out: "Hostile shades, here is your willing victim!" He then deliberately closed the doors of the tomb over himself, and by self-starvation opted to expel from his body the life that he had condemned by his own sentencing.'

15   This was the news that the slave brought, punctuated with extended sighs and occasional tears; his audience of country-workers was deeply moved. But they felt apprehensive at being under new ownership, and their sympathy ran deeper for the disaster which had struck their former master's house.

Accordingly they planned to run away. The head groom, who was charged with the horses and who upon Charite's strong recommendation had undertaken to look after me, loaded on my back and on those of the other beasts all the valuables that he kept stored in his cottage. He then carried them away, and abandoned his former abode. We carried on our backs young children, women, chickens, sparrows, kids, pups; and all those who had difficulty in walking and who hindered our swift departure exploited our feet to make the journey. The weight of my load was prodigious, but it did not dishearten me, for in joyful flight I was leaving behind the abominable fellow who sought to slice off my manhood.

We made our way over the rough ridges of a wooded mountain, and then journeyed through the plains extending beyond. As evening overshadowed our path, we came to a crowded and prosperous village. The inhabitants there tried to deter us from leaving in darkness or even in the early morning. They said that there were hordes of gigantic wolves plaguing all that district; they were burly and big-bodied, exceedingly fierce and savage, and were constantly hunting plunder in many areas. At that time they were blockading the very roads, and like highwaymen they attacked travellers as they passed by. Indeed, their mad hunger made them so savage that they stormed neighbouring farmhouses, and the fate suffered by unresisting cattle now overhung the human occupants themselves. They claimed that the road on which we were to travel was littered with half-devoured bodies, all gleaming white because the bones had been stripped of their flesh. Hence it was vital that we observe the greatest caution in resuming our journey, and take the most stringent care to travel in broad daylight, when the hour was well advanced and the sun was at its zenith. We should avoid the traps lurking round us on all sides, and negotiate the hazards at a time when the aggression of those foul beasts was tempered by the sun's rays. We should proceed not strung out in isolation, but in compact wedge-formation.

16   But our most negligent runaway leaders were rash in their blind haste, and fearful that we might be followed. They

disregarded this salutary advice, and without awaiting the morning light they drove us with full loads on to the road just after midnight. I was fearful of the danger of which we had been forewarned, so I then sought the innermost possible position, hiding myself to lurk unnoticed in the crowd of closely-packed beasts, and thus protecting my haunches against the attacks of those wild animals. There was general astonishment at the turn of speed with which I outpaced the horses accompanying us. Such acceleration was a mark of apprehension rather than eagerness on my part; indeed, I reflected that it was panic more than anything which had induced the celebrated Pegasus to take to the air, and that the tradition that he had wings was justified because he leapt upward as high as heaven in his fear of being bitten by the fire-breathing Chimaera. An additional reason for apprehension was that the shepherds who were herding us had equipped themselves as if for battle. One wielded a lance, another a hunting-spear, a third darts, a fourth a club; they also carried stones which the rugged path supplied in abundance. Some of them had sharp stakes, but most deterred the beasts with flaming torches. The only thing they lacked for a formal battle-line was a bugle.

However, our fears on this score were wholly groundless and superfluous, but we landed ourselves in a much stickier trap. The wolves were doubtless frightened off by the din raised by our close-knit group of young men, or at any rate by the glaring light of the torches, or they may have been plundering elsewhere. None of them attacked us, or were even in evidence some way off.

17 But we chanced to pass by an estate in which the farmhands mistook our large band for robbers. They were considerably exercised for their property as well as extremely frightened, so they set their dogs on us with the usual halloos and shouts of every kind. These animals were wild, huge, and more ferocious than any wolves or bears, and had been carefully reared as guard-dogs. Their native savagery was intensified by the din which their masters made. They charged at us, surrounded us on all sides, and leapt at us from

every angle, making no distinction between man and beast as they mangled us. Their sustained attacks left many of us lying on the ground. I swear that the sight you would have beheld there was worthier of pity than of the pen: that large pack of dogs was fiercely intent on tugging at those who fled, clinging to those who stood their ground, mounting on some who were prostrate, and in their progress through our entire column, sinking their teeth into everything and everyone.

18   This hazard was bad enough, but worse was to follow. Those countrymen posted themselves on rooftops and on the nearest hill, and sent rocks rolling full tilt on us. We were utterly at a loss to decide whether to take cover more against the dogs at close quarters or the rocks at long range. One of the rocks suddenly struck the head of a woman astride my back; she reacted to the pain by weeping and wailing, and by shouting to her husband the head-groom to come to her aid. He kept calling on the gods to witness what was happening, and as he wiped the blood from his wife, he raised his voice in complaint. 'Why are you attacking and oppressing us so cruelly? We are poor people struggling on our way. What booty do you cast your eyes on? What losses are you seeking to avenge? I cannot believe that you are beasts dwelling in caves, or barbarian rock-dwellers, that you take pleasure in shedding human blood!'

The words were scarcely out of his mouth when the heavy shower of stones ceased, and the storming attack of the dogs was quietened as they were called off. Then one of the estate-workers called out from the top of a cypress-tree: 'We are not brigands eager to plunder you. Our aim has been to avoid that same harsh treatment at your hands. You can now proceed untroubled and without interference.'

These were his words. But we embarked on the rest of our journey bearing the marks of many wounds. Some had been struck by stones, others bitten by the dogs; all of us were injured. After we had travelled a fair distance on the road, we reached a grove planted with tall trees and with delightful patches of green meadow. Our leaders decided to refresh themselves here with a brief rest, and to give more careful treatment to their bodies which had suffered various lacerations. So they sprawled out at various places on the ground, and hastened first to restore their wearied spirits, and then to apply different remedies to their wounds. One washed off the blood in the waters of a stream which flowed by; another reduced the swellings with sponges soaked in vinegar; a third bound his gaping wounds with bandages. This was how each looked after his own well-being.

19 While this was going on, an old man surveyed the scene from the top of a hill. Nanny-goats cropping the grass all around plainly showed that he was a herdsman. One of our number asked him if he had milk for sale, either still liquid or newly curdled into cheese. He shook his head over and over again. 'What?' he asked. 'Are your minds at this moment on food or drink or any sort of refreshment? Do none of you know about this place where you have taken rest?' With these words he rounded up his devoted sheep, turned on his heel, and retired to a distance. His comment and his precipitate departure considerably agitated our herdsmen. In their disquiet they were eager to enquire about the nature of the place, but there was no one to inform them. But then another old man, tall but weighed down with age, leaning with his whole weight on his stick and dragging his feet wearily along, approached in floods of tears along the road. When he sighted us, he wept copiously, touched the knees of each of the young men, and pleaded with them in these words:

20 'I implore you by your personal Fortunes and your guardian spirits to come to the aid of this destitute old man. If you do, I pray that you may reach my time of old age still strong and happy. Rescue my little one from death, and restore him to these grey hairs of mine. My grandson, my engaging companion on this journey, chanced to be trying to catch hold of a sparrow chirruping in a hedgerow, and he has fallen into a pit close by which lies open beneath the brambles. He is now in the greatest danger of his life. I know that he is alive, for I can hear him crying and repeatedly calling for his grandfather, but I cannot go to his rescue because of my poor bodily health, as you can see. But it would

be easy for you with the resource of your youth and strength to come to the aid of this most unhappy old man, and to save the life of that boy, who is the last of my descendants and the only one of my stock still surviving.'

21   As he pleaded in this way and tore at his grey hairs, the whole of our company pitied him. One in particular, more stout-hearted, younger, and physically stronger than the rest, had emerged unscathed from the earlier fracas. He jumped up smartly, and asked where the boy had tumbled in. When the old man pointed with his finger at some prickly brambles not far away, the young man briskly accompanied him there. Meanwhile we had restored ourselves, the beasts by eating our fodder and the humans by tending their needs, and we all took up our baggage and set out. To begin with the men repeatedly shouted after the young fellow, loudly calling on him by name, but then the long delay caused them disquiet, and they sent one of their number to summon him, to search out their comrade, to tell him it was time to leave, and to escort him back. The messenger returned after a short time, trembling and pale as boxwood. He had an extraordinary tale to tell about his fellow-slave: he had seen him lying prostrate, with a monstrous snake perched on top of him gnawing his flesh, so that the youth was now almost entirely gobbled up. There was not a sign anywhere of that unhappy old man. When they heard this, they connected it with the words of the shepherd, who had clearly been warning them against that inmate of this desolate region who was as old as himself. So they abandoned that baneful spot, and took to their heels in headlong flight, driving us along with frequent blows of their cudgels.

22   We finally reached a village after completing a long journey at top speed, and we rested there for the entire night. A quite noteworthy outrage had been committed there, and I am eager to recount it.

The extensive estate where we lodged was managed by a slave whose master had entrusted him with the entire supervision of the household. This bailiff was married to a fellow-slave in the same retinue, but was inflamed with passion for a free woman who lived beyond the estate. His wife burned with resentment at this adulterous liaison. She set fire to all her husband's account-books, and all that was stored in the granary. Still not satisfied at having avenged the slight to her marriage-bed by inflicting such damage, she next took drastic steps against the fruit of her own womb. She lassooed herself, and then wound the same rope round the baby whom she had borne some time before to that same husband. She then threw herself down into the deepest of wells, taking the small child with her. Their master took her death very badly. He seized the wretched slave whose licentious behaviour had been responsible for this appalling outrage, stripped him and smeared his whole body with honey. Then he bound him tightly to a fig-tree, in the rotting trunk of which resident ants were busy building their nests and scurrying to and fro in a continuous stream. Once they smelt the honey-sweet odour of his body, they clung fast to it, taking tiny but regular and continual bites from it. This torture continued over a long period, until his flesh and inner organs were gnawed away. So the bailiff was devoured, and the ants stripped his limbs bare, so that nothing but the bones were left adhering to that tree of death. They hung there, stripped of the flesh, gleaming starkly white.

23   So we abandoned this accursed resting-place as well, leaving the villagers to their heartfelt grief. We took to the road again, and for a whole day we travelled on routes which straddled a plain. We finally arrived exhausted at a populous and famous town. The shepherds escorting us decided to make this their permanent abode, for it seemed a safe place to hide from those who might be searching for them at some distance away; in addition, the plentiful abundance of grain was enticing. So for three days the pack-animals were rested and fed, to ensure that our appearance would fetch a better price, and then we were led to market. The auctioneer loudly announced the price of each beast, and the horses and other asses were bought by wealthy buyers, most of whom turned up their noses at me and passed by, leaving me forlorn and isolated. I became so irritated with people mauling me and

trying to assess my age from my teeth that I fastened my grinders into the foul-smelling hand of one individual who kept massaging my gums with his filthy fingers, and completely crushed it. This incident cooled the enthusiasm of prospective buyers among the crowd, for they thought me over-aggressive. Then the auctioneer, now hoarse from straining his tonsils and exercising his raucous voice, began to concoct amusing jokes about my prospects: 'For how long are we to try in vain to sell this nag? The poor old thing is feeble, his hooves are worn down, and the painful treatment he has suffered has made him unsightly. He is vicious too, for all his stupidity and lethargy. He is nothing better than a braying, worn-out sieve. So let us at any rate make a present of him, if we can find someone who does not object to wasting his fodder.'

24   With words like these the auctioneer raised guffaws from the bystanders. But that most malevolent Fortune of mine, whom I had failed to shake off in my flight through numerous regions, or to placate through the ills I had already suffered, turned her blind eyes on me again. Remarkably, she found me a buyer most suited to my grim misfortunes, and thrust him upon me. Let me outline his type: he was a catamite, and an old one at that, bald on top, with ringlets streaked with grey dangling round his head. He was representative of the meanest dregs of society, those people who parade through the streets of towns banging cymbals, shaking castanets, and carrying round the Syrian goddess whom they adduce to solicit alms. In his eagerness to purchase me, he asked the auctioneer where I hailed from; the man declared that I was a Cappadocian, and quite virile. When the other in turn asked my age, the auctioneer flippantly replied: 'The astrologer who drew his horoscope claimed that he was in his fifth year, but doubtless the ass is a better authority for his own age, since he registered for the census. I know that I am with forethought risking indictment under the Cornelian law if I sell you a Roman citizen as a slave, but why don't you buy this worthy and honest piece of goods? He will be able to offer you satisfaction both outdoors and indoors.' The loathsome purchaser, however, kept on posing one question after another

incessantly, finally asking with furrowed brow whether I was meek and mild.

25   The auctioneer replied: 'This is no ass you see; he's gelded, compliant in any service. He doesn't bite or lash out. You could believe that in this ass's skin there lurks an unassuming human being. You can readily observe this; just push your head between his thighs, and you'll easily establish what a massive length of endurance he has on offer!'

This was how the auctioneer exercised his wit at the expense of the greedy priest. But the other detected the tone of mockery, and with a show of indignation said: 'You lifeless deaf and dumb creature! You crazed auctioneer! I pray that the Syrian goddess our all-powerful universal mother, and holy Sabazius, and Bellona, and the Idaean mother and her Attis, and the lady Venus and her Adonis may blind you for making me the butt of your coarse witticisms! You surely do not imagine, you fool, that I can entrust the goddess to an untamed animal? Why, he might suddenly throw a fit and dislodge the statue of the goddess, and then I, poor queen, would have to rush around with my hair flying loose, seeking a doctor for my goddess as she lies prostrate on the ground!'

When I heard words like these, my first thought was to bound suddenly into the air as though crazed, so that he would lose interest in buying me, once he saw that I had a furious temper when roused. But the purchaser was keen, and forestalled my intention by at once forking out the price of seventeen denarii. My master readily accepted it, and gladly, for he had had enough of me. There and then he fastened a bridle of flax round my mouth, and consigned me to Philebus, the name of my new owner.

26   The priest took over his untrained servant, and dragged me off home. As soon as he reached the threshold, he shouted out: 'Look, girls, what a handsome wee slave I've brought for you!' The 'girls' were in fact a bunch of catamites. Their joy was immediate and ecstatic; they cried out discordantly in their cracked, hoarse, girlish voices, doubtless under the impression that some slave-boy had been procured to serve them. But when they saw that an ass was there in place of a man—and

not a hind for a maiden!—they turned up their noses, and taunted their master with various comments to the effect that it wasn't a slave which he'd brought, but a marriage-partner for himself. 'Just be sure not to devour this lovely little chick yourself!' they said. 'You must share him from time to time with your lovey-doveys.'

Whilst babbling to each other with remarks such as these, they secured me close to the manger. There was a quite well-built young man there, an expert piper; they had bought him at a slave-stand with the coins which they had collected. When they were carrying the goddess around outside, he would walk beside them playing the horn, but indoors his role was that of communal bedfellow, spreading his services around. As soon as he set eyes on me inside, he delightedly set lots of fodder before me, and said to me in happy tones: 'At last you have come to deputize for me in my most pitiable toil. I wish you long life. May you win the approval of our masters, and relieve the pressure on my now wearied loins.' As I heard these words, I now began to give thought to the fresh trials in store for me.

27   Next day the priests set out, clad in multicoloured garments and with features hideously made up; their faces were smeared with clay pigment, and their eyes were daubed with mascara. They had put on conical caps and saffron garments of linen and silk. Some wore white shirts decorated with purple stripes in spear-motifs pointing in different directions, and gathered up at the waist; they had yellow sandals on their feet. The goddess, who was attired in a garment of silk, they consigned to me to carry. Their arms were bared to the shoulder; they carried fearsome swords and axes; and they leapt about uttering ecstatic cries, for the pipe-music fired them to frenzied dancing.

After visiting several cottages in the course of their wanderings, they reached an estate belonging to a wealthy owner. As soon as they entered it they dashed forward frantically, making the place resound with their discordant wailing. For some time they bent their heads low and twisted their necks in supple movements, making their dangling locks rotate. Occasionally they would sink their teeth into their own flesh, and as a finale they each slashed their arms with the two-edged swords which they brandished. In the course of this performance, one of them behaved even more frenziedly. Drawing frequent breaths from deep within as though filled with the heaven-sent inspiration of a deity, he would pretend to be struck with madness—as if men visited by a divine presence are usually rendered feeble or sick, rather than raised to higher things!

28   But now observe how divine providence repaid him as he deserved. In loud, oracular tones he began lyingly to reproach and charge himself with having committed some wicked sin against the sacred tenets of his holy religion, and he proceeded to demand due punishment at his own hands for his sinful deed. He then seized the whip which these effeminates carry around as their distinctive possession. It is fringed with long, twisted tassels of wool, inset with several knuckle-bones from sheep. Wielding it, he scourged himself with lashes from this heavily knotted weapon, withstanding the pain of the blows in remarkable fashion by gritting his teeth. You could see the ground getting soaked with the filthy blood of the catamites as a result of the incisions of the swords and the blows of the whips. The sight made me considerably anxious, when I saw the blood gushing out in torrents from all these wounds, in case the stomach of the foreign goddess craved the taste of ass's blood, just as some people like to drink ass's milk.

Eventually exhaustion overtook them with this self-laceration, or at any rate they felt that they had had enough, so they called a halt to the torture. Many of those watching vied with each other in contributing coppers and even silver coins which the priests caught in the open folds of their garments. They also obtained a cask of wine, milk, cheeses, and a quantity of spelt and fine flour. Some people presented barley for the goddess's mount. All of this the priests raked in with greedy eagerness, stuffing it into sacks purposely brought for this windfall. They then heaped the sacks on my back, so that I doubled as a walking larder and a walking temple, for I was bowed down under the weight of the double burden.

29   During such wanderings as this they plundered the entire region. In one hill-village they felt so pleased with the size of their unusually large haul that they organized a celebratory banquet. By citing a false oracular utterance they extracted from some farmer the fattest of rams, so that when sacrificed it could fill the belly of the starving Syrian goddess. When their supper was elegantly laid, they visited the baths and returned from there spick and span, bringing with them as a dinner-guest a peasant of powerful physique, especially chosen for the capacity of his loins and lower parts. Those most filthy reprobates had no more than tasted a few greens prior to the meal proper when they were fired with unspeakable longing to perform the most despicable outrages of unnatural lust. They surrounded the young fellow on every side, stripped off his clothes, laid him on his back, and kept smothering him with their abominable kisses. My eyes could not long endure such evil conduct. I longed to cry out: 'O citizens, to the rescue!' but the only sound that came out was 'O!', without being supplemented by the other syllables and consonants. The 'O' was quite clear and strong, an apt expression for an ass, but the timing was inopportune.

The trouble was that several young men from a neighbour-ing village were searching for an ass stolen from them during the night. They were conducting a most thorough search of all the inns, and when they heard my braying coming from within our lodging, they thought that their plundered beast had been secreted in some remote corner of the dwelling. They burst suddenly in with a concerted rush to seize their property on the spot, and caught the priests red-handed engaged in those obscenely foul practices. They at once summoned the locals from all quarters, and pointed out to them this most degrading display, adding their sardonic praise of the priests' wholly unblemished chastity.

30   The priests were shattered by this notoriety, which was avidly circulated by word of mouth among the common folk, and which made them deservedly hated and loathed by all. So about midnight they gathered up all their belongings and furtively quitted the village. Before sunrise they had completed

a good part of their journey, and by daylight reached a
trackless, desolate region. There, after considerable discussion
among themselves, they made preparations to kill me. The
goddess whom I had carried was lifted off my back, and set on
the ground. They stripped me of all my blankets, tied me to an
oak-tree, and then flogged me with the whip strung with
sheep's knuckle-bones, until they all but finished me off. One
of them threatened to cut my hamstrings with his axe, because
my triumph over their lily-white virtue had so humiliated
them. But the rest, with an eye not to my welfare but to the
statue lying before them, decided that I must be kept alive. So
they loaded me up again with the baggage, and kept
threatening me with the flat of their swords until they reached
a famous town. There was a leading citizen there who was in
general a scrupulous person and who held the gods in especial
awe. He was roused by the clashing of the cymbals, the
beating of the drums, and the soothing measures of the
Phrygian chant. He came running to meet us, welcomed the
goddess with the hospitality of a votary, and installed us in the
precincts of his very spacious house. There he hastened to
appease the deity with most devout worship and with rich
sacrificial victims.

31   It was here, as I recall, that my life was exposed to the
greatest danger. One of the estate-workers had been out
hunting, and had sent in part of the bag, the plumpest haunch
of a huge stag, to his master as a gift. It had been carelessly
hung at a modest height behind the kitchen-door, and some
dog—as good a hunter as the estate-worker!—had stealthily
seized it and made off in haste, pleased with his prize and
escaping the eyes of those looking after it. When the loss was
discovered, the cook blamed his own carelessness, and shed
long and futile tears of lamentation. His master was pressingly
demanding his dinner. The unhappy cook, in a state of abject
fear, kissed his little son goodbye and seized a length of rope to
fashion a noose and encompass his own death. But his trusty
wife observed her husband's desperate danger. She fiercely
grabbed the deadly halter with both hands, and said to him:
'Has your panic in your present plight driven you out of your

mind? Haven't you noted that the gods with their foresight have provided you with a chance remedy to hand? If you have retained an atom of sense in this harshest of hurricanes imposed by Fortune, listen carefully to me. Take this ass, this new arrival, to some remote spot, and slit its throat. Tear off its haunch to make it resemble the one you have lost, cook it with due care, adding plenty of spicy flavours, and set it before the master in place of the venison.'

That most depraved scoundrel decided to save his skin at the price of my death. He lavishly praised the wit of his fellow-slave, and proceeded to sharpen his knives for the butchery which he was contemplating.

BOOK 9

With the Priests, the Baker, the Market-Gardener:
Four Tales of Cuckolding

1 This was how that foulest of executioners was equipping his
sacrilegious hands to slaughter me. But the onset of such
pressing danger prompted me to a plan of action, and without
indulging in lengthy reflection I decided to bolt and thus
avoid the threat of the butcher's knife. So I snapped the rope
which secured me, and at once charged out at full speed to
gain sanctuary, bursting along with rapid hoof-beats. I
negotiated the adjacent colonnade at speed, and propelled
myself without hesitation into the dining-room; where the
master of the house in company with the goddess's priests was
dining on the sacrificial meat. My unceremonious entry upset
several of the dinner-dishes, tables and lamps as I collided
with them. The master was annoyed at this unsightly havoc
wreaked on his furniture. He put me in the close charge of one
of his servants, regarding me as an ill-mannered, licentious
beast, and ordered him to confine me in some securely barred
place to ensure that I could not disrupt their peaceful feasting
with similarly wanton behaviour a second time. Having
cleverly protected myself by this smart trick so that I was
delivered from the clutches of the butcher, I was delighted at
being confined in a prison which guaranteed my safety. But
the truth is that if Fortune is hostile, nothing can turn out
auspiciously for any person alive. The economy of divine
providence is foreordained, and cannot be undermined or
changed by any wise plan or sage remedy. So that very
stratagem which seemed to have gained me safety for the time
being, now unleashed a further great hazard—indeed, it spelt
instant destruction.

2 Suddenly a slave burst into the dining-room as the guests
chatted amiably. His face was contorted with fear as he
reported to his master that a mad bitch had just burst in from

the nearest lane through the rear gate with incredible violence. She had attacked the hunting-hounds with the most flaming fury, and had then made for the stable close by and assaulted several of the pack-animals equally savagely. To crown all, she had not left even the men unscathed: Myrtilus the muleteer, Hephaestio the cook, Hypnophilus the chamberlain, Apollonius the physician, and indeed several other members of the household had all been mangled and bitten in various places as they tried to fend the animal off. A number of the pack-animals had been affected by her poisonous bites and were turning rabid like the dog.

This news at once struck the diners with dismay, for they thought that I was likewise infected and out of control. They seized any weapons that came to hand, and encouraged each other to ward off such a destructive menace to the community. So they came after me, though they rather than I myself were in the grip of that diseased madness. They would undoubtedly have butchered me limb from limb with the lances or hunting-spears and with the double-edged axes which the servants had urgently provided, but I got wind of this sudden storm of danger, and at once burst into the sleeping-quarters allotted to my owners as their lodging. They then closed and barred the doors behind me and blockaded the place, intending to wait until I was dead after being gripped and consumed by the tenacious fury of the deadly plague. This turn of events had at last liberated me, and I welcomed the boon of my isolation. I threw myself on a made-up bed, and enjoyed what I had lacked for many a day, the sleep of a human being.

3   My weariness was dispelled by the soft bed, and it was broad daylight when I arose fully refreshed. The men had remained awake all night keeping watch on me, and I could hear them exchanging views such as these about my condition: 'Are we to believe that the poor ass is still violently possessed by continuing madness?' 'No, he must be quite dead, now that the savage effect of the poison has intensified.' They suspended these differing opinions by exploring the situation. When they put their eyes to a crack in the door, they saw me standing at my ease, sound and self-possessed. So then they seized the

initiative and opened the doors to investigate more fully whether I was now docile. One of them proved to be my heaven-sent redeemer; he pointed out to the rest that the way of proving my sound health would be to offer me a full dish of fresh water to drink. If I drank the water without concern in the normal way, they would know that I was healthy and free of all disease. On the other hand, if on sighting and tasting the water I showed revulsion and sought to avoid it, they would realize that the baneful madness still persisted. This, he said, was the usual diagnostic technique, also recommended in ancient books.

4   The suggestion met with their approval, and a large vessel of clear water was hastily fetched from a nearby stream. With continuing hesitation they set it before me. I did not linger in advancing to meet them; I bent to it quite thirstily, plunged in my entire head, and proceeded to drain the water which was truly my salvation. I then endured with equanimity the clapping of their hands, the twisting of my ears, the tugging at my muzzle, and such other tests as they sought to apply until I could clearly give proof to them all of my controlled behaviour, which was the polar opposite of their lunatic assumptions.

In this way I had avoided a double danger. Next day I was again burdened with the temple-spoils, and led on to the road with the rattles and cymbals to form a peripatetic begging-outfit. After we had wandered round to several cottages and hill-villages, we halted at a hamlet which according to the residents' account was built among the tumbling relics of a once wealthy city. We were accommodated at the nearest inn, and there we heard a witty story which I should like you too to hear. It concerns the cuckolding of an indigent man.

5   This fellow lived a hard life in grinding poverty. What little pay he obtained to keep body and soul together was gained by performing manual work. He had a slip of a wife who was likewise poverty-stricken, but she had a bad name for being extremely promiscuous. One day, after her husband had left early for a job which he had undertaken, her barefaced lover at once crept stealthily into her lodging. He and the wife were

quite untroubled as they practised love's wrestling-holds. But then the husband, blissfully ignorant and entertaining no suspicions of his wife's conduct even at that stage of their marriage, unexpectedly returned to the house. Finding the entrance already closed and barred, he thought highly of his wife's chaste behaviour. He hammered on the door and whistled to announce his arrival. Then that clever woman, who was quite resourceful in such unsavoury circumstances, freed the lover from her close embraces, and craftily hid him in a corn-jar lying half-buried in a corner, with nothing else in it. Then she opened the door, and greeted her husband as he entered by speaking to him sharply.

'Is this how I find you,' she asked, 'strolling about idly at leisure? Why are you not attending to your usual work to ensure our livelihood and to make provision for our daily bread? Here am I, working desperately night and day, spinning wool till my arms ache, to see that our hovel has a lamp to light it if nothing more. How much happier my neighbour Daphne is! There she is, roistering with her lovers, flushed with wine and food from early morning!'

6   This rattled her husband. 'Whatever do you mean?' he asked. 'It's true that our foreman has a lawsuit on his hands and has given us the day off, but I've still made provision for our supper today. Just take a look at that corn-jar. It's for ever empty, occupying all that space to no purpose. The only contribution it makes is to get in the way of our daily round. I have sold it to a buyer for six denarii, and he is on the point of stumping up for it and taking it with him as his property. So why not buckle to and lend me a hand to dig it out and pass it over at once to the buyer?'

That guileful woman improvised, and with a shameless guffaw replied: 'What a splendid husband, what a keen man of business I have here! I'm merely a house-bound woman, but I've already sold for seven denarii what he has disposed of for less!' The husband was delighted at this raised bid. 'Who', he asked, 'has offered so much for it?' She answered: 'You silly man, he has already climbed down into the jar to take a good look and ensure that it is in good shape.'

7   The lover, duly prompted by the woman's words, emerged smartly. 'Do you want the candid truth, ma'am?' he asked. 'This jar of yours is very old. It's been knocked about and has gaping cracks in several places.' He then turned to her husband, pretending not to know who he was. 'I don't know you, little man,' he said, 'but why don't you look sharp and hand me a lamp? Then, when I've scraped off the dirt inside, I can take a careful look at the jar to see if it is serviceable. Or do you think that my money grows on fruit-trees?' That sharp-witted, admirable husband, as gullible as ever, lit a lamp without delay, and said: 'Step out, brother; stand here and relax till I clean it out properly, and then I'll show it to you.' As he spoke, he stripped off, took the lamp down inside, and began to scrape the long-standing grime from the mouldering jar.

Then that handsome lover-boy the adulterer laid the workman's wife face down over the jar, bent over her, and screwed her without fear of interruption. Meanwhile she thrust her hand into the jar, and with the wit of a lady of easy virtue made a fool of her husband. With her finger she pointed out various places that needed cleaning, until the job was completed both above and below. She took the seven denarii, while the hapless workman had to put the jar on his shoulders and carry it to the adulterer's lodging.

8   Those priests, veritable models of chastity, lingered in that place for a few days, growing fat on the citizens' generosity, and stuffing themselves with the abundant profits from their prophecies. There they devised a novel source of gain. They composed one oracular response to cover a number of situations, and in this way made fools of several people who consulted them on diverse matters. This was the response:

> Why do the harnessed oxen cleave the field?
> To make the seeds a luxuriant harvest yield.

Then, if questioned by people who happened to be arranging a marriage, their answer was that this response accorded with their situation: the couple should be 'harnessed' for marriage and for begetting the 'seeds' of children. If a potential buyer of property made enquiry of them, the reply was that 'oxen', 'harnessing', and flourishing fields of seedlings were being aptly prophesied for them. If a person was troubled about departing on a journey and consulted the divine auspices, the priests claimed that the most docile of all four-footed beasts were now 'harnessed' and standing ready, and that gain was being promised him by the 'yield' from the 'field'. If a man about to engage in battle or to pursue a gang of robbers enquired whether his foray would be successful, they would claim that the efficacious prophecy made his victory secure, for the necks of the enemy would be 'harnessed' beneath the yoke, and most abundant and 'luxuriant' profit would be forthcoming from depredations from the foe. By such crafty, guileful prophecy they had raked in quite a sum of money.

9 However, the non-stop enquiries they received made them weary, and they grew tired of offering explanations. So they took to the road again. The journey was considerably worse than the night-long travelling which we had earlier completed, for the road was deeply pitted with steep ruts, awash with stagnant marsh-water in some places, and in others slippery with foul mud. The result was that my legs were bruised through numerous collisions and constant tumbles before I succeeded finally in emerging on to level paths in an exhausted state.

But suddenly a band of horsemen descended on us from the rear. With great difficulty they halted the mad gallop of their horses. Then they set about Philebus and the rest of his comrades with a will. They grabbed them by the throat, called them impious and obscene, and from time to time gave them a good pummelling with their fists. They then hand-cuffed them all, and in menacing tones repeatedly demanded that they produce without delay a golden goblet which was the ill-gotten gain of the crime which they had committed. They claimed that the priests had furtively abstracted it from the very shrine of the Mother of the Gods, under the pretence of performing solemn ceremonies conducted in secret; and that then before it was broad daylight they had quitted the city-limits, blithely imagining that they could evade punish-

ment for such a monstrous crime by their stealthy departure.
10   One of them did not fail to lay his hand on my back, and
after groping around in the very bosom of the goddess whom I
was carrying, he uncovered and extracted the golden goblet
before the eyes of all. But those most depraved creatures were
not to be confounded or abashed even when confronted with
their most impious crime. Instead they indulged in forced
laughter and joking, saying: 'What harsh, unworthy treatment we are getting! So often innocent people find their heads
in a noose! To think that for the sake of one mere cup, which
the Mother of the Gods bestowed on her sister the Syrian
goddess as a guest-present, we ministers of religion are being
tried for our lives as if we were criminals!' But this and
similarly stupid blusterings were of no avail, for the villagers
escorted them back, and at once tied them up and locked
them in the local Bridewell. The goblet and indeed the statue
which I had been carrying were deposited in the temple-
treasury, and consecrated there.

Next day they brought me out, and the auctioneer
announced that I was for sale once more. A baker from a
neighbouring hill-town purchased me for seven sesterces more
than Philebus had earlier paid for me. He also bought some
corn, and at once loaded me up with it in heavy quantity. He
then led me up a steep path, which sharp stones and assorted
brushwood made hazardous to negotiate, to the mill which he
used for grinding the corn.

11   In the mill there were several pack-animals turning
millstones of varying dimensions by repeatedly circling them.
They worked not only during the day but also throughout the
night, sleeplessly producing flour by incessant rotation of the
machinery. My new master, however, doubtless fearing that
I would baulk at my first apprenticeship to slavery, made
generous provision for me; he gave me a holiday on that first
day, and filled my manger to the brim with fodder. But that
blessed period of leisure and abundant food did not extend
longer, for early next day I was appointed to what seemed the
largest of the millstones. I was blindfolded, and at once
pushed on the curving course of the circular track, so that I

was to retrace my steps over the identical path within the orbit of the circumscribed limits, and thus go a-wandering but without deviating. But I had not so far forgotten my native wit and wisdom as to lend myself readily to this apprenticeship to the trade. Though in my earlier life among men I had often watched millstones being rotated in this way, I stood rooted to the spot in feigned astonishment, as if I were without experience and knowledge of their working. My thinking was that I would be regarded as unsuitable and quite useless for duties of this kind, and would at worst be deputed to some lighter labour, or even left to forage at leisure. But the cunning which I deployed was vain and damaging. Several men armed with sticks at once surrounded me; being blindfolded I was still unsuspecting. Suddenly, at a given signal and with concerted shouts they rained a shower of blows on me, and the din they made so confused me that I abandoned my entire tactic, and at once showed the greatest skill in applying my whole weight to the rope round my neck, and in making the rounds with alacrity.

12   This sudden improvement in my attitude roused the whole crowd of workmen to laughter. Once the greater part of the day was over (by then I was reduced to exhaustion), they unhooked me from the grinding-machine, removed the horse-collar from my neck, and set me in front of the manger. Though I was extremely tired, urgently in need of restoring my strength and on the point of collapse through hunger, my habitual curiosity and my considerable apprehension kept me rooted there. So I deferred my meal of abundant fodder, and took some pleasure in observing how this unprepossessing bakery was run.

Great heavens, what poor specimens of humanity the men were! Their entire bodies formed a pattern of livid bruises. Their backs, which bore the marks of the whip, were not so much covered as shaded by torn shirts of patchwork cloth. Some wore nothing except a thin covering over their private parts; all were clad in such a fashion that their bodies were visible through the rags they wore. They had letters branded on their foreheads, half-shaved heads, and chains round their ankles. Their faces were a ghastly yellow, and their eyes had contracted in the smoke-filled gloom of that steaming, dank atmosphere, making them half-blind. They resembled boxers who coat themselves with dust when they fight, for their bodies were a dirty white from the oven-baked flour.

13   As for my fellow-beasts, what can I say, what words can I use to describe those superannuated mules and enfeebled geldings surrounding the manger with their heads bent low as they munched the piled-up straw? Their necks, pockmarked with running sores, were twitching; their limp nostrils gaped wide from constant bouts of coughing; their chests were a mass of raw patches from the continual rubbing of their rope-harnesses; their flanks were exposed to the bone from constant beatings; their hooves were distended and misshapen through their incessant circling of the millstones; their entire skins were coarse with age and scurvy emaciation.

Such were the members of the baker's establishment, and I feared that I too would be emulating their grisly example. As I recalled the happy state of the Lucius of old, now reduced to a most precarious level of existence, I dropped my head in depression. Nowhere at hand was there any consolation for my pain-wracked existence, except that my innate curiosity did something to restore me, for no one took any account of my presence; they all did and said whatever they liked without inhibitions. That godlike creator of ancient poetry among the Greeks, when seeking to depict a man of the greatest circumspection, was justified in singing of him who had attained the highest virtues by visiting many cities and gaining acquaintance with various peoples. Indeed, I myself now gratefully recall my existence as an ass, for when I was concealed in the ass's covering and was tried by varying fortunes, I gained a knowledge of many things, though admittedly I was less wise.

14   From that experience I have decided to let you in on an outstandingly good and attractively elegant story, on which I now embark.

The baker who had bought me was in all respects a decent and quite sober fellow, but the luck of the draw had given him the most evil wife, easily the worst woman in the world. So he had to endure the most excruciating torments affecting his bed and his home. I swear that even I constantly grieved in silence for his lot. There was not a single vice which that most despicable woman did not possess; every conceivable wickedness had accumulated in her mind as in some filthy cesspool. She was crabbed and crotchety, libidinous and bibulous, obdurate and obstinate. Her greed was evident in her base thieving, her prodigality in her unsightly extravagance. She was a foe to fidelity, and made war on chastity. In addition, she despised and ground beneath her heel the powers of heaven; instead of adhering to a sure faith, she sacrilegiously feigned bold awareness of a deity whom she proclaimed to be the only God. By devising empty ceremonies she misled the people at large, and deceived her hapless husband by devoting herself to early-morning drinking and day-long debauchery.

15   This was the nature of the woman, and the rancour with which she victimized me was amazing. Even before daylight, while she still lay in bed, she would loudly order the novice-ass to be harnessed to the mill-wheel. As soon as she quitted her bedroom, she would insistently designate me for repeated whipping before her eyes. When the other pack-animals were turned loose to enjoy their meal at the proper time, on her instruction I was allowed access to the manger only much later. This harsh treatment had greatly intensified my native curiosity about her behaviour. I divined that a young man was visiting her chamber with some regularity, and I was extremely keen to set eyes on his face, if only the covering over my head allowed my eyes a glimpse of him at some moment, for I would have had sufficient wit one way or another to expose the immoral activities of that most disgusting female.

There was an old woman who attended her in her sexual escapades and acted as go-between in her extra-marital affairs. All day and every day she was her inseparable companion. First thing at breakfast, and then as they poured out undiluted wine for each other, the old hag and her mistress would launch preliminary attacks and devise deceitful plots with cunning intrigues to achieve the undoing of the wretched husband. Though I was utterly furious with Photis for the error she made in changing me into an ass when intending to turn me into a bird, I was nevertheless heartened by one consolation at least in my hideous deformity: I was endowed with massive ears, and even at a distance I could very easily overhear all that was going on.

16   So it was that one day my ears caught these words of that audacious old hag: 'Mistress, you must yourself come to a decision about this lazy, fear-ridden boyfriend whom you acquired without my approval. He shrinks like a coward from the wrinkled frown of that boorish and loathsome husband of yours, and because of this he frustrates your eager embraces through a lack of urgency in his limp love-making. How much better is the young Philesitherus! He is handsome, generous, energetic; he never rests in challenging the precautions which husbands vainly take. I swear that he is the only man who deserves to enjoy the favours of every married woman. He alone merits a golden crown on his head, if for no other reason than that of late he showed outstanding resource in cuckolding a jealous husband. Listen to this, and then contrast the differing temperaments of the two lovers.

17   'You know, I think, a man called Barbarus, one of our town-councillors, the man they call Scorpion because of his needling ways? His wife comes of a good family and is outstandingly beautiful. He has taken the most stringent measures to confine her in his house under elaborate supervision.' The baker's wife answered this last query. 'Of course,' she said. 'I know them well. You are speaking of my friend Arete. I was at school with her.' 'Well, then,' said the hag, 'do you know the full story about her and Philesitherus?' 'I haven't heard a word of it,' replied her mistress. 'I'm most eager to know about it, so please, mother, reveal all the details in order.' So without delay that garrulous old gossip began her tale.

'This man Barbarus was preparing to go on a journey he had to make, and was anxious to ensure his dear wife's chaste behaviour by taking the most careful precautions. So he gave secret instructions to his confidential slave Myrmex, who was a byword for his outstanding loyalty, and entrusted him with the entire supervision of his mistress. He threatened to clap the slave in irons and imprison him for life, and finally said he would have him put to death violently and shamefully, if any man so much as touched Arete with his finger in passing. He backed this threat with an oath sworn by all the gods in heaven. He accordingly set out on his journey with his mind at rest, leaving Myrmex at home neurotic and frantic with anxiety as he shadowed the wife with the utmost vigilance.

'Myrmex was on tenterhooks, his attention riveted on his task. He refused to allow his mistress to go out anywhere, and when she busied herself spinning wool at home, he would sit close by her, refusing to leave her side. Equally when she had to go out late in the day to take her bath, he would stick close to her, clutching the hem of her cloak. So he performed his duty and maintained the trust reposed in him with exemplary prudence.

18   'But the dazzling beauty of that married lady could not be kept hidden from the eager and watchful eye of Philesitherus. The very challenge of her reputation for chastity, and of the excessive and extraordinary precautions taken to guard her, acted as a spur and kindled his excitement. He was ready to perform or to endure anything, and he harnessed all his powers to overcome the strict routine of the household. He was convinced of the frailty of human loyalties, believing that all obstacles could be surmounted by money, and that even doors of adamant are often breached by gold. He seized the opportunity of finding Myrmex alone, confided his love-feelings to him, and imploringly sought from him the remedy for his harsh pain. He claimed that unless he gained the object of his desire with all speed, he was resolved and ready to embrace imminent death. The meeting could easily be arranged, so Myrmex should have no fears; for when evening fell, he could rely on the darkness and creep in alone, heavily cloaked and muffled, and be away again in no time. After pressing these and other similarly persuasive arguments, he finally inserted a solid wedge to prise violently open the extremely stiff resistance mounted by the slave. He extended

his hand and showed him some spanking new gleaming gold pieces; twenty of them he would like Myrmex to pass on to the girl, and ten he was delighted to offer to Myrmex himself.

19   'Myrmex bridled at this unprecedentedly shameful proposal. He put his fingers to his ears and bolted. Yet the glowing gleam of gold was ever before his eyes. Though he put a distance between himself and Philesitherus, and winged his way homeward at full speed, he could still visualize those beautiful, gleaming coins, and in his mind he already possessed that rich haul. The poor slave had the strange sensation of tossing mentally on a sea of troubles, his thoughts tearing him apart; he was pulled one way and dragged the other towards opposing resolutions. Loyalty lay on one side, profit on the other; torture lay with the one, and gratification with the other. In the end gold prevailed over fear of death. His longing for the lovely lucre did not diminish with time; baneful greed preoccupied him even in the night-hours, with the result that though his master's threats confined him to the house, the gold summoned him outside. Finally he swallowed his shame and brooked no further delay, and accordingly he presented the suitor's proposal to the ears of his mistress.

'The lady was fickle by nature. She followed her inclinations, and at once put her chastity at the service of the accursed metal. Myrmex was overjoyed, and rushed off to the man who had subverted his loyalty, eager not only to obtain but merely to handle the money, the sight of which had caused his downfall. In a paroxysm of joy he informed Philesitherus that his own great exertions had brought the suitor's longings to fruition, and he at once demanded the promised reward. Myrmex clutched the golden currency with a hand which had never known the feel even of copper.

20   'When the night was well advanced, he led that lively lover unaccompanied to the house, and escorted him with head well covered to his mistress's bedroom. With unfamiliar embraces they were just seeking favourable omens for their untried love, and as naked combatants were embarking on their first campaign under Venus, when to the general surprise the husband unexpectedly appeared at the gate of his house; he

had exploited the cover of darkness to arrive unobserved. He banged and shouted and battered the doors with a stone. The delay in answering made him suspicious, and he threatened Myrmex with dire punishment. The slave was panic-stricken at this unexpected reverse; in his craven fear he felt utterly resourceless, and the only excuse which he could offer was that the darkness of night was hindering him from finding the key which he had carefully hidden away. Meanwhile Philesitherus had heard the commotion, and hastily put on his shirt, but in the confusion he raced from the bedroom without his slippers. Finally, Myrmex inserted the key in the lock and opened the door to his master who was still calling the gods to witness. While Barbarus rushed to the bedroom, the slave sent Philesitherus hastily and stealthily on his way, and felt reassured once he was safely beyond the threshold. He locked up the house, and returned to bed.

21   'But when dawn broke and Barbarus was leaving the bedroom, he noticed the unfamiliar slippers under the bed; Philesitherus had been wearing them when he crept in. The material evidence made Barbarus suspect what had occurred, but he did not reveal to his wife or to any of his household the resentment he felt. He removed the slippers and stealthily hid them under his clothes. He brusquely ordered Myrmex to be put in chains by his fellow-slaves, and dragged to the forum. He then made his way swiftly there, grumbling repeatedly under his breath. He was sure that the evidence of the slippers could easily put him on the track of the adulterer. With face livid and eyebrows furiously raised, he strode angrily along the street. Behind him followed Myrmex, burdened with chains; though his guilt had not been clearly established, he was having a bad attack of conscience, and was weeping and howling desperately in a vain attempt to elicit pity. Suddenly at this vital moment Philesitherus confronted them. Though he was pursuing some other business, this sudden sight gave him pause. But he was not apprehensive. He recalled the gaffe which he had made in his hurried exit, and inferring all that had happened thereafter, his brain at once summoned all its habitual resourcefulness. He brushed the slaves aside, and

made for Myrmex, shouting at the top of his voice. He rained his fists on the slave's cheeks, but pulled his punches as he cried: "You dissolute, lying blackguard! I only pray that your master here, and all the powers of heaven which you have been summoning with rash oaths, may bring you to a sticky end as your evil character deserves! You stole my slippers from me yesterday at the baths. By God, you thoroughly deserve to keep those chains about you till they wear out, and to endure the darkness of a dungeon as well."

'Barbarus was taken in by the timely trick of that forceful young man; indeed, as his spirits rose, he was lulled into gullibility. So when he got back home, he summoned Myrmex, forgave him with his whole heart, handed over the slippers, and advised him to return them to their owner from whom he had stolen them.'

22   The old woman had got as far as this in her prattling when her mistress interrupted: 'She's a lucky lady to enjoy the uninhibited approaches of such a determined companion! Just think of poor me; the friend I've met up with jumps even at the noise of the mill, and at the sight of that scurvy ass over there.' The old woman replied: 'I'll soon win that eager lover over completely, and strengthen his resolve; I'll have him here for you, true to his pledge.' She then promised also to return in the evening, and hurried out of the chamber. That chaste wife at once prepared a meal fit for a Salian priest, decanted a vintage wine, and seasoned fresh meat with sausages. Finally, when the table was groaning with food, she awaited the adulterer's coming as if he were some god. Luckily for her, her husband was dining out at the house of the laundryman near by.

As the day was now reaching its close, I was at last freed from my collar, and restored to the relaxation of the manger. But to tell the truth, I was thankful not so much for this relief from toil as for the uncovering of my eyes, which enabled me to watch all the manœuvres of that criminal woman without hindrance. By now the sun had glided down beneath the ocean, and was giving light to the regions of the world below the earth. At this moment that rash adulterer arrived, cleaving to the side of that most depraved old hag. He was still a mere boy; his cheeks shone smooth and bright, and he was himself still a source of pleasure to male lovers. The woman welcomed him with a flood of kisses, and bade him recline at the board laid before him.

23   But just as the young man was raising his preliminary glass of wine and his first mouthful of food to his lips, the husband approached, returning much earlier than expected. That model wife uttered savage curses against him, praying that he might break both his legs. The lover turned pale, and trembled with fright. A wooden tub chanced to be lying upended there; its usual purpose was for holding sifted flour. She pushed him out of sight under it. Then with her native guile she affected innocence of her base behaviour, and assumed an untroubled countenance. She asked her husband whatever was the reason for his leaving his closest friend's dining-table and returning home at that early hour. He was depressed, and sighed repeatedly. 'I just could not bear the disgraceful, outrageous behaviour of that wicked wife of his, so I cleared off. Ye gods! A married woman like her, so trustworthy and sober, and yet she has blackened her reputation with a most unholy scandal. I swear by holy Ceres here that even now I can scarcely believe my eyes when I consider the sort of woman she is.'

That most shameless woman's interest was roused by these words of her husband, and in her eagerness to know what had happened, she kept loudly demanding that he reveal the entire story from the beginning. She did not stop pressing him until her husband complied with her wish, and recounted the disgrace attending the household of another, all unaware of the situation in his own.

24   'My friend the laundryman has a wife who has always seemed a highly moral woman, priding herself on her good reputation and managing her husband's domestic affairs with due modesty. But then she threw herself into the arms of some adulterer, for whom she conceived a secret passion. She has often been meeting him for stealthy embraces, and at the very time when the two of us were arriving from the baths for dinner, she was having it off with that same young fellow. So

our arrival caused her sudden panic, and she had to improvise a plan. She hid him in the bottom of a wicker cage; it was built upright with wooden slats intertwined, and clothes were hanging round it to be bleached with the white sulphur fumes coming from the cage. Since she thought that he was now quite safely hidden there, she stopped worrying, and joined us at table. But meanwhile the young man was being choked and enveloped by that most acrid and oppressive smell of sulphur. He couldn't get his breath, and began to feel dizzy, and the natural effect of the powerful sulphur was to make him sneeze repeatedly.

25   'The first time the husband heard a sneeze coming from behind his wife's back, he thought it came from her, and he uttered the conventional "Bless you" over her. The same thing happened again, and was repeated several times until he was alerted by the excessive sneezing and finally tumbled to the truth. He at once shifted the table, lifted off the cage, and dragged out the young fellow, who was gasping repeatedly and could scarcely breathe. The laundryman was seething with anger at the dishonour done to him; he called for his sword, and gave every sign that he would have killed the youth by slitting his throat, if I had not given thought to the danger which we both faced, and with difficulty restrained him from launching a wild attack. I maintained that this enemy of his would shortly die from the severe effects of the sulphur alone, without our incurring responsibility for his death. The laundryman cooled down, not at my persuasion but through the force of circumstances, for the adulterer was now barely alive. He dragged him out into the nearest alley. I then exercised some quiet persuasion with the wife, and finally induced her to go away for a little while and to lodge in the meantime with some female friend away from the shop, until in due course her husband's blazing anger had subsided. He was so inflamed and furious that he undoubtedly planned to inflict some more damaging harm on his wife and himself. So I have come back home; revulsion drove me from my friend's table.'

26   As the baker recounted these details, the woman with her

long history of wantonness and shamelessness kept cursing the laundryman's wife, uttering oaths of condemnation; she called her disloyal, shameless, and in short a disgrace to her entire sex for having banished her modesty, ground beneath her heel the contract of the marriage-bed, and begrimed her husband's home with the notoriety of the brothel. She said that the woman had dispensed with the worthy role of wife, and won for herself the title of prostitute; such women should be burnt alive.

But she herself was mindful of her own secret vulnerability and sullied conscience; and so that she could more speedily free her adulterer from his cramped position in his hiding-place, she repeatedly urged her husband to retire to bed earlier than usual. But since his abrupt departure had interfered with his dinner and he was extremely hungry, in courteous tones he demanded a dinner at home instead. The woman hastily if unwillingly placed before him the food which she had intended for another.

As I reflected on this dreadful woman's earlier misbehaviour and her present persistence in it, I was seething inwardly, and pondered carefully within myself whether I could somehow uncover and expose her deceit, and render help to my master by kicking away the cover and revealing to the eyes of all the lover who was crouching under the tub like a tortoise.

27   In the end divine Providence looked kindly on my anguished concern for the insult dealt to my master. All the beasts of burden had been put in the charge of a lame old man, who began to herd us to the nearest pool to drink, as the hour of day now prescribed. This routine provided me with the opportunity for which I had devoutly prayed, for as I passed the tub I noticed the tips of the adulterer's fingers protruding through a narrow opening in his hollow cover. With a fierce sideways thrust of my hoof I stamped on them until they were thoroughly squashed, and the unbearable pain finally forced him to raise a tearful shout. He pushed the bin off him, and cast it aside; being thus restored to the gaze of the uninitiated, he revealed the character of that infamous woman.

The baker, however, was not greatly concerned at his wife's loss of her chastity. To calm the boy, who had turned deathly pale and was trembling, he assumed a benevolent and kindly look as he began to talk to him. 'Have no fear, son, of any grim retribution from me. I am no barbarian with unsightly, rustic manners; I shall not finish you off with deadly sulphur-fumes, like the vindictive laundryman. I shall not invoke the rigour of the law, and indict you on a capital charge of adulterous behaviour, for you are such a charming and beautiful wee boy; instead, I shall share you with my wife. I shall not contest ownership so as to partition our estate, but rather seek to divide you between us, so that without any argument or dispute the three of us may agree to share the one bed. I have always lived in such harmony with my wife that following the guidance of the philosophers, our tastes are identical. But equity does not permit a wife to exercise more authority than a husband.'

28   With caressing words like these he led the way to bed. The boy followed, though reluctantly. While that most chaste of wives was locked in another room, the baker had the boy to himself in bed, where he enjoyed the sweetest possible revenge for the damage done to his marriage. But as soon as the sun's bright wheel ushered in the day, he summoned two of his strongest slaves, and when they had hoisted the boy high, he beat his buttocks with a rod, and questioned him: 'What? Do you, still a boy so soft and tender, seek to deprive lovers of the bloom of your youth, and instead make free-born women your target? Do you pollute lawfully joined marriages, and at your early age claim the title of adulterer?'

Following these and other rebukes, and after giving him a good hiding as well, he kicked him out of the house. So that stoutest of all adulterers unexpectedly got away in one piece, but his swift departure was painful because those white buttocks of his got a pounding both during the night and by day. The baker punished his wife too; he gave her notice of separation, and at once drove her out of his house.

29   That lady's natural propensity for wickedness was reinforced by deeper anger at this contemptuous treatment,

however much she deserved it. In her annoyance, she reverted to her old tricks, and was fired to have recourse to practices naturally favoured by women. She took great pains to seek out an old woman who was believed able to achieve any purpose by spells and witchcraft. She implored her with many prayers, and showered her with numerous gifts, as she sought one or other of two requests: either that her husband relent and she be reconciled to him, or if the witch could not achieve this, that he should meet a violent end through the agency of a spectre or some dread power. Then the witch, who was endowed with supernatural faculties, made a preliminary assault, as yet deploying only the rudimentary weapons of her art; by these she tried to divert the deeply resentful spirit of the husband, and to direct him towards feelings of love. But when this attempt on him turned out differently from her expectation, she grew irritated with the divine powers which she had invoked. She was goaded by the scorn which the baker displayed, as well as by the profitable reward promised, so she began to threaten the very life of that most wretched husband, to bring about his death by rousing the ghost of a woman slain by violence.

30   But perhaps, diligent reader, you will censure my version of events with an argument of this kind; how could you, clever ass though you were, ascertain as you claim what these women were secretly hatching, when you were enclosed within the confines of the bakery? Listen, then, and I will explain to you how this inquisitive fellow disguised as a beast discovered all that was done to achieve the destruction of my master the baker.

Suddenly about noon a woman made her appearance in the bakery. She was dishevelled as if she were on trial and deeply distressed. Her body was only half-covered by a pitiable patchwork garment; her feet were bare and unshod; her unsightly complexion was drawn, and pale as boxwood; her greying hair was disordered, blackened by ashes sprinkled over it and hanging low to cover most of her face. In this guise she laid her hand gently on the baker, and led him off to his bedroom as if she wished to converse with him in private. She closed the door, and remained there for a considerable time. But by now the workmen had finished grinding all the grain which they had been handling, and they needed to obtain a fresh supply. The favoured slaves on duty outside the bedroom called to their master, and asked for a fresh supply to grind, but when he made no response to their loud and repeated shouts, they began to hammer harder on the door. The fact that it was so securely barred made them suspect that something was very seriously wrong, so they bent back or broke off the hinges by powerful thrusts of their shoulders, and finally forced their way in. The woman was nowhere to be found, and they saw their master strung up on a beam, hanging there already dead. They freed him from the noose round his neck, and lowered his body. They then tended it with the final washing, brutally beating their breasts and keening loudly; once these rites to the dead were completed, they accompanied the hearse in large numbers, and consigned him to the grave.

31   Next day his daughter came running from the nearest hill-village, where she had resided for some time following her marriage. In her grief she tugged at her unbound hair, and repeatedly beat her breasts with her fists. Though no member of the household had told her of the tragedy, she had learnt all that had happened. The sorrowing image of her father had appeared to her in sleep, his neck still encircled with the noose, and had revealed to her all the details of her stepmother's criminal behaviour—the adultery, the witch-craft, and his descent to the realm of the dead when constrained by the ghost. After the daughter had abused her person with lengthy demonstrations of grief, she was finally checked by the concerted action of the household, and suspended her mourning. On the ninth day after death, the formal ritual at the tomb was duly completed, and as heiress she then sold by auction the household slaves, the furniture, and all the beasts. Thus unbridled Fortune, operating through the uncertainties of an auction, distributed the possessions of one household into various hands. So it happened that I was purchased for fifty sesterces by a poor

and insignificant market-gardener. As he remarked, the price was high, but he intended to make a living by making me share his labours with him.

32   The situation seems to demand of me an explanation of the routine of this new form of my slavery. My master was accustomed to load me up early in the morning with a consignment of vegetables, and to drive me to the nearest town; when he had delivered the produce to those who bought it, he would return to the allotment riding on my back. While he was bent over the servile tasks of digging, watering, and his other jobs, I restored my strength with untroubled rest. But now the stars were advancing on their ordered paths, and the year on its returning journey through the allotted days and months had bent its course beyond the pleasant autumn harvest towards the wintry frosts of Capricorn. During this time of unceasing rain and dew-laden nights, I was housed in an unroofed stall beneath the open sky, and was in agony with the constant cold; for my master was extremely poor, and could not buy a blanket or thin coverlet for himself, let alone for me. He resigned himself to lodging within the leafy enclosure of his tiny hut. Moreover, when in the early morning I stepped out with no shoes on my feet, and trod on extremely cold mud and on sharp patches of ice, I suffered torment. I could not fill my belly even with the usual fodder, for my master and I ate equal amounts of similar food, which was far from filling. It consisted of mouldering, bitter lettuces which had gone to seed so long ago that they looked like brooms, and because they were long past their best, they had a rotting and bitter taste, exuding a muddy juice.

33   One night an estate-owner from a neighbouring village was finding it hard to find his way through the darkness of a black, moonless night, and he was drenched with heavy rain. So he was prevented from journeying straight home, and turned aside into our modest allotment, for his horse was now exhausted. He was welcomed in friendly fashion as the circumstances demanded, and though the refreshment was Spartan rather than luxurious, he was anxious to repay the generosity of his host. So he promised to give him from his

lands some grain and olive-oil, and two casks of wine as well. My master promptly mounted my bare back, taking with him a sack and some empty wineskins, and embarked on a journey of about seven miles. On completing this distance, we reached the estate I mentioned, where the genial host at once allowed my master to share a handsome meal.

As they chatted with each other and passed the winecups to and fro, a quite astonishing portent occurred. One of the flock of hens came running through the middle of the yard, cackling with the characteristic squawk which indicated her eagerness to lay an egg. Her master eyed her, and said: 'What a good, productive servant you are! For quite a time now you have laid an egg every day to fatten us up, and I see that it is your intention to provide our first course today as well.' Then he turned to a slave. 'Come on, boy,' he said, 'put the basket in which the hens lay their eggs in its usual corner.' But when the slave had seen to this as ordered, the hen ignored the usual bed for laying, and deposited its load before the very feet of the master. The egg was premature, and to be the cause of the greatest anxiety, for she did not lay it in the form familiar to us. It was a fully grown chicken, with feathers, claws, eyes; it was even cheeping, and at once began to shadow its mother.

34   But a similar, much more sinister portent then appeared, such as would rightly cause any person to shudder. Under the very table which bore the remains of the supper, the earth yawned open, and from its depths gushed a towering fountain of blood. Great showers of drops flew out from it, and spattered the table with gore. Then, at the very moment when the company was stupefied with astonishment and terror at these warnings from heaven, a servant came running from the wine-cellar to report that the wine, which had earlier been apportioned out after fermenting, was bubbling up again with boiling heat in all the casks, exactly as if a roaring fire had been lit beneath them. In the meantime a weasel was also seen dragging a dead snake in its mouth out into the open, and a green frog leapt out of the mouth of a sheepdog. Then that very dog was attacked by a ram close by, and had its throat

severed by a single bite. All these portents, and others like them, caused the master and his whole household the greatest consternation, and totally paralysed their minds. They could not decide what to do first and what next, with what number and what kind of sacrificial victims to seek to conciliate the heavenly powers.

35   In this stupor as they awaited some grisly and fearful outcome, a young slave came rushing in, and reported to the estate-owner calamities so great that they could not have been worse. This master boasted three grown-up sons, all well educated and endowed with modest manners. They had long been friendly with a poor man living in a small cottage. Now this tiny residence abutted upon a huge, rich estate owned by a powerful neighbour. He was a rich young man of illustrious descent, who however exploited for evil purposes the fame of his ancestors. He had a powerful band of dependants, and was able to do in the community whatever he wished. He kept treating his needy neighbour like an enemy, launching attacks on his humble property by slaughtering his cattle, driving off his oxen, and trampling down his crops when they were still ripening. Having by then stripped him of all his modest possessions, he was attempting even to force him off his poor holding. He raised a groundless suit over boundaries, and claimed for himself the other's entire property. The peasant was in general an inoffensive person, but now that he had been stripped bare by the greed of this rich neighbour, he sought to keep his ancestral soil if only for his own grave. So with considerable apprehension he invited a large gathering of friends so that they could witness the demarcation of the boundaries. Among the rest were the three brothers, anxious to afford such little help as they could to their friend in his grievous plight.

36   But that crazed estate-owner was not in the least frightened or even troubled by the presence of many citizens. He had not restrained his plunderings, and now he did not seek even to restrain his language. When those friends made gentle representations and sought to soften his hot temper with soothing words, he suddenly uttered a most solemn oath by

his own life and that of his dear ones: he swore that he regarded the presence of all those intermediaries as of trifling importance, and finally claimed that his slaves would hoist that neighbour of his up by the ears, and at once sling him out of the cottage into the furthest distance. These words induced impassioned anger to seize the hearts of all the listeners. Then one of the brothers made a prompt and somewhat franker response: it was no use the magnate's relying on his wealth and making threats with despotic arrogance, for even poor people were in general accustomed to enjoy protection from the haughty treatment of the rich through that defence of the laws accorded to free men.

These words fed the man's vile temper as oil feeds a flame, as sulphur feeds a fire, as a whip goads a Fury. His madness now advanced to the furthest pitch. He shouted that he bade them all be hanged, their laws as well, and then he commanded his sheepdogs to be released. These guardians of the estate were fierce and huge; they were in the habit of devouring carcases left lying in the fields, and were trained to bite passing travellers without discrimination. He ordered them to be set upon the peasant's supporters and egged on to kill them. No sooner were they roused and fired by the customary signal from the shepherds than they were goaded to ungovernable madness; their discordant barking inspired terror as they made for the men, inflicting all kinds of wounds as they tore and mauled them. Even those who bolted they did not spare, but pursued them all the more viciously.

37   In the course of this mêlée as the panicking crowd was being butchered, the youngest of the three brothers stubbed his toes and tripped over a rock. As he fell headlong to the ground, he provided a shameful feast for those savage and most fierce dogs, for they at once took possession of their prostrate prey, and tore the poor young fellow to pieces. When the other brothers heard his dying cries, they were appalled, and rushed to rescue him. They covered their left arms with their cloaks, and sought to defend their brother and to drive off the dogs by showering them with stones. But they could neither wear down nor overcome their ferocity, with the result

that the most wretched youth was mangled and died on the spot. The last words which he uttered were a plea that they should exact revenge from that most depraved man of wealth for the death of their younger brother.

Then I swear that the surviving brothers did not so much abandon hope of their safety as totally disregard it. They made a rush at the rich proprietor, and blazing with anger they assaulted him wildly, pelting him with a shower of stones. Though covered in blood, he was experienced in the role of assassin from many such despicable deeds in the past. He hurled his spear and pierced one of the pair clean through the breast. Though he was mortally wounded with no breath of life left in him, the young man did not sink to the ground; as the spear passed right through him, the greater part of it emerged through his back, and the force of the impact made it stick in the earth, so that it kept his body upright, stiff and in balance. Meanwhile one of the rich man's slaves, a tall, strong individual, came to the aid of his murderous master. He fired a stone at long range, aiming at the right arm of the third youth, but without success; to the general surprise the stone fell harmlessly by, merely grazing the tips of his fingers.

38   That happier outcome gave the most resourceful youth some slight hope of revenge. He pretended that his hand was disabled, and he cried to that most cruel young proprietor: 'Enjoy, then, the destruction of our entire family, feed your insatiable cruelty on the blood of three brothers, celebrate a splendid triumph over your fellow-citizens stretched out here. But realize that though you deprive this poor man of his possessions, and extend your boundaries without limit, you will none the less have to live with a neighbour. As for this right hand of mine, which would gladly have severed your head, it too hangs useless, shattered by the malevolence of fate.'

That crazed thief was already provoked, but these words drove him wild. He grabbed his sword and eagerly advanced to slaughter with his own hand that most unhappy youth. But the man he challenged was no more of a coward than himself. Quite contrary to the aggressor's anticipation, the young man put up unexpected resistance. He seized the other's right arm in a terrier-like grip, raised his weapon high, and with great force struck the rich man repeatedly until he squeezed the wicked life out of him. Then, to escape the violence of the slaves who rushed on him, he at once boldly cut his own throat with the dagger which was still dripping with the enemy's blood.

These were the events foreshadowed by those portentous prodigies and reported to that most wretched master. Encompassed by all these disasters, the old man could not utter a word, or even shed a silent tear. He seized the knife with which he had just divided the cheese and the other dishes of the meal among his guests, and following the example of his most unfortunate son he too slashed his throat repeatedly, until he slumped with bent head over the table, and with a stream of fresh blood washed away the stains left by the gore of that earlier portent.

39   The market-gardener expressed his sorrow for this extremely sudden collapse of the family's prosperity, and also bitterly lamented his own misfortunes. Having paid for his meal with his tears, and repeatedly wrung empty hands, he at once mounted me, and made his way back on the road by which we had come. But even that return journey proved disastrous for him, for a tall fellow accosted us. His uniform and his behaviour showed that he was a legionary soldier. In a haughty, supercilious voice he demanded to know where the gardener was taking the unladen ass. My master was still distracted with grief, and in any case did not understand Latin, so he tried to pass without replying. The soldier could not control his habitual arrogance; he angrily interpreted the other's silence as an insult, struck him with the vine-staff that he carried, and knocked him off my back. The gardener then grovellingly replied that through ignorance of the language he could not understand what the centurion was saying. So the soldier questioned him in Greek: 'Where are you taking this ass of yours?' The gardener replied that he was making for the nearest town. 'Well, I need this beast's help,' said the soldier. 'He must take his place with the other beasts, and transport

the baggage of my commanding officer from that fortress near by.'

Then he at once laid hands on me, seized the halter with which I was led, and began to drag me off. The gardener wiped his head clean of the blood which poured from the wound caused by the previous blow, and spoke submissively a second time. He pleaded with that comrade-in-arms to behave more courteously and temperately, and swore that such behaviour would crown his hopes with success. 'In any case,' he added, 'this ass is a lazy beast, and he bites as well; and then he has a nasty malady that makes him tumble, so that he can barely carry a few handfuls of vegetables from my allotment near by. He gets tired, and his breath is laboured, so still less would he be able to cope with carrying heavier loads.'

40   But he then realized that the soldier, impervious to all his pleas, was even more determined to put an end to his life, for he had now turned the vine-rod round, intending to split the gardener's head with the knob at the thicker end. So my master had recourse to hasty measures of defence. He pretended that he was trying to grasp his opponent's knees to arouse his pity, so he bent low in suppliant fashion. But he then seized both his feet, raised him high, and brought him down heavily to earth. He then proceeded to assault his entire face, hands and ribs with his fists, elbows, teeth, and a stone which he grabbed from the road. From the moment that he lay prostrate on the ground the centurion could not fight back or offer any resistance. He had to content himself with repeated threats that if he got back on his feet, he would cut him into little pieces with his sword. The gardener took note of his words, snatched the sword from him, threw it as far away as he could, and resumed the attack on him with still fiercer blows. The soldier was flat on his back, and hindered by his wounds; he could devise no means of ensuring his survival, so he took the only course available to him, and pretended to be dead.

The gardener then took the sword with him, mounted my back, and headed directly for the town. Without even a thought of visiting his allotment, he went to lodge with a close friend of his, to whom he told the whole story. He begged this friend's help in his hour of danger, asking that he should conceal his ass and himself long enough for him to keep out of sight for two or three days, and thus escape indictment on a capital charge. His host was not unmindful of their long-standing friendship, and readily took us in. My feet were roped together, and I was dragged upstairs into the attic. The gardener stayed in the shop downstairs, where he crept into a chest and hid there, with the lid closed over his head.

41   I later learnt that after some time the soldier arrived in town looking as if he were the worse for a heavy bout of drinking. He was tottering along, incapacitated by the pain of his many wounds, and just managing to support himself on his staff. He was too embarrassed to say a word to any of the townsfolk about his sluggish inability to defend himself, but he silently nursed his grievance, and when he encountered some fellow-soldiers he divulged to them his unhappy experience. They agreed that he should lie low for a time in his quarters, for apart from the indignity which he had suffered, the loss of his sword made him fear the implications of his oath as a soldier. Meanwhile they said that now that they had obtained particulars of how to identify us, they would take pains to seek us out and exact revenge.

Inevitably there was a traitorous neighbour to lay information that we were hidden in that place. The soldiers then sent for the magistrates. They falsely claimed that on the road they had lost a very valuable silver vessel belonging to their commanding officer, that a gardener had found it and refused to give it back, and that he was holed up in the house of a friend of his. The magistrates, on hearing of this loss and its association with the commander's name, came to the door of the lodging where we were staying. They loudly ordered our host to surrender us—for, they said, it was beyond dispute that he was concealing us—or else face the danger of a capital indictment. But in his zeal for the safety of his friend whom he had promised to help, he was not in the least deterred. He laid no information about us, and maintained that he had not even set eyes on the gardener for several days. The soldiers swore

oaths to the contrary by the emperor's life-spirit, claiming
that he was hiding there and in no other place. The
magistrates eventually decided to put the man's resolute
denial to the test by mounting a search. So they sent in lictors
and other state-officials, and ordered them to give the whole
premises a rigorous examination, probing one corner after
another. They reported back that there was no sign of any
man or indeed of the ass within the threshold of the dwelling.

42   A more contentious argument then broke out on both sides.
The soldiers kept calling on Caesar to witness that their
assertions about us were well grounded, while the home-
owner denied the charge, and supported his stance by
repeated oaths invoking the majesty of the gods. This
argument conducted with noisy altercations reached my ears,
and being a naturally inquisitive ass imbued with restless
impulses, I craned my neck and tried to peer out through the
small window to see what all the noise was about. It so
chanced that one of the soldiers caught a glimpse of my
shadow, and called all of them to witness it on the spot. At
once a great hubbub arose. Some of them immediately
mounted the stairs, laid their hands on me, and dragged me
down as though I were under arrest. All their doubts were
now banished, and they searched in every nook and cranny.
On opening the chest, they found the wretched gardener.
They hauled him out and consigned him to the magistrates;
then they escorted him to the city gaol, where he was
doubtless to suffer execution. They could not stop laughing
and joking at my peering out; this is the origin of the much-
quoted proverb about the peeping ass and its shadow.

BOOK 10

Tales of Wicked Women: Pleasant Life with the Cooks Leads to Public Humiliation

1 I have no knowledge of what befell my master the gardener next day. But the soldier, who had endured at his hands such a gratifying beating for his excessive aggression, unharnessed me and led me out of the stable without encountering any opposition. He then loaded me with his luggage from what I assumed were his quarters, and led me out on the road, duly adorned and equipped in military fashion, for I carried a helmet which gleamed brightly, a shield which glittered still further afield, and also a lance with a notably long shaft. He had carefully set these on top of his high-piled baggage as though he were serving with the army on campaign; not, I imagine, because this conformed with battle-orders at the time, but in order to terrorize wretched travellers. Once we had made a fairly easy journey through the plain, we reached a small town where we lodged at the house of a town-councillor rather than at an inn. The soldier at once put me in charge of a slave, and dutifully left to report to his superior, who commanded a thousand armed troops.

2 It was there a few days later, as I recall, that a wicked and appalling crime was committed. I record it in this book so that you can read of it as well.

The master of the house had a son, whose good education had made him a model of filial devotion and decent behaviour; he was the kind of son you would have wished to have for yourself. His mother had died many years before, and his father had married again. By this second wife he had another son who had just celebrated his twelfth birthday. This stepmother became dominant in her husband's house through her beauty rather than her good character. Because she was either libidinous by nature or was drawn to the most heinous wickedness as the victim of fate, she cast her eyes on her stepson. You should know, gentle reader, that you are now to read a tragedy and no mere anecdote; you are to rise from the comic sock to the tragic buskin.

As long as the love which that woman nurtured was in its first stages and undeveloped, she was able to suppress her slight blushes, and to resist in silence Cupid's as yet mild onset. But once her whole heart was filled with the fire of madness, that love grew wild and boiled up out of control, so that she now caved in before the god's fierce onslaught. She made a pretence of illness, falsely claiming that her heart's wound was a physical malady. We all know that sick people and lovers suffer precisely the same impairment of health and appearance; they are alike hideously pale, their eyes droop, their knees are unsteady, their sleep is disturbed, and their sighs grow stronger as the torture lingers on. You might have thought that the storm-tossed symptoms of this lady too were the effect merely of the heat of fever, except that she kept weeping as well. Alas, how ignorant are the minds of physicians! What do throbbings of the veins denote, or changes of colour, or laboured breathing, or frequent tossing and turning from one side to the other? Great heavens, how easy it is to diagnose! You need not be a practising physician as long as you have experience of love's longings, when you observe someone who is not running a temperature yet is all aflame.

3   So it was that in her inability to contain her madness, the wound struck deeper. So she broke her long silence, and ordered that her son be summoned to her presence. She would gladly have expunged that title of son had she been able, so as not to be reminded of her shame. The young man did not defer his obedience to his sick parent's command. He made for her chamber with a brow puckered with an old man's concern, for this was an obedience which in a sense he owed to his father's wife and his brother's mother. She, however, was exhausted by the tortured silence which she had endured for so long; she was, so to say, aground on the shallows of doubt, so that every greeting which she thought apt for conversation at that moment she would in turn dismiss. Even now, as her

sense of shame faded, she was hesitant about how best to begin. The young man for his part even at that moment had no suspicion that anything was amiss; with modest demeanour and without prompting he asked her the causes of her present illness. She then seized the baneful chance of their being alone together to become reckless. She burst into floods of tears, covered her face with the hem of her robe, and addressed a few words to him in a trembling voice.

'You yourself are the entire cause and source of my present suffering, but you are also the remedy and my sole chance of salvation. Those eyes of yours have inveigled themselves through my own eyes into the depths of my heart, and are kindling in my marrow the keenest of flames. So have pity on me, because I am wasting away because of you. Do not let reverence for your father hold you back in any way, for you will be the very means of keeping alive his wife now on the point of death. It is because I see his likeness in your face that my love for you is fitting. You can rest fully assured that we are by ourselves; you have sufficient leisure to perform what you must do. The deed that goes unseen is as if it's never been.'

4   The youth was thrown into confusion by this sudden, outrageous proposal. But though he felt immediate abhorrence at such evil behaviour, he thought it best not to make things worse by a harsh and untimely repudiation, but rather to soften the blow and put her off with a guarded promise. This he accordingly wrapped in many words. He vehemently urged her to be of good heart, and to devote herself to the recovery of her health until some journey of his father granted them free scope for their pleasure. He then at once retired from his stepmother's sight which he found abhorrent. He reflected that this great calamity to his house needed further counsel, so he at once referred the matter to his aged tutor, a man of acknowledged sobriety. The outcome of their lengthy discussion was that the safest course seemed to lie in avoiding raging Fortune's storm by precipitate flight.

But the woman could not endure even slight delay. With remarkable cunning she at once invented some pretext to induce her husband to make an immediate and pressing journey to widely scattered estates. Thereupon her mad hope, which had now reached its height, impelled her boldly to demand the lustful encounter which the youth had pledged. But by pleading various pretexts he avoided the sight of her which he had come to abhor. Finally, the variety of excuses which he sent made her realize clearly that he was reneging on his promise to her, and with inconstant fickleness she translated her impious love into a hatred far more impious. She at once took aboard a favourite slave who had accompanied her as part of her dowry. He was a most wicked fellow, free of all scruples in performing any crime. She shared with him her treacherous designs; the course which seemed best to them was to rob the wretched youth of his life. So the scoundrel was at once dispatched to obtain poison taking instant effect, which he carefully diluted with wine to encompass the death of that blameless stepson.

5   While the guilty pair were conferring about the apt moment for offering him the poisoned drink, it chanced that the younger boy, that most debased woman's own son, arrived home after a morning devoted to his studies. After eating his lunch, he felt thirsty, and when he came upon the glass of wine in which the poison lurked, he at once drained it in his ignorance of the secret conspiracy. No sooner had he drunk the deadly draught prepared for his brother than he fell lifeless to the ground. The boy's escort was devastated by this sudden collapse of the boy, and at once with cries of distress summoned the mother and the whole household. Once the poisoned drink was identified as the cause of the misfortune, those present variously assigned the responsibility for the outrageous crime. But that cruel woman, whose vindictiveness as a stepmother was beyond compare, remained untroubled by the bitter death of her son, by guilt at the murder of her kin, by the disaster to the family, by the grief of her husband, or by the harrowing funeral rites. Instead she exploited the disaster of the household to gain revenge. She at once sent a runner to report to her husband on his journey the disaster which had befallen his house; then, when he returned

from his journey with all speed, she put on the boldest of faces, and pretended that her son had been cut off by poison administered by her stepson. In a sense this was not a lie, since the boy had pre-empted the death intended for the young man. But the fiction she told was that the younger brother had been wickedly murdered by her stepson because she had refused to yield to the immoral lust in which he had tried to have his way with her. Even this monstrous lying did not satisfy her, for she added that he had also threatened her with his sword for exposing his evil deed.

That unhappy father was then devastated by the double death of his two sons, and was bitterly storm-tossed on a sea of troubles. He had to watch his younger son being buried before his eyes, and was totally convinced that the other would be condemned on charges of incest and murder of kin. To crown all, the feigned mourning of the wife he loved so much was driving him to utter hatred of his own child.

6   The funeral procession and burial of his son had scarcely been completed when straight from his funeral-pyre the old man burst frantically into the market-place. He was still staining his cheeks with fresh tears, and tugging at his grey hairs, now grimy with ashes. In ignorance of that wicked woman's deceit, with tears and prayers—even grasping the knees of the city-councillors—he there indulged the full gamut of his emotions to encompass the destruction of his remaining son. He claimed that the youth had committed incest in his father's chamber, that he was a murderer of kin by causing a brother's death, and that in threatening the murder of his stepmother he was an assassin. In his grief the father had roused the council and the common folk to such feelings of pity and anger that they sought to waive the tedium of a formal trial with its clear proofs provided by the prosecution and its studied evasions offered by the defence. Instead they all loudly demanded that this public scandal be publicly punished and buried under a hail of stones.

The magistrates meanwhile were apprehensive of danger to themselves, in case from these small evidences of indignation, disaffection should develop into the collapse of public order.

So in part by pleas to the councillors and in part by restraining the common folk, they sought to have judgment duly done in the traditional manner, with the claims of both sides scrutinized before proclamation of the sentence, in accord with the civil law. No person, they said, should be condemned unheard, as happened among savage barbarians or in an arbitrary tyranny; so grim a precedent should not be bequeathed to posterity in time of peace.

7   This healthy advice prevailed, and the herald as instructed immediately announced that the councillors should assemble in the council-chamber. They at once took their usual places according to the order of precedence. On a further proclamation from the herald the prosecuting counsel entered first; finally the defendant too was summoned and escorted in. Following the procedures of Attic law observed on the Areopagus, the herald forbade the advocates in the case either to utter preambles or to arouse pity.

That this was the procedure I gathered from overhearing several conversations, but since I was in my manger away from the scene, I cannot know of or report to you the pressing arguments of the prosecutor, or the points on which the defendant sought acquittal—in short, the speeches and exchanges. What I did discover for certain I shall record in writing here.

Once the opposing statements of the speakers were concluded, it was decided to establish the truth and reliability of the charges by definite proofs rather than to allow inferences in so important a case to rest on suspicions. Above all, it was necessary at all costs to put in the witness-box the slave who alone was said to know that events had occurred as claimed. That gallows-bird was not a whit disconcerted by the uncertain outcome of such an important case, or by the sight of the crowded chamber, or even by personal feelings of guilt. He began to claim and proclaim as truth the story which he had invented: that the youth in anger at being rejected by his stepmother had summoned him; that in seeking to avenge that slight, he had bidden the slave kill her son; that he had promised a huge reward for his silence; that he had threatened him with death if he refused; that the youth had mixed the poison with his own hand, and had then given it to the slave to administer to his brother; that he then suspected that the slave had withheld the cup as proof of the crime, and had not played his part; and that in the end the youth had administered it to the boy with his own hand. Once the rascal had recounted all this without the slightest apprehension as though it were the gospel truth, the case was concluded.

8   Not one councillor had remained so fair-minded towards the young man as not to find him clearly guilty and to condemn him to be sewn in the sack. All their pens alike inscribed the one word 'guilty', and following the invariable custom, their identical votes were about to be consigned to the bronze urn. Once the voting-pebbles had been lodged there, and the affair (and the defendant's fate) was decided, nothing could be subsequently changed, for power over his life passed into the hands of the executioner. But then one of the councillors, a physician whose known honesty and outstanding authority excelled that of the rest, covered the mouth of the urn with his hand to prevent anyone idly dropping in his pebble. Then he addressed these words to the council:

'My happy boast is that my past life has met with your approval, and I refuse to countenance what would be a clear case of murder, since the defendant has been arraigned on false charges. You are under oath as you pass judgment, and I will not let you perjure yourselves through being deceived by the lies of a cheap slave. Nor can I trample underfoot my own obligation to the gods by beguiling my conscience and pronouncing a wrong sentence. So learn from me the facts of the case.

9   'Not long ago this gallows-bird made an approach to me. He was anxious to procure some swift-acting poison, and offered me a hundred gold pieces for it. He said that it was required for a sick person who was in the painful throes of a wasting and incurable disease, and was eager to withdraw himself from the torture of a continuing existence. I saw through the wicked scoundrel as he blustered and offered his implausible explanation. I was convinced that he was plotting

some crime, yet I did give him a potion. Yes, I gave him a potion, but I did not there and then accept the price which he offered, for I was guarding against a future enquiry. I said to him: "In the event that any of these gold pieces which you offer me turns out to be counterfeit or not one hundred per cent gold, kindly put them in this wallet, and seal them up with your ring. Then tomorrow they can be verified in the presence of a dealer." This pretext persuaded him to put his seal on the bag of money. When he was brought before the court, I at once ordered one of my servants to pick up the bag from my shop and to bring it here at the double. See, it has been brought here, and I now display it to you. The slave can examine it and identify his seal. So how can the brother be accused of procuring this poison when the slave purchased it?'

10 The scoundrel was then gripped by violent trembling, and his natural complexion turned deathly pale. A cold sweat seeped over all his limbs. Then he began to shift uncertainly from one foot to the other. First he scratched the front of his head, and then the back; with his mouth half-closed he stammered and muttered such ridiculous nonsense that not a single person could reasonably regard him as innocent. But then his native cunning reasserted itself, and with great insistence he kept denying the truth of the physician's account, and accused him of lying. When the physician realized that not only the sanctity of the law but also his own honesty was being openly damaged, he redoubled his efforts and strove to rebut the scoundrel, until on the magistrate's instructions the city-officials seized the hands of that vilest of slaves, pulled off his iron ring, and compared it with the seal on the wallet. They matched, and this confirmed earlier suspicions. The wheel and rack were then wielded in the Greek manner to torture the slave, but he remained steadfast with remarkable obstinacy, and yielded neither to blows nor even to fire.

11 Then the physician exclaimed 'By heaven, I will certainly not allow you to exact punishment from this innocent youth, for it would be impious. Nor will I permit this slave to make sport of our legal processes, and escape punishment for this

criminal outrage. I shall offer you clear proof of the actual
facts. When this blackguard was eager to procure this deadly
poison, I did not regard it as appropriate to my profession to
provide anyone with the means of death, for my apprenticeship had taught me that the purpose of medicine was to
restore people to health. However, I feared that if I refused to
give it to him, my untimely rejection would minister to his
crime, for he would purchase the deadly potion from some
other person, or in the final extremity perform the impious
deed with a sword or some other weapon. So I gave him
mandragora, which is a mere soporific; the drug is well known
for its reliable knock-out effect, for it induces sleep almost
indistinguishable from death. It is hardly surprising that this
scoundrel, in his utter desperation and awareness of the final
punishment which ancestral custom has appointed for him,
should readily endure these tortures which are light by
comparison. But if the boy did indeed drink the potion mixed
by my hands, he is still alive. He is peacefully sleeping, and as
soon as he has shaken off his torpid sleep, he will return to the
bright light of day. But if he has been killed, or if death has
overtaken him, you can investigate other causes of his
demise.'

12   Following the old man's speech delivered on these lines, it
was decided to investigate. They made their way to the tomb
at once with great urgency, where the boy's body had been
laid. There was no city-councillor, no member of the ruling
class, no individual even from the common folk whose
curiosity did not impel him to flock there. Then the father
removed the lid of the coffin with his own hands. Just then his
son shook off the deadly sleep, and rose from the realms of the
dead. His father hugged him close; the joy of the moment
deprived him of speech. He led the boy out before the people's
eyes; still tightly bound and wrapped in his funeral garments,
he was brought to the courtroom. So now the crimes of that
most villainous slave and that still more villainous woman
were out in the open; the bare truth was visible for all to see.
The stepmother was condemned to exile for life, and the slave
was hoisted on the gallows. By general accord the gold pieces

were awarded to the good apothecary as a reward for that timely soporific. As for the aged father, the celebrated and famed stresses of Fortune ended in a manner worthy of the divine Providence that shaped them; in a short period of time, in fact in one brief moment, he suddenly became the father of two grown sons, after enduring the perils of childlessness.

13　　I myself at that time was adrift on the waves of my destined fate. The soldier had procured me and laid claim to me without payment, for no one had sold me to him. But now in due obedience to the command of his commanding officer, he was to convey a letter written to the great emperor at Rome. So he sold me for eleven denarii to two brothers in the locality who were slaves, and whose master was quite rich. One of them was a confectioner who baked bread and honey-buns, and the other a cook, who would braise the meat until it was tender, and spice it with especially tasty sauces. The brothers lived together, sharing a common lodging. Their purpose in buying me had been to have me carry the numerous vessels necessary for the various needs of their master as he travelled over different regions. So I was adopted as a third lodger accompanying the two brothers, and at no time did I find Fortune so accommodating; for in the evening, after luscious dinners had been served on most exquisite dishes, my masters would bring back numerous left-overs to their modest abode. One of them would carry the sizeable remains of pork, chicken, fish, and all sorts of meat, while the other brought bread, cakes, pastries, tarts, biscuits, and several other honeyed sweetmeats. Once they had locked up their lodging and departed to the baths to freshen themselves up, I used to stuff myself to repletion on these god-given feasts, for I was not such a fool or complete ass as to dine on prickly hay and leave all that delicious food untouched.

14　　For quite a time I got away handsomely with my crafty pilfering, for up to that point my thieving was cautious and quite modest. I contented myself with rather few delicacies from so many, and the brothers had no suspicion that an ass was playing tricks on them. But then my confidence at being unobserved grew greater. I began to dispose of all the choicest left-overs, and to select and lick clean the more luscious sweets. Nagging suspicion pricked the minds of the brothers, but even at that stage they did not suspect me of such behaviour, but began systematically to seek out the person guilty of these daily thefts. In the end they even started to blame each other for this disgraceful thieving. They took more diligent note, instituted closer watch, and kept careful count of the left-overs. Finally, one of them threw restraint to the winds and accosted the other.

'It is unfair and indeed uncivilized of you to steal the choicer left-overs every day, to sell them secretly to increase your savings, and then to demand an equal division of what is left. So if our joint association is not to your liking, we can continue to live as brothers in all other ways, but abandon this link by which we share and share alike; for I see that the cause of my complaint is subjecting me to heavy losses and is engendering considerable antipathy between us.' The other interjected. 'Heavens, I like this brazen cheek of yours! Every day you have been quietly stealing the left-overs, and now you have got your grumble in before mine, which all this time I have been nursing and bemoaning in secret so as not to appear to accuse my own brother of mean thieving. But it is good that we have both spoken out, and that we are seeking a means of stemming our losses, for if this silent resentment between us continued, it would result in the strife that befell Eteocles.'

15   Having exchanged these and similar rebukes, they both swore that they were wholly guiltless of any deceit or pilfering, and agreed that they must use every means of detecting the thief who was causing their joint loss. They assured each other that the ass in the lodging by himself could not be attracted to such foodstuffs, yet every day the choicest morsels were nowhere to be found. Nor was it possible that their room was being invaded by monster flies like those Harpies of old which used to plunder the banquets of Phineus.

Meanwhile I was feasting on this generous fare, and waxing fat on this abundance of human food. My body had now filled out to a generous plumpness, my hide had become juicily soft and greasy, and my coat was well nourished, with a handsome sheen. However, my enhanced physical beauty was the cause of a signal blot on my reputation. The brothers' interest was aroused by my enlarged frame, for they noted that the hay remained wholly untouched day by day. So they concentrated their attention wholly on me. They pretended to depart to the baths at the normal hour, and as usual closed the doors behind them. But then they spied on me through a tiny hole, and saw me tucking into the feast which was spread around. They no longer worried about the losses they were sustaining; they were astonished at the portentous spectacle of an ass as gourmet, and they split their sides with uncontrollable laughter. They summoned a fellow-slave, and then a second, and then several more, and let them observe the indescribable gluttony of the slow-witted ass. In the end they were all overcome by such loud and unrestrained laughter that it reached the ears of their master as well, as he was passing by.

16   He then asked what was so funny as to rouse the laughter of the household, and when he was told the reason, he also took a look through the same crack and was extremely diverted. He too began to laugh so loudly that he got the belly-ache. He then opened the door, stood beside me, and watched me openly. Now that at last I was finding Fortune's face smiling more benevolently on me, my confidence was boosted by the pleasure I was giving to the present company. So with total unconcern I continued happily eating. Eventually the master of the house was so pleased by this unusual sight that he ordered me to be led—in fact, he guided me with his own hands—to his dining-room. There he ordered the table to be laid, and every variety of freshly-prepared foodstuffs and untouched dishes to be set before me. I had already had an elegant sufficiency, but I wished to ingratiate myself and make myself more acceptable to him, so I attacked the food placed before me as if I were famished. They gave detailed thought to the food which would be particularly repugnant to an ass, and then set this before me to test my docility. There were meats spread with silphium, fowl sprinkled with pepper,

and fish swimming in some foreign sauce. Meanwhile the dining-room reverberated with the loudest laughter.

Then some wit present said: 'Give this dining-guest of ours a drop of wine.' The master responded to this witticism: 'That joke of yours, you scallywag, is not such a mad idea. It's quite possible that our fellow-guest will be glad to take a cup of sweet wine as well. Hey, boy, take this gold beaker, and wash it well. Then mix in some wine and honey, and offer it to this self-invited guest of mine. Tell him too that I've already drunk his health.' The guests were roused to intense expectation. I was not in the least perturbed; with a leisurely and quite good-humoured gesture, I screwed the edges of my lips into a ladle-shape, and drained the large cup at a single gulp. A din broke out as they all bade me good health.

17   The master of the house was so overjoyed that he summoned his slaves who had bought me, and gave instructions to pay them the purchase-price four times over. Then he put me in the care of a freedman of his, of whom he greatly approved and who had a fair sum of money tucked away, and instructed him to look after me carefully. The freedman fed me up in a quite civilized and friendly fashion, and to win the greater esteem of his patron, he took great pains to divert him with the tricks which I had performed. First he taught me to recline at table, leaning on my elbow, and then to wrestle and also to dance with my forefeet off the ground; and most wonderful of all, to respond to words with a sign, for I would indicate refusal by tossing back my head, and acceptance by a nod. If I was thirsty, I would demand a drink by turning to the wine-steward and winking with each eye successively. All these promptings I obeyed with the greatest ease; in fact I could have performed them without instruction, but I was afraid that if I did a number of tricks without coaching as if I were human, they might think that this presaged something sinister, slaughter me as a monstrous prodigy, and throw me as rich fare to the vultures.

By now the story had circulated widely, and my marvellous tricks had brought my master fame and renown. 'That's the man', people would say of him, 'who keeps an ass as a companion and guest at table. The creature wrestles, and dances, and understands human language, and indicates its feelings by motions of the head.'

18   I must first tell you—in fact I should have mentioned it at the outset, but I'll do it now—who the man was, and where he came from. My master's name was Thiasus, and his native city was Corinth, the capital of the entire province of Achaea. His ancestry and social rank had entitled him to rise step by step up the ladder of offices, and he was now in line for the quinquennial magistracy. To show that he was worthy of receiving these badges of office, he extended his generosity more widely, with the promise of a gladiatorial show affording a three-day spectacle. In his eagerness for public fame, he had at that time even visited Thessaly to obtain there the most notable beasts and gladiators of renown, and now that he had made all his arrangements and purchases to his satisfaction, he was preparing to return home. He rejected his gleaming coaches and relegated his handsome four-wheelers, some of which were covered and some open; they were drawn along unoccupied at the rear of his column. He also disdained the Thessalian horses and his other Gallic beasts, though their noble stock attaches high monetary value to them. Instead, he decked me out with gold trappings, purple housings, crimson covers, silver bridle, embroidered belt and tinkling bells; then he mounted me, and from time to time would address me with most affectionate words. Among several other remarks, he claimed that he was absolutely charmed at having in me both a dinner-companion and a means of transportation.

19   After completing our journey, partly by land and partly by water, we reached Corinth, where great crowds of citizens gathered. My impression was that they were not so much anxious to honour Thiasus as to take a good look at me; for there too I had become so celebrated that I was a source of considerable profit to the man in charge of me. When he realized that so many were eager and extremely enthusiastic to view my tricks, he locked the door and let them in one at a time. By charging admission, he routinely raked in quite a bit each day.

Among the crowd that gathered was a married lady of position and wealth. Like the rest, she paid to watch me, and as a result was diverted by my various tricks. Gradually constant admiration developed into a strange longing for my person. She could devise no remedy for her insane lust; she burningly desired my embraces like some asinine Pasiphaë. The outcome was that she bargained with the keeper, offering a large sum for the right to sleep with me for a single night. The keeper was not in the least concerned whether I could be the source of any pleasure to her. He was merely concerned with his own profit, so he agreed.

20 When we had finished dinner and had retired from the master's dining-room, we found the married lady already in attendance; she had been waiting in my room for some time. Heavens, what splendid preparations she had made! Four eunuchs were busily laying a bed for us on the ground, with pillows bulging with soft feathers making an airy base. Over these they carefully spread coverlets of gold braid adorned with Tyrian purple, and on top they laid other pillows; these were quite tiny, but there were several of them, the kind that refined women usually rest their chins and necks on. They did not postpone the pleasures of their mistress by lingering long, but closed the doors of the chamber and made off. Within, candles gleamed brightly, and illumined for us the darkness of the night.

21 The lady then stripped herself stark naked, removing even the band which confined her lovely breasts. She stood close to the light, and from a pewter jar anointed herself with large quantities of, oil of balsam. She then rubbed generous measures of it with much more enthusiasm on me; she also applied frankincense to my nostrils. Then she kissed me hard—not the sort of kisses casually offered in the brothel, whether by harlots demanding money or customers refusing it, but those sincerely offered from the heart. She also addressed me most affectionately, with 'I love you', 'I want you', 'You are my only love', 'I can't live without you', and the other phrases with which women both rouse their partners and attest their own feelings. She then grabbed my halter, and

made me lie as I had learnt to do; it was readily done, for I envisaged nothing new or difficult in prospect, especially as I was to enjoy the embraces of so beautiful and passionate a woman, and this after so long a time. My zeal was enhanced by the fact that I had soused myself with a bellyful of the finest wine, and the perfume with its heady scent had roused in me a longing to copulate.

22   But I was sorely exercised and considerably fearful, wondering how I could mount such a fragile lady with my four hulking legs; how I could embrace such soft and shining limbs fashioned of milk and honey with my hard hooves; how I could kiss such small red lips steeped in the liquid of ambrosia with my huge mouth, which was so misshapen and ugly with its teeth like rocks; finally, how that woman could admit my massive penis, however much she yearned for it from the tips of her toes. I felt sorry for myself, for if I split that noble woman apart I should be thrown to the beasts and incidentally grace my master's show. Meanwhile she was repeatedly whispering gentle endearments, pressing constant kisses, and uttering rapturous sounds with devouring eyes; and as climax she murmured 'I have you, I have you, my fond dove, my sparrow.' As she spoke, she showed that my reservations were needless, and my fear unfounded; for she hugged me as closely as she could, and admitted me absolutely all the way. Whenever I withdrew my buttocks in an attempt to spare her, she would lunge madly towards me, seize my back, and cling to me in a still closer grip. Ye gods, I began to think that I had not the strength to satisfy her, and to believe that the mother of the Minotaur had succeeded in extracting pleasure from her lowing lover! After that sleepless night of activity, the woman shrank from being seen in daylight and retired, having agreed on the same fee for the next night.

23   My keeper was not reluctant to bestow these pleasures as the lady ordained, in part because of the large payment he was receiving, and partly to set up a new diversion for his master. Without delay he informed him of our sexual performance. The master rewarded his freedman lavishly,

and booked me in for his public show. But that worthy bed-mate of mine could not be hired because of her high rank, and no other lady could be induced to participate in spite of the considerable reward. So he obtained a woman of low repute who by decree of the governor had been condemned to be thrown to the beasts. She was to appear in company with me in the theatre before the people, and publicly demonstrate her chaste behaviour there. The story that I heard of how she merited this punishment was as follows.

This woman had a husband whose father was to travel abroad. On his departure he instructed his wife, who was carrying the burden of pregnancy and was the mother of the young husband, that if she gave birth to a child of the weaker sex, the baby was to be killed at once. But when a baby girl was born in the absence of her husband, she was induced by the innate love which mothers have for their offspring to disobey her husband. She gave the girl to neighbours to rear, and when her husband returned she told him that the baby was a girl and had been disposed of. But when the girl matured to her full womanhood, making it necessary that a date be set for her marriage, the mother could not bestow on her daughter the dowry appropriate to her birth without the knowledge of her husband. So she did the only possible thing. she revealed the hidden secret to her son, for she greatly feared that by some mischance he might succumb to the pressures of youthful ardour, and fall in love with his sister in the blissful ignorance which she shared. The young man was a model of family devotion; he scrupulously observed both obedience to his mother and his duty to his sister, and by hiding his motives behind an apparent display of common kindness, he discharged the duty demanded by the blood-relationship. He admitted the girl into the protection of his home as if she were a neighbour abandoned and orphaned of the support of her parents, and later he entrusted her in marriage to a very close and much loved friend, bestowing on her a dowry most generously from his own pocket.

24   However, these most suitable arrangements so religiously made could not escape Fortune's deadly intent, for at her

prompting, savage jealousy at once guided its course to the young man's house. For there and then this wife of his—she was the one now to be exposed to the beasts as a result of these events—first began to suspect this girl to be a rival for her bed, and her supplanter; and then her suspicion turned to hatred, and hatred thereafter led to her ambushing the girl in the most cruel of death-traps.

The foul deed which she eventually devised was this: she secretly commandeered her husband's ring, and set off to the country. She then dispatched a favourite slave, one faithful to her but deserving ill of the goddess Good Faith, to report to the girl that the young man had gone to his country house, and was summoning her to join him; she should come with all speed, he added, alone and unaccompanied. To ensure that the sister would not hesitate to come, she gave the slave the ring which she had secretly taken from her husband, and which when displayed would authenticate the message. The girl obeyed the instruction of her brother (this relationship with him was known to her alone), and having also identified the seal shown to her, she made lively haste, journeying alone as ordered. But once the girl had tumbled into the trap laid with such deep deceit, and was caught in the snare in which she had been ambushed, that worthy wife lost all control under the pricks of lustful fury. First she stripped her husband's sister naked, and gave her a severe whipping. Then, as the girl cried out the truth, that the wife's boiling rage at having a rival in love was unjustified, and repeatedly screamed that the young man was her brother, the wife assumed that her whole story was a tissue of lies, and she killed her most cruelly by thrusting a white-hot brand between her thighs.

25   Then the girl's brother and husband both hastened there, roused by the tidings of this cruel death. In their different ways they mourned and wept over the girl, and consigned her to burial. Her youthful brother could not endure with equanimity the wretched and wholly unjustified death of his sister. He was stricken to the heart with grief, and flushed with the baleful fury of the keenest resentment. In consequence he was fired with such fiercely flaming fever that he

now seemed to require medical treatment as well. His wife, who had long since forfeited the title as well as the loyalty of a wife, made an assignment with a physician whose lack of integrity was notorious; he was well known for the battles which he had fought, and the many palms of victory which he had won, for he could number many trophies as the work of his right hand. She at once promised him fifty thousand sesterces if he would sell her a quick-acting poison, so that she could procure her husband's death. When the bargain was struck between them, he made a pretence of dispensing the celebrated potion called by more learned people 'The Health-offering', a drug necessary for easing gastric pains and dissolving bile; but in its place he substituted another draught, 'The Proserpina-offering'. Then, in the presence of the household and of several friends and relatives, the physician handed the cup, carefully mixed with his own hand, to the sick man.

26   But that shameless woman now sought both to remove her associate in crime, and to recoup the money which she had promised him, so she placed a restraining hand openly on the cup. 'You are the best of physicians,' she said, 'but you must not offer this draught to my dearest husband until you yourself have taken a good drink of it, for how can I be sure that there is no harmful poison secreted in it? As a man of circumspection and learning, you above all can scarcely be offended if I, as a scrupulous wife concerned for my husband's health, show such necessary devotion to him.'

The physician, thrown into sudden turmoil by the un-expected and desperate boldness of this ruthless woman, was put totally out of his stride, and because of shortage of time was deprived of the leisure for a measured reply. So rather than incur suspicion of a guilty conscience by displaying any fear or hesitation, he took a good drink of that same potion. The young man was reassured by this, and he too took the cup and drank the proffered medicine. The physician, after concluding his immediate business in this way, made to return home with all speed, in his haste to counteract the harmful effect of the poison he had taken by means of a potion which would save his life. But that ruthless woman continued with the same impious determination with which she had begun, and refused to allow him to move an inch from her sight until, as she put it, the potion had been absorbed, and the effects of the medicine were patent. Finally, wearied with his numerous lengthy appeals and protestations, she reluctantly let him leave. Meanwhile that hidden and destructive poison was raging all through his internal organs, and had penetrated deep into his marrow. By this time he was grievously affected, and he reached home only with the greatest difficulty, plunged into a comatose stupor. He had just time to recount the entire circumstances to his wife, and to instruct her at least to demand the promised payment for the twin deaths, before that most responsible of physicians after violent convulsions yielded up his life.

27   The young man likewise failed to hold on to life, and met his death from the same mortal causes while his wife shed crocodile tears. Following his burial, and after the few days during which funeral services are offered to the dead had elapsed, the physician's wife arrived to demand payment for the two deaths. The woman continued true to her nature; she expunged the true face of honesty, but superimposed its outward appearance, and she answered the doctor's wife with soothing words. She promised everything lavishly and abundantly, and stated that she would pay the appointed price without delay if only the other agreed to give her a little of the potion to carry through the job which she had begun.

I need say no more. The physician's wife was trapped in the noose of this most wicked deceit, and she readily consented. To ingratiate herself still further with that woman of wealth, she hastened to collect the entire box of poison from her home, and gave it to her. The murderess had now obtained ample means of committing her crimes, and she extended her bloodstained hands far and wide.

28   She had a young daughter by the husband whom she had recently murdered, and she was intensely irritated by the fact that the laws bestowed the requisite right of inheritance upon this little girl. In her avid desire for the daughter's entire

patrimony, she began to threaten her life as well. In her awareness that unscrupulous mothers obtain inheritances when their children die, she showed herself to be the same sort of mother as she had proved a wife. She contrived a meal suited to the occasion, and with the same poison prostrated both the physician's wife and her own daughter. The baleful drug made short work of the little girl's soft and tender internal organs, and put an end to her frail life. But the physician's wife first began to suspect the truth when that abominable potion began to storm around her lungs on its destructive journey. Her suspicions were confirmed when her breathing became laboured, so she made straight for the governor's house. There with loud cries she invoked the good faith of the governor, and raised an outcry among the citizens, since she intended to expose such monstrous crimes. She at once succeeded in opening both the house and the ears of the governor to listen to her. Then, after carefully recounting from the very beginning all the heinous deeds of that most cruel woman, she was suddenly gripped by a dizziness that clouded her mind. Her lips which had been half-open she locked tightly together; a continued whistling sound was heard as her teeth clamped upon each other, and then she fell lifeless before the governor's very feet.

This governor was a man of experience, and he did not permit such manifold outrages committed by that venomous serpent to fester through passive delay. He at once had the woman's personal servants arrested, and by applying torture he extracted the truth from them. He then decreed that she be exposed to the wild beasts, a punishment less than she deserved, but no other fitting mode of torture could be devised.

29   This, then, was the woman with whom I was to be joined publicly in marriage. It was with great anguish and considerable anxiety that I awaited the day of the show. I repeatedly felt the urge to contrive my own death rather than be defiled by the contagion of that female criminal, and feel the ignominy of disgrace at a public show. But without the resource of a human hand or fingers, I was quite unable to

draw a sword with the round stump of my hoof. In this extreme calamity I sought consolation in one slight and extremely slender hope: spring now dawning was adorning all nature with blossoming buds, clothing the fields in bright crimson. Roses were bursting out from their thorny clothing, exuding a fragrance like cinnamon, and gleaming brightly. They could transform me back to the Lucius of old.

The day appointed for the show was now at hand. As I was led to the theatre, a crowd of people cheering in procession attended me. During the preliminaries of the show, devoted to mimic dances by performers on the stage, I was posted before the gate. There I found it pleasant to munch the luxuriant grass sprouting at the very entrance to the theatre. From time to time I refreshed my inquisitive eyes by gazing through the open gate at the highly pleasing spectacle afforded by the show. Boys and girls in the first flower of blossoming youth were embarking on the Greek Pyrrhic dance. They looked strikingly beautiful in their gleaming garments as they made their expressive entry. They were marshalled in lines, and moved round beautifully in their circling steps. At one moment they would glide sinuously round to form a circle, at another they would link with each other in slanting column; next they would wedge themselves into a hollow square, and then open out into separate groups. But when the closing note of the trumpet brought their complex manoeuvres to an end as they danced to and fro, the curtain was raised, the backcloths were folded away, and the stage was set.

30   A mountain of wood had been constructed with consummate workmanship to represent the famous mountain which the poet Homer in his song called Mount Ida. It was planted with thickets and live trees, and from its summit it disgorged river-water from a flowing fountain installed by the craftsman's hands. One or two she-goats were cropping blades of grass, and a youth was acting out control of the flock. He was handsomely dressed to represent the Phrygian shepherd Paris, with exotic garments flowing from his shoulders, and his head crowned with a tiara of gold. Standing by him appeared a radiant boy, naked except for a youth's cloak

draped over his left shoulder; his blonde hair made him the
cynosure of all eyes. Tiny wings of gold were projecting from
his locks, in which they had been fastened symmetrically on
both sides. The herald's staff and the wand which he carried
identified him as Mercury. He danced briskly forward,
holding in his right hand an apple gilded with gold leaf, which
he handed to the boy playing the part of Paris. After
conveying Jupiter's command with a motion of the head, he at
once gracefully withdrew and disappeared from the scene.
Next appeared a worthy-looking girl, similar in appearance to
the goddess Juno, for her hair was ordered with a white
diadem, and she carried a sceptre. A second girl then burst in,
whom you would have recognized as Minerva. Her head was
covered with a gleaming helmet which was itself crowned with
an olive-wreath; she bore a shield and brandished a spear,
simulating the goddess's fighting-role.

31   After them a third girl entered, her beauty visibly unsurpassed. Her charming, ambrosia-like complexion
intimated that she represented the earlier Venus when that
goddess was still a maiden. She vaunted her unblemished
beauty by appearing naked and unclothed except for a thin
silken garment veiling her entrancing lower parts. An
inquisitive gust of air would at one moment with quite
lubricious affection blow this garment aside, so that when
wafted away it revealed her virgin bloom; at another moment
it would wantonly breathe directly upon it, clinging tightly
and vividly outlining the pleasurable prospect of her lower
limbs. The goddess's appearance offered contrasting colours
to the eye, for her body was dazzling white, intimating her
descent from heaven, and her robe was dark blue, denoting
her emergence from the sea.

      Each maiden representing a goddess was accompanied by
her own escort. Juno was attended by Castor and Pollux, their
heads covered by egg-shaped helmets prominently topped
with stars; these Castors were represented by boys on stage.
The maiden playing this role advanced with restrained and
unpretentious movements to the music of an Ionian flute
playing a range of tunes; with dignified motions she promised

the shepherd to bestow on him the kingship of all Asia if he awarded her the prize for beauty. The girl whose appearance in arms had revealed her as Minerva was protected by two boys who were the comrades in arms of the battle-goddess, Terror and Fear; they pranced about with swords unsheathed, and behind her back a flutist played a battle-tune in the Dorian mode. He mingled shrill whistling notes with deep, droning chords like a trumpet-blast, stirring the performers to lively and supple dancing. Minerva with motions of the head, menacing gaze, and writhing movements incisively informed Paris that if he awarded her the victory for beauty, her aid would make him a doughty fighter, famed for the trophies gained in wars.

32   But now Venus becomingly took the centre of the stage to the great acclamation of the theatre, and smiled sweetly. She was surrounded by a throng of the happiest children; you would have sworn that those litle boys whose skins were smooth and milk-white were genuine Cupids who had just flown in from sky or sea. They looked just the part with their tiny wings, miniature arrows, and the rest of their get-up, as with gleaming torches they lit the way for their mistress as though she were *en route* to a wedding-banquet. Next floated in charming children, unmarried girls, representing on one side the Graces at their most graceful, and on the other the Hours in all their beauty. They were appeasing their goddess by strewing wreaths and single blossoms before her, and they formed a most elegant chorus-line as they sought to please the Mistress of pleasures with the foliage of spring. The flutes with their many stops were now rendering in sweet harmony melodies in the Lydian mode. As they affectingly softened the hearts of the onlookers, Venus still more affectingly began gently to stir herself; with gradual, lingering steps, restrained swaying of the hips, and slow inclination of the head she began to advance, her refined movements matching the soft sounds of the flutes. Occasionally her eyes alone would dance, as at one moment she gently lowered her lids, and at another imperiously signalled with threatening glances. At the moment when she met the gaze of the judge, the beckoning of her arms

seemed to hold the promise that if he preferred her over the other goddesses, she would present Paris with a bride of unmatched beauty, one like herself. There and then the Phrygian youth spontaneously awarded the girl the golden apple in his hand, which signalled the vote for victory.

33   You individuals who are the lowest form of life—I should call you rather sheep of the courts, or more aptly still, vultures in togas—why are you amazed that all jurymen nowadays trade their verdicts for money, seeing that when the world began, this suit conducted between deities and men was corrupted by grace and favour? This country bumpkin, chosen as judge in the plans laid by Jupiter, sold that first verdict for lustful gain, and thereby destroyed the whole of his race. And heavens, it was no different in the notorious dispute that followed between famed Greek leaders: Palamedes, who excelled in learning and knowledge, was condemned for treason on false charges, and again the mediocre Odysseus was given the verdict over Ajax, greatest of warriors and a man unsurpassed in martial bravery. Again, what sort of trial was that conducted before those shrewd Athenian legislators who were teachers of every form of knowledge? That old man possessed divine foresight; the god of Delphi pronounced him pre-eminent in wisdom before all other mortals. Yet was he not encompassed by the deceit and envy of a most wicked clique on the grounds that he was corrupting the youth, when in fact he was bridling and restraining them? And was he not executed by the juice of that baleful plant, stamping on his fellow-citizens the stigma of enduring disgrace? For even today outstanding philosophers prefer his most sacred school to all others, and in the loftiest pursuit of happiness they swear by his name.

But I would not wish any of you to censure this onset of my indignation with the unspoken reflection: 'What? Shall we now endure that ass making pronouncements to us on philosophy?' So I shall return to the story at the point where I left it.

34   Once Paris had completed that judgement of his, Juno and Minerva retired from the stage, downcast and apparently

resentful, indicating by gestures their anger at being rejected. Venus on the other hand was elated and smiling, and registered her joy by dancing in company with the entire chorus. At that moment a stream of saffron mixed with wine shot high in the air from the peak of the mountain. It issued from a hidden pipe, and as it coursed downward, it spread in a fragrant shower over the she-goats grazing all around, until the dye improved their colour by transforming their native grey into yellow. Then, as the entire theatre was permeated by the delightful scent, an abyss in the earth opened up and swallowed the wooden mountain.

A soldier now made his hasty way up the centre aisle to procure the woman from the state prison, as the crowd was now demanding her; she was the one who I mentioned had been condemned to the beasts for her manifold crimes, and assigned to the distinction of a wedding with me. A bed was being meticulously laid, doubtless to serve as our nuptial couch; it gleamed with Indian tortoiseshell, was stuffed with masses of feathers, and adorned with a coverlet of silk. Shame at the prospect of public copulation, and disgust at being besmirched by this foul female criminal, afflicted me, but I was in an agony of torment also through fear of death. I reflected that when we were joined close in sexual embraces, any beast dispatched to kill the woman could not prove to be so wisely discriminating, so skilfully trained, or so moderately self-denying as to tear to pieces the woman lying at my side, and to spare me because I had not been condemned and was innocent.

35   By now my anxiety was aroused not by a sense of shame but by regard for my very safety. So while my keeper was preoccupied and busy as he carefully arranged the couch, and the entire slave-retinue was concentrating on provision of the hunting-scene to follow, or wholly diverted by the pleasurable scene on stage, I was granted free scope for my deliberations, for no one considered that a tame ass like me needed very much watching. I edged unobtrusively forward until I reached the nearest gate; then I took off at full gallop. I covered a good six miles at top speed, and reached Cenchreae.

This is a town celebrated as part of the notable colony of the Corinthians, and is lapped by the Aegean sea and the Saronic gulf; there is also a harbour there which affords the safest refuge for ships, and great crowds of people throng there. So I gave these gatherings a wide berth, and chose a secluded beach where I stretched out and rested my weary body in the bosom of softest sand, close to the spray thrown up by the waves. The sun's chariot had by now bent its way past the last turning-point of the day; I surrendered myself to the silence of the evening, and sweet sleep descended on me.

BOOK 11

Salvation, and Conversion to Isis

1 A sudden fear aroused me at about the first watch of the night. At that moment I beheld the full moon rising from the sea-waves, and gleaming with special brightness. In my enjoyment of the hushed isolation of the shadowy night, I became aware that the supreme goddess wielded her power with exceeding majesty, that human affairs were controlled wholly by her providence, that the world of cattle and wild beasts and even things inanimate were lent vigour by the divine impulse of her light and power; that the bodies of earth, sea, and sky now increased at her waxing, and now diminished in deference to her waning. It seemed that Fate had now had her fill of my grievous misfortunes, and was offering hope of deliverance, however delayed. So I decided to address a prayer to the venerable image of the goddess appearing before my eyes. I hastily shook off my torpid drowsiness, and sprang up, exultant and eager. I was keen to purify myself at once, so I bathed myself in the sea-waters, plunging my head seven times beneath the waves, for Pythagoras of godlike fame proclaimed that number to be especially efficacious in sacred rites. Then with tears in my eyes I addressed this prayer to the supremely powerful goddess:

2 'Queen of heaven, at one time you appear in the guise of Ceres, bountiful and primeval bearer of crops. In your delight at recovering your daughter, you dispensed with the ancient, barbaric diet of acorns and schooled us in civilized fare; now you dwell in the fields of Eleusis. At another time you are heavenly Venus; in giving birth to Love when the world was first begun, you united the opposing sexes and multiplied the human race by producing ever abundant offspring; now you are venerated at the wave-lapped shrine of Paphos. At another time you are Phoebus' sister; by applying soothing remedies you relieve the pain of childbirth, and have brought

teeming numbers to birth; now you are worshipped in the
famed shrines of Ephesus. At another time you are Proserpina,
whose howls at night inspire dread, and whose triple form
restrains the emergence of ghosts as you keep the entrance to
earth above firmly barred. You wander through diverse
groves, and are appeased by varying rites. With this feminine
light of yours you brighten every city and nourish the
luxuriant seeds with your moist fire, bestowing your light
intermittently according to the wandering paths of the sun.
But by whatever name or rite or image it is right to invoke
you, come to my aid at this time of extreme privation, lend
stability to my disintegrating fortunes, grant respite and peace
to the harsh afflictions which I have endured. Let this be the
full measure of my toils and hazards; rid me of this grisly,
four-footed form. Restore me to the sight of my kin; make me
again the Lucius that I was. But if I have offended some deity
who continues to oppress me with implacable savagery, at
least allow me to die, since I cannot continue to live.'

3   These were the prayers which I poured out, supporting
them with cries of lamentation. But then sleep enveloped and
overpowered my wasting spirit as I lay on that couch of sand.
But scarcely had I closed my eyes when suddenly from the
midst of the sea a divine figure arose, revealing features
worthy of veneration even by the gods. Then gradually the
gleaming form seemed to stand before me in full figure as she
shook off the sea-water. I shall try to acquaint you too with
the detail of her wondrous appearance, if only the poverty of
human speech grants me powers of description, or the deity
herself endows me with a rich feast of eloquent utterance.

To begin with, she had a full head of hair which hung
down, gradually curling as it spread loosely and flowed gently
over her divine neck. Her lofty head was encircled by a
garland interwoven with diverse blossoms, at the centre of
which above her brow was a flat disk resembling a mirror, or
rather the orb of the moon, which emitted a glittering light.
The crown was held in place by coils of rearing snakes on
right and left, and it was adorned above with waving ears of
corn. She wore a multicoloured dress woven from fine linen,

one part of which shone radiantly white, a second glowed yellow with saffron blossom, and a third blazed rosy red. But what riveted my eyes above all else was her jet-black cloak, which gleamed with a dark sheen as it enveloped her. It ran beneath her right arm across to her left shoulder, its fringe partially descending in the form of a knot. The garment hung down in layers of successive folds, its lower edge gracefully undulating with tasselled fringes.

4   Stars glittered here and there along its woven border and on its flat surface, and in their midst a full moon exhaled fiery flames. Wherever the hem of that magnificent cloak billowed out, a garland composed of every flower and every fruit was inseparably attached to it. The goddess's appurtenances were extremely diverse. In her right hand she carried a bronze rattle; it consisted of a narrow metal strip curved like a belt, through the middle of which were passed a few rods; when she shook the rattle vigorously three times with her arm, the rods gave out a shrill sound. From her left hand dangled a boat-shaped vessel, on the handle of which was the figure of a serpent in relief, rearing high its head and swelling its broad neck. Her feet, divinely white, were shod in sandals fashioned from the leaves of the palm of victory. Such, then, was the appearance of the mighty goddess. She breathed forth the fertile fragrance of Arabia as she deigned to address me in words divine:

5   'Here I am, Lucius, roused by your prayers. I am the mother of the world of nature, mistress of all the elements, first-born in this realm of time. I am the loftiest of deities, queen of departed spirits, foremost of heavenly dwellers, the single embodiment of all gods and goddesses. I order with my nod the luminous heights of heaven, the healthy sea-breezes, the sad silences of the infernal dwellers. The whole world worships this single godhead under a variety of shapes and liturgies and titles. In one land the Phrygians, first-born of men, hail me as the Pessinuntian mother of the gods; elsewhere the native dwellers of Attica call me Cecropian Minerva; in other climes the wave-tossed Cypriots name me Paphian Venus; the Cretan archers, Dictynna Diana; the

trilingual Sicilians, Ortygian Proserpina; the Eleusinians, the ancient goddess Ceres; some call me Juno, others Bellona, others Hecate, and others still Rhamnusia. But the peoples on whom the rising sun-god shines with his first rays—eastern and western Ethiopians, and the Egyptians who flourish with their time-honoured learning—worship me with the liturgy that is my own, and call me by my true name, which is queen Isis.

'I am here out of pity for your misfortunes; I am here to lend you kindly support. End now your weeping, abandon your lamentation, set aside your grief, for through my providence your day of salvation is now dawning. So pay careful attention to my commands. The day to be born of this night has been dedicated to me in religious observance from time immemorial. Now that the storms of winter are stilled, and the tempestuous waves of the ocean are calmed, the sea is now safe for shipping, and my priests entrust to it a newly built vessel dedicated as the first fruits of our journeys by sea. You are to await this rite with an untroubled and reverent mind.

6   'As the procession forms up, a priest at my prompting will be carrying a garland of roses tied to the rattle in his right hand. So without hesitation part the crowd and join the procession, relying on my kindly care. Then, when you have drawn near, make as if you intend to kiss the priest's hand, and gently detach the roses; at once then shrug off the skin of this most hateful of animals, which has long been abominable in my sight. Do not be fearful and regard any of these commands of mine as difficult, for at this moment as I stand before you I am also appearing to my priest as he sleeps, and am instructing him what to do following this. At my command the close-packed crowds will give way before you. In the midst of the joyous ritual and the jolly sights, no one will recoil from your ugly shape, nor put a malicious complexion on your sudden metamorphosis, and lay spiteful charges against you.

'What you must carefully remember and keep ever locked deep in your heart is that the remaining course of your life until the moment of your last breath is pledged to me, for it is only right that all your future days should be devoted to the one whose kindness has restored you to the company of men. Your future life will be blessed, and under my protection will bring you fame; and when you have lived out your life's span and you journey to the realm of the dead, even there in the hemisphere beneath the earth you will constantly adore me, for I shall be gracious to you. You will dwell in the Elysian fields, while I, whom you now behold, shine brightly in the darkness of Acheron and reign in the inner Stygian depths. But if you deserve to win my divine approval by diligent service, you will come to know that I alone can prolong your life even here on earth beyond the years appointed by your destiny.'

7   When she had reached the close of her sacred prophecy, that invincible deity retired to keep her own company. Without delay I was at once released from sleep. With mingled emotions of fear and joy I arose, bathed in sweat, utterly bemused by so vivid an epiphany of the powerful goddess. I sprinkled myself with sea-water, and as I meditated on her important commands, I reviewed the sequence of her instructions. At that moment the clouds of dark night were dispersed, and a golden sun arose. There and then groups of people filled the entire streets, darting here and there in quite exultant devotion. My personal sense of well-being seemed to be compounded by a general atmosphere of joy, which was so pervasive that I sensed that every kind of domestic beast, and entire households, and the very weather seemed to present a smiling face to the world. For a sunny, windless day had suddenly succeeded the previous day's frost, so that even the birds were enticed by the spring warmth to burst tunefully into sweet harmonies, as with their charming address they soothed the mother of the stars, the parent of the seasons, the mistress of the entire world. Why, even the trees, both those fertile with their produce of fruit, and the barren ones content with the provision of mere shade, expanded under the southerly breezes, and smiled with the budding of their foliage; they whispered sweetly with the gentle motion of

their branches. Now that the great din of the storms was stilled, and the waves' angry swell had subsided, the sea quietened and controlled its floods, while the sky dispersed the dark rain-clouds and shone with the cloudless and bright brilliance of its light.

8   And now the outrunners of the great procession formed up to lead the way, each most handsomely adorned in the garb of his choice. One had buckled on a belt, and was playing the soldier; a second had tucked up his cloak, and his high boots and spears identified him as a huntsman; a third was wearing gilded shoes, a silk gown, costly jewellery, and a wig, and was mincing along impersonating a woman; a fourth was conspicuous with greaves, shield, helmet, and sword; you would have thought that he was emerging from a school of gladiators. A fifth who made his appearance was guying a magistrate, with the rods of office and a purple toga; a sixth was pretending to be a philosopher with his cloak and staff, sandals, and a goatee beard. Two others were carrying different types of rod, the one playing the fowler with bird-lime, the other the angler with his hooks. I saw also a tame she-bear dressed up as a matron, being carried along in a chair, and a monkey in the woven cap and saffron garment that Phrygians wear, carrying a golden cup to ape the shepherd-boy Ganymede; and an ass with wings stuck to its shoulders ambling along beside a feeble old man, so that you might have labelled the one Pegasus and the other Bellerophon, and enjoyed a hearty laugh at both.

9   While the participants in these comic diversions for the townsfolk were prancing about here and there, the special procession in honour of the saviour goddess was being set in motion. Some women, sparkling in white dresses, delighting in their diverse adornments and garlanded with spring flowers, were strewing the ground with blossoms stored in their dresses along the route on which the sacred company was to pass. Others had gleaming mirrors attached to their backs to render homage to the goddess as she drew near them, and others with ivory combs gestured with their arms and twirled their fingers as if adorning and combing their queen's

tresses. Others again sprinkled the streets with all manner of perfumes, including the pleasing balsam-scent which they shook out in drops. Besides these there was a numerous crowd of both sexes who sought the favour of the creator of the celestial stars by carrying lamps, torches, tapers and other kinds of artificial light. Behind them came musical instruments, pipes and flutes which sounded forth the sweetest melodies. There followed a delightful choir of specially chosen youths clad in expensive white tunics, who kept hymning a charming song composed to music by a talented poet with the aid of the Muses; the theme incorporated chants leading up to the greater votive prayers to follow. In the procession too were flautists dedicated to the great god Sarapis; the pipes in their hands extended sideways to their right ears, and on them they repeatedly played the tune regularly associated with their temple and its god. There were also several officials loudly insisting that a path be cleared for the sacred procession.

10   Next, crowds of those initiated into the divine rites came surging along, men and women of every rank and age, gleaming with linen garments spotlessly white. The women had sprayed their hair with perfume, and covered it with diaphanous veils; the men had shaved their heads completely, so that their bald pates shone. With their rattles of bronze, silver, and even gold, they made a shrill, tinkling sound. Accompanying them were the stars of the great world-religion, the priests of the cult who were drawn from the ranks of famed nobility; they wore white linen garments which fitted tightly across their chests and extended to their feet, and they carried striking attributes of most powerful deities. Their leader held out a lamp gleaming with brilliant light; it did not much resemble those lanterns of ours which illumine our banquets at night, but it was a golden, boat-shaped vessel feeding quite a large flame from an opening at its centre. The second priest was similarly garbed; he carried in both hands the altar which they call the 'altar of help', a name specifically bestowed on it by the providential help of the highest goddess. A third priest advanced, bearing a palm-branch, its leaves finely worked in gold; he carried also the staff of Mercury. A

fourth priest exhibited a deformed left hand with palm
outstretched, symbolizing justice; since it was impaired by
nature and endowed with no guile or cunning, it was thought
more suited to represent justice than the right hand. He also
carried a small golden vessel rounded like a woman's breast,
from which he poured libations of milk. A fifth priest bore a
winnowing-fan of gold, fashioned from laurel-twigs, and a
sixth carried an amphora.

11   Immediately behind marched gods who deigned to advance
on human feet. Here was Anubis, the awesome go-between of
gods above and subterranean dwellers; with face part-black,
part-golden, tall and holding his dog's neck high, he carried a
herald's staff in his left hand, and brandished a green palm-
branch in his right. Hard on his heels followed a cow rearing
upright, the fertile representation of the goddess who is
mother of all; a member of the priesthood held it resting on his
shoulders, and he bore it with a flourish and with proud gait.
Another carried the box containing the mysteries and
concealing deep within it the hidden objects of that august
religion. Yet another priest bore in exultant arms the
venerable image of the supreme deity. It was not in the shape
of a farm-animal or bird or wild beast or the human form
itself, but in its ingenious originality it inspired veneration by
its very strangeness, for it expressed in a manner beyond
description the higher religious faith which has to be cloaked
in boundless silence. Fashioned from gleaming gold, this was
a small vase skilfully hollowed out on a perfectly rounded
base, with remarkable Egyptian figures fashioned on its outer
surface; it had not a high neck, but it projected into a long
spout extending into a beak. On its other side a handle was set
well back in a broad curve, and above it was an asp coiled in a
knot, the striped swelling of its scaly neck rearing high.

12   Suddenly the blessings promised by that most supportive
deity came near. A priest approached bearing with him my
future fortune and my very salvation. Exactly in keeping with
the divine promise, his right hand held an adorned rattle for
the goddess and a crown of flowers for me; the crown was
fittingly, God knows, a crown of victory, for after enduring

countless exhausting toils and after surviving numerous
hazards, I was now through the providence of the highest
goddess overcoming Fortune, who had grappled with me so
fiercely. But though seized with sudden joy, I did not bound
forward at an uncontrolled gallop, for obviously I feared that
the tranquil course of the ritual would be disturbed by the
sudden charge of a four-footed beast. Hesitantly and with
subdued steps such as a man might make, I gradually worked
my body sideways, and crept slowly nearer as the crowd
parted, doubtless at the command of the goddess.

13   What happened next made me realize that the priest
recalled the divine message which he had received the
previous night. He registered astonishment at how the task
laid upon him had materialized; he halted abruptly, stretched
out his right hand unprompted, and dangled the garland
before my very face. Then in trembling haste (for my heart
was beating wildly), I seized with greedy mouth the garland
which gleamed with its texture of beautiful roses. I was eager
to see the promise fulfilled, so with even greater eagerness I
bolted it down. Nor was I cheated of that promise from
heaven, for my ugly animal form at once deserted me. First
my unsightly bristles disappeared, and then my thick skin
thinned out; my fat belly contracted; the soles of my feet
extended into toes where the hooves had been; my forefeet
became hands equipped for two-footed tasks; my long neck
shrank, my face and head became round, my projecting ears
resumed their earlier modest shape; my rocklike teeth were
restored to human size, and my tail, earlier the chief cause of
my distress, totally disappeared.

The crowd stood amazed, and the devotees paid homage to
the demonstrable power of the greatest deity and to this
wonder-working which corresponded with the visions of the
night; aloud and in unison as they raised their hands to
heaven they acclaimed this notable kindness of the goddess.

14   As for me, total astonishment rendered me speechless. My
mind was unable to contain so sudden and boundless a joy,
and I dithered, wondering what it would be best for me to say
first, and how I could make first use of my new-found voice;

what words I should use to launch auspiciously my tongue reborn, and how and at what length I should express my thanks to the great goddess. But the priest, who by some divine inspiration was aware of all my calamities from the start, took the initiative, though he too was deeply moved by the extraordinary miracle. With a nod he signalled an instruction to hand me a linen cloth to cover my nakedness, for as soon as the ass had stripped me of his accursed skin, I had jammed my thighs tightly together and placed my hands discreetly over them. So far as a naked man could, I had used nature's resources to cover myself decently. Thereupon one of the consecrated band quickly tore off his upper garment and hastily threw it over me. Then the priest, eyeing my appearance with astonishment, gazed on me indulgently with what I swear was a godlike look, and spoke these words.

15   'Lucius, the troubles which you have endured have been many and diverse. You have been driven before the heavy storms and the heaviest gales of Fortune, but you have finally reached the harbour of peace and the altar of mercy. Your high birth, and what is more, your rank and your accomplished learning have been of no avail to you whatever. In the green years of youth, you tumbled on the slippery slope into slavish pleasures, and gained the ill-omened reward of your unhappy curiosity. Yet somehow Fortune in her blind course, while torturing you with the most severe dangers, has in her random persecution guided you to this state of religious blessedness. So she can now head off and muster her most savage rage in search of some other victim for her cruelty, for hostile chance has no influence over those whose lives our majestic goddess has adopted into her service. Have brigands, or wild beasts, or slavery, or those winding, wholly crippling journeys to and fro, or the daily fear of death been of any avail to Fortune's malice? You have now been taken under the protection of Fortune with eyes, who with the brilliance of her light lends lustre even to the other gods. Show now a happier face in keeping with your white garment, and join the procession of the saviour goddess with triumphal step. Let unbelievers see

you, and as they see you let them recognize the error of their ways; for behold, Lucius is delivered from his earlier privations, and as he rejoices in the providence of the great Isis, he triumphs over his Fortune. But to ensure your greater safety under closer protection, enrol in this sacred army to which you were invited to swear allegiance not long ago. Consecrate yourself from this moment to the obedience of our religion, and of your own accord submit to the yoke of service. Once you have begun to serve the goddess, you will then better appreciate the reward of your freedom.'

16   This was how that remarkable priest phrased his prophecy. Then he fell silent, showing signs of weariness as he recovered his breath. I then took my place in the sacred procession and walked along, keeping close attendance on the sacred shrine. I was recognized, indeed I was the cynosure of all eyes; the whole community singled me out with pointing fingers and nods, and gossiped about me: 'Today the venerable power of the almighty goddess has restored him to the ranks of men. How happy, how blessed three times over he is! Doubtless through the purity and faith of his former life he has deserved such sovereign protection from heaven, and in consequence he had been in a manner reborn, and has at once pledged himself to the service of her cult.'

Meanwhile amid the din of joyous prayers we edged our way slowly forward and drew near to the sea-shore, at that very place where as Lucius-turned-ass I had bivouacked the previous day. There the gods' statues were duly set in place, and the chief priest named and consecrated to the goddess a ship which had been built with splendid craftsmanship, and which was adorned on all its timbers with wonderful Egyptian pictures. Holding a flaming torch, he first pronounced most solemn prayers from his chaste lips, and then with an egg and sulphur he performed over it an elaborate ceremony of purification. The bright sail of this blessed craft carried upon it woven letters in gold, bearing those same petitions for trouble-free sailing on its first journeys. The mast was of rounded pine, gloriously tall and easily recognized with its striking masthead. The stern was curved in the shape of a goose, and gleamed with its covering of gold leaf. In fact the whole ship shone, polished as it was in clear citrus-wood.

Then the entire population, devotees and uninitiated alike, vied in piling the ship high with baskets laden with spices and similar offerings, and they poured on the waves libations of meal soaked in milk. Eventually the ship, filled with generous gifts and propitious offerings, was loosed from its anchor-ropes and launched on the sea before a friendly, specially appointed breeze. Once its progress had caused it to fade from our sight, the bearers of the sacred objects took up again those which each had brought, and they made their eager way back to the temple, following in tidy order the same detail of procession as before.

17   Once we reached the temple itself, the chief priest, those who carried the gods' images, and those previously initiated into the august inner sanctuary were admitted into the chamber of the goddess, where they duly set in place the living statues. Then one of the company, whom they all termed the scribe, stood before the entrance and summoned an assembly of the *pastophori*; this is the name of the sacred college. There from a high dais he first recited from a book formulaic prayers for the prosperity of the great emperor, the senate, the knights, and the entire Roman people; then for sea-travellers and for ships journeying within the bounds of our imperial world. Next he announced in the Greek language and according to Greek ritual the ceremony of the launching of the ships. The applause of the people that followed showed that this speech was well received by all. Then the folk, ecstatic with joy, brought up boughs, branches and garlands, and having kissed the feet of the goddess (her statue, wrought from silver, was attached to the temple-steps), they departed to their homes. But my enthusiasm did not permit me to separate myself by more than a nail's breadth from that spot, and I gazed intently on the image of the goddess as I pondered my earlier misfortunes.

18   Meanwhile, however, swift Rumour had not been idle or slow in winging her way. She had been prompt in recounting throughout my native region that blessing of the provident

goddess which was so worthy of veneration, as well as my own remarkable history. As a result, family friends, household slaves, and my closest blood-relatives dispelled the grief which had afflicted them at the false report of my death, and in raptures of sudden joy they all hastened with various gifts, wishing to set eyes on me at once as one returned from the dead to the light of day. I had despaired of ever seeing them again, so I was likewise restored by their presence. I accepted their kind offerings with gratitude, for my friends had considerately ensured that I had a generous allowance to cover clothes and living expenses.

19   So I dutifully spoke to each of them, and briefly recounted my earlier hardships and my present joys. But then I made my way back to feast my eyes on the goddess, for this gave me the greatest delight. I rented a dwelling within the temple-precinct, and made a temporary home for myself there, devoting myself to the goddess in service as yet unofficial, but associating closely with the priests and constantly worshipping that great deity. No single night, no siesta passed which was not haunted with the vision and advice of the goddess. By numerous sacred commands she decreed that since I had been so inclined for some time, I should now at last undergo initiation. Though I was eager and willing, a kind of religious fear held me back, for I had carefully enquired about the difficulties of such religious service—the quite demanding abstinence prescribed by the rules of chastity, and the need to control with careful circumspection a life subject to many chance events. So through pondering these problems repeatedly I somehow kept postponing a decision, in spite of my enthusiasm.

20   One night the chief priest appeared to me in a dream, offering me an armful of gifts. When I asked the meaning of this, he replied that they had been sent to me as my belongings from Thessaly, and that there had also arrived from the same region a slave of mine by the name of Candidus. On awakening I pondered this vision long and repeatedly, wondering what it meant, especially as I was convinced that I had never had a slave of that name. But

whatever the prophetic dream portended, I thought that in any case this offering of belongings gave promise of undoubted gain. So I was on tenterhooks, beguiled by this prospect of greater profit as I awaited the morning opening of the temple. The gleaming curtains were parted, and we addressed our prayers to the august image of the goddess. The priest made his rounds of the altars positioned there, performing the liturgy with the customary prayers, and pouring from a sacred vessel the libation-water obtained from the sanctuary of the goddess. With the ceremony duly completed, the initiates greeted the dawning of the day, and loudly proclaimed the hour of Prime. Then suddenly the slaves whom I had left at Hypata, when Photis had involved me in those notorious wanderings, appeared on the scene. I suppose that they had heard the stories about me; they also brought back that horse of mine which had been sold to various owners, but which they had recovered after recognizing the mark on its back. This caused me to marvel more than anything else at the perspicacity of my dream, for quite apart from getting confirmation of its promise of profit, by its mention of a slave Candidus it had restored to me my white horse.

21   This event made me perform my diligent service of worship more conscientiously, for these present blessings offered a pledge of hope for the future. Every day my longing to be admitted to the mysteries grew more and more, and I repeatedly greeted the chief priest with the most ardent requests that he should at last initiate me into the secret rites of the sanctified night. But he was in general a sober character, well known for his adhesion to a strict religious routine, and he treated me in the same way as parents often restrain their children's untimely desires. In a gentle and kind way he postponed my pressing request, whilst at the same time calming my agitation with the comforting expectation of a rosier future. He explained that the day on which a person could be initiated was indicated by the will of the goddess, that the priest who was to perform the sacred ritual was chosen by the foresight of that same goddess, and in addition the expenses necessary for the ceremonies were indicated in

the same instruction. His advice was that I, like the others, should observe all these rules with reverent patience. It was my duty to take stringent precautions against both over-enthusiasm and obstinacy, avoiding both faults so as not to hang back when summoned, nor to push forward unbidden. Not one individual in his community was so depraved in mind, or so enamoured of death as to undertake that ministry in a rash and sacrilegious spirit, without having received the call individually from his mistress; for that would incur a guilt that spelt death. Both the gates of hell and the guarantee of salvation lay in the control of the goddess. The act of initiation itself was performed as a rite of voluntary death and of salvation attained by prayer; indeed, it was the will of the goddess to select persons when their span of life was complete and they were poised on the very threshold of their final days. Such people could be safely entrusted with the profound mysteries of the sect. By her providence they were in some sense reborn, for she set them back on the course of renewed health. So I too was to submit to heaven's command, even though I had for long been named and designated for that blessed ministry by the notable and manifest favour of the great deity. Like the other worshippers, I should meanwhile abstain from profane and unlawful foods, to allow myself worthier access to the hidden secrets of that most hallowed religion.

22   Once the priest had pronounced on the issue, I did not mar my allegiance by impatience, but in humble peace and praiseworthy silence I concentrated on performing the service of the sacred cult with diligence for several days. The saving kindness of the powerful goddess did not fail or torture me with lengthy delay, but in the darkness of the night by commands by no means dark she clearly warned me that the day I had always desired had arrived, on which she would bestow on me my greatest ambition. She also explained how much I needed to contribute to pay for the ceremonies; and she appointed Mithras himself, her own high priest, to carry out the ritual, since she said that he was joined to me by some divine conjunction of our stars.

I was invigorated by these and the other kindly commands of the supreme goddess. Before it was fully daylight, I abandoned my bed and hurried straight to the priest's lodging. I met him with a greeting just as he was leaving his chamber. I had decided that I would demand initiation into the sacred rites more insistently than usual because it was now apparently my due. But as soon as he set eyes on me, he anticipated me with the words: 'Lucius, how lucky and blessed you are! The worshipful deity honours you so greatly with her kindly favour!' He added: 'So why now stand idle there, the cause of your own delay? The day for which you longed in your constant prayers has dawned, when at the divine commands of the goddess with many names you are to be admitted through my agency to the most holy mysteries of our sacred rites.' That most genial old man then put his hand in mine, and led me to the portals of that most splendid temple. He performed the task of opening the temple in accord with the solemn ritual, and performed the morning sacrifice. Then from a hidden recess in the shrine he extracted some books headed with unfamiliar characters. Some were in the shapes of every kind of animal, and served as summaries of formulaic phrases. Others were knotted and twisted into wheel-shapes, or intertwined like vine-tendrils at the top, to prevent their being read by inquisitive non-initiates. From these books the priest recited to me the preparations necessary for conducting the initiation.

23   At once I energetically made the necessary preparations regardless of expense. Some I purchased personally, and others through my friends. The priest now told me that the required moment had come, so he led me to the baths close by in company with a group of initiates. First I was ushered into the normal bath. Then the priest first asked for the gods' blessing, and cleansed me by sprinkling water all over me until I was wholly purified. I was then escorted back to the temple. Two-thirds of the day had now elapsed; the priest set me before the very feet of the goddess, and gave me certain secret instructions too sacred to divulge. Then he commanded me openly, for all to witness, to discipline my pleasures in

eating for the ensuing ten days, taking no animal flesh and drinking no wine.

I duly observed these commands with respectful self-discipline. The day now came which was appointed for my promise to the gods, and as the sun bent its course and ushered in the evening, suddenly crowds of initiates gathered from every side, and in accord with ancient custom they each paid me honour with a variety of gifts. Then all the non-initiates were removed to a distance. I was shrouded in a new linen garment, and the priest took my hand and led me into the heart of the sanctuary.

Perhaps the reader's interest is roused, and you are keen to enquire about the ensuing words and actions. I would tell you if it were permitted to reveal them; you would be told if you were allowed to hear. But both your ears and my tongue would incur equal guilt; my tongue for its impious garrulity, and your ears for their rash curiosity. I will not keep you long on tenterhooks, since your anxiety is perhaps motivated by religious longing. So listen, and be sure to believe that what you hear is true. I drew near to the confines of death and trod the threshold of Proserpina, and before returning I journeyed through all the elements. At dead of night I saw the sun gleaming with bright brilliance. I stood in the presence of the gods below and the gods above, and worshipped them from close at hand. Notice, then, that I have referred to things which you are not permitted to know, though you have heard about them. So I shall recount only what can be communicated without sacrilege to the understanding of non-initiates.

24   Morning came, and the rites were completed. I emerged sacramentally clothed in twelve garments. Though the clothing is quite germane to the ritual, there is no bar to my mentioning it, because at the time there were numerous persons present to see it. I took my stand as bidden on a wooden dais set before the statue of the goddess at the very heart of the sacred shrine. The linen garment that I wore made me conspicuous, for it was elaborately embroidered; the expensive cloak hung down my back from the shoulders to the heels, and from whatever angle you studied it, I was adorned

all round with multicoloured animals. On one side were Indian snakes, and on the other Arctic gryphons begotten by a world beyond this in the shape of winged birds. This garment the initiates call 'Olympian'. In my right hand I wielded a torch well alight; a garland of glinting palm-leaves projecting like the sun's rays encircled my head. When I was thus adorned to represent the sun and set there like a statue, the curtains were suddenly drawn back, and the people wandered in to gaze on me. Subsequently I celebrated a most happy birthday into the sacred mysteries; there was a pleasant banquet and a gathering of witty guests. There was also a third day of celebration with a similar programme of ceremonies, including a sacred breakfast and the official conclusion to the initiation.

For a few days I lingered on there, for I enjoyed the indescribable pleasure of gazing on the divine statue. I had pledged myself to Isis for the kindness which I could not repay. Finally, however, at the behest of the goddess I wound up my thanks, admittedly not expressed fully, but humbly and as far as my poor abilities allowed, and I prepared my long-delayed journey home. Even then the bonds of my most ardent yearning were hard to break. So finally I crouched before the image of the goddess, and for long rubbed her feet with my cheeks. With rising tears and frequent sobs I addressed her, choking on and swallowing my words.

25 'O holy, perennial saviour of the human race, you are ever generous in your care for mortals, and you bestow a mother's sweet affection upon wretched people in misfortune. No day, no period of sleep, no trivial moment hastens by which is not endowed with your kind deeds. You do not refrain from protecting mortals on sea and land, or from extending your saving hand to disperse the storms of life. With that hand you even wind back the threads of the Fates, however irretrievably twisted. You appease the storms raised by Fortune, and restrain the harmful courses of the stars. The gods above cultivate you, the spirits below court you. You rotate the world, lend the sun its light, govern the universe, crush Tartarus beneath your heel. The stars are accountable to you,

the seasons return at your behest, the deities rejoice before
you, the elements serve you. At your nod breezes blow, clouds
nurture the earth, seeds sprout, and buds swell. The birds
coursing through the sky, the beasts wandering on the
mountains, the snakes lurking in the undergrowth, the
monsters that swim in the deep all tremble at your majesty.
But my talent is too puny to sing your praises, and my
patrimony is too meagre to offer you sacrificial victims; I have
neither the richness of speech, nor a thousand mouths and as
many tongues, nor an endless and uninhibited flow of words
to express my feelings about your majesty. Therefore I shall
be sure to perform the one thing that a pious but poor person
can do: I shall preserve your divine countenance and your
most holy godhead in the recess of my heart, and there I shall
for ever guard it and gaze on it with the eyes of the mind.'

This was the sense of my prayer to the highest deity. I then
embraced Mithras, the priest who was now my father. I clung
to his neck and kissed him repeatedly; I begged him to pardon
me for being unable to offer him worthy recompense for such
great kindnesses.

26   After remaining for some time prolonging my words of
thanks, I eventually parted from him. I hastened by the
shortest route to set eyes once more after this long lapse of
time on my ancestral home. A few days later the powerful
goddess moved me to pack my bags in haste, and to board
ship. I set out for Rome, and very quickly arrived safe and
sound through the favour of a following wind at the harbour of
Augustus. From there I speeded along by carriage, and on the
evening of 12 December I reached the sacred city. After that
there was no task which I undertook with greater enthusiasm
than my daily prayers addressed to the supreme godhead of
queen Isis, who is appeased with the utmost reverence under
the title of Campensis, which is adapted from the location of
her temple. In short, I became a regular worshipper there, a
stranger to the shrine but an adherent of the cult. By now the
great sun had completed his year's course through the circle of
the zodiac, when the watchful care of the beneficent deity
again broke into my sleep to advise me a second time of the

need for initiation and sacred ritual. I wondered what she was putting in hand, what coming event she was proclaiming. My surprise was natural, for I believed that my full initiation had been performed long ago.

27   As I debated this religious difficulty in my own mind, and further scrutinized it with the advice of initiates, I became aware of a new and surprising aspect: I had been initiated merely into the rites of the goddess, but had not as yet been enlightened by the sacred mysteries of that great god and highest father of the gods, the unconquered Osiris. The nature of this deity and his cult was closely aligned to, and in fact united with, hers, but there was the greatest difference in the mode of initiation. Hence I ought to consider that I was being asked to become the servant of this great god as well.

The issue did not for long remain undecided, for next night one of the initiates appeared in a dream before me clad in linen garments. He was bearing thyrsus-rods and ivy, and certain objects which must not be revealed. These he set before my household gods, and then settled himself on my chair, and gave notice of a sumptuous religious banquet. To allow me to recognize him by a clear identification-mark, he walked gingerly with hesitant step, for his left heel was slightly misshapen. In view of this clear intimation of the gods' will, the entire cloud of my uncertainty was dispelled. As soon as my early-morning respects to the goddess had been paid, I began to ask each and everyone with the greatest animation whether anyone had a walk as in my dream. Confirmation was forthcoming, for I at once set eyes on one of the *pastophori* who coincided exactly with the vision of the night, not only by the evidence of his foot, but also by the rest of his build and by his dress. I later discovered that he was called Asinius Marcellus, a name quite relevant to my transformation. I approached him there and then; he was well aware of what I was about to say, for he had been already similarly instructed to conduct the initiation. The previous night he had had a vision: while he was adorning the great god with garlands, he had heard from the statue's mouth (this is the means by which Osiris proclaims the future of individuals) that a man from

Madauros who was quite poor was being sent to him, and that he must at once initiate him into his divine rites. By the god's providence this man would gain fame in his studies, and the priest himself would obtain a rich reward.

28   This was how I pledged myself to the rite of initiation, but my slender means with which to meet expenses delayed my aspiration. The expense of travel had reduced my modest capital, and the cost of living in Rome greatly exceeded my outgoings in the province. Harsh poverty was therefore the stumbling-block; as the old proverb has it, I was trapped and tortured 'twixt axe and altar'. None the less, the god continued to put repeated pressure on me. To my great embarrassment there were frequent attempts to cajole me, and finally came the command direct. So I scraped up just enough money by parting with my paltry wardrobe. This had been the specific instruction I received: 'If you were embarking on some activity for pleasure, you would certainly not hesitate to part with your shabby clothes; so now that you are embarking on these noble rites, do you hesitate to resign yourself to a poverty which you can never regret?'

Therefore I made the detailed preparations; for a second time I happily confined myself to a meatless diet for ten days, and I also shaved my head. I gained enlightenment in the nocturnal mysteries of the highest god, and now with full assurance I regularly attended the divine services of this kindred religion. It brought the greatest consolation to me during my time abroad, and equally important, it furnished me with a more opulent standard of living. This was not surprising, for I made a little money in the courts by pleading in the Latin language, and was attended by the wind of favouring Success.

29   Only a short time elapsed when I was again confronted by unexpected and quite remarkable commands from the deities, compelling me to undergo yet a third initiation. At this point the concern that gripped me was not trivial; I was quite troubled in mind as with some anxiety I pondered these issues: what was the point of this strange, unprecedented instruction of the gods? I had now undergone initiation a

second time, so what was lacking to make it complete? 'I suppose', I reflected, 'that the two priests performed the ceremony in my case incorrectly or incompletely.' I swear that I even began to take a jaundiced view of their good faith. But while I tossed on the tide of such speculation, and was being driven to the point of madness, a kindly apparition of the god in a prophetic utterance at night explained the situation to me.

'You should not be apprehensive at this long series of initiations, or believe that some element has been previously omitted. On the contrary, you should be delighted and overjoyed at this continual favour of the deities. You should glory in the fact that on three occasions you will have a role scarcely granted once to any other mortal, and you can rightly believe that you will be ever blessed as a result of your three inductions. A further sacred initiation is necessary in your case, for as you must now reflect, the garb of the goddess which you donned in the province continues to rest in the temple there. The result is that here at Rome you cannot wear it for worship on feast days; when bidden you cannot appear in the radiance of those blessed vestments. So with joyful heart and at the prompting of the great gods you must be initiated once more, and I pray that this induction may be blessed and auspicious for you, and bring you saving help.'

30   In this way the majestic persuasion of the god-sent dream declared what I must do. So without relegating or idly deferring the business, I at once reported the gist of my vision to my priest. Without delay I submitted to the abstemious and meatless diet, and by voluntary abstinence I exceeded the period of ten days laid down by the eternal law. I made generous provision for the initiation, providing all that was required with religious zeal rather than by calculation of my possessions. I swear that I had no regrets whatever about the hardship and expense; there was no reason for such regrets, since the bountiful provision of the gods had now made me comfortably off through the legal fees I was receiving.

Only a few days later Osiris, the god preferred before great gods, highest of the greater deities, greatest of the highest, ruler of the greatest, seemed to bid me welcome during the hours of sleep. He had not transformed himself into any other human shape, but deigned to address me in person with his own august words. He told me not to hesitate to continue as now with my celebrated advocacy in the lawcourts, and not to fear the aspersions of malignant men nettled by the expertise in my legal activities which was attained by strenuous application. So that I should not be one of the rank and file attending to his rites, he appointed me to the college of the *pastophori* and also one of the quinquennial administrators. So I had my head completely shaved once more, and gladly performed the duties of that most ancient college, founded as long ago as the days of Sulla. I did not cover or conceal my bald head, but sported it openly wherever I went.

EXPLANATORY NOTES

BOOK 1

1.1 *Milesian mode*: Hanson persuasively suggests that the story opens 'as if in the middle of a literary discussion'. The epithet 'Milesian' connotes entertaining anecdote of a risqué kind. See further, S. Trenkner, *The Greek Novella in the Classical Period* (Cambridge, 1958), 172 ff.; T. Hägg, *The Novel in Antiquity* (Oxford, 1983), 186 ff. Apuleius lulls the reader into the belief that the romance is to be an entertainment and nothing more.

Egyptian paper . . . Nile: a teasing hint is being offered about Egyptian connections with the romance, which do not become fully explicit until the final book.

my antique stock: Apuleius now assumes the persona of Lucius, as if on stage (see Introd. § IV). The claim to wholly Greek blood, and to ancestral connections with the leading Greek cities of Athens, Corinth, and Sparta, is to be referred to Lucius the I-narrator, not to Apuleius. It is not until 11.27 that Apuleius of Madauros merges himself with his hero Lucius.

circus-rider: the image of the circus-rider leaping from one horse to another may signify the technique of inserting anecdotes or additional episodes into the frame of the Greek story. See Introd. §§ III–IV.

it ^will delight you: for the problems of identifying the spokesman in this introductory chapter, see n. 23 to the Introduction.

1.2 *Sextus*: the apparently casual reference to Sextus, tutor of Verus (co-emperor, 161–9), and to his uncle Plutarch, who in his *De Iside* reconciles Isiac worship with the philosophy of Plato, is important in the development of the fable; see Introd., p. xxxi.

1.4 *Painted Porch*: this was the covered colonnade adorned with paintings which was situated by the Athenian agora, and was the site of the Stoic school. There is an additional hint here of the philosophical connections of the hero Lucius.

the god carries round with him: the god of healing, Asclepius, is conventionally represented in art with a staff round which a serpent is entwined.

1.5 *sun-god*: for the oath by the sun, cf. Homer, *Il*. 3. 277.

Aegium: this city, one of the leaders of the Achaean League, lay in the Peloponnese immediately south of the Corinthian Gulf. Some modern translators confuse it with Aegina.

Lupus: 'Mr Wolfe', a name suggesting the business predator.

1.6 *Socrates*: doubtless the name is intended to be ironical, in view of the lack of practical wisdom which he demonstrates.

Aristomenes: the name, reserved for the heart of the story, has again an ironical ring, since it means 'One of heroic strength'.

1.7 *Larissa*: an ancient town on the river Peneius, lying directly on the route southward from Macedonia.

Meroë: the significance of the name is disputed. Some suggest a connection with the word for unmixed wine (*merum*), because of the traditional association of witches with drinking. Others less cogently see a coded reference to Isiac worship, because the island of Meroë in the Nile had a temple to Isis (Juvenal, 6. 527, 13. 163).

1.8 *She can . . . light up hell itself*: with this catalogue of disorders in nature achieved by witchcraft, compare Lucan 6. 461 ff.

Ethiopians . . . Antipodeans: 'Both lots of Ethiopians' connote dwellers at the eastern and western bounds of the world. Cf. Homer, *Od*. 1. 23 f.; J. Y. Nadeau, *CQ* (1970), 339 ff., esp. 347. The reference to Antipodeans may have been awakened by Plato, *Timaeus*, 63a and Plutarch 869c.

1.9 *elephant*: elephants take 22 months to bring forth their young, but popular belief extended the pregnancy to ten years; cf. Pliny, *NH* 8. 28.

1.10 *Medea*: in Euripides' *Medea*, Jason decided to desert Medea in favour of Creon's daughter. In revenge Medea sent the bride a present of a cloak which fastened on her flesh, and a crown from which issued a stream of devouring fire (line 1186).

1.12 *Panthia*: the name connotes 'All-divine'.

Endymion: the young hunter solicited nightly by Selene (the moon; cf. Plato, *Phaedo* 72c, Cicero, *Tusc*. 1. 92, etc.).

Ganymede was plucked from Mt. Ida by an eagle to become Jupiter's cup-bearer (Ovid, *Met.* 10. 155 ff. etc.).

Ulysses: for the classic account of Odysseus' departure from Calypso, see Homer, *Od.* 5.

1.13 *be sure not to float away*: others render *caue . . . transeas* in the positive sense ('Take care to travel back to the sea'). My translation regards it as an instruction to stop the flow of blood and not to float away upon it.

urine: in addition to the humiliation which the gesture imposes on Aristomenes, such urination could be a magical practice to prevent him making his escape; cf. Petronius, *Sat.* 57.

1.16 *my dear little bed*: it has frequently been noted that the address to the bed parodies a Roman prayer (see e.g. Scobie's edition of Book I). Evocation of Sallust, *Jug.* 14. 22 has also been suggested.

1.18 *disturbing dreams*: cf. Cicero, *Div.* 1. 60.

1.20 *elegant tale*: this story of Aristomenes and Socrates does not appear in *Lucius or the Ass* (henceforward *Onos*); it is part of the patterning of the fable introduced by Apuleius himself. Ironically, Lucius accepts the truth of the story but fails to apply the lessons of Socrates' sexual submission and Aristomenes' curiosity (see 1. 12 above) to his own circumstances.

1.21 *Milo*: in the *Onos* the host is named Hipparchus. He is by no means as miserly as Milo; Apuleius has developed the comic characterization considerably.

Demeas: the man's name in the *Onos* is Decrius Decrianos. Apuleius may have chosen the name Demeas to evoke Demea, the stern parent in Terence's *Adelphi* who closely superintends his son's behaviour.

1.22 *Corinth*: Lucius here specifies his native region; cf. also 2. 12. In the *Onos*, he hails from Patrae. H. J. Mason, *Phoenix* (1971), 165, suggests that Apuleius designates Corinth to evoke the permissive society which Lucius finally renounces.

1.23 *Hecale*: King Theseus was entertained by the aged Hecale before he joined combat with the bull of Marathon (cf. Plutarch, *Theseus*, 14). The fact that Lucius' father bears the same name perhaps suggests that he is an Athenian.

Photis: in the *Onos* the maid's name is Palaestra ('Miss Wrestling-ground'), a title associated with prostitutes. Photis evokes the Greek word for light, not so much connoting 'the dangerous light of eroticism and magic' (so Lancel, *AHR* (1961), 146) as identifying her as the counterpart of Lucius, whose name evokes *lux* in Latin.

1.24 *twenty denarii*: there are 4 sesterces to the denarius, so that the price was reduced to 80 sesterces.

tomorrow: no such intimation is made next day to Pythias; this is one of the many loose ends in the romance.

aedile: the aedile's duty included supervision of the market.

1.25 *this performance*: this episode at the market does not appear in the *Onos*, and has almost certainly been inserted by Apuleius himself. Some scholars (G. Drake, *Papers in Language and Literature* (1969), 356; P. Grimal, *RÉA* (1971), 343 ff.) see it as a coded reference to Isiac ritual, but it is better regarded as literary entertainment, recalling satirical treatments of the lordly behaviour of municipal magistrates (cf. Horace, *Sat*, 1. 5. 34 ff., Juvenal, 10. 100 ff.).

BOOK 2

2.3 *Plutarch's household*: n. on 1.2 above, *Sextus*.

Byrrhena: in the *Onos*, the lady is called Abroea.

2.4 *rock*: reading *rupe* for *rure* in *F* and Robertson.

Actaeon . . . Diana: the significance of this description of the statuary (absent from the *Onos*) now becomes clear. Actaeon was changed into a stag because he gazed with curiosity on Diana's naked form; this is a warning to Lucius about the dangers of curiosity, which he disregards with the catastrophic result of transformation into an ass. Byrrhena's next remark, 'All that you see is yours', is therefore charged with irony.

2.5 *the goddess*: Diana, represented in the statuary, is identified with Hecate, goddess of witchcraft.

Pamphile: the name means 'lover of all'; in the *Onos* the witch is not named. The parallel between the *libido* of Pamphile and that of Meroë in Aristomenes' story in Book I should be noted.

2.7   *slices of meat*: a further dish is mentioned here, but the Latin is hopelessly corrupt.

stood to attention: there is a joking reminiscence of Virgil, *Aen.* 2. 774 here: 'obstipui, steteruntque comae.'

2.8   *criterion of beauty*: an autobiographical element may intrude here. In his *Apology* 4. 11, Apuleius defends himself against the charge of playing the dandy with his long hair. His obsessive interest in hair emerges again at 5. 22 and 11. 3 in descriptions of the hair of Cupid and Isis. See J. Englert and T. Long, *CJ* (1972–3), 236 ff.

that belt of hers: for the belt of Aphrodite/Venus, see Homer, *Il.* 14. 215 ff., where its effect is detailed when Hera borrows it to have her way with Zeus.

Vulcan: Venus' marital relations with Vulcan are not always idyllic, but doubtless Apuleius has in mind Virgil, *Aen.* 8. 369 ff., where Vulcan is a slave to her charms.

2.11 *Lake Avernus*: the entry-point to Hades on the Bay of Naples (Virgil, *Aen.* 6. 237 ff.).

2.12 *Corinth*: see n. on 1.22 above, *Corinth*.

Chaldaean visitor: the Chaldaeans, dwelling close to the Persian Gulf, had such fame as astrologers that their name became synonymous with the profession; hence this visitor need not have been a foreigner.

several books: Apuleius sports with the reader, who is enjoying the 'unbelievable tale'.

2.13 *Diophanes*: the name suggests 'prophesying through Jupiter'.

Cerdo: 'Mr Profit'.

fee for the prophecy: the fee is high when we recall that Lucius paid only 20 denarii for his fish at 1. 24.

2.16 *hot water*: for this regular practice in antiquity, cf. e.g. Horace, *Odes* 3. 19. 6.

fetials: the college of fetials, 20 in number, had the formal task of declaring war on behalf of the Roman state; see *OCD*, 'Fetiales'.

2.17 *She even ... concealment*: she skittishly imitates the pose of Venus rising from the waves, a favourite subject in ancient art.

2.18 *taking the auspices*: Lucius describes the love-engagement in the language of military metaphor, as the Roman love-elegists do. Just as a Roman commander consulted the gods before battle by taking the auspices, so Lucius consults Photis before departure.

2.20 *Thelyphron*: the point of the name ('With a Woman's Mind') becomes clear in 2. 23, where Thelyphron depicts himself as a manly figure, but the bubble is later pricked.

2.21 *Miletus*: the city is chosen as the provenance of the story-teller because of its association with the Milesian tale; see n. on 1.1 above, *Milesian mode*.

celebrated province: the phrase suggests that Thessaly was still part of Achaea (it was joined to Macedonia in the Antonine period). But this is no index either to the date of composition or indeed to the date of the *mise-en-scène* at Larissa, since Thelyphron is recounting an incident of some years earlier.

2.22 *sun-god . . . Justice*: the sun (Apollo) and Justice (Themis or Dike) were associated at Delphi; see Pausanias, 10. 5.

gold pieces: the *aureus* was worth 25 denarii or 100 sesterces; see n. on 2.13 above, *fee for the prophecy*, to evaluate the comparative value of the proposed fee.

2.23 *Harpies*: these grisly creatures, half-bird half-woman, symbolically describe the rapacious witches of Thessaly.

Lynceus . . . Argus: Lynceus was an Argonaut famed for his keen sight (cf. e.g. Horace, *Epistles*, 1. 1. 28). Hundred-eyed Argus was commissioned by Juno to keep watch on Io, whom she had spitefully changed into a heifer when Jupiter impregnated her (Ovid, *Met*. 1. 625 ff.).

2.25 *in the garden*: reading *in hortulos* (Helm; *mosculos F*; *musculos* Robertson).

god of Delphi: Apollo, famed for his prophetic powers.

2.26 *Philodespotus*: 'Master-lover'.

future misfortune: Thelyphron's friendly offer was interpreted as a suggestion that there would be further corpses to guard.

Aonian: 'Aonian' is a learned term for 'Boeotian'; the reference is to Pentheus of Thebes, who in Euripides' *Bacchae* was torn to pieces for showing contempt to Dionysus. The Pipleian poet Orpheus (the adjective refers to his haunt near

Pieria, the Macedonian spring sacred to the Muses) suffered a similar fate.

2.28 *Zatchlas*: the introduction of the Isiac priest, the meaning of whose name is obscure (for possible interpretations, see Gwyn Griffiths, *Apuleius of Madauros*, 39 and 351; G. Drake, *Papers in Language and Literature*, 12), explains why Apuleius has incongruously stitched this surprise ending on to the tale of Thelyphron's mutilation. That main story is clearly a further warning to Lucius not to dabble in the occult; Zatchlas' raising of the corpse is to be visualized as contrapuntal to the vicious practices of the witches (so J. Tatum, *TAPA* (1969), 501) and a demonstration of the proper application of magical powers.

Coptus . . . Memphis . . . Pharos: the shrine of Coptus in upper Egypt had a god Min sometimes regarded as the son of Isis (Gwyn Griffiths, *Apuleius of Madauros*, 211). Isis herself had a shrine at Memphis. For the connection of Isis with Pharos, the island off Alexandria with the famous lighthouse, see Gwyn Griffiths, 43 (with bibliography). The rattle formed part of the appurtenances of Isis.

2.29 *Furies*: Apuleius perhaps evokes Lucan, 6. 719 ff. There the witch Erichtho recalls to life a soldier slain at Pharsalus; when he is as reluctant as the husband here. Erichtho summons the Furies Tisiphone and Megaera.

2.31 *joyful ritual*: though links have been suggested with the cult of Gelōs at Sparta mentioned by Plutarch (*Lys.* 25. 4; *Cleom.* 30. 1), or with the Roman festival of the Hilaria (D. S. Robertson, *JHS* (1919), 114) this Festival of Laughter is probably a purely imaginary one, invented to serve the purpose of his story by Apuleius; it further underlines the dangers of magic which Lucius continues to disregard.

flowing mantle: the joke reads lamely in English. It was the custom to deck out statues of the gods on feast-days; Lucius proposes to adorn the god Laughter with a literary tribute.

2.32 *Geryon*: the three-formed Spanish giant, slain by Hercules as one of his twelve labours; see n. on 3.19 below. When Apuleius makes Byrrhena claim that the Festival of Laughter was inaugurated 'in the early days of the city' (ch. 31) he is perhaps evoking Evander's account of the festival of Hercules at Pallanteum in Virgil, *Aen.* 8.

BOOK 3

3.1   *Aurora*: parody of epic descriptions of daybreak ('Rosy-fingered Dawn' appears more than twenty times in Homer; cf. Virgil, *Aen.* 12. 77) is one of Apuleius' amusing literary pleasantries. The technique reappears in the eighteenth-century novels of Fielding and others.

fame: see 2.12 above.

3.2   *ceremonies of purifications*: in the ceremony of lustration preceding a sacrifice (*Amburbium*, round the city, *Ambarualia* round the fields; see R. M. Ogilvie, *The Romans and their Gods* (London, 1969), 88 f.), the victims were led round in procession.

They even … to observe the proceedings: compare Apuleius' description of the crowds thronging the theatre at Carthage (*Flor.* 16. 11 ff.).

3.3   *time allowed for speaking*: the clepsydra, a regular feature in Roman courts from the first century BC (see e.g. Cicero, *Brutus*, 324, *Fin.* 4. 1; Pliny, *Ep.* 2. 11. 14), is described to lend comic verisimilitude to the trial.

addressed the assembly: as part of this literary entertainment, Apuleius presents two high-flown forensic utterances. For analysis of them, see van der Paardt's Commentary, ad loc.

3.7   *Sun … Justice*: see 2.22 and n. ad loc., *sun-god … Justice*.

3.9   *a wheel*: for the wheel as a Greek mode of torture, cf. Cicero, *Tusc.* 5. 24.

Proserpina and Orcus: the deities of the underworld.

3.11 *in honour of Laughter*: see n. on 2.31 above, *joyful ritual*.

statue: throughout his romance, Apuleius playfully incorporates autobiographical touches into Lucius' portrayal; for similar distinctions of statues granted to him, see *Flor.* 16; Augustine, *Ep.* 138. 19.

3.12 *the deity*: this is Risus, god of laughter.

3.15 *sacred cults*: there is more autobiographical intrusion here; Apuleius boasts of being initiated into Greek cults at *Apol.* 55, whereas Lucius elsewhere makes no such claim until he is initiated as Isis' votary in the final book.

3.17 *eastern side*: the eastern side, facing the rising sun, is especially important in magic; cf. 2.28 above.

unintelligible letters: these are the *tabellae defixionum*, tablets inscribed with *carmina* to entice a lover; cf. Virgil, *Ecl.* 8. 66 ff.

3.18 *mad Ajax*: in the *Ajax* of Sophocles, the hero is demented by the award of the arms of Achilles to Odysseus, and he slaughters a flock of sheep under the delusion that they are the Greek leaders.

utricide: 'A Skin-slayer'.

3.19 *Hercules' twelve labours*: for the twelve labours of Hercules, including the slaughter of the three-formed giant Geryon and the bringing up to the upper world of the three-headed Cerberus, see Ovid, *Met.* 9. 182 ff.

the embraces of matrons: Lucius' claim that he has previously spurned the embraces of matrons indicates a descent into sensuality in succumbing to the charms of Photis. In the patterning of his sinning, the 'servile pleasures' of sex precede his witnessing of magic; both are condemned by the priest of Isis at 11.15 as the cause of his sufferings.

3.21 *an owl*: for similar transformations by magic into birds, cf. Ovid. *Met.* 14. 388 ff., *Amores* 1. 8. 13.

3.22 *axe my own limbs*: this proverbial expression is equivalent to 'cutting one's own throat'; cf. Petronius, *Sat.* 74.

two-legged Thessalian wolves: the *lupulae* are the nymphomaniac witches who could gain control over Lucius if he became a bird.

3.26 *nefarious and abominable woman*: it is important to note that Photis the sex-object is responsible for Lucius' fall from grace; Apuleius stresses that Lucius has no regard for the girl beyond the sexual satisfaction she affords him.

hospitality and a decent lodging: the Latin (*loca lautia* are the hospitable lodgings afforded to visiting ambassadors at Rome) registers a mild joke impossible to reproduce in English.

Jupiter . . . Faith: for Jupiter as god of hospitality, see Ovid, *Met.* 10. 224; also 7.16 below. Faith (Fides) his companion is said to have quitted the earth with other deities at Juvenal, 6. 1 ff.

3.27 *Epona*: for this goddess, cf. Juvenal, 8. 157; she was prominent in Africa, where she was connected especially with beasts and their grooms (cf. Tertullian, *Apol.* 16; Minucius Felix, *Oct.* 28. 7).

For how long: apparently in parody of the exordium to Cicero's First Catilinarian.

3.29 *Jupiter whom we all know*: Robertson (*PCPS* 1926, 133 ff.) suggests that this refers to Caesar just invoked, but this is not borne out by what follows.

the bit: reading *frena* with Puteanus in preference to *faena* (Robertson; *foena F*) which is rarely found in the plural.

BOOK 4

4.2 *Success*: the Romans deified many abstract concepts. Apuleius may have had in mind Varro's invocation to the gods of country life in the exordium to his *Res Rusticae* (1. 1. 6), where Bonus Euentus is hymned—'without whom there is frustration, not cultivation'. Cf. also the statue of the goddess mentioned by Pliny, *NH* 34. 77.

laurel-roses: probably *nerium oleander* rather than the modern rhododendron; for its noxious effect on cattle, cf. Pliny, *NH* 16. 79, 24. 90.

4.4 *compassionate discharge*: Apuleius uses the Latin term (*causaria missio*) humorously to amuse his Roman audience. The *causarii* were soldiers invalided out of the army (Livy 6. 6. 14).

4.6 *subject and occasion demand*: this is parody of the conventional exordium used by historians when describing the location of an operation; cf. Sallust, *Jug.* 17. 1; Livy 26. 42. 7.

reception room: the atrium of a Roman house was the reception-room into which a guest first entered. Apuleius humorously suggests that the sheep-pen served this purpose for the robbers' cave.

4.8 *Centaurs at table*: reading *Centaurisque cenantibus* (Helm; *tebcinibus Centaurisque F*, *Centaurisque semihominibus* Robertson). For the feast of Perithous, king of the Lapiths, a Thessalian tribe, see Homer, *Od.* 21. 295 ff., Ovid, *Met.* 12. 210 ff.

eight feet richer: a comic formulation for the acquisition of Lucius-turned-ass and his horse.

Lamachus: a famous Athenian general of this name fought in the Sicilian expedition during the Peloponnesian War (cf. Thucydides, 6. 8. 2, 6. 101. 6). The name is jokingly attached to the bandit-leader.

4.9 *seven gates*: 'Seven-gated' was the traditional epithet for Thebes in epic (Homer, *Il*. 4. 406, *Od*. 11. 263, etc.), another literary pleasantry.

Chryseros: 'Mr Gold-lover.'

public services and shows: for this duty imposed on wealthy Greek citizens, cf. *OCD*, 'Liturgy'.

4.11 *the sea*: in burying Lamachus at sea, Apuleius appears to have forgotten that the bandits' operation was inland at Thebes; in addition, he may be evoking Thucydides 2. 43. The 'entire element' is water, one of the four elements.

4.12 *Alcimus*: 'Mr Valiant'.

rib-cage . . .: parody of Virgil, *Aen*. 12. 508 is evident here.

4.13 *Demochares*: 'Mr People-pleaser'.

4.14 *Eubulus*: emending *Babulus* (*F*; 'Mr Babbler') to Eubulus ('Mr Good-Counsellor') with Bursian and Robertson. Some scholars suggest that the episode of the bear-impersonation that follows parodies Virgil's account of the Wooden Horse in *Aen*. 2; see most recently S. A. Frangoulidis, *PP* (1991), 95 ff.

4.15 *Thrasyleon*: 'Mr Bold-Lyon'.

4.16 *Nicanor*: the name ('Victorious') is not significant, as Nicanor's role is minor.

4.20 *Cerberus*: the three-headed dog guarding the entrance to the underworld represents by metonymy Hades itself.

4.21 *We repeatedly reflected*: such laments for the departure of deities from the world are a frequent feature in earlier literature. See Hesiod, *WD* 200 (the departure of Aidōs); Catullus, 64. 384 ff.; Juvenal, 6. 1 ff.

4.22 *Salian priests*: the luxurious feasts enjoyed by these priests of Mars were proverbial; cf. Cicero, *Att*. 5. 9. 1; Horace, *Odes*, 1. 37. 2, etc.

4.26 *Attis or Protesilaus*: Attis, votary of the goddess Cybele, was prevented from marrying by being castrated by the goddess;

see Ovid, *Fasti*, 4. 221 ff. with Frazer's note. Protesilaus' marriage to Laodamia was cut short when he was summoned to fight at Troy, where he was the first Greek to die (Ovid, *Met.* 12. 68).

4.28 *They would . . . upright thumb*: this was the gesture of adoration known as *proskunēsis* (cf. Apuleius, *Apol.* 56).

sprung from . . . frothing waves: for the myth of the birth of Venus, see Hesiod, *Theog.* 195 ff. There is a play on the name Aphrodite and the Greek word for foam (*aphros*).

4.29 *Paphos, Cnidos . . . Cythera*: these were centres of traditional worship of Aphrodite in Cyprus, Asia Minor, and off the coast of the Peloponnese respectively. At this point Apuleius visualizes the locale of the story as mainland Greece.

soliloquy: the physical manifestations of Venus' anger are described with evocations of Poseidon's fury in the *Odyssey* (5. 285) and Juno's in the *Aeneid* (7. 292).

4.30 *Here am I . . .*: the angry soliloquy is a composite of Lucretius, 1. 2 and Virgil, *Aen.* 7. 308 ff.

shepherd: this was Paris, who in the contest on Mt. Ida preferred the beauty of Aphrodite to that of Hera and Athena (cf. Paus. 5. 19. 1). He received Helen as his reward, and thereby brought on Troy the hostility of the spurned goddesses.

4.31 *the host of Venus' companions*: for the Nereids, Homer, *Il.* 18. 37 ff., Virgil, *Aen.* 5. 285 f.; Portunus, the old god of harbours, Cicero, *ND* 2. 26, Ovid, *Fasti*, 6. 547 (equating him with Palaemon); Salacia, Roman goddess of the sea-waves, Varro, *LL* 5. 72; Palaemon, the Greek sea-god, Cicero, *ND* 3. 39, Virgil, *Aen.* 5. 283; Tritons, attendants of Neptune, Virgil, *Aen*, 5. 824, etc.

4.32 *Milesian tale*: though the old hag is depicted as telling the story, Apuleius destroys the dramatic illusion with this genial reference to himself. Mention of the Milesian Tale, echoing the introductory chapter to the romance, preserves the mask of entertainment over the hidden purpose of edification; see Introduction p. xxiv ff.

4.33 *Lydian mode*: see 10.32 and n.

BOOK 5

5.6   *sacrilegious curiosity*: this key-phrase in the *conte* (and in the romance as a whole) made a deep impression on Apuleius' fellow-countryman Augustine; see my paper in *G&R* (1988), 73 ff.

5.8   *golden house*: perhaps evoking the celebrated palace of Nero at Rome.

5.9   *bars and chains*: at the outset of the story, the sisters had contracted 'splendid marriages' (4.32). Such inconsistencies reflect the author's tendency to write for the moment, here to underline the sisters' jealousy.

5.11 *he will be mortal*: the child when born proves to be female (6.24), another inconsistency.

5.17 *monstrous dragon*: this is a highly Virgilian snake; see especially *Georg.* 3. 425 ff.

       Pythian oracle: here referring to the oracle at Miletus (see 4.32), not at Delphi. Apollo ('Pythian' because he slew the dragon Python) was the god common to both.

5.24 *slipped down to earth exhausted*: the Platonist flavour of the *conte* is at its most pronounced here, when Psyche (the soul) aspires to union with the divine but is weighed down by the body (*Phaedrus*, 248c is close).

5.26 *take your goods and chattels with you*: Apuleius here uses the formal terms for divorce ('tibi res tuas habeto'; cf. Gaius, 24. 2. 2) and for the solemn form of marriage (*confarreatae nuptiae*) to divert his Roman readers.

5.27 *fell ... in the same way*: the deaths of the sisters can be visualized in the Platonist sense as the sloughing-off of bodily attachments, as Psyche seeks to attain union with the divine.

5.29 *your father's estate*: these are further technical pleasantries with which Apuleius regales his learned Roman readers. It was perfectly possible in Roman law for a mistress to adopt a slave; cf. F. Norden, *Apuleius und das römische Privatrecht* (Leipzig, 1912), 74.

5.30 *stepfather*: Apuleius makes humorous play with Venus' marital problems. Though married to the lame Vulcan, she had a liaison with Mars during which the couple were caught red-handed by the angry husband (cf. Ovid, *Met.* 4. 171 ff., *AA* 2. 561 ff.).

insult . . . expiated: the abusive comments heaped by Venus on Cupid here, and the ensuing conversation with Ceres and Juno, evoke the scene in Apollonius Rhodius, 3. 93 ff., where Hera and Athena are the participants.

BOOK 6

6.2 *begged Ceres' favour*: Demeter/Ceres was the deity at the centre of the Eleusinian mystery-religion. Psyche's litany here incorporates references to the myth of Proserpina, daughter of Ceres, who was borne off by Dis in his chariot ('the car which snatched') and imprisoned in Hades ('the earth which latched') during each winter, but was allowed to return to earth each summer. The myth symbolizes the death and rebirth also enacted in the case of Lucius in the liturgy of Isis in the final book.

6.4 *Sister and spouse . . .*: the litany to Juno envisages her syncretistically. Her Greek counterpart Hera has ancient connections with Samos and Argos (see *OCD*, Hera), and she is identified with the Carthaginian tutelary goddess Tanit. The river-god at Argos, Inachus, was the father of Io, whose myth was enacted in the liturgy of Isis. Juno's Greek title ('Yoking Goddess') and her Latin name 'Lucina' signal her roles as goddess of marriage and of childbirth respectively.

legislation: again the learned joke. Such legislation was enshrined in Roman law; see Introduction, n. 15.

6.6 *Heaven admitted his daughter*: Venus is the daughter of the sky-god Ouranos/Jupiter; in Apuleius' philosophical vision, as a lesser deity she lives on a lower level than her father.

6.7 *Jupiter . . . did not refuse her*: the sportive evocation of Homer, *Il.* 1. 528 is noteworthy here.

6.8 *metae Murciae*: this was the 'Murcian turning-point' in the Circus Maximus at Rome, so called because it was close to the temple of Venus Murcia. The indifference to geographical coherence (hitherto the action has centred on Greece and the Aegean) in the interests of momentary joking for a Roman audience is characteristic.

Habit: so called because 'Habit furthers love' (Lucretius, 4. 1283).

Orcus: see 3.9 and n. ad loc.

6.13 *Cocytus*: the house of Venus, where this instruction is given, is situated close to Taenarus (see 6.18); this is the modern Cape Matapan at the southernmost point of the Peloponnese. Psyche enters the region of the dead from there. The waterfall feeds into the Stygian world below. The language here is Virgilian, drawing on *Aeneid*, 6 to evoke the *katabasis* of Aeneas (*Aen.* 6. 323, 327). The motif of drawing water is from Hesiod, *Theog.* 782 ff., where Zeus sends Iris for the water which seals the oaths taken by the gods.

6.15 *cupbearer to Jupiter*: for the eagle's rape of Ganymede from Mt. Ida, see Ovid, *Met.* 10. 155 ff.

6.19 throughout this section there are verbal evocations of Aeneas' journey through the underworld in *Aeneid* 6.

6.22 *former role*: Cupid is a schizoid character, now sober lover and now wanton boy. He reverts to this second persona to win Jupiter's support against Venus.

lex Iulia: this law, passed under Augustus in 18 BC, made adultery a criminal offence for the first time. See Jane F. Gardner, *Women in Roman Law and Society* (London, 1986), 127 ff.

You have transformed my . . . countenance: see Ovid, *Met.* 6. 103 ff. for these various shapes adopted by Jupiter as depicted on Arachne's tapestry.

6.23 *liable to a fine*: another playful touch: such fines for non-attendance were imposed in the senate at Rome and increased in the Augustan age; cf. Cassius Dio, 54. 18. 3, 55. 3. 2.

6.24 *his personal cup-bearer*: for Ganymede, see n. on 6.15 above.

Pleasure: for the connection implicit here with Lucius' 'pleasure beyond telling' in his mystical union with Isis, see 11.24 and Introduction, p. xl.

6.25 *I was standing close by*: in *Onos* 22, the bandits make only two journeys, and Lucius goes with them on the first. Apuleius describes three journeys, on the first of which Lucius does not go. This allows him to overhear the story of Cupid and Psyche, grafted by Apuleius on to the main story.

6.26 *fear had lent wings*: an evocation of Virgil, *Aen.* 8. 224.

6.27 *Dirce*: wife of the Theban king Lycus, was tied to the horns of a bull by Amphion and Zethus, sons of Antiope, because she had planned a similar punishment against their mother; see Hyginus, 7 f.

6.28 *four-footed gallop*: a reminiscence of Virgil, *Aen.* 11. 875.

6.29 *Phrixus etc.*: for the flight of Phrixus, who sought to escape from his stepmother on the back of a ram, see Hyginus, 2 f. For Arion on the dolphin, Herodotus, 1. 24; for Europa and the bull, Ovid, *Met.* 2. 833 ff. etc.

6.30 *Pegasus*: the winged horse, born from Medusa's blood when the Gorgon's head was severed by Perseus, and later ridden by Bellerophon to slay the Chimaera, is the theme of Ovid, *Met.* 4. 785 ff.

6.31 *The first ... second ... third*: these are the punishments prescribed in the *Digest* (48. 19, 16, 10) for captured bandits. The speakers propose punishments which they themselves would suffer if captured. See T. N. Habinek, 'Lucius' Rite of Passage', in *Materiali e discussioni per l'analisi dei testi classici* (Pisa, 1990), 66.

BOOK 7

7.5 *Haemus ... Theron*: the names are a play on Mt. Haemus, the Thracian mountain expressive of the brigand's height, and on the Greek verb to hunt, reflecting the father's profession.

7.6 *Plotina*: Apuleius may have chosen the name because of Hadrian's virtuous wife Pompeia Plotina (see Pliny, *Paneg.* 83 f.). Her childlessness, in contrast to the fecundity of this lady, could be interpreted as Apuleian humour. Others note the similarity to Hypsicratea, wife of Mithridates of Pontus in Val. Max. 6. 5.

Zacynthus: he was to spend his exile in this island off the west coast of Greece.

7.7 *Orcus*: see 3.9 and n. ad loc.

7.8 : in the abbreviated Greek version (*Onos* 26), there is no trace of this story of Plotina and the escape of 'Haemus', who is later to be revealed as Charite's bridegroom Tlepolemus. Apuleius may have inserted the story so that the reader can interpret it as a coded message to Charite that her ordeal with the bandits would soon be ended. Haemus' description of his escape on an ass is a possible pointer to Charite's later departure on the back of Lucius.

dowry: the word has ironical implications. The true commitment of 'Haemus' is to his bride Charite, not to the bandits.

7.10 *secretary of the robbers' chest*: the Latin phrase wittily evokes the imperial office of finance established by Hadrian; cf. *SHA*, Hadrian, 20. 6.

Salian priests: see 4.22 and n. ad loc.

7.11 *wine he had sampled*: for this as erotic practice, see Ovid, *Amores*, 1. 4. 33 f.

7.12 *Tlepolemus ... Charite*: the names of the bridal couple, Tlepolemus ('Enduring Warrior') and Charite ('Grace') do not appear in the *Onos* and have probably been invented by Apuleius.

7.14 *Bactrian camel*: since the Bactrian camel has two humps, it was able to store more food than the Arabian species; see Aristotle, *Hist. Anim.* 498b–499a; Pliny, *NH* 8. 67.

7.16 *Jupiter*: see 3.26 and n. ad loc.

king of Thrace: this refers to Diomedes of Thrace, later fed to his own horses by Hercules; see Diodorus Siculus 4. 15. 3 f.

7.26 *Bellerophon*: by equating the traveller with Bellerophon, the ass comically identifies himself with Pegasus; see 6.30 and n. ad loc.

7.27 *the boy's mother burst into my stable*: Apuleius sets the scene for the incongruous Ciceronian oration to follow; see Introduction, p. xxix.

despicable manner: a reference to the *senatus consultum Silanianum* (AD 10), by which a slave was required to aid an endangered master (*Digest* 29. 5).

7.28 *Althea*: Ovid, *Met.* 8. 425 ff., describes how Meleager slew his mother's brothers, and how in revenge his mother Althea caused his death. The Fates had decreed that his life would end when a firebrand was burnt, and she thrust it into the fire.

BOOK 8

8.1   *historical narrative*: Apuleius deliberately undercuts the dramatic impact of his narrative with this preliminary announcement of the literary genre. For the sources of the story, see n. on 8.14 below.

Thrasyllus: 'Mr Desperado'. He is modelled on Sallust's Catiline; cf. *Cat.* 5 and 14 f.

8.6   *The crime . . . misfortune*: this description is virtually a mosaic of Virgilian phrases. Note especially the Virgilian Fama (Rumour) (cf. *Aen.* 4. 172 f., 195 f., 9. 474 f., 11. 139 ff.) and Charite's wild behaviour which evokes that of Dido (4. 298 ff.).

8.7   *Liber*: the Latin god Liber (equated with Dionysus/Bacchus) was the youthful deity of the vintage. Charite's choice of the god closest in appearance to her dead husband allows her to indulge in devotions to Tlepolemus which might otherwise scandalize her family and friends. Virgil's Dido likewise commemorates her husband Sychaeus in his own shrine (*Aen.* 4. 457 f.); perhaps Apuleius has also in mind the story of Protesilaus and Laodamia; see B. L. Hijmans, *Mnem.* (1986), 358 f.

8.8   *his name*: see n. on 8.1 above, *Thrasyllus*.

disclose his unspeakable treachery: there is no need to assume that Thrasyllus divulges his role as assassin. It is merely the proposal of marriage that disquiets her; his part in the death of her husband is revealed to her later in her dream.

the shade of Tlepolemus: the Virgilian evocation continues; compare Sychaeus' appearance in a dream to Dido at *Aen.* 1. 353 ff.

8.9   *months still to elapse*: the period of mourning prescribed for a husband's death varied between ten months and a year; see the Groningen commentary (ed. Hijmans etc.) on this book.

8.13 *Dry your untimely tears . . .*: compare Dido's farewell speech at *Aen.* 4. 653 ff.

8.14 : this tragic story of Charite has been introduced by Apuleius, for in the Greek version she and her husband are accidentally drowned (*Onos* 34). Several themes from earlier literature have been stitched together to compose the story.

The hunting episode evokes the Atys story in Herodotus 1. 34 ff., and the Adonis story in Ovid, *Met.* 10. 710 ff. Charite's reactions are modelled on those of the demented Dido (see nn. on 8.6, 7, 13 above). Plutarch, *Mul. Virt.* 257 e–f has the similar story of the murdered husband and the wife Camma's revenge. The scene at the tomb is reminiscent of Haemon's behaviour in Sophocles, *Antigone* 1231 ff. (note the Haemus–Haemon coincidence). Apuleius exhibits his literary virtuosity.

8.16 *Pegasus*: see 6.30 and n. ad loc.

8.17–18 : neither this nor the following anecdote appears in the *Onos*; Apuleius, it seems, has inserted them to depict the hostile world into which Lucius has fallen as punishment for his sin.

8.22 *I am eager to recount it:* this story too bears all the marks of an Apuleian insertion, the intermingled themes of marital infidelity and magic recall the twin failings of Lucius.

8.23 *famous town*: in the *Onos*, the town is Beroia in Macedonia, but Apuleius leaves the itinerary vague since he is to diverge from the Greek version at the forthcoming climax.

jokes about my prospects: for Apuleius' literate readers the joking includes parody of Cicero's *exordium* in his First Catilinarian

braying, worn-out sieve: *ruderarium cribrum*: *ruderarium* ('rubbishy') has the punning connotation of 'braying' (from *rudere*); the two meanings are impossible to combine in one word in English. The sieve would be made from the ass's hide.

8.24 *Syrian goddess*: this is Atargatis, whose cult was widespread in Greece from the third century BC onward. An inscription to her has been found at Beroia (see note on 8.23, *famous town*, above). By the first century AD the cult had reached Rome, for Nero became a follower (Suetonius, *Nero*, 50).

virile: Cappadocia was renowned for virile men (Petronius, 63. 5). There is sexual innuendo in this remark to the catamite priest.

census: Roman citizens were required to register for tax purposes.

Cornelian law: no such *lex Cornelia* forbidding the sale of citizens as slaves is known; it is probably 'un nom de fantaisie' (Vallette in the Budé edition, ad loc.)

8.25 *Syrian goddess . . . Adonis*: for the Syrian goddess, see note on 8.24 above. Sabazius was a Phrygian–Thracian deity with functions similar to those of Dionysus (Cicero, *ND* 3. 58 with Pease's note). Bellona was the Roman goddess of war. The Idaean Mother is Cybele, the Magna Mater whose priest Attis castrated himself in ecstasy (Catullus, 63). For Adonis beloved by Venus, see Ovid, *Met.* 10. 710 ff.

poor queen . . . hair flying loose: the catamite makes himself feminine, comically investing his baldness with hair.

seventeen denarii: compare the prices later paid for the ass: to the baker (9.10), 'seven sesterces more' (= 18¾ denarii in all); to the market-gardener (9.31), 50 sesterces (= 12½ denarii); to the cooks (10.13), 11 denarii (allegedly a hasty sale; in the *Onos* the price was 25 drachmas/denarii).

Philebus: 'The rev. Love-Boyes' (McLeod).

8.26 *a hind for a maiden*: the literary touch is Apuleius' addition; substitution of a hind for a maiden in propitiatory sacrifice evokes the spurious close of Euripides' *Iphigenia in Aulide*. The phrase became proverbial for unexpected substitution (Achilles Tatius, 6. 3. 3).

At last you have come: this may be a take-off of Anchises' greeting to Aeneas in the Elysian Fields (Virgil, *Aen.* 6. 687 f.).

8.27–8: Lucretius 2.614 ff. has clearly inspired this lengthy description of the wild behaviour of the catamite priests.

8.28 *ass's milk*: taken as a remedy for various illnesses; cf. Pliny, *NH* 28. 125.

8.30 *Phrygian chant*: this mode of music was associated especially with the flute, played in orgiastic ritual in honour of Bacchus or Cybele.

BOOK 9

9.1 *divine providence*: it is clear that Fortune is represented as that aspect of divine Providence which brings trials and reverses in its train; see 11.15 n.

9.2 *Myrtilus etc.*: this episode of the mad dog does not appear in the *Onos*, and these comically apt names have been coined by

Apuleius himself. Myrtilus is the name of a mythological charioteer (Hyginus, 224); Hephaestio evokes Hephaestus, god of fire; Hypnophilus in Greek means 'sleep lover', an apt name for a chamberlain; and Apollonius derives from Apollo, god of healing.

9.4 *temple spoils*: this reference to temple-spoils is puzzling until we reach 9.9, where it becomes clear that Apuleius has omitted from the Greek story an episode in which the priests stole a golden bowl from a shrine; see *Onos* 41.

cuckolding: the succession of stories about cuckolded husbands which now follows is inserted by Apuleius to demonstrate the infidelities of the unregenerate world in which he now roams. The first story was appropriated by Boccaccio in the *Decameron*, where it becomes the second story of the seventh day (Peronella and the lover in the tub).

9.8 *oracular response*: this, and the jocular interpretations of it, do not appear in the *Onos*; they read like a characteristic Apuleian insertion.

9.9 *Mother of the Gods*: Cybele, the Magna Mater.

9.10 *Bridewell*: Apuleius uses the term 'Tullianum' for the gaol. This was the Roman dungeon allegedly built by Servius Tullius in the Regal period. Apuleius cites it to amuse the Roman reader.

consecrated there: in *Onos* 41, the statue of Atargate is more aptly lodged in another temple, presumably one consecrated to Atargate rather than to Cybele.

Philebus . . . paid for me: see 8.25 and n. ad loc., *seventeen denarii*.

9.13 *godlike creator*: Homer, whom Lucius paraphrases (cf. *Od.* 1. 1 ff.) in singing Odysseus' praises.

9.14 *the only God*: clearly the jibe of worshipping 'the only God' and the other practices mentioned here are directed against an adherent of either Judaism or Christianity. Given the hectic growth of Christianity in North Africa in the late second century (see Introduction, p. xxxix), Christianity seems the likelier target.

9.16 *audacious*: reading *intimidae* (Helm; *timidae F*, Robertson).

Philesitherus: 'Master Love-chaser'.

9.17 *Arete*: 'Mrs Virtue', an ironical title.

Myrmex: the word means 'ant' in Greek, an apt name for the busy servant.

9.18 *breached by gold*: in this moralizing story of the power of gold, Apuleius flaunts his knowledge of Horace, *Odes*, 3. 16. 9 ff., where gold is said to make its way through ministers and stone walls. The image of the wedge a little later also evokes this ode.

9.22 *Salian priest*: see note on 4.22.

laundryman: the interrelated stories of the baker's wife and the laundryman's wife which follow are, like the earlier story in 9.5, incorporated into the *Decameron*, where they become Novella 10 of the fifth day (Pietro di Vinciolo and Ercolano).

mere boy: note the inconsistency in the character of Philesitherus, a more mature and adventurous figure in the earlier tale. Apuleius always writes for the moment, and a changed persona is necessary in this new anecdote.

9.23 *Ceres here*: since this episode takes place at the baker's, it is fitting that a statue of Ceres, goddess of corn, has a place there.

9.25 *we both faced*: a charge of collusion in the murder would have implicated the baker.

9.26 *eyes of all*: Apuleius seems to be so carried away with the mimic nature of this drama that here and at the end of the next paragraph he appears to forget that the sole persons present, other than Lucius, are the baker and his wife.

9.27 *vindictive laundryman*: thus the three stories of cuckolded husbands are drawn together. 'I am no barbarian' puns on the name of Barbarus, the husband in 9.17.

equity: these legal quips, as we note in the Introduction (pp. xxix f), are a frequent means of amusing sophisticated Roman readers, well acquainted with the laws of property.

9.31 *on the ninth day*: the *novendiale sacrificium* took place at the tomb on the ninth day after death, and a funeral banquet followed; cf. Tacitus, *Ann.* 6. 5.

price was high: but lower than that paid for Lucius earlier (note on 8.25, *seventeen denarii*).

9.32 *Capricorn*: the sun enters Capricorn at the winter solstice in December.

9.33 *One night*: no trace of the following episode appears in the *Onos*; we can be reasonably certain that it is Apuleius' own insertion, since the citation of the horrific prodigies adds a further Roman touch of a literary nature to the narrative.

9.39 *his own misfortunes*: the gardener no longer had any prospect of receiving the produce promised him by the bereaved proprietor.

vine-staff: this was the symbol of the centurion's rank and authority; see Tacitus, *Ann.* 1. 23.

9.42 *The peeping ass and its shadow*: the proverb is found in Menander's fragmentary play *The Priestess* (fr. 246 K). It seems to have developed from two earlier expressions, 'Because of an ass's gaze', and 'Concerning an ass's shadow'; for conjectural explanations of these, see Gaselee's note in the earlier Loeb edn. of *The Golden Ass* (tr. Adlington), ad loc. The incident is found in the Greek story (*Onos*, 49), but Apuleius exploits it to lay further emphasis on the curiosity of the hero.

BOOK 10

10.2 *I record it in this book*: this long anecdote, not in the *Onos*, appears to have been inserted by Apuleius as a further depiction of the fallen world into which the hero is plunged.

sock . . . buskin: the promise of high tragedy (the sock is the low shoe of the comic actor, the buskin the high boot of the tragic player) is not fulfilled, for the episode ends happily. Apuleius merely announces that the theme of the stepmother infatuated with her stepson is inspired by Euripides' *Hippolytus* and Seneca's *Phaedra*.

undeveloped: the Latin (*Cupido paruulus*) recalls Virgil, *Aen.* 1. 715. The lady's subsequent behaviour contains further evocations of Virgil's Dido, and of the Phaedra of Seneca and Ovid, *Heroides*, 4.

Alas . . . physicians: echoing Virgil's 'heu uatum ignarae mentes!' (*Aen.* 4. 65), in the apt context of Dido's love-sickness; cf. also Petronius, 42. 5.

colour: retaining *coloris* with *F*, *Robertson* against *caloris*, in view of 'not running a temperature' in the following sentence.

10.3   *It is because . . . fitting*: cf. Seneca, *Phaedra*, 646 f.

10.7   *the Areopagus*: at Athens, the ancient court for trying homicide. For the procedure, see D. M. MacDowell, *The Law in Classical Athens* (London, 1978), 116 ff. For the injunction against irrelevance, cf. Lysias 3. 34; Aristotle, *Rhet.* 1354ᵃ; and other references in MacDowell, 43.

10.8   *sewn in the sack*: this was the traditional penalty prescribed by the Twelve Tables. The convicted parricide was enclosed in a sack with a dog, a cock, a snake, and an ape, and drowned. This method of execution had long been abandoned. See *OCD*, *parricidium*.

10.10   *Greek manner*: cf. note on 3.9, *a wheel*.

10.11   *purpose of medicine*: Hippocrates, 1. 299: 'Neither will I administer a poison to anyone when asked to do so, nor will I suggest such a course.'

Mandragora: (or mandrake) was commonly used as a narcotic in surgical operations. For the ancient texts, see C. B. Randolph, *Proc. American Acad. of Arts and Sciences* (1905), 487 ff.

10.13   *eleven denarii*: in the *Onos*, 46, the price was 25 drachmas/ denarii; Apuleius freely changes the sums paid for the transaction.

master was quite rich: the owner is from Thessalonica in the *Onos*, but Apuleius makes him a Corinthian (see 10.18 below) for the purposes of the climax of the story.

10.14   *savings*: a slave at his master's discretion could purchase his freedom by accumulating his *peculium*; see T. Wiedmann, *Greek and Roman Slavery* (Beckenham, 1981), 52.

Eteocles: the fratricidal strife between Eteocles and Polynices, sons of Oedipus, at Thebes is prominent in Aeschylus, *Seven Against Thebes*, and Sophocles, *Antigone*.

10.15   *Phineus*: the blind Phineus was constantly robbed of his meal by the Harpies, a theme appearing on vase-paintings and in Apollonius Rhodius, 2. 180 ff.

10.16   *silphium*: this plant associated with Cyrene (Catullus, 7. 4; Pliny, *NH* 19. 38) was used for both culinary and medicinal purposes.

10.17 *four times over*: at *Onos*, 48, the master pays only twice as much; Apuleius' underlines the lavish spending of his new master.

on my elbow: Adlington thoughtfully misrenders 'on my tail'; the absurdity of 'elbow' seems not to have occurred to the author of the *Onos* or to Apuleius.

10.18 *Thiasus*: the name suggests 'The Reveller', befitting the man who mounts the show; the *Onos* calls him Menecles.

quinquennial magistracy: the two principal officers of the municipality (*duouiri*) received this honorific title every fifth year.

10.19 *Pasiphaë*: wife of king Minos of Crete; she conceived a passion for a bull, and the fruit of their union was the Minotaur.

10.22 *lowing lover*: see the previous note.

10.23 *The story . . .*: this anecdote too has apparently been inserted by Apuleius; see note on 10.2 above.

killed at once: in Roman law a father had the right to rear or to expose a child (*Digest*, 28. 2. 11; see Jane F. Gardner, *Women in Roman Law and Society* (London, 1986), 155).

10.27 *funeral services*: see note on 9.31, *on the ninth day*.

10.29 *Pyrrhic dance*: initially a war-dance in armour, this became a more general choral performance; it is apt here, for the contest on Mt. Ida precipitated the Trojan War in which Pyrrhus was prominent (Virgil, *Aen.* 2. 469 ff.).

10.30 : The pageant that follows, described in Apuleius' most florid style, does not appear in the *Onos*. The theme of Venus' victory is the ironical prelude to the bestial copulation scheduled to follow.

10.31 *Castor and Pollux*: Juno's stepsons; Leda after being visited by Jupiter in the form of a swan gave birth to them in an egg; they were known as the Castors.

the Dorian mode: considered manly, and thus apt for Minerva, whereas the Ionian was thought effeminate; cf. Plato, *Rep.* 399a, *Laches*, 188d.

10.32 *the Lydian mode*: likewise rejected by Plato as effeminate (*Rep.* 398e).

10.33 *vultures in togas*: Apuleius amuses his readers with this disparaging address to Roman lawyers.

Palamedes: condemned on the evidence of a forged letter planted by Odysseus (Virgil, *Aen.* 2. 82 with Williams's note; Ovid, *Met.* 13. 308 ff.). The contest between Odysseus and Ajax for the arms of Achilles, Ovid, *Met.* 13. 1 ff. These examples may have occurred to Apuleius because they appear in Plato's account of the trial of Socrates (*Apol.* 41b), which is mentioned next here.

That old man: for Socrates' execution in 399 BC, and the judgement of the Delphic oracle that 'no man was wiser', cf. Plato, *Apol.* 24b ff. and 21a.

they swear by his name: Apuleius has himself in mind as a prominent Middle Platonist; Introd. pp. xv ff.

10.35   *took off at full gallop*: at this point Apuleius departs radically from the Greek story to incorporate the novel climax of conversion to Isis. In the Greek version, Lucius gulps down roses carried by the attendant at the Thessalonican games, is restored to manhood, and retires home after being humiliatingly rejected by the matron who was obsessed with him as an ass.

Cenchreae: excavations at Cenchreae have uncovered a shrine with Egyptian motifs which must be one of the temples mentioned by Pausanias 2. 4. 6 (see Gwyn Griffiths's edn. of Book 11, 18 ff.).

BOOK 11

11.1   *seven times*: for such importance attached by Pythagoreans (and subsequently by Platonists) to the number seven, see W. K. C. Guthrie, *A History of Greek Philosophy*, vol. 1 (Cambridge, 1962), 303 f.

supremely powerful goddess: Lucius recognizes the moon as the one deity in various guises, but does not make the specific identification with Isis until 11.5 below.

11.2   *Ephesus*: this is Diana/Artemis, who in her role as Lucina presides over childbirth.

Proserpina: Hecate/Proserpina is depicted in Greek art with three bodies or heads; she is identified as 'the three-formed goddess' with Diana and Luna at Horace, *Odes* 3. 22. 3, and Virgil speaks of the 'Virgin's triple countenance' (*Aen.* 4.

511). Here her roles as Proserpina and Luna are acknowledged.

11.3–4: this description of the robes and accessories of the goddess is modelled on the statuary of Isis; virtually all the details recorded here can be paralleled from the statues. See Gwyn Griffiths's edn. of Book 11, ad loc.

11.5 *variety of . . . titles*: like the prayer of Lucius in 11.2 above, this aretalogy falls into four sections of three phrases each. The syncretism is characteristic of second-century Isiac worship. The Phrygians ('first-born' according to Herodotus, 2. 2) worshipped Cybele at Pessinus. Athena/Minerva is called 'Cecropian' because Cecrops was the legendary first king of Athens. Paphos in Cyprus had a celebrated shrine of Aphrodite/Venus. Cretan Dictynna is identified with Artemis/Diana in the Greek dramatists (see Guthrie, *The Greeks and their Gods* (London, 1950), 105). The Sicilians ('trilingual' because of the successive incursions of Carthaginians, Greeks, and Romans) worshipped 'Ortygian' Proserpina because Ortygia is the island off Syracuse, and the goddess was carried off to Hades from Sicilian fields. The Rhamnusian goddess is Nemesis, worshipped at Rhamnus near Marathon. 'Eastern and western Ethiopians' translates *utrique* (so Robertson; *arique F*); for the sense see note on 1.8, *Ethiopians . . . Antipodeans*.

this rite: the *nauigium Isidis*, celebrated on 5 March and hence inaugurating the sailing-season, is described in 11.16.

11.6 *spiteful charges*: Lucius might have feared that those observing his change of shape would charge him with the capital offence of magic.

Elysian fields: like Anchises, father of Aeneas, Lucius is to enjoy the state of natural bliss attained in this region of Hades.

11.8 *Ganymede*: see note on 1.12, *Endymion*.

Pegasus and Bellerophon: see note on 6.30.

11.9 *votive prayers*: presumably those uttered at 11.17.

Sarapis: (or Serapis) frequently replaces Osiris as husband of Isis in the Hellenistic period, but is mentioned in the romance only here, whereas Osiris appears at 11.27 and 30. Osiris is considered by some as the 'Greek' title, Sarapis as the 'foreign' name, but they are regarded as the same god.

11.10 *staff of Mercury*: Anubis bears similar objects in the next chapter, so this must be a priest of his; like Mercury, he is the guide of souls to Hades. (Apuleius carried round a statue of Mercury, and sacrificed in private to it; see *Apol.* 63. 3.)

11.15 *Fortune with eyes*: here Apuleius evokes the composite figure of Isis-Fortuna, who in her Hellenistic guise is accompanied by the cornucopia and rudder as symbols of her provision and guidance. The Fortune of the Greek novels, who has so unremittingly persecuted Lucius, is blind and malignant, equated with Typhon; Isis-Fortuna by contrast is the saving power with sight and foresight.

11.16 *sacred shrine*: presumably the altar described in 11.10.

egg and sulphur: for their use in purification ceremonies, see Ovid, *AA* 2. 330.

11.17 *living statues*: perhaps 'living' because represented by humans (as is the case with Lucius when initiated at 11.24). But the Latin *spirantia* can mean 'lifelike'.

sacred college: Lucius himself is admitted to the college of 'shrine-bearers' (11. 30), a lower order 'on the borderline between priests and temple-servants' (Gwyn Griffiths).

entire Roman people: unlike Christianity, the Isiac religion is now comfortably established at Rome.

11.18 *my native region*: at 2.12, Lucius stated that his home was in Corinth where he now is; cf. 1.22.

11.20 *Candidus*: 'white'. The 'belongings' promised are presumably the slaves.

11.22 *Mithras*: the name suggests a connection between the ritual of Mithras and that of Isis; 'an atmosphere of friendly syncretism' (Gwyn Griffiths). Winkler, 245, is unnecessarily taken aback, regarding it as 'like introducing the Pope, and calling him Martin Luther'. But the cult-figures of paganism unite in the face of the emergent Christian threat.

unfamiliar characters: the Egyptian hieroglyphs would be unfamiliar to a Greek.

11.24 *Olympian*: presumably so-called because the initiates have a rapport with the Olympian gods. The Arctic or Hyperborean epithet attached to the gryphons reflects the tradition that they came from the far north (Herodotus, 4. 13, 32; Pliny, *NH* 10. 70. 136). On the garb, see Gwyn Griffiths, ad loc.

11.26 *the harbour of Augustus*: constructed close to Ostia, had been built under Augustus; see R. Meiggs, *Roman Ostia* (Oxford, 1960), 54 ff., 153 ff.

Campensis: the temple was called Campensis because it lay on the Campus Martius; see Josephus, *Ant.* 18. 65 ff.; S. B. Platner and T. Ashby, *Topographical Dictionary of Ancient Rome* (Oxford, 1929), 283 ff.

11.27 *Osiris*: as Isis' husband, he was closely associated with her ritual. The epithet 'unconquered' commemorates his victory over Seth-Typhon, and may have been influenced by Mithras' title *Sol invictus*.

pastophori: see note on 11.17, *sacred college*.

a name quite relevant: Asinius is cognate with *asinus*, an ass.

Madauros: Apuleius' native city (Introd. p. xi); thus at the climax of his novel the author identifies himself with his hero.

11.28 *twixt axe and altar*: for the saying, reflecting the plight of the sacrificial victim, cf. Plautus, *Captiui*, 617.

11.30 *pastophori*: see note on 11.17, *sacred college*.

quinquennial administrators: for this honorific title awarded to the chief officials of the municipality every fifth year, see note on. 10.18. Presumably the usage was extended to temple-wardens.

days of Sulla: scholars speculatively connect Sulla's cult of Fortune with worship of Isis, but there is no other evidence than this for his establishment of the college.

INDEX AND GLOSSARY OF NAMES

THE WORLD'S CLASSICS

A Select List

BEN JONSON: Five Plays
Edited by G. A. Wilkes

LEONARDO DA VINCI: Notebooks
Edited by Irma A. Richter

HERMAN MELVILLE: The Confidence-Man
Edited by Tony Tanner

PROSPER MÉRIMÉE: Carmen and Other Stories
Translated by Nicholas Jotcham

EDGAR ALLAN POE: Selected Tales
Edited by Julian Symons

MARY SHELLEY: Frankenstein
Edited by M. K. Joseph

BRAM STOKER: Dracula
Edited by A. N. Wilson

ANTHONY TROLLOPE: The American Senator
Edited by John Halperin

OSCAR WILDE: Complete Shorter Fiction
Edited by Isobel Murray

VIRGINIA WOOLF: Mrs Dalloway
Edited by Claire Tomalin

A complete list of Oxford Paperbacks, including The World's Classics, OPUS, Past Masters, Oxford Authors, Oxford Shakespeare, and Oxford Paperback Reference, is available in the UK from the Arts and Reference Publicity Department (BH), Oxford University Press, Walton Street, Oxford OX2 6DP.

In the USA, complete lists are available from the Paperbacks Marketing Manager, Oxford University Press, 200 Madison Avenue, New York, NY 10016.

Oxford Paperbacks are available from all good bookshops. In case of difficulty, customers in the UK can order direct from Oxford University Press Bookshop, Freepost, 116 High Street, Oxford, OX1 4BR, enclosing full payment. Please add 10 per cent of published price for postage and packing.